PRAISE FOR BESTSELLING AUTHOR

JULIE KAGAWA

'Katniss Everdeen better watch out'
—*Huffington Post* on *The Immortal Rules*

'Julie Kagawa is one killer storyteller'
—MTV's *Hollywood Crush* blog

'Julie Kagawa's Iron Fey series is the next *Twilight*''
—*Teen.com*

'Fans of Melissa Marr...will enjoy the ride'
—*Kirkus Reviews* on *The Iron Queen*

'wholly satisfying'
—*Realms of Fantasy* on *The Iron Queen*

'a book that will keep its readers glued to the pages until the very end'
—*New York Journal of Books* on *The Iron Daughter*

'*The Iron King* surpasses the greater majority of dark fantasies'
—*teenreads.com*

Also by ***Julie Kagawa***
from

The Iron Fey series
(in reading order)

THE IRON KING
WINTER'S PASSAGE *(eBook)*
THE IRON DAUGHTER
THE IRON QUEEN
SUMMER'S CROSSING (eBook)
THE IRON KNIGHT
IRON'S PROPHECY (eBook)
THE LOST PRINCE

Coming soon

THE IRON TRAITOR

Blood of Eden series

THE IMMORTAL RULES
THE ETERNITY CURE

THE ETERNITY CURE

The legend continues

A BLOOD OF EDEN NOVEL

JULIE KAGAWA

Published in Great Britain 2013
Mira Ink, an imprint of Harlequin (UK) Limited,
Eton House, 18-24 Paradise Road,
Richmond, Surrey, TW9 1SR

ISBN 978 1 848 45185 8

47-0513

Mira Ink's policy is to use papers that are natural, renewable and recyclable products and made from wood grown in sustainable forests. The logging and manufacturing processes conform to the legal environmental regulations of the country of origin.

Printed and bound by
CPI Group (UK) Ltd, Croydon, CR0 4YY

To Natashya, for encouraging me to kill my darlings.
And to Nick, for everything else.

Part I

HUNTER

CHAPTER 1

I smelled blood as soon as I walked into the room.

A blast of snow-laced air accompanied me, swirling around my black coat, clinging to my hair and clothes as I shoved back the door. The space beyond was small and dirty, with rotting tables scattered about the floor and steel drums set at every corner, thick smoke pouring from the mouths to hover near the roof. An ancient ceiling fan, half its blades broken or missing, spun limply, doing little to disperse the choking air.

Every eye in the room turned as I stepped through the frame and, once settled on me, didn't glance away. Hard, dangerous, broken faces watched intently as I passed their tables, like feral dogs scenting blood. I ignored them, moving steadily across the creaky floorboards, feeling nails and chips of glass under my boots. I didn't need to take a breath to know the air reeked of sweat and alcohol and human filth.

And blood. The scent of it clung to the walls and floors, soaked into the rotting tables, smeared in dark stains across the wood. It flowed through the veins of every human here, hot and heady. I heard several heartbeats quicken as I made my way to the counter, felt the eager stirrings of lust and hunger, but also the hint of fear, unease. Some of them, at least, were sober enough to guess the truth.

The man behind the counter was a grizzled giant with a snarl of scar tissue across his throat. It crept up his neck and twisted the left corner of his lip into a permanent scowl. He eyed me without expression as I took a seat on one of the moldy bar stools, resting my arms on the badly dinged counter. His gaze flicked to the hilt of the sword strapped to my back, and one of his eyelids twitched.

"I'm afraid I don't have the type of drink you're looking for," he said in a low voice, as his hands slid under the bar. When they came up again, I knew they wouldn't be empty. *Shotgun, probably,* I guessed. *Or maybe a baseball bat.* "Not on tap, anyway."

I smiled without looking up. "You know what I am."

"Wasn't difficult. Pretty girl walking into a place like this either has a death wish or is already dead." He snorted, shooting a dark look at the patrons behind us. I could feel their hooded gazes even now. "I know what you want, and I'm not about to stop you. No one here will miss these idiots. You take what you have to, but don't trash my bar, understand?"

"Actually, I'm just looking for someone," I said, knowing I didn't have a lot of time. The dogs at my back were already stirring. "Someone like me. Bald. Tall. Face scarred all to hell." I finally looked up, meeting his impassive gaze. "Anyone like that come through here?"

A muscle worked in his jaw. Beneath his grimy shirt, his

heartbeat picked up, and a sheen of sweat appeared on his brow. For a moment, he seemed torn about whether he should pull out the gun or whatever he had beneath the counter. I kept my expression neutral, unthreatening, my hands on the bar between us.

"You've seen him," I prodded carefully. He shook himself, then turned that blank stare on me.

"No." The reply seemed dragged from somewhere deep within. "*I* didn't see him. But..." He glanced at the men behind me, as if judging how much time we had, before shaking his head. "About a month ago, a stranger came through. No one saw him enter, and no one saw him leave. But we found what he left behind."

"Left behind?"

"Rickson and his boys. In their home. From one end of it to the other. They said the bodies were so scattered they never found all the pieces."

I bit the inside of my lip. "Did anyone see who did it?"

"Rickson's woman. She lived. At least, until she blew her brains out three days later. But she said the killer was a tall, pale man with a face scarred like the devil himself."

"Anyone with him?"

The barkeep frowned then shook his head. "No, she said he was alone. But he carried a large black bag with him, like a body bag. That's all we could get out of her, anyway. She wasn't terribly coherent, if you know what I mean."

I nodded, drawing back, though the words *body bag* sent a chill through my stomach. *I'm getting closer, though.* "Thank you," I murmured, sliding off the stool. "I'll be going now."

That's when I felt the arm on my shoulder.

"Oh, you're not leaving yet, little girl," murmured a voice in my ear, hot and rancid. A large hand reached down and gripped my wrist, hard enough to bruise, if I could still bruise. "It's too cold outside. Come over here and keep us warm."

A smile tugged at one corner of my mouth. *Finally. Took you long enough.*

I looked at the barkeep. He met my gaze, then very deliberately turned and walked toward the back room. The man next to me didn't seem to notice; his arm slid down my back and curled around my waist, trying to drag me away. I didn't budge an inch, and he frowned, too drunk to realize what was happening.

I waited until the barkeep vanished through the door, letting it swing shut behind him, before I turned to my assailant.

He leered at me, the stench of alcohol coming off him in waves. "That's right, little girl. You want some of this, don'cha?" Behind us, a few more patrons were starting to get up; either they wanted in on the fun, or they thought they could take me out together. The rest watched behind their tankards, tense and wary, smelling of fear.

"Come on then, bitch," the man beside me said, and grabbed my other arm, his face mean and eager. "Let's do this. I can go all night."

I smiled. "Can you now?" I said quietly.

And lunged at him with a roar, sinking my fangs into his throat.

When the barkeep returned, I was already gone. He would find the bodies—the ones stupid enough to stay and fight—lying where they had fallen, a couple in pieces, but most of them still alive. I had what I'd come for. The Hunger had been sated, and better here, in this outpost full of bandits and murderers, than anywhere else. Better these kinds of men than an innocent family or an old couple huddled together in the ruins of an isolated cabin, trying to keep warm. I was a monster who killed and preyed on human life; I could never escape that, but at least I could choose what kind of lives I took.

Outside, the snow was falling again. Thick flakes clung to my eyelashes and cheeks and stuck to my straight black hair, but I didn't feel them. The bitter chill couldn't touch someone who was already dead.

I gave my katana a flick, causing a line of crimson to spatter to the ground. Sliding it into the sheath on my back, I started walking, my boots crunching over frozen mud. Around me, the wood and tin shanties were silent, dark smoke leaking from windows and chimney stacks. No one was out tonight; the humans were all inside, huddled around steel drums and bottles, keeping fire and alcohol between them and the icy cold. No one would see the lone teenage girl in the long black coat, walking down the path between shanties. Just like the town's other visitor, I'd come, taken what I needed and vanished back into the night. Leaving carnage behind me.

About a hundred yards away, a wall of corrugated steel and wire rose into the air, dark and bristling. It was uneven in places, with gaps and holes that had been patched and repatched and finally forgotten about. A flimsy barrier against the creatures that lurked outside the wall. If things continued here with no change, this little outpost would eventually vanish off the face of the earth.

Not my problem.

I leaped to the roof of a shanty leaning against the wall, then over the wall itself, landing lightly on the other side. Straightening, I gazed down the rocky slope to the road that had led me here, now invisible beneath the snow. Even my footsteps, coming in from the east, had vanished beneath the layer of white.

He was here, I thought as the wind whipped my face, tugging at my hair and coat. *Barely a month ago. I'm getting closer. I'm closing the gap.*

Dropping from the cliff, I fell the twenty feet, coat flapping behind me, and landed at the edge of the road, grunting as my body absorbed the shock. Stepping onto the rough, uneven pavement, feeling it crumble under my boots, I walked to where the road split, weaving off in two directions. One path curved away, circling the tiny outpost before heading south; the other continued east, toward the soon-to-be-rising sun.

I gazed down one direction, then the other, waiting. And just like at the last crossroads I'd hit, it was there again. That faint pull, telling me to continue northeast. It was more than a hunch, more than a gut instinct. Though I couldn't explain it completely, I knew which direction would lead me to my sire. *Blood calls to blood.* The killings I'd found on my travels, like the unfortunate family in the settlement behind me, only confirmed it. He was traveling fast, but I was catching up, slowly but surely. He couldn't hide from me forever.

I'm still coming, Kanin.

Dawn was a couple hours away. I could cover a lot of ground before then, so I started off once more, heading down the road toward an unknown destination. Chasing a shadow.

Knowing we were running out of time.

★★★

I walked through the night, the wind icy in my face, unable to numb my already cold skin. The road stretched on, silent and empty. Nothing moved in the darkness. I passed the tangled remains of old neighborhoods, streets vacant and overgrown, buildings crumbling under the weight of the snow and time. Since the plague that wiped out most of humanity and the rabid outbreak soon after, most cities had been reduced to empty husks. I'd found a few settlements scattered here and there, humans living free despite the constant threat of rabids or invasion from their own kind. But the majority of the population existed in the vampire cities, the great, walled-in territories where the coven provided food and "safety" in exchange for blood and freedom. The humans in the vampire cities were nothing more than cattle, really, but that was the price of vampire protection. Or, that's what they wanted you to believe. Monsters existed on both sides of the wall, but at least the rabids were honest about wanting to eat you. In a vampire city, you were really just living on borrowed time, until the killers who smiled and patted you on the head finally showed their true colors.

I should know. I was born there.

The road stretched on, and I followed as it snaked through white forests grown up around sprawling towns and suburbs, until the sky turned charcoal-gray and sluggishness began to drag me under. Heading off the road, I found a faded ranch house choked with weeds and brambles. They grew up through the porch and coiled around the roof, smothering the walls, but the house itself seemed fairly intact. I eased my way up the steps and kicked open the door, ducking inside.

Small furry creatures scurried into the shadows, and a cloud of snow rose from my entry, swirling across the floor. I spared a glance at the simple furniture, covered in dust and cobwebs, strangely undisturbed.

On the wall closest to me sat an old yellow sofa, one side chewed by rodents, spilling dirty fluff over the floor. Memory stirred, a scene of another time, another house like this one, empty and abandoned.

For just a moment, I saw *him* there, slumped against the cushions with his elbows on his knees, pale hair glimmering in the darkness. I remembered the warmth of his hands on my skin, those piercing blue eyes as they gazed at me, trying to figure me out, the tightness in my chest when I'd had to turn away, to leave him behind.

Frowning, I collapsed to the sofa myself and ran a hand over my eyes, dissolving the memory and the last of the frost clinging to my lashes. I couldn't think of him now. He was in Eden with the others. He was safe. Kanin was not.

I leaned back, resting my head on the back of the couch. Kanin. My sire, the vampire who'd Turned me, who'd saved my life and taught me everything I knew—he was the one I had to focus on now.

Just thinking of my maker caused a frown to crease my forehead. I owed the vampire my life, and it was a debt I was determined to repay, though I could never understand him. Kanin had been a mystery from the very start, from that fateful night in the rain when I'd been attacked by rabids outside my city's walls. I'd been dying, and a stranger had appeared out of nowhere, offering to save me, presenting me with the choice. Die…or become a monster.

Obviously, I'd chosen to live. But even after I'd made my decision, Kanin hadn't left. He'd stayed, teaching me what it meant to be a vampire, making sure I knew exactly what I had chosen. I probably wouldn't have survived those first few weeks without him.

But Kanin had secrets of his own, and one night the darkest of them caught up to us in the form of Sarren, a twisted vampire with a vendetta. Dangerous, cunning and completely out of his mind, Sarren had tracked us to the hidden lab we were using as a hideout, and we were forced to flee. In the chaos that had followed, Kanin and I were separated, and my mentor had vanished back into the unknown from where he'd come. I hadn't seen him since.

But then the dreams began.

I rose, the cushions squeaking beneath me, and wandered down a musty hallway to the room at the end. It had been a bedroom at one point, and the twin bed in the corner was far enough away from the window to be out of the sun if it came creeping into the room.

Just to be safe, I hung a ratty blanket over the sill, covering the pane and plunging the room into shadow. Outside, it was still snowing, tiny flakes drifting from a dark, cloudy sky, but I wasn't taking any chances should it clear up. Lying back on the bed, keeping my sword close, I stared at the ceiling and waited for sleep to claim me.

Vampires don't dream. Technically, we are dead, our sleep that of a corpse, black and depthless. My "dreams" were of Kanin, in trouble. Seeing through his eyes and feeling what he felt. Because in times of extreme duress, pain or emotion, blood called to blood, and I could sense what my sire was feeling. Agony. Sarren had found him. And was taking his revenge.

My eyes narrowed as I recalled the very last one.

My throat is raw from screaming.

He didn't hold back last night. He was toying with me before, just showing me the edge of his deranged cruelty. But last night, the true demon came out. He wanted to talk, tried to get me to talk, but I wasn't going to oblige him. So he made me scream instead. At one point, I looked down at my body, hanging like a piece of flayed meat from the ceiling, and wondered how I was still alive. I've never wanted to die so badly as I did then. Surely hell would not be as bad as this. It was testament to Sarren's skill, or perhaps insanity, that he kept me alive when I was doing my best to die.

Tonight, though, he is oddly passive. I woke, as I had countless nights before, hanging by my wrists from the ceiling, mentally preparing myself for the agony that would come later. The Hunger is a living thing, devouring me, a torment all in itself. Lately I see blood everywhere, trickling from the ceiling, oozing past the door. Salvation always beyond reach.

"It's no use."

His voice is a whisper, slithering out of the darkness. Sarren stands a few feet away, watching me blankly, his pale face a web of scars. Last night, his eyes glowed feverishly bright as he screamed and railed at me, demanding I talk, answer his question. Tonight, the dead, empty look on his face chills me like nothing else.

"It's no use," he whispers again, shaking his head. "You're right here, right at my fingertips, and yet I feel nothing." He slides forward, touching my neck with long, bony fingers, his gaze searching. I don't have the strength to jerk away. "Your scream, such a glorious song. I

imagined how it would sound for years. Your blood, your flesh, your bones—I imagined it all. Breaking them. Tasting them." He runs a finger down my throat. "You were mine to break, to peel apart, so I could see the rotted soul that lies beneath this shell of meat and blood. It was to be a magnificent requiem." He steps back, his expression one of near despair. "But I see nothing. And I feel…nothing. Why?" *Whirling away, he stalks to the nearby table, where dozens of sharp instruments glint in the darkness. "Am I doing something wrong?" he murmurs, tracing them with a fingertip. "Is he not to pay for what he has done?"*

I close my eyes. What he has done. *Sarren deserves to hate me. What I did to him, what I was responsible for—I deserve every torment he heaps on my head. But it won't make things right. It won't put an end to what I caused.*

As if reading my thoughts, Sarren turns back, and the gleam in his eyes has returned. It burns with searing intensity, showing the madness and brilliance behind it, and for the first time, I feel a stirring fear through the numbing agony and pain.

"No," he whispers slowly, in a daze, as if everything has suddenly become clear. "No, I see now. I see what I must do. It is not you *that is the source of the corruption. You were merely the harbinger. This whole world is pulsing with rot and decay and filth. But, we will fix it, old friend. Yes, we will fix it. Together."*

His hand skims the top of the table to the very end, picking up the item on the corner. It isn't bright like the others—shiny metal polished to a gleaming edge. It is long, wooden, and comes to a crude, whittled point at the end.

I shiver, every instinct telling me to back away, to put distance between myself and that sharp wooden point. But I can't move, and Sarren approaches slowly, the stake held before him like a cross. He is smiling again, a demonic grin that stretches his entire ravaged face and makes his fangs gleam.

"I can't kill you, yet," he says, touching my chest with the very tip of the stake, right over my heart. "No, not yet. That would spoil the ending, and I have a glorious song in mind. Oh, yes, it will be magnificent. And you…you will be the instrument on which I compose this symphony." He steps forward and pushes the tip of the stake into my chest, slowly, twisting it as it sinks beneath my skin. I throw back my head, clenching my jaw to keep the scream contained, as Sarren continues. "No, old friend. Death is still too good for you. We're just going to send you to sleep for a while." The stake continues to slide into my flesh, parting muscle and scraping against my breastbone, creeping closer to my heart. The wood becomes a bright strip of fire, searing me from the inside. My body convulses and starts to shut down. Darkness hovers at the edge of my vision—hibernation pulling me under, a last effort at self-preservation. Sarren smiles.

"Sleep now, old friend," he whispers, his scarred face fading rapidly as my vision goes dark. "But not for long. I have something special planned." He chuckles, the empty sound following me down into blackness. "You won't want to miss it."

The vision had ended there. And I hadn't had any more dreams since.

I shifted on the bed, bringing the sword close to my chest, thinking. I'd tracked Sarren to one place he *had* been: a rotted-out ruin of a house in an empty suburb, a long flight of steps leading down to the basement. The scent of Kanin's blood had hit me like a hammer as soon as I'd opened the door. It had been everywhere—on the walls, on the chains that hung from the ceiling, on the instruments spread over the table. A dark stain had marred the floor right below the metal links, making my stomach turn. It didn't seem possible that Kanin had survived, that *anything* could have survived that macabre dungeon. But I had to believe that he was still alive, that Sarren wasn't finished with him just yet.

My hunch had been confirmed when, as I'd explored further, I'd discovered the stiff, decaying bodies of several humans tossed casually in a closet upstairs. They had been drained of blood, their throats cut open instead of bitten, a stained pitcher sitting on a table nearby. Sarren had been feeding Kanin, letting him heal between sessions. Closing the door on the pile of corpses, I'd felt a deep stab of sympathy and fear for my mentor. Kanin had made mistakes, but no one deserved that. I had to rescue him from Sarren's sick insanity, before he drove my sire completely over the edge.

Gray light was beginning to filter through the holes in the blanket over the window, and I grew evermore sluggish in response. *Hang in there, Kanin,* I thought. *I'll find you, I swear. I'm catching up.*

Although, if I was honest with myself, the thought of facing Sarren again, seeing that blank, empty smile, the fevered intensity of his gaze, terrified me more then I cared to admit. I remembered his face through Kanin's eyes, and though I hadn't noticed it in the dream, I'd later recalled the film across his left eye, pale and cloudy. He'd been blinded there, and recently. I knew, because the pocketknife that had been jammed into his pupil the last time I saw him…was mine.

And I knew he hadn't forgotten me, either.

CHAPTER 2

Four months ago, I walked away from Eden.

Or, more accurately, I was forced out. Much like Adam and Eve getting kicked out of their infamous garden, I had reached Eden with a small group of pilgrims only to be turned away at the gates. Eden was a city under human rule, the only one of its kind, a walled-in paradise with no monsters or demons to prey on its unsuspecting citizens. And I was the monster they feared most. I had no place there.

Not that I would've stayed, regardless. I had a promise to keep. I had to find someone, help him, before his time ran out.

So, I'd left Eden and the company of the humans I'd protected all the way there. The group I'd left was smaller than the group I'd first joined; the journey had been hard and dangerous, and we'd lost several along the way. But I was glad for the ones who'd made it. They were safe, now. They no longer had to worry about starvation or cold, being chased by raiders or stalked by vampires. They no longer had to fear the rabids, the vicious, mindless creatures that roamed the land after dark, killing anything they came across. No, the humans who'd made it to Eden had found their sanctuary. I was happy for them.

Though, there was…one…I regretted leaving behind.

The sky was clear the following night, spotted with stars, a frozen half-moon lighting the way. The wind and the crunch of my boots in the snow were the only sounds keeping me company. As always, while walking alone through this quiet, empty landscape, my mind drifted to places I wished it wouldn't.

I thought of my old life, my human one, when I was simply Allie the street rat, Allie the Fringer, scraping out a meager existence with my old crew, facing starvation and exposure and a million other deaths, just to declare that we were "free." Until the night we'd tempted fate a bit more than usual and had paid for it with our lives.

New Covington. That was the name of the vampire city where I was born, grew up and ultimately died. In my seventeen years, I hadn't known anything else. I'd known nothing of the world beyond the Outer Wall that kept out the rabids, or of the Inner City, where the vampires lived in their dark, gleaming towers, looking down on all of us. My whole existence had consisted of the Fringe, the outer ring of New Covington where the human cattle were kept, herded in by fences and branded with tattoos. The rules were simple: if you were branded—Registered to the masters—you were fed and somewhat taken care of, but the catch was, you were owned. Property. And that meant you had to donate blood on a regular basis. If you were Unregistered, you were left to fend for yourself in a city with no food and no supplies except the ones the masters allotted; but at least the vamps couldn't take your blood unless they caught you themselves.

Of course, you still had to worry about starving to death.

Back when I was human, I'd struggled with hunger every day. My life had revolved around finding food and little else. There had been four of us in my small gang—me, Lucas, Rat and Stick. We had all been Unregistered; street rats, beggars and thieves, living together in an abandoned school and barely scraping by. Until one stormy night when we'd ventured beyond the Outer Wall to find food…and became the hunted ourselves. It had been stupid to step outside the protection of New Covington, but I'd insisted, and my stubbornness had cost us everything. Lucas and Rat had been killed, and I'd been pulled down and torn apart by a pack of rabids. My life should've ended that night in the rain.

In a way, I guess it had. I'd died that night in Kanin's arms. And now that I was a monster, I could never go back to the life I'd known. I'd tried, once, to contact a friend from my old life, the boy named Stick whom I'd looked after for years. But Stick, seeing what I'd become, had screamed and fled from me in terror, confirming what Kanin had always told me. There was no going back. Not to New Covington, not to my old life, not to anything that was human. Kanin had been right all along. He was always right.

I thought of him often, of the nights we'd spent in the secret lab beneath the vampire city where I was born. His lessons, teaching me what it meant to be a vampire, how to hunt and fight and kill. The humans I'd preyed on, their screams, the warm blood in my mouth, intoxicating and terrible. And

Kanin himself, who'd taught me, in no uncertain terms, what I was—a vampire and a demon—but also that my path was my own; that I had a choice.

You are a monster. His voice was always so clear in my head, as if he was standing right next to me, his dark eyes boring into my skull. *You will always be a monster—there is no turning back from it. But what kind of monster you become is entirely up to you.* That was the lesson I clung to most, the one I swore I'd never forget.

But Kanin had another rule as well, one I hadn't remembered so clearly as the first. The one about humans, and becoming attached...

And just like that, my traitor mind shifted to a lean figure with jagged blond hair and solemn blue eyes. I remembered his smile, that lopsided grin meant only for me. I remembered his touch, the heat that radiated from him when we were close. His fingers sliding over my skin, the warmth of his lips on mine...

I shook my head. Ezekiel Crosse was human. I was a vampire. No matter what I felt, no matter how strong my feelings, I could never separate the urge to kiss Zeke from the desire to sink my fangs into his throat. That was another reason I'd left Eden without saying goodbye, without letting anyone know where I was going. I couldn't be near Zeke without putting his life in danger. Eventually, I would kill him.

It was better to be alone. Vampires were predators; the Hunger was always with us, the craving for human blood that could take over at any time. Lose yourself to the Hunger, and the people around you died. It had been a hard lesson for me to learn, and one that I did not ever want to repeat. It was always there—that fear that I would slip, that the Hunger would take over again and when I came back to myself I would have killed someone I knew. Even the men I preyed on—bandits, raiders, marauders, murderers—they were all still human. They were living beings, and I killed them to feed myself. To keep myself from attacking others. I could choose what kind of people I preyed on, but in the end, I had to prey on someone. The lesser of the two evils was still evil.

Zeke was too good to be dragged down by that darkness.

Deliberately, I forced my thoughts away from Zeke before they grew too painful. To keep myself distracted, I concentrated on the pull, the strange tug that I still didn't understand, even now. Awake, I barely felt it; only in sleep could I sense Kanin's thoughts, see through his eyes. Or, at least, I could before that last vision, when Sarren had driven a wooden stake into Kanin's chest, sending him into hibernation.

I couldn't feel Kanin's experiences anymore. But when I concentrated, I did know which direction would lead me to my sire. I did that now, emptying my mind of all other thoughts, and searched for Kanin.

The pull was still there, a faint pulse to the east, but… something was wrong. Not dangerous or threatening, but there was an odd sensation in my gut, that nagging feeling you get when you know you've forgotten something and you just can't remember what. Dawn was still hours away; I wasn't in danger of being caught outside in the light. There was nothing I could have left behind except my sword, and that was strapped firmly across my back. Why, then, did I feel so uneasy?

A few minutes later, it hit me.

The pull I was following, that strange but unerring sense of *knowing,* was slowly splitting off, moving in different directions. I stopped in the middle of the road, wondering if I was mistaken. I wasn't. There was still a strong pull to the east, but also a fainter one, now, to the north.

I frowned. Two directions. What could it mean? And where was I supposed to go, now? The feeling to the east was stronger; I just barely felt the compulsion to the north, but it was definitely there. Impossible as it seemed, I had come to a crossroad. And I had no idea where to go.

Did Kanin free himself, somehow? Is he fleeing north, and I'm tracking Sarren down alone? It doesn't seem likely that Sarren would be the one to run. Upon reflection, my frown deepened, the sense of worry and unease growing stronger. Is *it Sarren? Would I even feel anything from him? We're not blood kin, we're not related in any way that I know of. What's going on here?*

Utterly bewildered, I stood in the center of the road trying to decide what to do, which direction to follow. I was still new to this vampire-blood-tie thing and had no idea why there would be two pulls instead of one. Had Sarren fed from Kanin, perhaps? Was it possible that Sarren *was* related to me and my sire in some distant past, centuries ago?

It was a mystery, and one I had no way to solve. In the end, I continued east. Indecision and doubt still nagged at me as the other sense of *knowing* continued to pull away, but I couldn't be in two places at once; I had to pick a direction and keep going. So I chose the stronger of the two urges, and if it led me right to a pissed-off, psychotic vampire eager to peel the skin from my bones, then I would just have to deal with that bump when I got there.

★★★

When I woke the next evening, the second pull had shifted completely to the west. I ignored it and my doubts and continued eastward. For two more nights, I walked through unending forest and rotted towns, my only company the road and the occasional flash of wildlife in the darkness. Deer were abundant out here, as were raccoons, opossums and the odd mountain lion stalking its prey through the trees and broken houses. They didn't bother me, except to give me the evil eye, and I left them alone, as well. I wasn't Hungry, and animal blood, as I'd learned the hard way, did nothing to satisfy the monster within.

The snow and heavy woodlands continued, the road I traveled strangled on either side with vegetation that split the pavement and pushed its way up through the cracks. Eventually, though, the road widened, and dead cars began to appear, rusty hulks of metal beneath the snow, growing more numerous as I traveled. I was approaching a city, and my instincts prickled a warning. Most empty towns and suburbs were just that, broken and deserted, with crumbling houses lining silent, overgrown streets. But the cities, once a place of thousands of humans living side by side, were overrun with a different species now.

The road widened even more, became a highway, stubbornly pushing back the choking forest. More vehicles appeared, turning the road into a maze of rusted metal and glass, though only on the side of the highway leaving the city. I kept to the other, empty lane, passing the endless stream of dead, smashed cars, trying not to look inside, though sometimes it was impossible not to see. A skeleton lay against the steering wheel of a crumpled car, half-buried in the snow that drifted through the broken windshield. Another dangled beneath a charred, overturned truck. Thousands of people, trying to leave the city all at once. Had they been fleeing the plague, or the madness that came soon after?

The road wound through the sprawling city streets, piled high with snow and coated with a thick layer of ice. I left the car-choked main road and entered the empty side streets, finding it easier to navigate the smaller paths.

After crossing a windy bridge over a sullen gray river, I stumbled upon a huge marble building, relatively clear of vegetation and strangely undisturbed. Curious, and because it was in the same direction of the pull I'd been following, I headed toward it then made my way along the outer wall. Half the roof had fallen in, and a couple of the enormous pillars surrounding it were crushed and broken. An entire corner had crumbled away, and rubble was strewn across the floor. I ducked inside, gazing around cautiously.

The room, for its enormous size, was quite empty. Nothing lived here, it seemed, except the single owl that swooped out from the high, vaulted ceiling when I came in. Marble pillars lined the room, and I could make out words carved into the walls on both sides, though they were too cracked and eroded to read.

Against the back wall, looming up to an impossible height, was a statue. An enormous statue of a man sitting on a marble chair, his wrists resting against the arms. One of his hands was missing, and there were many small cracks in his stony features, but he was surprisingly undamaged. The marble chair had been streaked with paint, scrawled with ugly words that continued up the wall, and one corner of the statue was blackened, as if burned. But the man in the chair was still noble looking despite the damage. His great, craggy face peered down, looking right at me, and it was eerie, standing there beneath the stone gaze of a giant. As I backed toward the exit, the hollow eyes appeared to follow me out. Still, I thought it was a kind face, one that didn't belong in this time. I wondered who he had been, to be immortalized in such a way. There were so many things about the time Before that I didn't know; huge statues and marble buildings that seemed to serve no purpose. All very strange.

Outside, I paused to get my bearings. Straight ahead, a rectangle of cracked cement stretched away from the bottom of the steps. Leaves and branches were frozen beneath a layer of ice filling the shallow pool, and the rusty hulk of a car lay on its side at the edge.

And then, I saw the strangest sight yet. Beyond the steps, directly in front of me, a huge white tower rose into the night. It was ridiculously thin and pointed, a pale needle scraping the clouds, looking as if a strong breeze could blow it over.

And that faint pull was drawing me right toward it.

I hurried down the steps and skirted the edges of the pool, my boots squelching in mud, weeds and slush. Past the cement, the land dissolved into swampy marshland filled with brush, reeds and puddles of icy water. As I drew closer and the tower loomed overhead, I realized that the tug, the pull I'd been tracking for months, was stronger than it had ever been. Though it wasn't coming from the tower itself; rather, from another large white building, barely visible over a canopy of trees beyond.

Resolved that my prey was so close, I stalked forward, pushing through weeds and brush.

And stopped.

Several hundred yards from the tower, past a crumbling street lined with rusty cars and across another swampy lawn, a bristling fence rose out of the ground to scar the horizon. About twelve feet tall, made of black iron bars topped with coils of barbed wire, it was a familiar sight. I'd seen many walls in my travels across the country—concrete and wood, steel and stone. They were everywhere, surrounding every settlement, from tiny farms to entire cities. They all had one purpose, and that purpose was right in front of me, preventing any further advances tonight.

A huge swarm of spindly, emaciated creatures crowded the fence line, hissing and snarling, baring jagged fangs. They moved with a jerky, spastic gait, sometimes on all fours, hunched over and unnatural. Their clothes—the few that had them anyway—were in tatters, their hair tangled and matted. Chalky skin was stretched tightly over bones, and the eyes in the gaunt, bony faces reflected the soullessness behind them. A blank, dead wall of white.

Rabids. I growled softly and eased back into the shadow of a tree. They hadn't seen me yet. As I huddled behind the trunk, watching the shambling horde, I noticed a weird thing. The rabids didn't rush the fence or try to scramble over it, though they could have easily clawed their way to the top if they tried. Instead, they skulked around the edge, always a few feet away, never touching the iron bars.

Even more curious now, I peered past the rabid horde through the fence and clenched my fists so hard the nails dug into my palms.

Looming above the gates, beyond the iron barrier, a squat white building crouched in the weeds. The entrance to the place was circular, lined with columns, and I could make out flickering lights through the windows.

And I knew.

He's in there. If I had a heartbeat, it would be thudding loudly now. I was so close. But who would it be? Who would I run into, once I finally caught up? Would I meet my sire, and would he be surprised to see me? Would he be angry that I'd tracked him down? Or would I run into a dangerous, terrifyingly insane vampire all too eager to torture me to death?

Guess I'll find out soon enough.

The breeze shifted, and the awful, dead stench of the rabids hit me full force, making me wrinkle my nose. They weren't going to let me saunter up and knock on what was probably the local vampire Prince's door. And I couldn't fight the whole huge swarm. A few of the savage creatures I could deal with, but taking on this many ventured very close to suicide. Once was enough, thanks. I'd dealt with a massive horde like this one outside the gates of Eden, and survived only because there had been a large lake nearby, and rabids were afraid of deep water. Vampire or not, even I could be dragged under and torn apart by sheer numbers.

Frowning, I pondered my plan of attack. I needed to get past the rabids without being seen. The fence was only twelve feet tall; maybe I could vault over it?

One of the rabids snarled and shoved another that had jostled it, sending it stumbling toward the fence. Hissing, the other rabid put out a hand to catch itself, grabbing on to the iron bars.

There was a blinding flash and an explosion of sparks, and the rabid shrieked, convulsing on the metal. Its body jerked and spasmed, sending the other rabids skittering back. Finally, the smoke pouring off its blackened skin erupted into flame and consumed the monster from the inside.

Okay, definitely not touching the fence.

I growled. Dawn wasn't far, and soon I would have to fall back to find shelter from the sun. Which meant abandoning any plans to get past the gate until tomorrow night. I was so close! It irked me that I was mere yards from my target and the only thing keeping me from my goal was a rabid horde and a length of electrified metal.

Wait. Dawn *was* approaching. Which meant that the rabids would have to sleep soon. They couldn't face the light any better than a vampire; they would have to burrow into the ground to escape the burning rays of the sun.

Under normal circumstances, I would, as well.

But these weren't normal circumstances. And I wasn't your average vampire. Kanin had taught me better than that.

To keep up the appearance of being human, I'd trained myself to stay awake when the sun rose. Even though it was very, *very* difficult and something that went against all my vampire instincts, I could remain awake and active if I had to. For a little while, at least. But the rabids were slaves to instinct and wouldn't even try to resist. They would vanish into the earth, and with the threat of rabids gone, the power that ran through the fence would probably be shut off. There'd be no need to keep it running in the daytime, especially with fuel or whatever powered the fence in short supply. If I could stay awake long enough, the rabids would disappear and the fence would be shut off. And I'd have a clear shot to the house and whoever was inside it. I just had to deal with the sun.

It might not be wise, continuing my quest in the daylight. I would be slow, my reactions muted. But if Sarren was in that house, he would be slow, too. He might even be asleep, not expecting Kanin's vengeful daughter to come looking for him here. I could get the jump on him...if I could stay awake.

I scanned the grounds, marking where the shadows were thickest, where the trees grew close together. Smartly, the area surrounding the fence was clear of brush and trees. Indirect sunlight wouldn't harm us, but it was still unpleasant, even in the shade, knowing that if the light shifted or a gust of wind tossed the branches, you'd be in a great deal of pain.

As the sky lightened and the sun grew close to breaking the horizon, the horde began to disappear. Breaking away from the fence, they skulked off to bury themselves in the soft mud, their pale bodies vanishing beneath water and earth. The grounds surrounding the fence emptied swiftly, until there wasn't a rabid to be seen.

I leaned against the trunk of a thick oak, fighting the urge to follow the vicious creatures beneath the earth. It was still madly difficult to remain conscious as the sun rose into the sky. My thoughts felt sluggish, my body heavy and tired. But my training to remain above ground, even when our greatest enemy poked its head above the trees, paid off, and I was still standing when the last stubborn rabid disappeared beneath the earth. Still I waited until the sun had nearly risen above the trees, to allow time for the fence to be shut off. It would be hilariously tragic if I avoided the rabids, avoided the sun, only to be fried to a crisp on a damn electric fence because I was too impatient. About twenty or so minutes after the horde disappeared, the faint hum coming from the metal barrier finally clicked off. The fence was down.

Now came the most dangerous part.

I pulled my coat over my head and tugged down the sleeves

so they covered my hands. Direct sunlight on my skin would cause it to blacken, rupture and eventually burst into flame, but I could buy myself time if it was covered.

Still, I was *not* looking forward to this.

All my vampire instincts were screaming at me to stop when I stepped out from under the branches, feeling the weak rays of dawn beating down on me. Not daring to look up, I hurried across the grounds, moving from tree to tree and darting into shade whenever I could. The stretch closest to the fence was the most dangerous, with no trees, no cover, nothing but short grass and the sun heating the back of my coat. I clenched my teeth, hunched my shoulders and kept moving.

As I approached the black iron barrier, I scooped up a scrap of metal and hurled it out in front of me. It arced through the air and struck the bars with a faint clatter before dropping to the ground. No sparks, no flash of light, no smoke. I didn't know much about electric fences, but I took that as a good sign.

Let's hope that fence really is off.

I leaped toward the top, feeling a brief stab of fear as my fingers curled around the bars. Thankfully, they remained cold and dead beneath my hands, and I scrambled over the fence in half a second and landed on the other side in a crouch.

In the brief moment it took me to leap over the iron barrier, my coat slipped off my head. My relief at being inside the fence without cooking myself was short-lived as blinding pain seared my face and hands. I gasped, frantically tugging my coat back up while scrambling under the nearest tree. Crouching down, I examined my hands and winced. They were red and aching from just a few seconds in the sunlight.

I've got to get inside.

Keeping close to the ground, I hurried across the tangled,

snowy lawn, feeling horribly exposed as I drew closer to the building. If someone pushed aside those heavy curtains in front of the huge windows, they would most definitely spot me. But the windows and grounds remained dark and empty as I reached the curving wall and darted beneath an archway, relieved to be out of the light.

Okay. Now what?

The faint tug, that subtle hint of *knowing,* was stronger than ever as I crept up the stairs and peeked through a curtained window. The strange, circular room beyond was surprisingly intact. A table stood in the center with several chairs around it, all thankfully deserted. Beyond that room was an empty hallway, and even more rooms beyond that.

I stifled a groan. Finding one comatose vampire in such a huge house was going to be a challenge. But I couldn't give up.

The glass on the windows was shockingly unbroken, and the window itself was unlocked. I slid through the frame and dropped silently onto the hardwood floor, glancing warily about. Humans lived here, I realized, a lot of them. I could smell them on the air, the lingering scent of warm bodies and blood. I wondered why the scent didn't knock me down the second I came into the room. If Sarren was here, he'd likely paint the walls in their blood.

But I didn't run into *any* humans, alive or dead, as I made my way through the gigantic house, and that worried me. Especially since it was obvious this place was well taken care of. Nothing appeared broken. The walls and floor were clean and uncluttered, the furniture, though old, was sturdy and carefully arranged. The Prince who lived here either had a lot of servants to keep this place up and running, or he was incredibly dedicated to cleaning.

I continued to scan the shadows and the dozens of empty rooms, wary and alert, searching for movement. But the house remained dark and lifeless as I crept up a long flight of steps, down an equally long corridor, and stopped outside the thick wooden door at the end.

This is it.

Carefully, I grasped my sword and eased it out, being sure the metal didn't scrape against the sheath. Getting here had been way too easy. Whoever was on the other side of that door knew I was coming. If Sarren was expecting me, I'd be ready, too. If Kanin was in there, I wasn't leaving until I got him out safe.

Firmly grasping the door handle, I wrenched it to the side and flung the door open.

A figure stood at the back wall, waiting, as I'd feared. He wore a black leather duster, and his arms, crossed lazily over his chest, were empty of weapons. Thick, dark hair tumbled to his shoulders, and a pale, handsome face met mine over the room, lips curled into an evil smile.

"Hello, sister," Jackal greeted, his gold eyes shining in the dim light. "It's about time you showed up."

CHAPTER 3

"Jackal," I whispered, as the tall, lean vampire sauntered toward me. I remembered when I'd seen him last, the self-declared Prince of a flooded raider city, its residents as dangerous and ruthless as himself. He had gone through a lot of trouble to capture the humans I'd traveled with, three years of searching the roads, of having his men comb the countryside. And once Jackal had found them, he hadn't been above sacrificing them, one by one, to get what he wanted. Zeke and I had managed to rescue our group from Jackal's demented clutches, but several had died in the process, and the pain of that failure to save them still haunted me.

Why was Jackal here now? The last I'd seen of him, he had been shoved out of a thirty-story window—after, I remembered quite clearly, he'd jammed a wooden stake into my stomach. I didn't have fond memories of the raider king, and I knew Jackal wasn't terribly happy with me, either.

Then the implication hit me like a brick in the chest, and

I stared at him in horror. Kanin was our sire, having Turned the both of us. The raider king was my "blood brother," and *blood called to blood*. No wonder there had been two pulls. If Jackal was here, then *he* was the presence I'd been following. Not Kanin. Not Sarren. I'd chosen to track the wrong lead.

I gripped my sword so hard the hilt bit into my palm, and I would've snarled in frustration had Jackal not been twenty feet away. Who knew how far Sarren had extended his lead now? Months of searching, of trying to close the gap and find my sire, all for nothing! The psychotic vampire still had him and could be on the other side of the world for all I knew.

And here I was, trapped in this house with my brother, who probably wanted to kill me.

"I've been waiting for you, sister." Jackal smiled as he approached, fangs gleaming. His duster billowed behind him, and I caught a glint of metal beneath. "You took your sweet time, didn't you? And after the Prince of Old D.C. told all the guards and house staff to hide in the basement to let you through, just in case you were Hungry, you still had to skulk through the house like a common burglar. Didn't it seem a bit odd, not running into anyone?"

Now I did snarl at him, baring my fangs. "What are you doing here, Jackal?"

"Visiting the Prince," Jackal said mildly, and shrugged. "Waiting for you." He continued to grin at me, smug and dangerous. "Oh, what's the matter, sister? Did you not expect me? Were you hoping to run into someone else?"

"I was, actually," I shot back, and took a step forward, raising my sword. "But I'll take care of you before I go looking for him again. Let's get on with it."

"Let's not," said a low voice, and a new presence entered the room, closing the door behind her. A tall, statuesque woman gazed down at me with large black eyes. Full red lips stood out sharply against her dusky skin, and her hair floated around her face like a dark cloud. "If you and Jackal are going to fight," she said in a throaty voice, "then wait until tonight and do it outside. I'd rather not have you throwing each other around and breaking furniture."

"Azura." Jackal smiled, waving a hand at me. "This is my lovely little sister."

"I gathered that," the vampiress said, not returning the smile. To me, she said, "Please put your weapon away. If you are going to remain in my house, you will do so on civil terms. I would hate to have you thrown out to face the sun."

I felt trapped, staring them down. Two vampires, one of whom was still a Prince and probably a Master. I was all too happy to fight Jackal again, but I doubted I could take them both. The female had that same calm, cool air of another vampire I knew, another Master, and I could feel the power in that deceitfully slender form.

I sheathed my blade cautiously, still keeping a wary eye on Jackal, who looked far too pleased with this whole situation. "What's going on?"

"Azura is an old…acquaintance of mine," Jackal said, shooting the vampire woman a sultry look. Other than a raised eyebrow, she did not respond. "I thought, since I was passing through, I would her pay a visit. Of course, once I sensed you coming, I thought I'd stick around and wait for you."

"If you're looking for a fight, I'll be glad to give you one."

"Trust me, sister. Nothing would make me happier." Jackal

bared his fangs in an evil grin, and I tensed, ready to draw my sword again. "I would love to tear the head from your neck and stick it on the wall outside, but I promised Azura I would behave." He jerked his head at the vampire woman, who continued to watch us both with detached amusement. "Besides," Jackal continued, "I thought you might be interested to know what I discovered about Kanin and Sarren."

That threw me. I narrowed my eyes, staring him down. "How do you know about that?"

"Oh, come on." Jackal crossed his arms. "You're not the only one looking for our dear sire. Kanin and I need to have a little talk, but that freak Sarren is making it difficult. Did you actually come here looking for them?" He shook his head, either in admiration or disgust. "What would you have done if it had been Sarren you stumbled onto, and not me? You think you're a match for him, little sister? He would have turned you inside out."

"So what are *you* doing?" I challenged. "Hiding out here, hoping Sarren gets bored or tired of tormenting Kanin? Don't want to take on Sarren yourself?"

"Damn straight," Jackal returned with a flash of fangs. "I'm not going after that psycho unless I have to. You think I'm bad?" He snorted and shook his head. "You haven't seen anything until you've met crazy Sarren. And you sure as hell won't be able to take him on alone. Not even Kanin wanted to cross paths with him. He'll completely destroy you."

I blinked, startled at the underlying fear in Jackal's voice. It sounded like he had run into Sarren before, as well, or maybe Kanin had simply warned him about Psycho Vamp and his eternal vendetta. Whatever the reason, hearing Jackal's warning made me even more reluctant to face Sarren and more desperate to get Kanin away from him.

"Listen to your brother," Azura broke in, startling me. "He is correct. We all have heard of Sarren and his cruelty, his ruthlessness, his brilliance even through his madness. When I heard that he was in the city, I ordered my humans to not leave the house even during the day, and ran the fence continuously until I was certain he was gone."

Damn. Even the Master vampire, the Prince of this city, was scared of Sarren. How strong was he, really? Or was he just an unpredictable nut job that no one wanted around, spouting creepy poetry and making everyone nervous?

Somehow, I doubted it. Sarren was cunning and dangerous enough to capture Kanin, the strongest vampire I knew. True, Psycho Vamp had been after him for a very, very long time, and it was partially my fault that he had found us, but still. If *Kanin* had succumbed to Sarren's cruel insanity, what would he do to me?

"So, why are you still here?" I demanded, glaring at Jackal. "You said you were waiting for me—here I am. What do you want?"

"I have a proposition for you."

Instantly suspicious, I stiffened, and Jackal sighed. "Oh, don't give me that look, sister. I'm a reasonable guy." He smiled dangerously. "You invaded my city, set it on fire, killed my men, and destroyed over ten years of careful planning, but that doesn't mean we can't reach an agreement."

"I have nothing to say to you," I growled. "There's nothing you can offer that will keep me here. I'm leaving. If you want a fight, try me again when the sun goes down."

"Well, that's a shame," Jackal replied, seeming unconcerned as I turned away. "Because I know what Sarren was looking for."

I paused a few feet from the hall. I could feel Jackal's smug, knowing grin at my back and, hating myself, turned slowly back around. "What are you talking about?"

"Like I said, Sarren came to Old D.C. looking for something. Showed up a few days before I did, then took off again with Kanin. I didn't follow, because I'm not stupid enough to take him on myself, and because I could feel you coming. So I thought I'd wait for you."

"You still haven't answered my question. Or given me any reason to stick around." I narrowed my eyes. "In fact, you have about five seconds to make your case before I walk out that door."

"Oh, trust me. You'll want to hear this." The former raider king crossed his arms, unconcerned. "You know how the rabids were created, don't you?" he asked. "That it was our dear sire, the noble Kanin himself, who sacrificed our own kind to seek a cure to the plague, only to have the humans screw everything up when they changed those vampires into rabids?"

"He told me."

"Good. Saves me the time of explaining everything." Jackal leaned against a bookcase. "Well, they didn't have just the one lab. The government had a few of them, scattered about the country, all frantically working to end the plague. And one of them is somewhere in this city." He grinned at my startled expression. "Yeah, Kanin once mentioned there was a hidden lab in the old capital, and when Sarren came sniffing around, I figured that's what he was looking for."

"Where is this lab?"

"No idea." Jackal shrugged. "Figured I'd talk to Azura, see if she knew anything about it. She thinks that it's underneath the city somewhere, down in the old tunnel systems that run belowground. Problem is, those tunnels are crawling with rabids, making it difficult to search for it. That's when I got the brilliant idea to wait until you showed up. I figured we'd cover more ground if we looked for it together."

It was my turn to snort. "And I'm going to agree to help you…why?"

"Because if you help me find the lab," Jackal returned, "I'll help you save Kanin."

"I don't need your help—"

"Yes, you do." He pushed himself off the bookcase, giving me an intense look. "You don't know Sarren. You don't know what he's capable of. You think you're going to storm his lair, take him out and rescue Kanin, but you're wrong. Sarren's a crazy bastard, and he's older and smarter than either of us. You want to stop him, you're going to need my help. We can always kill each other later, when we catch up to our sire. But if you want to see Kanin again, you're going to have to trust me."

"Because you have such a great track record in that department?"

"Oh, come on," Jackal said, smiling encouragingly. "Just because I staked you and tossed you out a window? Surely we can get past that little misunderstanding."

"No," I growled, feeling my fangs slip through my gums. "It's not what you did to me. You kidnapped and murdered my friends. You fed one of them to a rabid. You tortured a man to get what you wanted, and you are responsible for his death." I remembered the bloodstained arena, the cage in the center and the rabid pulling its victim down with chilling screams. My lip curled back from my fangs. "I should kill you now for what you did to them."

"Is that so?" Jackal regarded me intently. "Then tell me, my dear sister, how many have *you* killed? How many of my men died when you fled the city with your little 'friends,' hmm? How many throats have you torn out, how many humans have you ripped apart, because you couldn't control the Hunger? Or maybe I'm wrong." He tilted his head with a fake quizzical expression. "Maybe you're the first of our kind who doesn't need human blood to survive. If that's the case, then please, tell me now so I can apologize and be on my way." He looked at me expectantly with his eyebrows raised. I clenched my fists and glared back, and he nodded. "Who are you trying to fool? People are *food*. You know it as well as I do. So don't expect me to feel terribly guilty about killing your humans, not when you reek of blood and death. You're not any less of a monster then I am."

I growled, half tempted to lunge and cut that smirking head from his body. Zeke's father, Jebbadiah Crosse, deserved that much justice. So did Darren and Ruth and all the others we'd lost because of the raider king. But Azura took a single step forward, placing herself closer to me and Jackal, and I could feel her readiness to jump in if needed.

"Work with me here, sister," Jackal went on, his voice low and cajoling. "I'm not asking for much. I just want you to help me find the lab. Then we can go rescue the old man, but I need to find the lab first."

"That could take time," I argued. "Time I don't have. Time Kanin doesn't have. We have to get to him before—"

"Kanin is already dead," Jackal snapped. "Or as near to it as he can be. Sarren forced him into hibernation, and it's rare for us to come out of that. He isn't going to wake up anytime soon. And if Sarren wanted him truly destroyed, he would've done it by now."

"Why are you so eager to find this place?"

Jackal gave me a look of incredulous contempt. "You really have to ask me that?" He sighed and shook his head. "What have I been after this whole time? What was so important that I searched the country for three years to find that old preacher and his little congregation? What would bring me here, to ask for *your* help, when I had a whole army of raiders and minions ready to do my bidding? Think hard, sister. It's not that difficult."

I didn't have to think about it. "The cure," I whispered. Jackal smirked and nodded.

"Yeah. The cure. The end of Rabidism. That's a little more important than finding Kanin right now." He held up a hand as I glared. "I still want to find the old man," he told me. "Like I said, we need to have a talk. And I'm going to need your help to get him away from Sarren. So…you help me, and I'll do the same." He bared his fangs in a savage grin. "And then, after all that is out of the way, you can try to kill me, and I'll stick another stake in your gut and leave you for the rabids, what d'ya say?"

"Jackal," Azura said, sounding faintly exasperated, "if you wish this girl's cooperation, I suggest you stop taunting her. She is not one of your simple human thugs whom you can cower with a threat. If I am forced to kill her because of your uncharitable attitude, I will be very annoyed with you. Now…" She turned that dark, intense stare on me. "The sun is up, and I am very tired. If you two wish to continue your verbal sparring, I ask that you wait until evening. For now, I offer my home for as long as you have need of it."

"Um..." I hesitated, not sure what to make of this generosity, if I should trust it. Or her. But she was right. The sun was up, and unless I wanted to venture outside, I would have to take my chances. "Thank you."

Azura blinked slowly. "I would offer you the guest suite across from Jackal's, but I fear I might return to a war zone. So I will have William show you to one of the lower suites. We will continue this conversation tonight. And, girl..." Her dark gaze narrowed, turning ominous and threatening. "I can smell the blood on you. Do *not* eat my staff, or I will forget my hospitality long enough to remove the head from your neck, is that understood?"

I bit down a smirk. Diplomacy was necessary when dealing with Master vampires, and Princes especially; they did not deal well with sarcasm, I'd discovered. "Yes," I replied simply. "I understand."

Apparently satisfied, Azura turned to the door and raised a hand. One second later, a human in a black-and-white uniform stepped through the frame and bowed to me. "I will show you to your room," he said in a formal voice. "Please, follow me."

I shot Jackal one last glare and followed the human, trailing him down several long hallways and flights of stairs, my mind reeling. I had fully expected to find Sarren or my sire tonight; that it was Jackal threw a wrench in all my plans. I wasn't sure what to do next.

The human made his way unerringly through the massive house, until we came to a long hallway of doors. After pointing out the one to my room, the man bowed hurriedly and left, leaving me alone in the corridor. Still wary, I opened the door, revealing a small but lavishly furnished room. The bed, dresser, nightstand and table were old but meticulously cared for, polished to a dark shine and smelling faintly of chemicals. A pitcher and glass sat on the nightstand beside the bed, and the scent of warm blood roused my Hunger with a vengeance. I didn't trust Jackal at all, but it wouldn't hurt to take advantage of the Prince's hospitality, especially since it came in a cup and not the veins of a human.

I drained the pitcher, feeling the blood settle in my empty stomach and the sharp ache vanish for now. As my Hunger subsided, sleep took its place, dragging at my mind, weighing me down. After locking my door, I dragged the bulky dresser from its place against the wall and shoved it up against the frame. Maybe I was being paranoid, but I was not going to sleep in a strange house with two vampires, one of whom was *Jackal,* without some kind of precaution.

Satisfied that I'd at least have warning if someone came bursting through my door, I crawled atop the cool red sheets, not bothering to take off my coat or boots, and pondered what Jackal had said for as long as I could before succumbing to the darkness.

I woke the next evening with my sword in hand, having unsheathed and readied it as sleep finally dragged me under. Unfamiliar walls and furniture stared back at me as I rose, pausing a moment to remember where I was. A glance at the door revealed that it was still locked and barricaded, untouched. The pitcher sat empty on the end table, so no one had disturbed me while I slept—no servant, anyway.

As I sheathed my weapon, the previous night's conversation came back to me, making me frown. Jackal was here. My ruthless, murdering blood brother. I should leave. Better yet, I should kill him. We had a clear night sky and an empty lawn perfect for it. He'd kicked my ass the last time we'd fought, nearly killed me, but I was stronger now. If it came down to blows, this time I'd give him a hell of a fight.

But, if he was telling the truth, if the cure to Rabidism lay somewhere beneath our feet, no cost would be too high to find it. Much as I hated to admit it, Jackal was right. Charging in blind after Kanin wouldn't help him; I needed a plan if I was going to face Sarren. The help of another strong vampire was too great an opportunity to pass up.

Still, the thought of working with Jackal made my blood boil. I hadn't forgotten what he'd done to our group. He was cruel and vicious, and saw humans only as food or the means to an end. He killed without a second thought. He'd killed people I knew, people I considered friends.

Zeke would never consider letting him live.

I was still trying to decide what to do when a servant knocked timidly on the door, informing me that Master Azura and Master Jackal were waiting for me in the living room and to follow him please. After returning the dresser to its proper place, I followed the well-dressed human down the many hallways and up a flight of stairs before he paused outside a doorway and motioned me inside.

Azura and Jackal were there, of course, Azura sitting on a sofa with her long legs crossed, a wineglass of blood dangling between her fingers. Jackal slouched against the fireplace mantel, despite the flames flickering in the hearth, and the light cast his features in an eerie red glow. How he could stand being so close to the flames was baffling; I would never consider tempting fate like that. But then Jackal shot me a grin, smug and challenging, and I realized he was playing me. He knew the effect it would have on a vampire and was making sure I knew that he was not afraid.

"Oh, hey, the queen finally makes her appearance." Jackal raised his glass in a mocking salute before tossing the whole thing back in one swig. Azura gave him a disdainful look and sipped her drink. "So, little sister, are you ready to get this project underway?"

"I still haven't agreed to help you," I said, making Jackal sigh with impatience. "Why is that so surprising? As if I would agree to work with the guy who slaughtered my friends, who will probably stick a knife in my back as soon as I turn around."

"Don't think of it as helping *me,*" Jackal said in a reasonable voice. He didn't, I noticed, deny either accusation. "Think of it as helping Kanin. I, at least, will take any advantage I can get if I'm going to be facing Sarren."

I turned to Azura. "What do you think of all this?"

"Me?" Azura raised a thin eyebrow. "I don't care one way or the other. I'm just here to make sure you two don't turn my house inside out."

"Come on, sister," Jackal implored. "Let's not have a repeat of last night. You know this is the best way to help Kanin. And, admit it, you're just as curious as I am."

I glared at him. "Let's say I do agree to this, for now." His smirk grew wider, and I ignored it. "You said Sarren was searching for the lab, as well. Where do you think it could be?"

Azura uncrossed her legs and leaned forward, setting her

glass on the low table in front of the couch. "I had my people track down some old maps of the city and its subway systems," she said, smoothing a large sheet of paper over the wood. "They don't tell us exactly where to find a supersecret government lab, but I have a few good guesses."

Jackal remained where he was, but I crossed the room to the other side of the table, looking down at the paper on the surface. I'd never seen a map before and had no idea how to read one; it was a tangle of lines and scribbles that merged together into a chaotic mess. But Azura placed one dark red fingernail on a random line, tracing it across the page.

"The rabids," she began in her throaty voice, "keep to the subway tunnels in the daytime. At night, they emerge to hunt and stalk for prey, but usually return to the underground stations at dawn. Except for those few that cannot seem to leave my fence alone, at least. No one in this city ventures down into the tunnels, for any reason, at any time. It is not known exactly how many rabids are down there, but there are likely thousands of them. And this," she added, circling a place on the map with her finger, "is where we think the main nest is located." Withdrawing her hand, she glanced up at me. "That's where you're going to want to look for the lab."

"Why is that?"

"If this laboratory unleashed the rabid virus, it would have spread quickly. Hundreds, perhaps thousands of people would have been infected around that area. There would be a very high rabid population starting from that point and spreading outward."

"Wait a second." I frowned, thinking back to what Kanin had told me. "I thought the laboratory in New Covington was responsible for creating the rabids—they escaped, and that's how the rabid plague started."

"Is that what Kanin said?" Jackal snorted. "That's part of the story, but not the whole of it." He pushed himself off the wall and sauntered to an end table, grabbing a pitcher half-full of red and refilling his glass. Sitting comfortably in one of the armchairs, he took a large swallow from the glass and smiled at me.

"Have a seat, sister. Let me tell you exactly what happened, so you can fully appreciate the role our sire had in this whole fubar'ed situation." Jackal took another long, leisurely sip, waiting for me to sit down. I perched cautiously on the opposite chair.

"You know that Kanin captured vampires and handed them over to the scientists to experiment on," Jackal began, pleased now that he had an audience. It reminded me of his speech in the arena, standing in front of his army, the raiders cheering his name…right before he'd thrown Darren into the arena with a rabid for their entertainment. I could still hear Darren's screams as the rabid tore him apart. Rage flared, and I swallowed the growl rising to my throat, trying to concentrate on what the raider king was saying now.

"It was all in the interest of curing Red Lung," Jackal continued, oblivious to my sudden anger, "or that's what Kanin probably told himself while he was selling out his own kind. He would track down a likely target, stake them to send them into hibernation, then deliver them to the laboratories, where the scientists would do all the happy things scientists do to their hapless subjects."

I shifted uncomfortably in my seat, disturbed to think of

Kanin that way, even though I already knew about it. Or had thought I did, anyway.

"Thing was," Jackal continued, putting his boots up on the low, polished table, ignoring the glare from Azura, "New Covington wasn't the only lab searching for a cure. True, they were the one with the vampire patients, but they also shared their research with the other labs. And something happened here in D.C. to cause a massive rabid outbreak. Hundreds of people Turned within a matter of hours. We know the New Covington lab burned down and all the research was either taken or destroyed, but we don't know anything about the lab below this city. Is it still standing? Does it have the research from decades ago? What's been left behind, I wonder? The cure? Hopefully. But, what about the other things, the research on the plague and the virus and how Rabidism came to be?" Jackal's gold gaze narrowed, and something in that intense look made my skin crawl. "If any of that research is left behind, who is the very last person we'd want to stumble upon it? Sarren is brilliant and crazy and more than a little unstable. Think of all the nasty things he could do if he got his hands on that kind of information."

I shivered and felt the last of my protests dissolve. If Sarren was planning something, he had to be stopped. And if there was a cure to Rabidism, we had to find it. For better or worse, it appeared I would be working with my blood brother. For now, at least. I desperately hoped I was making the right choice and that Kanin would be able to hang on until we could get to him.

"I thought you would see it that way." Jackal smiled and rose, his duster falling behind him. "So, now that we're all finally on the same page, shall we get this party started?"

CHAPTER 4

The rabids were back, milling around the perimeter, but Azura showed us a tunnel that led from the house to an empty building beyond the fence. She wasn't sad to see us go, but provided us with maps, thermoses of blood and the reluctant offer that we could return if we absolutely had to.

"The subway is several blocks in that direction," Azura told Jackal, pointing to a spot on the half-open map. "It's the quickest way to get to the nest, but remember, once the sun rises, the tunnels will be crawling with rabids when they return underground to sleep. I suggest that you hurry. And try to stay off the streets. Use the rooftop—the rabids rarely think to venture off the ground."

"Thanks, darlin'," Jackal said, giving her a suggestive smile. "Maybe I'll drop by again someday, and we can 'reacquaint' ourselves when we have a little more time, eh?"

"Yes, just let me know when you're coming." Azura gave a tight smile. "I'll try to remember to turn the fence off for you."

"Minx." Jackal grinned, and Azura closed the door, shutting us out.

The city that lay beyond the fence was dark and eerie, overgrown with trees and bramble, as if a forest had grown up and smothered everything beneath. It was easy enough for two vampires to climb to the top of the nearest building and pick our way over loose shingles and gaping holes. Sometimes, where the space between buildings was too far to jump, we had to drop to ground level, but only until we could get to the next building and scale the walls. On the rooftops, the path was fairly clear, the moon lighting our way as we traveled above the streets, following Azura's map.

Below us was a different story.

Rabids roamed the tangled streets, skulking between cars, climbing out of windows, loping along crumbling sidewalks. They snarled and hissed at each other, blind in their rage and driven mad by the Hunger. There didn't seem to be any humans beyond the fence; I wondered if the ones in Azura's fortified house were the only humans left. An unfortunate cat tried scurrying across the road and was instantly pounced on by a rabid, who shoved the feline's head between his jaws and ripped it in two. The smell of blood drew several more rabids to the area, and a vicious fight erupted, with the rabids screaming and tearing at each other for the remains of the animal.

"You're not very talkative."

I ignored him, keeping my gaze straight ahead. Jackal strode easily next to me, sometimes glancing at the map as we traversed the rooftops.

"Nothing to say?" Jackal went on. "That's a surprise. You

were so verbose the first time we met. I must admit, I've killed a few siblings, but you're the first one I actually thought I could get along with." He sighed. "But then, of course, you killed my men and ran off with those humans I worked so hard to acquire. You and that boy." His voice took on a slight edge. "What was that kid's name again? The old preacher's son, the one the humans kept crying over, thinking he was dead? Something biblical, wasn't it? Jeremiah? Zachariah?"

Ezekiel, I thought, as my stomach went cold. *And there's no way I'm ever telling you about Zeke. I shouldn't be here, helping you. I should take my sword and shove it through your sneering face.*

"So, whatever happened to your humans?" Jackal inquired after several more minutes of tense silence. "Did they leave? Run away? After you went through so much trouble to get them out of my city?" He grinned. "Or did you wind up eating them all?"

"Shut up," I finally snapped, not looking at him. "They're safe. That's all you need to know."

"Oh?" I could feel his sneer, sense the gleeful smugness as we continued over the broken rooftops. "Got them to Eden, then? How very charitable of you." He grinned at my sharp glance. "What? Shocked that I know about Eden? Don't be. I always knew it was out there—a city with no vampires, just a bunch of fat little humans scurrying around, pretending to be in charge. I knew that old man was looking for it, too, and that, eventually, he would slip up and land right in my lap. He and his little band couldn't run from me forever, I just had to be patient. And it paid off—we finally got them. Everything was going to plan." His eyes narrowed. "Or, it was, until you showed up."

"Yeah, sorry to ruin your plans to take over the world."

"That is not true," Jackal said, sounding affronted. "I was trying to find a cure for Rabidism."

I snorted. Any living thing bitten by a rabid would Turn rabid itself, but that wasn't the only way to create one. Vampires, through the result of the mutated Red Lung virus, were all carriers of Rabidism, as well. Just biting or feeding from a human wouldn't Turn them, but for most of our kind, attempting to create a new vampire through the exchange of blood would birth not a vampire, but a rabid. Only the few Masters, the Princes of the cities, could spawn new offspring anymore, and even then, they were just as likely to spawn a rabid. Kanin, our sire, was a Master himself, but I was still very lucky to have made the transition to vampire instead of rising again as a monstrous, mindless horror.

"That old human was the key," Jackal went on, glaring at me now. "He had all the information we needed. The results the scientists had on the plague, the tests they ran, how the rabids were created, everything. I was trying to save our race, sister. I came so close, and you ruined it all."

"You were trying to cure Rabidism so you could turn your raider pets into a vampire army and take over everything," I shot back. "Don't even try to sell me the saint act. You're nothing but a scheming, bloodthirsty killer who's out for power. And by the way, where *is* that raider army of yours? Did they finally turn on you once you couldn't promise them immortality anymore?"

"Oh, don't worry, they're still there." Jackal's smile was not friendly. "It's fairly easy to govern a city that has no rules—the minions do what they please, and I don't stop them. But, with that old human dead, I had to come up with a new plan. That's when I thought you and I needed to have a little talk, and I certainly couldn't do that with a raider gang following me about the country." He shrugged. "They'll be there when I get back, *with* the cure. You haven't stopped anything, sister. You've just delayed things a bit."

"If there is a cure. We don't know if this lab created one or not, even a partial one."

"I would have shared it with you," Jackal said, sounding angry and hurt at the same time. "You and me, sister, we could've had it all. We could've had everything."

"I didn't want everything." I glared at him. "I didn't want your city, your minions, your schemes for power, any of it. I just wanted to get my friends to safety."

"Uh-huh." Jackal raised an eyebrow. "And how did that turn out? I don't see any of your 'friends' here now. Where are they? Back in their Eden, I suppose? Why didn't you hang around, if you're such great pals?" He snickered and went on before I could answer. "Here's what I think happened. You got the little bloodbags to Eden, like you said you would, but oh, they couldn't let a *vampire* into the city, now could they? That would just cause a panic, having a wolf walking among the sheep. So they either turned you away or drove you off. And your little friends, the humans that you rescued from the big bad raider king, the people you stuck your neck out for, they didn't do anything. Because they knew the others were right. Because you're a monster who kills humans to live, and no matter how much you tell yourself otherwise, that's all you'll ever be."

"Tell me again why I'm helping you?"

Jackal laughed. "You know I'm right, sister. You can deny it until the sky falls down, but you're only fooling yourself."

"You don't know me." He snickered again, and I whirled on him. "And another thing. Stop calling me 'sister.' We're not related just because Kanin sired us both. I have a name—Allison. Start using it."

"Sure thing, *Allison*." Jackal bared his fangs in a sneer. "But we both know the truth. Vampire blood is stronger than human ties—our blood links us together in a way they can't even imagine. Why do you think you could sense where I was, where Kanin is? Because you're getting stronger, and the stronger the vamp, the easier it becomes to know where the members of your particular family are at any time. That's why most covens are all members of the Prince's family, the ones he sired himself. He can sense where they are, and sometimes even what they're thinking. Makes it hard for them to turn on him. But the tie goes both ways."

"That's why we've been able to sense Kanin."

"Yep." Jackal looked off to the west as we started walking again. "And each other, to a lesser extent. But the strongest pull is toward our sire, or at least, it was until he went into hibernation. It doesn't work as well if the vampire is close to death, but it's still there."

"Why?"

"Because, in some small, subconscious way, Kanin is calling for us."

A couple hours later, we were no closer to finding the subway entrance than when we first started.

"Hmm." Jackal stopped at the edge of a roof, the open map

in both hands, turning it this way and that. "Well, damn. There's supposed to be an entrance to the subway somewhere on this street, but how the hell are you supposed to read a map if there are no damn signs?"

I let him fiddle with the map in silence and watched the pale forms of the rabids slipping through the shadows below. "Why would Sarren be looking for this laboratory?" I mused, softly so my voice didn't alert the monsters under our feet. "What do you think he wants?" Jackal gave a distracted grunt.

"Don't ask me. I'm not a psychotic maniac." He paused. "Well, not *as much* of a psychotic maniac. Okay, there's the Foggy Bottom metro entrance… Where the hell is the tunnel?" He glanced down at the street and sighed. "Maybe he's searching for the cure to Rabidism, too," he tossed over his shoulder. "Oh, but wait, you don't care about that, do you?"

A large group of rabids slid from between two buildings, directly below Jackal. He ignored both them and me as he studied the map. For a moment, I had the murderous thought of shoving him over the edge, letting him fall into the group of rabids, seeing if he could survive. The monster within approved of this plan, urging me to step forward, to attack when he wasn't looking. *Yes,* it whispered. *Do it. Jackal would, and he will someday. As soon as he doesn't need you anymore, he'll hit you from behind without a second thought.*

But that would make me just like him, wouldn't it?

The opportunity passed before I had a chance to decide. The rabid pack moved away, and the moment was lost. I watched them skulk across the street, hissing and snarling… and then vanish beneath a rubble pile.

I blinked. "Hey," I said, and Jackal lowered the map, watching as I walked to the edge of the roof and crouched down. "I think I found it."

We dropped carefully into the street, glancing around for rabids lurking behind cars or around buildings. Warily, we crossed the road and examined the spot where the pack had disappeared. The building next door had partially fallen, and the ground was strewn with broken glass, steel and cement. But beneath a collapsed overhang, a tiny, nearly invisible hole snaked down into the darkness.

Jackal grinned at me, hard and challenging. "Ladies first."

I bristled. The tunnel entrance sat quietly, like the open gullet of something huge and evil, waiting to swallow me whole. I crouched down and peered inside. Darkness greeted me, thick and eternal, difficult to pierce even with my vampiric night vision. Cold, dry air wafted from the crack, smelling of dust and rot and decay.

"What's the matter?" Jackal's smug voice echoed behind me. "Scared? Need your big vampire brother to go down first?"

"Shut up." Scowling, I reached back and drew my sword, sending a faint metallic rasp into the darkness. If something came leaping at me out of the black, I wanted to be prepared. Holding the hilt backward so that the flat of the blade pressed against my arm, I crouched down, rabid style, and slid into the hole.

My fingers touched rock and cold metal and, when I straightened, I found myself at the top of a long flight of stairs leading down into the unknown. The stairs, partially buried under earth and stone, were metallic, uneven and had a strange rippling effect to them, as if they hadn't been firmly grounded. If you looked at them a certain way, you could almost imagine they had once moved.

Jackal slid in behind me, feetfirst, dropping to the stairs with a grunt. "All right," he muttered as he straightened. Unlike me, he had to bend over slightly to avoid scraping his head on the ceiling. Being small did have its advantages sometimes. Shaking out the map, he squinted at it in the dark. "So, according to this, we have to take the red line North to get to the nest, which will be somewhere around this area…." He tapped the paper with a knuckle, looking thoughtful.

"Where, exactly?"

"Doesn't say."

"So we're going in blind. Searching for a lab that may or may not be there. In the middle of a nest of rabids who will trap us underground if we can't find a way out."

"Exciting, isn't it?" Jackal grinned and folded the map again. "It's moments like this that really make you appreciate immortal life. Don't you love it, sister? Doesn't it make you feel alive?"

"I'll pass, thanks." Sheathing my sword, I started down the stairs. "Right now, I'll settle for finding the lab and getting out of here in one piece."

The staircase descended deeper underground, opening into an enormous tunnel. The familiar rails lined either side of the platform, once having shuttled metal cars back and forth between stations, now quite empty. The ceiling of the huge domed tunnel was strange—a motif of concrete squares, some fallen in large chunks to the platform, stretching all the way down the corridor.

Jackal walked to the edge of the platform and dropped to

the tracks, peering down the tunnel. "No sign of rabids," he muttered. "At least not yet." He glanced at me over his shoulder. "You coming or not?"

I leaped onto the tracks behind him. "What's the matter, Jackal?" I sneered, wanting to repay him for that last quip. "Need me to hold your hand every time we go down a dark hole?"

He laughed, the sound bouncing off the domed roof of the ceiling, surprising me. "See, this is why I like you, sister. You and me, we're exactly the same."

I'm nothing like you, I thought, but his words continued to haunt me long after we entered the tunnel.

"Man, these things go on forever, don't they?"

I winced as his voice echoed loudly in the looming silence, a wave of noise traveling down the endless corridor. "Mind keeping it down?" I growled, listening for the shuffle of feet or the skitter of claws over rock, rabids alerted to our presence. We'd encountered a few of the monsters already, and I had no desire to cut my way through another wave. The dark subway tunnels reeked of them, their foul stench clinging to the walls. Nothing else moved here, not even rats. Sometimes, we encountered bodies of rabids, ravaged corpses torn apart by their own kind. Once, we came across what we thought was another dead body, only to have it leap at us with a shriek, swiping at us with its one remaining arm. Jackal seemed to enjoy these encounters, swinging the steel fire ax hidden beneath his duster with vicious force, crushing skulls and snapping bones with a savage grin on his face. I was far less enthused. I didn't want to be in this underground labyrinth of death, with this vampire I didn't like and certainly didn't trust. Because watching him fling himself at the rabids, grinning demonically as he tore them limb from limb, reminded me too much of myself. That thing that I kept locked away, the beast that goaded me into raw animal rage and bloodlust. The part that made us dangerous to every human we encountered.

The part that kept me from ever being with Zeke.

My blood brother grinned at me, swinging his bloody fire ax to his shoulder. "Aw, sister. Don't tell me you're scared of a few rabids."

"A *few* rabids is one thing. A massive horde in a narrow tunnel is another. And dawn is just a couple hours away." I glared down the crumbling cement tube in frustration. Old D.C.'s underground was a never-ending maze of tunnels and pipes and corridors that snaked and twisted and stretched away into the darkness. The night was waning, and the tunnels just went on and on, forever it seemed. We'd even stumbled into what looked like an underground mall, with ancient stores crumbling to rubble, strange items rotting on near-empty shelves. I'd once thought the sewers beneath New Covington were confusing; they were nothing compared to this. "Where is this stupid lab?" I muttered. "It feels like we've been walking in circles all night."

Jackal started to reply but suddenly paused, a slight frown crossing his face. "Do you hear that?" he asked me.

"No. What is it?"

He motioned me to be quiet, then crept forward again. The cement tube that we were walking down narrowed, and then I did hear something—something that raised the hair on my neck. If the low growls and hisses didn't rouse my suspicions, the dead, rotting stench that slithered down the tunnel confirmed it.

Weapons out, we eased forward, silent as death. Ahead of us, the tunnel abruptly ended in open air, and a rusty, narrow catwalk stretched out over nothing. Gripping my weapon, I followed Jackal to the edge of the catwalk and peered down, into the darkness.

"Shit," Jackal murmured, sounding faintly awed.

We stood at the edge of a massive round chamber, the walls soaring up a good fifteen feet above us. The narrow metal bridge, stretching to another tunnel on the opposite side, had to be at least two hundred feet across. The railings had rusted away completely, and the mesh floor had disintegrated in spots, but that wasn't what worried me the most.

Below us, about twenty feet down, the cement floor was a shifting, roiling carpet of pale bodies and jagged fangs. Rabids filled the chamber, growling, hissing, moving about the room like a swarm of ants. There were hundreds of them, maybe thousands, coming in from various tunnels and pipes near the ground. I hissed as their scent wafted up from the pit—blood and rot and decay and wrongness—and took a step back from the edge.

"Well," Jackal mused softly, watching the rabid swarm with vague amusement. "I think it's safe to say that we found the nest." He shook the catwalk experimentally. It creaked, rust and metallic flakes drifting down to the horde below. Thankfully, they didn't notice. "Doesn't seem very sturdy, does it? This is going to be interesting."

"You can't be serious."

"Do you see any other way across?" Jackal crossed his arms, shooting me a challenging smirk. "I thought you were so anxious to find the lab."

I smirked back. "Fine. After you, then."

He shrugged. Stepping onto the narrow bridge, he carefully eased out over the sheer drop, testing for weakness. The catwalk groaned but held, and he grinned at me.

"Afraid of heights, sister? Need me to carry you across?"

"Yeah, why don't you save the smart comments until you're on the other side?"

He rolled his eyes, turned, and began walking across the gap, moving with unnatural grace. Despite that, the catwalk creaked and groaned horribly under his weight. It shuddered and swayed, and I bit my lip, certain it would snap at any second and Jackal would plummet to his death.

Beneath us, the rabids had noticed the vampire trying to cross the bridge, and their shrieks and snarls rose from the pit as they surged forward, gazing up hungrily. Some of them began leaping for the catwalk, swiping at it with their claws, and though they couldn't quite make it, some of those leaps came frighteningly close.

After several long, tense moments, Jackal finally reached the other side. The hisses and screams from the rabids were deafening now, echoing through the chamber, as Jackal turned and beckoned me across with a grin.

Oh, dammit. Swallowing hard, I stepped to the edge and peered down again. The rabids saw me immediately and began flinging themselves at my end of the catwalk, slashing at the air. Trying to ignore them, I stepped onto the rickety metal walkway, feeling it shake and shudder under my feet. The end of the bridge seemed an impossible distance away.

One step at a time, Allie.

Keeping my gaze straight ahead, I started across the cat-walk, putting one foot in front of the other as lightly as I could. There were no railings to grab hold of; I had to make my way across on balance alone. The bridge swayed and groaned as I neared the center, carefully stepping over the gaping holes in the mesh floor. Through the gaps, the rabids churned below me, glaring up with dead white eyes and gnashing their fangs.

As I was nearing the end, trying to move faster but still keep my steps light, a rabid leaped up from the floor, lashed out, and struck the bottom of the catwalk with a metallic screech that lanced up my spine. The walkway jerked to the side, nearly spilling me off, then let out a deafening groan as one side of the bridge shuddered and twisted like paper.

Fear shot through me. I gave a frantic leap for the edge of the tunnel, just as the catwalk snapped and plummeted into the hordes below. I hit the wall a few inches from the edge and clawed desperately for a handhold, my fingers scrabbling against the smooth wall as I slid toward the wailing sea of death below.

Something clamped around my wrist, jerking me to a stop. Wide-eyed, I looked up to see Jackal on his stomach, one hand around my arm, his jaw clenched. His face was tight with concentration as he started to pull me up.

A reeking, skeletal body landed on my back, sinking claws into my shoulders, screaming in my ear. I snarled in pain, ducking my head as the rabid tore at my collar, trying to bite my neck. I couldn't do anything, but Jackal reached down with his other hand, drew the katana from its sheath on my back, and plunged it into the rabid. The weight clinging to me dropped away as the rabid screeched and fell back into the mob below, and Jackal yanked me into the tunnel.

I collapsed against the wall, staring at him as he glared down at the rabids. He…had just saved my life. Stunned, I watched him approach and hold the katana hilt out to me.

"So." His gold eyes shone as he gazed into mine. "I think I'm entitled to a smart comment or two now, don't you think?"

I took the sword numbly. "Yeah," I muttered as his smug look faded into something that wasn't completely obnoxious. "Thanks."

"No problem, little sister." The leer returned, making him look normal again. "Comment number one—how much do you weigh to snap the bridge like that? I thought you Asians were supposed to be petite and dainty."

Okay, moment over. I sheathed my blade and glared at him. "And here I *almost* thought you weren't a complete bastard."

"Well, that's your mistake, not mine." Jackal dusted his hands and gave the edge of the tunnel a rueful look. "Shall we continue? Before our friends start climbing each other to get to us? If that's the nest, the lab should be around here somewhere."

A clang from the pit below drew my attention. Walking to the edge, I peered out, just as a rabid landed on the tunnel rim with a snarl. As I snarled back and kicked the thing in the chest, sending it toppling back into the hole, I saw that the catwalk had fallen against the wall of the pit, and that rabids were scrambling up to leap into the tunnel. I drew my katana, slashing another out of the air as it flew at me, howling, but Jackal grabbed the back of my coat, yanking me away.

"No time for that! The whole nest will be up here in a second. Come on!"

The wails and shrieks intensified as more rabids entered the tunnel, snarling and baring their fangs. I spun, shrugging free of Jackal's grip, and we bolted down the passage, the screams of the monsters close behind.

A few miles from the nest, we didn't seem to be any closer to the hidden lab.

"You're just guessing now, aren't you?" I snapped at Jackal, who shot me an annoyed look over his shoulder as we ran.

"Sorry, I didn't see the big X with the words *Top Secret Government Laboratory* on the map, did you?"

A rabid dropped down from a breach overhead, hissing as it landing in front of us. Jackal whirled his ax, striking it under the jaw and smashing it aside, and we continued without slowing down. I could still hear the horde in pursuit, their screams echoing all around us, reverberating from everywhere. We had definitely poked a stick into a wasp nest, stirring them into a frenzy. We were in their world now, and they were closing in.

I snarled at the vampire's retreating back. "Yeah, well maybe you'd like to get that map out so we know where the hell we're going!"

We ducked through a door frame into yet another narrow cement corridor, rusted beams and pipes lining the walls and ceiling, dripping water on us from above. Jackal yanked the map from his coat and shook it open with a rustle of paper, scowling as the shrieks of the rabids echoed behind us.

"All right, where the hell are we?" he muttered, squinting at the map in the darkness, eyes narrowed in concentration. I glanced nervously at the hall we'd just come through, hearing the rabids draw closer, their claws skittering over the cement. Jackal began walking down the corridor, weaving around fallen beams and pipes, and I followed.

"You know they're right on our tail."

"First you want me to look at the map, now you're rushing me along. Make up your mind, sister." He walked by a tall square pillar that jutted out of the wall; two sliding doors stood half-open in the front, and a cold breeze wafted out of the crack. "Okay, there's the subway tunnels," Jackal muttered, walking a little faster now, holding the map close to see it in the dark. "And there's the entrance we came in... wait a second."

He stopped and half turned in the corridor, looking back the way we'd come. I followed his gaze, but saw nothing except empty hallway and rusty pipes, though I could still hear the rabids, getting closer.

"Um, where are you going?" I asked as Jackal began walking again, back toward the approaching horde. "Hey, wrong direction! In case you didn't know, we usually want to move *away* from certain death."

Jackal stopped at the long, square pillar jutting from the wall. "Yeah, I thought so," I heard him mutter. "This isn't on the map, and there shouldn't be anything down there. Get over here and look at this."

Against my better judgment, I jogged over to where Jackal

stood, staring at the doors. Cold, dry air billowed out of a gap that ran down the center, and Jackal gave a snort.

"He's been here."

"What? Sarren?"

"No, the boogeyman. Look." Jackal pointed to the sliding doors. The metal was crumpled along the edges, as if something had slipped ironlike fingers into the seam and pried them open.

I peered through the gap, following the narrow shaft as it plunged into the dark. It was a long, long way down.

A howl rang out behind us, and rabids spilled into the corridor, a pale, hissing flood. They screamed as they spotted us and charged, hurtling themselves over beams and around pipes, their claws sparking against the metal.

"Move, sister!" Jackal's voice boomed through the shaft, making my ears pound, and something shoved me through the opening. I leaped forward, grabbing thick cables as I dropped into the tube, catching myself with a grimace. Jackal squeezed through the doors and, instead of grabbing for the metal ropes, swung himself onto a rusty ladder on one side of the wall. He glanced over his shoulder and grinned at me.

"I'll meet you down there."

"You're lucky I can't reach you right now."

Jackal only laughed, but at that moment a rabid slammed into the door frame, hissing and gnashing its fangs across the gap separating us. With a shriek, it sprang forward, soaring through the air, grabbing the cables next to mine. Claws slashed at me, and I yelled, kicking at it as it we hung there, the metal ropes shaking wildly. Curved talons sparked off the cables, and I swung myself around the ropes, out of its reach.

The rabid shimmied through the cables like a grotesque monkey, lunging at my face with fangs bared. With a snarl, I threw up my arm, letting jagged teeth sink into my coat and skin, and then yanked it to the side, ripping the monster off the cables into empty air. It snatched desperately for another rope, missed and plummeted down the shaft, screaming. It was a long time before I heard the faint thud at the bottom.

More rabids crowded the door frame, their empty, dead eyes locked on me, but these seemed reluctant to take that leap. I looked around and saw Jackal already several yards below me, descending the ladder at shocking speed. Muttering dark promises under my breath, I began climbing down into the darkness.

The shaft went down at least a couple hundred feet, a pitch-black, claustrophobic tube that seemed to descend into the center of the earth. Even with my vampire sight, which turned complete darkness into shades of gray, I couldn't see the bottom or the top. It made me feel like I was dangling over a bottomless pit. I was relieved when I finally heard Jackal hit the bottom, sending a metallic thump up the shaft.

I slid down the remaining length of rope, landing on a square metal platform that swayed slightly under my weight. Gazing around, I discovered the platform wasn't attached to the walls of the tube; it appeared to be a large metal box at the bottom of the cables. A pale, broken body lay in the crack between the wall and the box, its skull smashed open on the corner.

Jackal stepped up, smirking, and I fought the urge to kick him in the shin. "Looks like we're on the right trail," he stated, pointing to a hatch in the center of the box that had already been pulled open. "After you."

Pulling my sword, I dropped through the hatch, landing inside the rectangular box, finding these doors shoved open, as well. Beyond the opening, a long hallway ended at two thick metal doors.

Jackal hit the floor beside me, his duster settling around him, and straightened, giving the entrance a shrewd look. "All right, you bastard," he muttered, walking forward. "What were you looking for down here?"

We went through the doors together, pushing them back, and stepped into a dark, chilling room. At first, it reminded me of the old hospital where Kanin and I had stayed in New Covington. Beds on wheels sat against the wall, sectioned off by rotted curtains, or lay tipped over on the ground. Shelves of strange instruments were scattered about, and bulky machines sprawled in the middle of the floor or in corners, knocked down and broken. Glass clinked under our feet as we maneuvered the maze of rubble and sharp objects,

I looked closer and saw that most of the beds had leather straps dangling from the sides, thick cuffs to restrain wrists and ankles. Pushing aside a moldy curtain, I jumped as a skeleton grinned at me from a bed, rotten leather restraints hanging on bony wrists. My stomach turned as I stared at the naked bones. What had happened here?

Jackal had already moved on, searching the hidden corners of the room, so I continued along a wall until I found another door. Unlike the others, this one didn't swing open at my touch. Why was it locked when none of the other doors had been? I braced myself and then lashed out with a kick, aiming for just beside the doorknob. There was a sharp, splintering crack, and the door crashed open.

It was an office, at least, it looked like one from the shelves and metal cabinets and large wooden desk in the corner. Unlike the rest of the lab, this one looked fairly clean and intact; nothing looked broken, and the furniture, though old and covered in dust, was still standing.

Except, there was a suspicious-looking dark spatter on the wall behind the desk and, when I walked around, I discovered a skeleton slumped in the corner, the threads of a long, once-white coat still clinging to him. One bony hand clutched a pistol.

Wrinkling my nose, I turned around and noticed a single book lying in the middle of the desk. Curious, I walked over and picked it up, examining the cover. It didn't have a title, and when I flipped it open, messy, handwritten pages sprang to light, instead of neat rows of typing.

Day 36 of the Human-Vampire experiment, the top line read.

All power is being redirected to keeping the lab up and running, so I am writing down my findings here, in case we lose it all. Then, if something happens to me, perhaps the project can continue from the notes I will leave behind.

We continue to lose patients at an alarming rate. Early tests with the samples from the New Covington lab have been disastrous, with our human subjects dying outright. We have not had a single patient survive the infusion of vampire blood. I hope the team in New Covington can send us samples we can actually work with.

—Dr. Robertson, head scientist of the D.C. Vampire Project

I shuddered. So, it sounded like the scientists here had been working with the New Covington lab, only they'd been experimenting on humans instead of vampires. That couldn't be good. I flipped a couple more pages and read on.

Day 52 of the Human-Vampire experiment,

The power grid in the city has gone down. We are running on the emergency backup generators, but we might have had our first breakthrough today. One of the patients that we injected with the experimental cure did not immediately die. She became increasingly agitated and restless minutes after receiving the injection, and appeared to gain the heightened strength of the vampire subjects. Interestingly, she became increasingly aggressive, to the point where her mental capacities appeared to shut down and she resembled a mad or rabid animal. Sadly, she died a few hours later, but I am still hopeful that a cure can be found from this. However, some of the younger assistants are beginning to mutter; that last experiment rattled them pretty badly, and I don't blame them for wanting to quit. But we cannot let fear hinder us now. The virus must be stopped, no matter what the cost, no matter what the sacrifice. Mankind's survival depends on us.

We're close, I can feel it.

A chill crawled down my spine. I turned the page and kept reading.

Day 60 of the Human-Vampire experiment,

I received a rather frantic message today from the lead scientist at the New Covington lab. "Abort the project," he told me. "Do not use any more of the samples on human patients. Shut down the lab and get out."

It was shocking, to say the least. That the brilliant Malachi Crosse was telling me to abandon the project.

I'm sorry, my friend. But I cannot do that. We are close to something, so very close to a breakthrough. I cannot abandon months of research, even for you. The samples that came in yesterday are the key. They will work, I am sure of it. We will beat this thing, even if I have to inject my own assistants with the new serum. It will work.

It must. We are running out of time.

I swallowed hard, then turned to the very last entry. This one was blotched and messy, as if the author had written it in a great hurry.

The lab is lost. Everyone is dead or will be dead soon. Don't know what happened, those monsters suddenly everywhere. Malachi was right. Shouldn't have insisted we go through with the last experiment. This is all on me.

I've locked myself in my office. Can't go out, not with those things running around. I only hope they don't find a way back to the surface. If they do, heaven help us all.

If anyone finds this, the remaining samples of the retrovirus have been placed in freezer number two in cryogenic storage. And if you do find them, I pray that you will have better success than I, that you will use them to find a cure for Red Lung and for this new monstrosity we have unleashed.

"Hey." Jackal appeared in the doorway before I could finish the entry. He jerked his head into the hall, serious for once. "I found something. And I think you'd better see this."

Taking the journal, I followed him, already suspecting what I would find. We swept through another pair of metal doors, into a small, bare room with tiled floors and walls. It was colder in here; if I were a human, my breath would be billowing out in front of me and bumps would be raised along my skin. Looking across the room, I saw why.

Four large white boxes stood along the back wall. They looked like bigger versions of normal refrigerators, except I'd never seen a working one before. One of the doors was open, and a pale mist writhed out of the gap, creeping along the ground.

Silently, I walked up to the door and pulled it back, releasing a blast of cold. Inside, rows of white shelves greeted me. The shelves were plastic and narrowly spaced, and tiny glass vials winked at me from where they stood in tiered holders.

Jackal stepped behind me. "Notice anything…missing?" he asked softly.

I scanned the shelves, and saw what he meant. Near the top, one of the layers was gone, as if it had been pulled out and never returned.

Jackal followed my gaze, his eyes darkening. "Somebody took something from this freezer," he growled. "None of the others are touched. And that someone was here recently, too. Now, who do you think that could be?"

I shivered and stepped back, knowing exactly who it had been. As I shut the door, my gaze went to the simple, hand-drawn sign taped to the front, just to confirm what I already knew.

Freezer 2, it read in faded letters.

Sarren, I thought, feeling an icy chill spread through my veins. *What the hell are you planning?*

"Well," Jackal muttered, crossing his arms. "I will say I am officially more disturbed than I was when we first started. I don't know what was in that freezer, but I can hazard a pretty good guess, which just seems all kinds of bad news." His voice was flippant, but his eyes gleamed dangerously. "There's no cure here, that's for certain. So, I guess the million-dollar question is—what would a brilliantly insane psychotic vampire want with a live virus, and where is he taking it now?"

Sarren had the Red Lung virus. The thought was chilling. What did he want with it? Where was he going? And how did Kanin figure into everything? At a loss, I looked down at the forgotten journal, at the unfinished entry on the last page.

I pray that this can be stopped. I pray that the team in New Covington is already working on a way to counter this. The lab there was designed to go into stasis if anything happened. It may be our only salvation now.

May God forgive us.

And I knew.

The journal dropped from my hands, hitting the floor with a thump. I felt Jackal's eyes on me, but I ignored him, dazed from the realization. If Sarren wanted to use that virus, there was only one other place he could go. The place I'd sworn I would never return to.

"New Covington," I whispered, as the path loomed unerringly before me, pointing back to where it all began. "I have to go home."

Part II

CAPTIVE

CHAPTER 5

There were no spotlights up on the Wall.

In New Covington, the Outer Wall was the city's shield, lifeline and best defense, and everyone knew it. The thirty-foot monstrosity of steel, iron and concrete was always lit up at night, with spotlights sliding over the razed ground in front of it and guards marching back and forth up top. It circled the entire city, protecting New Covington from the mindless horrors that lurked just outside, the only barrier between the humans and the ever-Hungry rabids. It was the one thing that kept the Prince in power. This was his city; if you wanted to live behind his Wall, under his protection, you had to consent to his rules.

In my seventeen years of living in New Covington, the Wall had never once been abandoned.

"Something is wrong," I muttered as Jackal and I stood on the outskirts of the kill zone, the flat, barren strip of ground that surrounded the Wall. Pits, mines and coils of barbed wire covered that rocky field, making it deadly to venture into. Spotlights—blinding beams of light that were rumored to have ultraviolet bulbs in them to further discourage rabids from coming close—usually scanned the ground every fifty feet. They were dark now. Nothing moved out in the kill zone, not even leaves blowing across the barren landscape. "The Wall is never unmanned. Not even during lockdowns. They always keep the lights on and the guards patrolling, no matter what."

"Yeah?" Jackal scanned the Wall and kill zone skeptically. "Well, either the Prince is getting lazy, or Sarren is wreaking his personal brand of havoc inside. I'm guessing the latter, unless this Prince is a spineless tool." He glanced at me from where he was leaning against a tree trunk. "Who rules New Covington anyway? I forgot."

"Salazar," I muttered.

"Oh, yeah." Jackal snorted. "Little gypsy bastard, from what Kanin told me. One of the older bloodlines, prided himself on being 'royal,' for all the good it did him here." He pushed himself off the tree and raised an eyebrow. "Well, this was your city, once upon a time, sister. Should we walk up to the front gate and ring the doorbell, or did you have another way in?"

"We can't just walk across the kill zone." I backed away from the edge, heading into the ruins surrounding the Wall, the rows of dilapidated houses and crumbling streets. There were still mines and booby traps and other nasty things, even if the Wall wasn't being patrolled. But I knew this city. I'd been able to get in and out of it pretty consistently, back when I was human. The sewers below New Covington ran for miles, and *weren't* filled with rabids like the Old D.C. tunnels. "The sewers," I told Jackal. "We can get into the city by going beneath the Wall."

"The sewers, huh? Why does this not surprise me?" Jackal followed me up the bank, and we wove our way through the tall weeds and rusted hulks of cars at the edge of the kill zone, back into the ruins. "You couldn't have mentioned this on the way?"

I ignored him, both relieved and apprehensive to be back. It had taken us the better part of a month, walking from Old D.C. across the ravaged countryside, through plains and forest and countless dead towns, to reach the walls of my old home. In fact, it would've taken us even longer had we not stumbled upon a working vehicle one night. The "jeep," as Jackal called it, had cut down our travel time immensely, but I still feared we'd taken too long. I hadn't had any dreams to assure me that Kanin was still alive, though if I concentrated, I could still feel that faint tug, urging me on.

Back to New Covington. The place where it all began. Where I'd died and become a monster.

"So, you were born here, were you?" Jackal mused, gazing over the blasted field as we skirted the perimeter. "How positively nostalgic. How does it feel, coming back to this place as a vampire instead of a bloodcow?"

"Shut *up,* Jackal." I paused, glancing at a broken fountain in front of an apartment complex. The limbless cement lady in its center gazed sightlessly back, and I felt a twinge of familiarity, knowing exactly where I was. The last time I'd seen New Covington, Kanin and I had been trying to get past the ruins into the forest before Salazar's men blew us to pieces. "I thought I was done with this place," I muttered, continuing past the statue. "I never thought I'd come back."

"Aw," Jackal mocked. "No old friends to see, then? No places you're just dying to revisit?" His mouth twisted into a smirk as I glared at him. "I would think you'd have *lots* of people you'd want to contact, since you're so fond of these walking bloodbags. After all, you're practically one of them."

I stifled a growl, clenching my fists. "No," I rasped as memory surged up despite my attempts to block it out. My old gang: Lucas and Rat and Stick. The crumbling, dilapidated school we'd used as our hideout. That fateful night in the rain… "There's no one here," I continued, shoving those memories back into the dark corner they'd come from. "All my friends are dead."

"Oh, well. That's humans for you, always so disgustingly mortal." Jackal shrugged, and I wanted to punch his smirking mouth. All through our journey from Old D.C., he'd been an entertaining, if not pleasant, travel companion. I'd heard more stories, pointed questions and crude jokes than I'd ever wanted to know about, and I'd gotten used to his sharp, often cruel sense of humor. Once I'd realized his remarks were purposefully barbed to get a rise out of me, it was easier to ignore them. We *did* almost come to blows one night, when he'd wanted to "share" an older couple living in an isolated farmhouse, and I'd refused to let him attack them. We'd gone so far as to draw weapons on each other, when he'd rolled his eyes and stalked away into the night, returning later as if nothing had happened. The next evening, three men in a black jeep had pulled alongside us, pointed guns in our direction and told us to get in the vehicle.

It had not gone well for them, but we did end up with that nice jeep. And with our Hunger temporarily sated, the tension between Jackal and me had been defused a bit. Of course, I still wanted to kick him in his smart mouth sometimes.

But he'd never brought up New Covington or my years as a human until now.

"So very fragile, these bloodbags," he continued, shaking his head. "You blink and another one has up and died. Probably better in the long run, anyway. I'm sure you got the whole *you must leave your past behind* lecture from Kanin."

"Jackal, just..." I sighed. "Just drop it."

To my surprise, he did, not saying another word until we reached the drainage pipe that led into the sewers. It was an odd feeling, sliding through the pipe, emerging into the familiar darkness of the tunnels. The last time I'd done this, I'd been human.

"Ugh." Jackal grunted, straightening behind me, wringing dirty water from his sleeves. "Well, it's not the nastiest place I've ever crawled through, but it's definitely up there. At least they're not in use anymore. From what Kanin told me, all the human crap in the city used to flow through these kinds of tunnels." He grinned as I gave him a sideways look. "Disgusting thought, ain't it? Kind of makes you glad you're not human anymore."

Without replying, I started down the tunnels, tracing invisible steps back toward the city.

We walked in silence for a while, the only sounds our soft footsteps and the trickle of water flowing sluggishly by our feet. For once, I was glad that I was a vampire and didn't have to breathe.

"So." Jackal's low, quiet voice broke the stillness. "How did you meet Kanin? It was here, right? You never told me much about you and him. Why'd he do it?"

"Do what?"

"Turn you." Jackal's eyes glowed yellow in the darkness of the tunnel, practically burning the side of my face. "He swore that he would never create another spawn after me. You must've done something to catch his attention, to make him break his promise." Jackal smiled, showing the very tips of his fangs. "What made you so special, I wonder?"

"I was dying." My voice came out flat, echoing down the tunnel. "I got caught outside the Wall one night and was attacked by rabids. Kanin killed them all, but it was too late to save me." I shrugged, remembering the terror, the phantom pain of claws in my skin, ripping my body apart. "I guess he felt sorry for me."

"No." Jackal shook his head. "Kanin never Turned humans just because he pitied them. How many humans do you think we've watched die in horrible and painful ways? If he offered to make you immortal, he must have seen something in you that he liked, made him think you could make it as a vampire. He doesn't bestow his 'curse' on just anyone."

"I don't know, then," I snapped, because I didn't want to talk about it anymore. "What does it matter? I'm a vampire now. I can't go back and change his mind."

Jackal raised an eyebrow. "Would you want to?"

His question caught me off guard. I thought of my life as a vampire, an immortal. How long had it been since I'd seen the sun, let it warm my face? How long since I had done anything truly human? I realized I didn't remember what real food tasted like anymore. The Hunger had completely infused my memories so the only thing I ever craved was blood.

And the most ironic thing? If Kanin hadn't Turned me, I would never have met Zeke. But being a vampire meant I could never be with him, either.

"I don't know," I said evasively, and heard Jackal's disbelieving snort. Of course, it was easy for him—he reveled in his strength and immortality, caring nothing for those he slaughtered along the way. A few months ago, I'd been so certain, but now…if it came back to that night, lying in the rain as my life slowly drained away, and a vampire asked me, once more, what I wanted…would my choice be the same?

"What about you?" I challenged, to get him off the subject. "Why did Kanin Turn you? Certainly not for your charming personality." He snorted a laugh. "So how did you meet Kanin? You two don't seem like you'd get along very well."

"We didn't," Jackal said easily. "Especially at the end, right before we parted ways. I guess you can say I was his biggest disappointment as a vampire."

"Why?"

He smiled evilly. "Oh, no. You're not getting my story that easily, sister. You want me to open up?" He grinned wider and pressed close, making me uncomfortable. His voice dropped to a low murmur. "You're going to have to prove that I can trust you."

"*You* can trust *me?*" I pulled back to glare at him, feeling my fangs press against my gums. "You're joking, right? I'm not the egotistical murdering bastard. I don't toss unarmed humans into cages with rabids and let them rip them apart for sport! I'm not the one who put a stake in my gut and threw me out a window."

"You keep harping on that," Jackal said with exaggerated patience. "And yet, you *are* a vicious, murdering vampire, sister. It's in your blood. When are you going to realize that you and I are exactly the same?"

We're not, I wanted to snarl at him, but a noise in the tunnels ahead made me pause. Halting, I put up a hand and looked at Jackal, who had stopped, as well. He'd heard it, too.

We eased forward, quietly but not too concerned with what we might find. Rabids rarely came down here; the Prince had sealed off all entrances into the sewers except a few, for the sole purpose of keeping them out of the city. Occasionally, a rabid would wander down here, but never for long, and never in the huge swarms we'd seen in Old D.C.

As we rounded a corner, there was a shout, and a flashlight beam shone painfully into my eyes, making me hiss and look away. Raising my arm, I peered back to see three pale, skinny figures standing at the mouth of the tunnel, gaping at us.

I relaxed. Mole men, as they were called, had been nothing but urban legends to me when I was a Fringer, just creepy stories we told each other about the cannibals living under the streets, until I'd run into a group of them one night in the tunnels. They were not, as some stories claimed, giant hairless rat-people. They were just emaciated, but otherwise normal, humans whose skin had turned pale and diseased from a lifetime of living in dark sewers. However, the stories about mole men preying on and eating fellow humans weren't entirely false, either.

That seemed a lifetime ago. This time, I was the thing they feared, the monster.

"Who are you?" one of them, a skinny human with scabs crusting his arms and face, demanded. "More topsiders, coming down to crowd our turf?" He stepped forward and waved his flashlight menacingly. "Get out! Go back to your precious streets and stop trying to invade our space. This is our territory."

Jackal gave him an evil, indulgent smile. "Why don't you make us, little man?" he purred.

"Knock it off." I moved forward, blocking his view of the humans before he could kill them. "What do you mean?" I demanded, as the three mole men crowded together, glaring at us. "Are people from the Fringe coming down here? Why?"

"Vampire," whispered one of them, his eyes going wild and terrified, and the others cringed. They started edging away, back into the shadows. I swallowed a growl, stepped forward, and the scabby human hurled the flashlight at my face before they all scattered in different directions.

I ducked, the flashlight striking the wall behind me, and Jackal lunged forward with a roar. By the time I'd straightened and whirled around, he had already grabbed a skinny mole man, lifted him off his feet and thrown him into the wall. The human slumped to the ground, dazed, and Jackal heaved him up by the throat, slamming him into the cement.

"That wasn't very nice of you," he said, baring his fangs as the human clawed weakly at his arm. "My sister was only asking a simple question." His grip on the human's throat tightened, and the man gagged for air. "So how about you answer her, before I have to snap your skinny neck like a twig?"

I stalked up to him. "Oh, that's a good idea, choke him into unconsciousness—we're sure to get answers that way."

He ignored me, though his fingers loosened a bit, and the human gasped painfully. "Start talking, bloodbag," the raider king said. "Why are topsiders coming down here? I'm guessing it's not because of your hospitality."

"I don't know," the mole man rasped, and Jackal shook his head in mock sorrow before tightening his grip again. The human choked, writhing limply in his grip, his face turning blue. "Wait!" it croaked, just as I was about to step in. "Last topsider we saw…he was trying to get out of the city…said the vampires had locked it down. Some kind of emergency. No one goes in or out."

"Why?" I asked, frowning. The human shook his head. "What about this topsider, then? He probably knows. Where is he now?"

The mole man gagged. "You…can't talk to him now, vampire. His bones…rotting in a sewer drain."

Horror and disgust curled my stomach. "You ate him."

"Oh, well, that's disgusting," Jackal said conversationally, and gave his hand a sharp jerk. There was a sickening crack, and the human slumped down the wall, collapsing face-first into the mud at our feet.

Horror and rage flared, and I spun on Jackal. "You killed him! *Why* did you do that? He wasn't even able to defend himself! There was no point in killing him!"

"He annoyed me." Jackal shoved the limp arm with a boot. "And there was no way I was going to feed on him. Why do you care, sister? He was a bloodthirsty cannibal who probably killed dozens himself. I did the city a favor by getting rid of him."

I snarled, baring my fangs. "The next human you kill in front of me, you'd better be ready for a fight, because I will come after you with everything I have."

"You're so boring." Jackal rolled his eyes, then faced me with a dangerous smile of his own. "And I'm getting a little tired of your holier-than-thou act, sister. You're not a saint. You're a demon. Own up to it."

"You want my help?" I didn't look away. "You want your head to stay on your neck the next time you turn your back on me?" His eyebrows rose, and I stepped forward, my face inches from his. "Stop killing indiscriminately. Or I swear, I will bury you in pieces."

"Yes, that worked out so well for you last time, didn't it? And it seems we keep having this conversation. Let me make something perfectly clear." Jackal, his eyes glowing a dangerous yellow, leaned closer, crowding me. I stood my ground. "If you think I'm afraid of you," he said softly, "or that I won't put another stick in your heart and cut off your head this time, you're only fooling yourself. I've been around a lot longer than you. I've seen my share of cocky vampires who think they're invincible. Until I rip their heads off."

"Anytime, Jackal." I reached back and touched the hilt of my sword. "You want that fight, just say the word."

Jackal stared at me a moment longer, then smiled. "Not today," he murmured. "Definitely soon. But not today." He stepped back, raising his hands. "Fine, sister. You win. I won't kill any more of your precious bloodbags. Unless I have cause, of course." He looked down at the dead mole man and curled a lip. "But if they come at me with knives or stakes or guns, all bets are off. Now, are we going to head into the city, or were you planning to hold hands with these cannibals and have a sing-along?"

I glanced once more at the broken corpse, wondering if his people would come for him and what they would do with his body if they did. Shying away from those thoughts, I stalked past Jackal and continued down the tunnel.

The rusty ladder that led up to the surface was exactly where I remembered it, and I felt another weird flicker of déjà vu as I pushed back the heavy round cover and emerged topside. Nothing had changed. The buildings were still there, dark and skeletal, falling to dust beneath vines and weeds. The rusted hulks of cars, their innards gutted and stripped away, sat decaying along sidewalks and half-buried in ditches. The vampire towers glimmered in the distant Inner City, as they had every night before this. Familiar and unchanged, though I didn't know what I'd expected. Maybe I'd thought things would be different, because *I* was so different.

"Huh," Jackal commented as he emerged from underground, gazing around at the crumbling buildings, the roots and weeds that grew over everything and pushed up through the pavement. "This place is a right mess, isn't it? Where is everyone?"

"Nobody stays out after dark," I muttered as we walked through the weed-tangled ditch, hopped the embankment and strode into the street. "Even though the vamps force the Registered humans to give blood every two weeks, and have plenty of bloodslaves in the Inner City, they still go hunting sometimes."

"Of course they do," Jackal said, as if that was obvious. "What fun is feeding from bloodbags you don't catch yourself? It's like having a stocked lake and never fishing from it."

I ignored that comment, nodding to the very center of the city, where the three vampire towers were lit up against the night sky. "That's where the Prince lives. Him and his coven. They never come down to the Fringe. At least, I never saw them when I lived here."

Jackal grunted, following my gaze. "According to vampire law, as visitors to the city, we're supposed to check in with the Prince," he muttered. "Tell him where we're from, what our business is here, how long we're staying." He snorted and curled a lip. "I don't really feel like playing by the little Prince's rules, and normally I would say 'the hell with it,' but that's going to be a problem now, isn't it?"

"Yeah," I agreed. I could feel the pull that drew me toward my sire. It was faint now, flickering erratically, as if Kanin was barely hanging on to life, but it still pulled at me, right toward the three towers in the center of New Covington. "He's in the Inner City." I sighed.

"Yep. And we'll probably run into Salazar's men while we're there. Could make searching for Kanin challenging if they decide we don't belong." Jackal grimaced as if speaking from experience. "Princes tend to be irrationally paranoid about strange vamps in their cities."

"We'll just have to take that chance." I gazed at the vampire towers and narrowed my eyes. "Salazar tried to kill Kanin and me both after he found us in the city." Jackal snickered, and I scowled at him. "He won't be too fond of *you,* either, because you're Kanin's blood. He hates Kanin with a vengeance."

"Everyone hates Kanin," Jackal said with a shrug. "All the old Masters know what he did, what he helped create. If we say we're looking for him, Salazar will probably assume we want to kill him. He doesn't have to know the truth."

"And what if he decides he wants to come with us and do the honors himself?"

"Salazar is a Master." Jackal smiled evilly. "It would be helpful to have a Master around when we run into Sarren—they can tear each other to pieces, and we can sneak out with Kanin. If we're lucky, they'll kill each other. If not…" He shrugged. "Then we'll just finish off the survivor when he's distracted."

"I don't like it."

"Why does that not surprise me?" Jackal's voice was flat. "What, exactly, is tripping you up here, sister? Having the Prince help us? Letting him fight our psychotically murderous vampire friend? Or is it the whole 'kick him when he's down' thing that's tweaking your conscience?" He shook his head. "Don't be so bloody naive. Salazar is a vampire, one who's lived a very long time and has become a Prince the old-fashioned way—by killing all his competition. He'll do exactly the same to us if he has the chance." He bared his fangs. "And you are going to have to start thinking like a vampire, my dear little sister, or you're never going to survive this world."

His words had an eerily familiar ring to them. I'd told Zeke Crosse the same thing once, that the world was harsh and unmerciful, and he wasn't going to survive if he didn't see it for what it was.

"All right," I snarled. "Fine. Let's go see the Prince, but I'm not spending any more time with him than we have to. We're here for Kanin, nothing else."

"Finally." Jackal rolled his eyes. "The shrew can see reason after all." Bristling, I was about to tell him what he could do with his reason, when a noise stopped me. A soft noise. One that, for whatever reason, raised the hair on the back of my neck.

We both turned to see a lone figure staggering down the street toward us.

CHAPTER 6

The human moved like it was drunk—shuffling, swaying from side to side, nearly tripping over its own feet. It would hit a car or the side of a building and lurch back, staggering and confused. I gave a soft growl, resisting the urge to pull away. Maybe because it reminded me of the animals bitten by rabids: stumbling around one moment, trying to eat your face off the next. Or maybe because there was just something *off* about it. Humans, even drunk humans, never ventured out this late at night. Save for a few of the more vicious gangs (and one very stubborn street rat who, incidentally, was no longer alive), all residents of New Covington fled inside when the sun went down. They had nothing to fear from rabids, of course, but wander the streets after dark, and you were just begging to be noticed by a vampire out hunting for live prey.

As the human drew closer, pawing blindly at its face, it tripped over a curb and fell, striking its head on the pavement. I saw its skull bounce on the asphalt, and the body collapse, twitching and gasping, in the gutter. At first, I thought it was dead, or at least dying.

Then, I realized it was laughing.

"Nice. Bloodbag's either too drunk to live or has gone right off the deep end," Jackal said, in what would've been a conversational tone if his fangs hadn't been showing through his gums. "I don't know whether to laugh or put it out of its misery."

At his voice, the human raised its head, regarding us with eyes that were as blank and glassy as a mirror. It was a woman, though it had been difficult to tell at first. Her hair had either been cut or torn out, as the top of her head was sticky with blood. Long gashes ran down both sides of her face, bleeding freely over her skin, but she didn't seem to notice the open wounds.

I resisted the urge to take several steps back. "Are you all right?" I asked, ignoring Jackal, who snorted. "You're hurt. What happened?"

The woman stared at me a second before her face contorted in a gaping, laughing scream. Baring bloodstained teeth, she lurched to her feet and charged me, swinging her arms. I leaped aside, and she ran headfirst into a cement wall, hitting the bricks with a muffled thump and reeling back. Shaking her head, she turned, spotting me through the curtain of blood running down her face, and shrieked with laughter.

As she lurched forward again, I drew my sword. At the sight of the weapon, she paused, still giggling, and suddenly clawed at her face, tearing open the already bleeding scars. More dark blood oozed down her cheeks.

"Is it...someone new?" she rasped, making my skin crawl. "Someone new, to make the burning stop?"

"What the hell—?" Jackal began, just as she lunged again, howling. Again, I dodged, but she followed me this time, swinging and flailing in complete abandon.

"Back off!" I snarled at her, baring my teeth. But the sight of fangs seemed to incense the human further. With a screech, she leaped, swiping at my face. I ducked her wild slashing and drove my sword hilt between her eyes, knocking her off her feet.

The human fell backward, her skull giving a faint crack as it hit the pavement again. She twitched, moaning, but didn't get up. Stepping past her body, I shot Jackal an evil look.

"Thanks for the help," I growled, and he smirked back.

"Hey, I am forbidden to kill any more bloodbags." Jackal crossed his arms and peered down at me, enjoying himself. "You were the one who told me to stop killing indiscriminately. I'm just following orders, here."

I bristled. "You can be such a—"

The woman screamed and, this time, I reacted on instinct, spinning around. As the human lunged for me, my blade sliced through ribs and out the other side, nearly cutting her in two. The body struck the curb with a wet splat, and though it thrashed and spasmed for a while as we watched it warily, it did not rise again.

Jackal and I exchanged a look as the body finally stopped moving. The night seemed deathly quiet and still.

"Okay." My blood brother nudged the corpse's leg with the toe of his boot. It flopped limply. "That's something completely new. Any guesses as to what that was all about?"

I peered down at the body, though I certainly wasn't going to touch it. "Maybe a rabid got in somehow," I mused. "Maybe that's why they shut down the city."

Jackal shook his head. "This wasn't a rabid. Look at it." He nudged the body, harder this time, flipping it over. He was right, and I had known it wasn't a rabid from the beginning. The rabids were pale, emaciated things, with blank white eyes, hooked fingernails and a mouthful of jagged fangs. This wasn't a rabid corpse. It looked perfectly human, except for the deep gouges down its cheek, and the wild, bulging stare.

"Smells human, too," Jackal added, taking a slow breath before wrinkling his nose. "Or at least, she doesn't smell dead. Not like they do. Though she must've been pumping herself full of *something* good, the way she put a hole through those bricks." He nodded at the cement wall, where the cracked indentation of a human skull sat in the middle of a bloody smear. "What did the crazy say to you? Something about making the burning stop?"

"Jackal," I growled, lifting my sword again. My blood brother looked up, following my gaze, and his eyes narrowed.

Across the street, two more humans shambled from a skeletal building, heads and faces torn, bright mad gazes searching the road. They muttered in low, harsh voices, garbled nonsense with only a few recognizable words. One of them held a lead pipe, which he banged on a line of dead cars as he crossed the street. Glass shattered and metal crumpled with hollow booms, ringing into the silence.

And then, another human emerged from an alleyway, followed by a friend.

And another.

And another.

More torn, bloody faces. More glassy eyes and mad, wild laughter, echoing all around us. The mob of humans hadn't seen us yet, but they were steadily drawing closer, and there were a lot of them. Their raspy voices slithered off the stones and rose into the air, making the hair on the back of my neck stand up. Vampire or no, I did *not* want to fight my way through that.

I snuck a glance at Jackal and saw that, for once, he was thinking the same. He jerked his head toward a building, and we quickly slipped away, ducking through a shattered window into the gutted remains of an old store. Dust and cobwebs clung to everything, and the floor was littered with rubble and glass, though the shelves were bare. Anything useful had been ripped out and taken long ago.

Outside the windows, the mob shambled about aimlessly. Sometimes they yelled at each other or no one, waving crude weapons at things that weren't there. Sometimes they shrieked and laughed and clawed at themselves, leaving deep bloody furrows across their skin. Once, a man fell to his knees and beat his head against the pavement until he collapsed, moaning, to the curb.

"Well," Jackal said with a brief flash of fangs, "this whole city has gone right to hell, hasn't it?" He shot me a dangerous look as we pressed farther into the building, speaking in harsh whispers. "I don't suppose the population was like this when you were here last, were they?"

I shivered and shook my head. "No."

"Nice. Well, if we're going to pay a visit to old Salazar, we need to hurry," Jackal said, glancing at the sky through the windows. "Sun's coming up, and I don't particularly want to be stuck here with a mob of bat-shit-crazy bloodbags."

For once, I agreed wholeheartedly.

Silently, we made our way through the Fringe, ducking into shadows and behind walls, leaping onto roofs or through windows, trying to avoid the crowds of moaning, laughing, crazy humans wandering the streets.

"This way," I hissed, and darted through a hole into an apartment building. The narrow corridors of the apartments were filled with rock and broken beams but were still fairly easy to navigate. Being inside brought back memories; when I'd lived here, I'd often taken this shortcut to the district square.

A moan drifted out of a hallway, stopping us. Sliding up against the wall, Jackal peered around a corner then quickly drew back, motioning for me to do the same. We both melted into the shadows, becoming vampire still, and waited.

A human staggered by, clutching a length of wood in one hand. He passed uncomfortably close, and I saw that he had clawed at his face until his eye had come out. Pausing, he glanced our way, but either it was too dark or his face was too ravaged for him to see clearly, for he turned his head and continued walking.

Suddenly, the one-eyed human staggered, dropping his club. Gagging, he fell to his hands and knees, heaving and gasping as if he couldn't catch his breath. Red foam bubbled from his mouth and nose, dripping to the ground beneath him. Finally, with a desperate choking sound, the human collapsed, twitched weakly for a moment and then stopped moving.

Jackal straightened, muttering a low, savage curse. "Oh, damn," he growled, more serious then I'd ever heard him sound. "That's why the city is locked down."

"What?" I asked, tearing my gaze away from the dead human. "What's going on? What is this?" Jackal stared at the human, then turned to face me.

"Red Lung," he said, making my blood freeze. "What you saw right there, those are the final symptoms of the Red Lung virus. Without the crazy muttering and tearing the eyes out, anyway." He shook his head violently, as if remembering. "I've never seen it, but Kanin told me how it worked. The infected humans would bleed internally, and eventually they would drown in their own blood, trying to throw up their organs. Nasty way to go, even for the bloodbags."

Dread gripped me. I glanced back at the body lying motionless in the hall, in the weeds poking through the floor, and felt cold. I remembered what Kanin had told me once, in the hidden lab when I first became a vampire. I'd asked him about the virus, why there was no Red Lung in the world anymore, if the scientists had found a cure. He'd given a bitter smile.

"No," Kanin said. "Red Lung was never cured. The Red Lung virus mutated *when the rabids were born. That's how Rabidism spread so quickly. It was an airborne pathogen, just like Red Lung, only instead of getting sick and dying, people turned into rabids." He shook his head, looking grave. "Some people survived, obviously, and passed on their immunities, which is why the world isn't full of rabids and nothing else. But there was no cure for Red Lung. The rabids destroyed that hope when they were created and escaped."*

And now, Red Lung had emerged again, in New Covington. Or a version of it had, anyway. Jackal and I exchanged a grave look, no doubt both thinking the same thing. *This* was what Sarren wanted, why he'd taken the virus samples. Somehow, he'd created another strain of the plague that had destroyed most of the world, and he'd unleashed it on New Covington.

The thought was terrifying.

Voices drifted out from the shadows, and we went still. The corpse in the hall had attracted another pair of humans from a nearby room. They poked it halfheartedly, asking crazy, nonsensical questions. When it didn't move, they quickly lost interest and shuffled back to the room, leaving it to rot at the mouth of the corridor.

We made our way through the apartments, slipping past the room with the crazy humans, and out to the street. I looked back and shuddered. "Why would he do this?" I whispered.

"Sarren doesn't need a reason for what he does." Jackal curled a lip in disgust. "He and his sanity parted ways a while back, and he's only gotten more deranged since. But this..." He gazed around the city and shook his head. "You bloody insane bastard," he muttered. "Why are you screwing with the food supply? We might not survive another epidemic."

Overhead, the sky was an uncomfortable navy blue, and most of the stars had faded. We didn't have a lot of time to reach the Inner City. "This way," I hissed at Jackal, slipping through the gap in the wooden fence surrounding the apartment. "It's still a good distance to the Sector Four gate."

We didn't quite make it.

I got us there as quickly as I could, of course. This was still my old neighborhood, my district. I had spent seventeen years of my life in this filthy, dilapidated ruin of a town, scavenging for food, dodging patrols, doing whatever it took to survive. This was my territory; I knew its quirks, its shortcuts, and where to go if I wanted to get somewhere quickly.

That wasn't the problem.

The problem was, back when I was human, everyone else had been human, too. The sane, rational, not-trying-to-kill-you kind of human. Now, the streets, the buildings, the side alleys and parking lots, were filled with infected madmen. Madmen who didn't fear vampires or pain or anything, and who would come at us, screaming, if they so much as saw our shadows move. Jackal and I cut several of these humans down as they flung themselves at us with a wild abandon almost like the rabids' single-minded viciousness. Other times, we would escape into the shadows, over walls, or onto the roofs where the infected couldn't follow. I'd never seen so many humans wandering the streets at night, and wondered where all the sane, noninfected people were. If there were any left at all.

A pink glow was threatening the eastern horizon when we finally reached the wall of the Inner City, fighting our way through another group of shrieking madmen to the big iron gates that led to the Prince's territory. Normally, the thick metal doors were heavily guarded, with soldiers stationed up top and two well-armed humans standing in front. Now, the gates were sealed tight, and no guards patrolled the Inner Wall. Nor did anyone respond to our shouts and banging on the doors. It seemed the Prince had drawn all his people farther into the city, leaving the Fringe to fend for itself.

Jackal swore and gave the gate a resounding kick. The blow made a hollow, booming sound that echoed down the wall, but the doors were thick, sturdy and designed to hold up to vampire attacks. They didn't even shake.

"What now?" he snarled, looking at the top of the Inner Wall, a good twenty feet straight up. Like the gates, the wall protecting the Inner City was built with vampires in mind. There were no handholds, no ledges to cling to, no buildings close enough to launch off. We wouldn't be getting into the city this way.

And dawn was dangerously close.

"Come on," I told Jackal, who glared at the wall as if he might take an ax to it when he came back. "We can't stay out here, and we're not getting in this way. I know a place where we can sleep—it's secure enough, we won't have to worry about crazy humans."

A woman staggered around a corner, her entire face an open, bleeding wound, and lunged at us with a howl. I dodged, letting her smack into the wall, then bolted into the Fringe again, Jackal following and snarling curses at my back.

Several streets and close calls later, with the sun moments away from breaking over the jagged horizon, I squeezed through a familiar chain-link fence at the edge of a cracked, overgrown parking lot. A squat, three-story building sat at the end of the lot, making a lump rise to my throat. *Home.* This had been home, once.

Then a searing light spilled over the buildings, turning the tops a blinding orange, and we ran.

Miraculously, no crazy humans waited in the parking lot to ambush us. After ducking through the doors into the shade of the hallway, I collapsed against the wall in relief.

"Nice place," Jackal remarked, slouched against the opposite wall, where a row of lockers rusted against the plaster. He gazed down the dark corridor, where rooms lined each wall, and curled a lip. "Let me guess—hospital? Or asylum."

"It's a school," I said, rolling my eyes. "Or it was, back before the plague." I pushed myself off the wall, feeling sluggish and tired now that the sun was out. "This way. There's a basement we used to hole up in when the vamps were out."

"We?" Jackal raised an eyebrow as we picked our way down the hall. I winced, realizing my slip, and didn't reply. "So," Jackal continued, gazing around with more interest, "this was where you lived as a bloodbag."

"You really like that term, don't you?"

"What?" Jackal looked confused.

"Bloodbag. That's all humans are to you." I turned down another hallway, one even more cluttered with rubble and fallen plaster. "You keep forgetting that you were one, once."

Now it was his turn to roll his eyes. "Look, sister. I've been a vampire for a long time now. Maybe not as long as Kanin, but definitely longer than you. Live a few decades, and yes, they all start to look the same. Like cows. Intelligent, talking pieces of meat." He ducked under a beam lying across the corridor, barely clearing it. "Granted, I didn't always see them that way, but time has a way of breaking down your convictions."

Surprised, I stopped and turned to blink up at him. "Really? You?"

"Does that shock you?" Jackal grinned, enjoying himself. "Yeah, sister. I was like you once. So worried about not hurting the poor defenseless humans, only taking what I needed, so scared about losing control." He shook his head. "And then, one night Kanin and I met a group of men who wanted to kill us. And we slaughtered them all. As easily as killing spiders." He grinned then, showing fangs. "Right then, I realized we were always meant to rule over humans. We could do whatever we wanted, and they couldn't stop us. Why deny your base nature? It's what we are.

"So, yes," he finished, still smirking at me. "I call humans 'bloodbags.' I don't need to know their names, or if they have a family, or what their favorite color is. Because I'm either going to outlive them, or I'm going to tear their throats open and suck them dry. And life got a lot simpler once I realized that."

"You gave up," I accused. "It just got too hard to fight it anymore."

"Did you ever think there was a reason for that? Because we're not supposed to! Why would I want to keep fighting my instincts?"

"You don't have to be a murdering bastard to be a vampire."

Jackal snorted. "You don't believe that," he mocked. "Not even *Kanin* believed that, and he was the biggest softhearted prick I ever came across. Before you, anyway." He sneered at my dark look. "But, go ahead. Keep telling yourself your pretty little lies. I just hope I'm there when it all comes crashing down around you."

We'd reached the end of the hall, and I pulled open the rusty metal door that led to the basement. Memories continued to haunt me as I made my way down the stairs, into the cement walled rooms of the school's lowest floor. This was where the gang and I had retreated whenever there was trouble—a rival gang, a vampire in the area, an unexpected patrol. The door could be barred from the inside, and the thick walls and floor made it hard for anything to get at us. Of course, now that I was a vampire, it was chilling to realize how easily I could have blown through that flimsy barrier, locked or not. And with no other way out of the basement, whoever came down here would be trapped.

Shutting the door, I let the bar clang into place. Hopefully, the crazies outside were not as strong as a vampire, because sleep was clawing at the edges of my mind. Jackal, gripping the railing like he, too, was in danger of falling over, looked around the dark, cold room.

"Where exactly do you expect us to sleep?"

"I don't care," I slurred, moving carefully down the steps. "Pick a corner. Just leave me alone." I found the spot behind several low-hanging pipes where I'd kept a ratty quilt for myself, and found it was still there. Drawing it over my shoulders, I sat down with my back to the corner and unsheathed my sword beneath the quilt. When we were traveling, we'd separated at dawn to bury ourselves in the frozen earth, hidden and safe from each other. Having him in the same room with me as I lay exposed and helpless made me nervous.

Jackal was still wandering around, looking for a place to lie down. I stayed awake as long as I could, listening to his footsteps, waiting for him to find a spot. I forced myself to keep my eyes open, fighting the sluggish pull threatening to draw me under, until the noises ceased.

Finally. Leaning my head against the wall, I let my eyes slip shut, and had just started to relax when his dark chuckle echoed out of the darkness.

"I know you're still awake."

"Good for you. Shut up and go to sleep."

Another snicker. "What you have to ask yourself," he continued, "is whether I'm the type who would stay awake long enough to kill you after you fall asleep, or if I'm an early riser who would kill you before you wake up."

"If you want your head to stay on your neck, you'd better be neither," I growled, though his words sent a cold spear of dread through my stomach. My hands tightened on my sword hilt, and Jackal laughed somewhere in the darkness, unseen.

"I'm just kidding, sis," he said. "Or am I? Something to think about, before you fall asleep. Nighty-night, then. Sleep tight."

I struggled to stay awake awhile longer, knowing I was playing right into Jackal's twisted sense of humor, yet unable to stop myself. I couldn't see Jackal, couldn't hear him, so I didn't know if he had already fallen asleep, if he was lying awake snickering to himself, or if he was waiting for me to drift off so he could creep over and quietly rip off my head.

I really, really hate him, was my last thought before I finally succumbed to the inevitable blackness.

CHAPTER 7

Hunger.

Nothing exists but Hunger.

There is no food here. No food, just stone and steel and darkness. Bars around me, chains on my wrists, pulling me to the wall. Can't move, can't stay here. Need to hunt, need food, prey, blood!

No.

No, calm yourself, Kanin. Think. You felt them, when you woke up. They're here. Both of them. The girl and the lost one. What are their names? Can't remember.

So Hungry.

"Welcome back, old friend."

Movement beyond the bars. He *is here; I can feel his cold black eyes on me, sense his smile. I growl, the noise vibrating around us, low and threatening. I hear his hissing chuckle.*

"Can you hear it?" His face floats between the bars, eyes closed, as if listening to music somewhere above us. "Can you hear the screams? Smell the fear, the taint of despair? This is only the beginning, you

know. Only the first test. And we are in the perfect place to watch everything unravel." He opens his eyes, smiling at me. "Oh, but I can feel the Hunger in you, old friend. It's eating you alive, isn't it? Sadly, your fate is no longer in my hands."

I lean forward, trying to reach him, to pull him through the bars and tear him in half. The shackles bite into my wrists, holding me back. He chuckles again, then draws away, pale face melting into the shadows beyond the cell.

"Goodbye, Kanin. I've enjoyed the times we had, but now, I have a greater purpose. I know you will not think of me much beyond this, but I will remember you. I will remember you most fondly. Farewell, old friend."

I opened my eyes, then jerked back, bashing my head against the concrete. Jackal was crouched in front of me, a faint smirk on his face, his eyes narrowed and contemplative. I brandished my sword in a flash of steel and fangs, but he leaped back, the blade missing him by centimeters.

"Dammit, Jackal!" I surged upright, keeping my weapon between me and the sadistic raider king. "What are you trying to pull? Do that again and I'll cut that stupid grin of yours in half!"

"Too easy, sister." Jackal's smirk widened, showing fangs. "You're far too trusting. I could have twisted your little head right off your neck, and you wouldn't have felt a thing." He demonstrated with his hands, then shook his head in mock disappointment. "You've got a lot to learn, I'm afraid."

"Well, you won't be the one teaching me." I sheathed my sword and turned away, still bristling from having him that close. Sadistic, obnoxious vampire. He got under my skin sometimes, but that was probably what he wanted, to keep me off balance, on edge. A sick game he liked to play.

"Or maybe," Jackal added, "you're just feeling sluggish because you didn't sleep well. Bad dreams?" When I looked at him sharply, he nodded, serious for once. "You saw him, too, didn't you? The old bastard is still hanging on."

"Yeah." I let myself feel that tiny sliver of hope, of relief. "He's still alive."

"Yep. Looks like Sarren brought him out of hibernation after all. Tough old geezer—some of us never come out of it."

"Any idea where he could be? It looked like he was underground somewhere, maybe a prison or a..."

I trailed off, frowning. Jackal started to reply, but I held up my hand, stopping him. Soft shuffling noises drifted to me across the room, coming from outside the barred door. I jerked my head at the entrance just as the handle turned and the door shook, as if something was trying to force its way inside.

Silently, I readied my sword, and Jackal picked up a rusty lead pipe from the floor, not bothering to return to wherever he had slept for his ax. At my nod, he glided up the steps and put his hand under the bar, looking back at me. I inched up, raising my sword, and nodded for him to open it.

Jackal wrenched off the bar and threw open the door. I lunged forward, sweeping my blade down, expecting to see a bloody-faced lunatic on the other side.

Something yelped and threw itself backward, and I pulled my blow up short, barely stopping in time. The body landed in an ungainly sprawl on the floor, a ragged human with shaggy brown hair and huge dark eyes. I felt a brief, faint stab of recognition, like I should know him from somewhere, but I couldn't place it. He gaped at us, fear and horror spreading across his face, before he scrambled away like a thin, ragged spider, arms and legs pumping frantically.

Jackal lunged past me, grabbed the kid by his ragged shirt and hauled him off his feet. "Where do you think you're going, little rat?" He yanked him back into the room. The kid howled, flailing wildly, and Jackal shook him once, hard enough that his head jerked back on his neck. "Hey now. None of that god-awful screeching. You'll attract the crazies wandering around out there. Wouldn't want to have to rip your tongue out through your teeth, would we?"

"Jackal," I snapped, closing the door and stalking back into the room. "Let him go."

He gave me a bored look, then dropped the gasping human unceremoniously on the floor. The kid, probably no more than thirteen, if I had to guess, scuttled backward until he hit a wall, then continued to gape at us with huge, terrified eyes.

"Take it easy," I said, stepping toward him slowly, ignoring the sudden flare of Hunger. The demon within growled impatiently, urging me to pounce on this boy and feed, but I forced it back. I recognized the skinny frame, the rags, the way his eyes darted everywhere, looking for a way out. He was an Unregistered. Just like I had been.

"Relax," I told him again, trying to sound calm and reasonable. "We're not going to hurt you, or...eat you. Just calm down."

"Oh, shit!" he panted, pressing himself to the corner, his gaze riveted on me. "It's true, then! That kid wasn't lying. You're *her!* You really did become a vampire!"

I stared at him. "How did you—?"

It hit me then, where I knew this boy from. He wasn't just a random street rat, he was part of Kyle's gang, a group of rival Unregistereds who had lived within our sector and scavenged the same territories. I'd seen him in passing a few times when I'd been human; the Unregistered gangs of the Fringe did not mingle and usually left each other alone. We weren't enemies, exactly. We'd warn other Unregistereds of sweeps and patrols, and if another group was scavenging a particular territory, we'd avoid that section for a day or two. But in our section of the Fringe, Kyle's gang had been our biggest competition for food and resources, and the truce between us had been tense in those final few days.

Of course, they must've been thrilled when they heard we were all killed by rabids. Myself included. Even if I didn't truly die, I could no longer be a part of that world. Their competition was gone. None of us had made it back to the city alive.

Except for one.

"Stick," I whispered, and stepped forward, advancing on the human. He cringed, looking terrified, but I didn't care anymore. "That kid you're talking about," I demanded, "was his name Stick? What happened to him? Is he still around?"

Is he still alive?

"That little pisswad?" The boy curled his lip, pure disgust filtering through the terror for a moment. "Nah, he's not around here anymore. He's gone. No one's seen him since the night you attacked our hideout."

I wasn't attacking your hideout, I wanted to say. *I was just looking for Stick.* But I knew the human wouldn't believe me. And besides, it didn't matter now. Stick was gone. The boy I'd looked after nearly half my life, the person I'd thought was my friend when I was human, had sold me out to the Prince when he'd discovered what I was. Kanin had cautioned me not to go after him, not to see him again, but I'd ignored his warnings and tried to contact my sole remaining crew member one last time.

I really should've known better. Stick had taken one look at what I was, screamed in terror and run away. Straight to the Prince and his followers, apparently. As if all our years of friendship, all those times I'd risked my neck for him, kept him safe, kept him fed and alive at my own expense, meant nothing.

I thought I'd buried that pain when I fled the city, but it ached, a dull, nagging throb somewhere deep inside. Still, I couldn't focus on the past. If this kid was uninfected and sane, maybe there were other humans who had escaped the chaos, too.

"Are there more of you?" Jackal broke in, thinking the same thing, apparently. The kid hesitated, and he added in a perfectly civil tone, "You realize your potential to be useful is the only thing keeping you alive right now, yes?"

"Yeah." The human spat the word, glaring at us with a mix of fear and hatred. "Yeah, there are more of us. Down in the tunnels beneath the city. We moved there when all the craziness started. The bleeders stay topside, for the most part."

"So that was what the mole man was talking about," I mused. "Topsiders coming down into their turf." I looked at the kid again. "Don't you have trouble with them? They're not happy about you pushing into their territory."

He shrugged. "We can take our chances with the crazies

or the cannibals. The mole men clans leave us alone if we're in a group. And the boss knows the tunnels pretty well, at least, the ones that are clan territory."

The tunnels. I suddenly remembered that, when I had been here with Kanin, some of the underground passages had led into the Inner City. I'd never seen them of course, never went looking for them, back when I was human. But rumors existed of places where you could creep into the vampires' territory, as dangerous and suicidal as that was. Back when I became a vampire, Kanin had shown me a way beneath the Inner Wall, through a network of old sewers and subway tunnels, right into the heart of the Inner City. But the underground was a maze, stretching for miles beneath the city streets, thousands of tunnels that all looked the same. Even if we could reach the old hospital, I didn't think I could retrace the steps Kanin had used to get past the wall. But, that path *did* exist, somewhere.

We couldn't get into the Inner City through the gates. And traveling the underground seemed a hell of a lot safer than staying topside with the "bleeders."

"Are you thinking what I'm thinking?" Jackal muttered behind me.

I nodded. "You said there is someone who knows the way through the tunnels," I told the kid, who winced, as if he knew what I was going to say next. "Take us to him."

"Show up with two bloodsuckers?" He went even paler, shaking his head frantically. "No, I can't! Everyone will freak out. And then they'll kill me for bringing you there."

I could feel Jackal's fanged smile without even seeing it. "Die then, or now, bloodbag. Your choice."

"Shit." The kid dragged a hand across his face. "All right,

fine. I'll take you there…if you promise not to kill me after. There are plenty of other humans down there if you get Hungry—suck on one of them, okay? I'll even point out the stupid, gullible ones. Just don't eat me."

Though I didn't let it show, I felt a flicker of disgust, hypocritical as it was. His answer shouldn't have surprised me. I'd grown up on the streets with the same attitude, the same survival instincts. In the Fringe, it was everyone for himself. No matter what, you did whatever it took to survive. I knew that. I'd *lived* that.

But then I'd met Zeke and his small group, and everything changed. They'd accepted me, a virtual stranger, as one of their own, no strings, no expectations. With the exception of their hardened leader, they'd looked out for each other, taken care of one another. And the boy whom I'd first thought naive and blind and idealistic must've rubbed off on me, because when faced with the choice to leave or risk my life for the group, my survival instincts had gone out the window. And I'd found I actually gave a damn about them all.

It had been a shock to learn there were other ways of living. It had been even more of a shock to know that I could still care, that I was willing to jeopardize my own existence for others. Now we were back in the Fringe, and the philosophy *everyone for himself* still held true. But, at least in my old gang, we hadn't sold other humans out to the vampires. Until Stick, anyway. It seemed Kyle's group had no such convictions.

Jackal grinned at me. "Ah, human loyalty. It's such an inspiring thing, isn't it, sister? Makes you wonder how we ever came out on top." He glanced at the Unregistered, who blinked, unaware that he'd just been insulted, and his smile grew wider. "Better hurry, little bloodbag, and lead us to your friends. I'm feeling kinda Hungry now."

The parking lot had a couple bleeders shambling about, muttering to themselves, but we were able to sneak around them without too much trouble. The scent of fresh blood, streaming from their faces and arms, hung on the breeze like invisible ribbons, rousing the demon within. I didn't realize I was staring at the back of our guide's neck until I felt my fangs poking my bottom lip and forced the Hunger down.

"When did this start?" I asked the kid once we were clear of the school. Partly because I was curious and partly to keep myself occupied, to focus on something other than my bloodlust. "The sickness, the craziness. How long has this been going on?"

"Not long." He glanced over his shoulder, as if surprised I was talking to him like a normal person. "Maybe two weeks, give or take a couple days? I dunno exactly—it's hard to tell underground."

"Why hasn't the Prince done anything?"

"He has." The kid snorted. "He's pulled all his pets and guards back into the Inner City and shut the doors on the rest of us. You try to get past the gates, they shoot you on sight. Food trucks have stopped coming, too." He shrugged, a hopeless, angry gesture. "Guess he's just waiting for everyone to die out here."

A human stumbled down the road, dragging a blanket behind him and reeking of blood, and my Hunger stirred restlessly. We waited in the shadows until the human shambled by. "You could get sick up here, too," I said to our guide after the bleeder lurched around a corner. "You're not worried about that?" He shrugged again and continued leading us through the streets.

"Not much choice. Like I said, we can take our chances up here with the bleeders, or starve in the tunnels. What would you do, if there was no food anywhere?" He spared me another glance and shook his head. "Guess you don't understand anymore. Vampires don't have that problem, do they?"

Oh, I understand more than you think.

We slipped through an overgrown street, where weeds, brush and large trees had cracked pavement and grown up through the ancient husks of cars. The vegetation covering the sidewalk and surrounding buildings was so thick it was like hacking through a forest. The Unregistered kid wove through the tangled undergrowth with an innate familiarity; he'd done this before, and often.

Ducking around the skeletal remains of a van, he stopped and cast a wary look around the shadows before dropping to a crouch in the bushes. Shoving a tire away, he brushed back a clump of weeds, revealing a small, perfectly round hole in the middle of the road. Another entrance to the maze of tunnels that ran beneath New Covington. I wondered how I—or rather, how Allie the Fringer street rat—had missed this one.

The Unregistered kid dug in his grimy pockets and pulled out a tiny flashlight, the beam barely visible as he poked it down the hole and peered around. "Looks like it's clear," he muttered, pulling it back out and inching close to the hole, preparing to drop inside. "Wait here a second, I'll make sure it's safe, then give you the heads-up when it's clear."

"Not so fast." I reached out and snagged the kid by the

shirt, dragging him back. "Don't think I'm stupid. I was one of you once, remember?" He started to protest, but I shoved him toward Jackal, who grabbed him by the collar. "I'll head down first, and the two of you can follow."

The kid looked back at Jackal and paled. "You're leaving me alone with *him?*"

"He won't try anything." I narrowed my eyes at the other vampire. "Right?"

"Me?" Jackal smiled, showing fangs. "I am the epitome of self-control and restraint, sister. Your bleeding heart must be rubbing off on me."

I rolled my eyes, drew my weapon and dropped into the hole.

My vampire sight adjusted almost instantly to the pitch blackness, showing me an endless concrete tunnel, dripping walls and crumbling bricks. Something small and furry skittered up a pipe and vanished into a crack, but other than that, the sewers were empty and still.

"Clear," I called back, sheathing my katana.

The kid dropped quite suddenly from the opening, as if he'd been shoved, and sprawled out on the concrete with a yelp of pain. I scowled and glared at Jackal as he dropped through a moment later, landing lightly and brushing off his sleeves.

"All righty," he announced, ignoring my glare. "Here we are in the sewers again, my favorite New Covington vacation spot. So thrilled to be here." He fixed the Unregistered with a dangerous smile. "Well, don't just stand there, tunnel rat. Give us the tour."

"Uh. Yeah," the kid said, rising warily to his feet. His eyes darted about, constantly alert in a way that was far too familiar. "Follow me."

We walked in silence for a bit. I stayed close to the human, watching him carefully, ready to grab him if he got the idea to bolt. Though he'd promised to lead us to the other Unregistereds, I had no doubt he would dart into the nearest drain or crack or dark hole if he got the chance. Unregistereds were opportunists, and the ones who survived did so any way they could. Stealing, lying, making promises they never intended to keep, just to stay alive. I would've done the same thing, if I was still human, still a street rat like this kid.

Kid? Street rat? I realized I didn't even know his name. Not that I particularly cared; I doubted he would've asked my name if the roles were reversed. But thinking of him as just a human, just a nameless street rat—that was something that the vampires did.

"You never told me your name," I said, surprising the kid, who looked back cautiously. "You know me—it seems all the Unregistereds know my name and what happened to me. What do they call you?"

"Roach," muttered the kid after a moment. "They call me Roach."

Jackal laughed. "Well, isn't that fitting."

"Are Kyle and Travis still around?" I asked, ignoring Jackal. They'd known me before I'd become a vampire—not well, but they would still recognize me when they saw me.

But Roach shook his head. "Nah, they're both dead."

I wasn't shocked at his bluntness, or his casual shrug, but it was sobering to hear yet two more people I knew were gone. "What happened?"

"Sickness took them. This way." Roach ducked down a narrow, half-circular tunnel, low and claustrophobic, sludgy water oozing across the floor. His voice echoed in the small space around us. "Travis died first, but Kyle turned into a bleeder and went crazy on us. That's when we knew we had to get off the streets. The new guy moved us all into the tunnels to avoid the crazies. He's probably gonna be pissed I went off alone again. Hang on a second. We're here."

A rusty grate covered the other end of the tunnel, and flickering yellow light filtered through the slats. I could see a form silhouetted against the grate, ragged and thin, probably on guard duty. He spun as our footsteps echoed down the tunnel, shining a flashlight through the grate. Roach flinched, throwing up an arm as the beam hit him in the face.

"Just me, stupid! Open the door."

The light flickered to me and Jackal. I peered through the haze and saw an older boy, lean and black, his dark eyes narrowed suspiciously. "Who are they?"

"What the hell does it look like?" Roach continued without missing a beat. "Fringers I met topside. People who aren't ripping their faces off. I figured the boss would want me to bring them down here."

"He's pissed at you, Roach." The beam slid back, and the guard lifted a heavy iron bar that had been placed across the grate cover. "You know we're not supposed to go up there alone, especially now."

"Yeah, yeah. Tell me something I don't know."

With an earsplitting screech, the grate opened. Roach passed the guard, who eyed me and Jackal warily but didn't say anything, and led us to a rusty staircase beyond the tunnel. The rickety-looking stairs rose from the concrete floor, spiraled up a narrow shaft and continued into the black.

"Um, they're pretty shaky," Roach said, glancing hopefully back at us. "Probably best we go one at a time—don't want 'em collapsing underneath us, right?"

Jackal chuckled. "Devious little bloodbag, isn't he? I don't know whether to be amused or insulted."

"Nice try," I said, and gestured him forward. "Keep going. We'll be right behind you."

Roach shrugged and continued up the stairs.

The steps *were* pretty shaky, creaking and groaning under our weight, but they held. We came out of the hole into a large room with cement floors and walls. Crumbling posts held up a low ceiling, and massive cylindrical machines, completely encased in rust, created a narrow corridor down one wall.

"What is this place?" I mused.

"Sub-basement," Jackal echoed behind me. "Or an old boiler room. We're probably below a factory or something." He took a long, deep breath and smiled, showing his fangs. "Ah, the stench of human misery. Can you smell it, sister?"

I didn't know what a boiler room was, and I wasn't going to ask, having bigger worries right now. Jackal was right—the scent of warm-blooded humans was everywhere, even overpowering the smells of rust and mold and greasy smoke. The hot smell of blood, wrapped around the scent of fear and hopelessness and despair, roused the Hunger from its restless hibernation. It made me want to melt into the darkness, to slide between the aisles and wait for an unsuspecting human to walk by, then yank it back into the shadows, never to be seen again.

"Keep it together," I growled, as much to myself as to the vampire next to me. His eyes shone a luminous yellow in a way I didn't like at all, and I glared at him. "We're here for their help, not a snack."

"Perish the thought." Jackal waved a hand in a vague gesture. "I was simply making an observation. What were *you* thinking of?"

Ignoring him, I trailed Roach down an aisle, the squat, rusty machines lining either side like rotund guardians. Flickering orange light danced over the floor between them, the low crackle of a fire echoing off the barrels. Leaving the maze of machinery, we entered a large open space, where a scattering of blankets, boxes and rag piles surrounded a dying fire.

Half-starved humans milled through the shadows cast by the flames, or huddled close to the fire, shivering. The cold had stopped affecting me long ago, and I didn't think about it anymore, but I realized it must be freezing for them down here. The Fringer that I had been, however, approved. Well hidden, underground, a lot of places to hide. Yeah, Allie the street rat would've liked this place. Whoever had chosen this secure little haven knew what they were doing.

Of course, that didn't account for vampires being allowed past the gates.

"Okay," Roach whispered, glancing at me over his shoulder, "I got you here. You'll let me go now, right?"

I scanned the shivering crowd of humans and frowned. "Who's in charge?"

"Um..." Roach gazed around the camp, too. "There," he said, pointing to one side. "Our fearless leader."

I followed his hand to where a pair of humans stood at the edge of the light, talking in low voices with their backs to us. One of them was unremarkable, thin and ragged and dirty, like all the others. The second human, however, wore sturdier clothes, boots and a black combat vest like I'd seen on some of the Prince's guards. A heavy pistol was holstered to his belt, and across his back was a strange weapon I'd never seen before. It looked like someone had taken a bow and arrow—something I'd only read about before—and attached it to the end of a gun. A long wooden spike lay nestled in the strange weapon, and it sent a chill through my stomach.

"Son of a bitch," Jackal muttered behind me. "The bastard has a crossbow. Well, *someone* is prepared to run into vampires, aren't they?"

Something clicked in my head, and the world seemed to stop. *No,* I thought, dazed. *It can't be. He can't be here now. It's not possible.*

But it was, and I knew who it was, even before he turned around. Blond, blue eyed, lean and tall, like he'd stepped right out of my memory, out of my dreams, and into existence.

"Zeke," I whispered as his piercing, familiar gaze met mine across the room. "What the hell are you doing here?"

CHAPTER 8

Ezekiel Crosse. The adopted son of Jebbadiah Crosse, the fanatical preacher who'd led a group of pilgrims across the country on a search for the mythical city of Eden. Zeke, the human who'd fought so hard to get his people to safety, whom I had left behind at the gates of Eden. The boy I thought I'd never see again, and certainly not *here,* hundreds of miles from that island, in the territory of a vampire Prince.

Zeke, the boy I couldn't get out of my head, who'd haunted my thoughts even though I knew I'd done the right thing, leaving him behind. Who had kissed me, knowing what I was. Who had offered his own blood to save my life when I lay close to death.

Who was supposed to be safe in Eden now.

He looked older, somehow, more mature, though it had been less than a year since I'd seen him last. His pale hair was shorter, not quite so shaggy, and though he was still lean and muscular, he'd lost the gaunt, wasted look of someone barely eating enough to live. He looked healthy and confident and strong, and achingly familiar.

"Allie." Zeke's voice was a breath, a whisper; I barely caught it even with my vampire hearing. It brought a storm of memories—our first meeting in the dead town, our first kiss, his hot, sweet blood spreading over my tongue. Everything about him came flooding back, and I stood there, reeling in the tide of emotion. Zeke was *here,* not in Eden with the others. He was right in front of me.

For a moment, Zeke stared back, blue eyes wide with shock, hope, relief...and something else.

But then, they flickered to the vampire standing beside me. And changed.

Recognition, followed by disbelief and rage. Those blue orbs turned icy cold, and a blank mask slammed down across his features. In one smooth movement, he stepped away and yanked the weapon from his back. I heard the hiss as he drew the string and leveled that deadly wooden point at Jackal's chest.

"Zeke, wait!"

I lunged in front of him as Jackal snarled, the animalistic sound booming through the chamber. Humans shrieked in terror, scattering like birds as they realized what had snuck into their safe little haven. Roach darted away, vanishing into the shadows as pandemonium erupted around us.

"Everyone, freeze!" Zeke's sharp, commanding voice rose over the chaos, stilling the panic. The frantic movement around us slowed as Zeke continued to hold the weapon on me and Jackal. "Stay where you are," Zeke went on, casting a split-second glance around the chamber. His voice rang with authority, composed yet firm. "Be calm, all of you. Do not move unless I give the word."

Smart move. Zeke knew vampires, some of it from me. He knew that we were predators, and that fear, panic and frantic movements could set us off, goad us into giving chase. I felt my own demon rise up, sensing prey, eager to hunt and kill. I forced it down, trying to stay calm, focused. But it was hard, caught between a wooden stake and a volatile, murderous vampire, with the smell of blood and fear thick in the air. I felt balanced on a razor's edge, and needed only a tiny push for everything around me to explode in violence.

Behind me, Jackal chuckled, soft and menacing. "Well, isn't this fun," he crooned, making me want to kick him in the groin. "Tell me, human. How many of these little bloodbags do you think I can kill before you get that shot off?"

I glared back at him, hoping Zeke would not rise to that challenge. "Shut up! You are not helping!"

He shrugged. "Sorry. Kind of hard to think when you have a crossbow pointed in your direction. Makes me a little twitchy."

"If you hadn't noticed," I growled, trying to keep my voice calm, "that crossbow is pointed at *me*. Because I was stupid enough to jump in front of you. Don't make me regret it even more."

"Allison." Zeke's voice was hard. My heart sank, and I turned to face those cold blue eyes. They glittered with anger, with shock and betrayal, as he shook his head. "Please tell me you have a valid reason for being here with *him*."

He spat the word like a curse. I didn't blame him—Jackal had kidnapped Zeke's family. He'd murdered Zeke's friend,

Darren, to set an example. He was responsible for the death of Zeke's father, Jebbadiah Crosse. He was a ruthless, brutal, cold-blooded killer, and Zeke had every reason to hate him.

So why am I standing here, protecting him?

"Zeke, please…"

"Zeke," Jackal growled behind me, as if just figuring something out. "*Ezekiel.* Ezekiel Crosse. Son of a bitch, you're the kid the old bastard was talking about. You're the old man's son!"

Shit. I spun, but Jackal hit me hard, shoving me aside. I struck the cement floor just as the snap of the crossbow string rang out in the brief moment of silence. Jackal ducked, moving with the inhuman speed of our kind, and the deadly spike zipped by him, missing his face by centimeters. As I cursed and shot to my feet, he roared, baring his fangs, and went for Zeke.

I shot after him, praying to make it there in time. As Jackal closed the distance, Zeke dropped the crossbow and yanked a long wooden spike from a slot in his armored vest. Jackal snarled, but Zeke stood his ground, raising the stake in his fist as the vampire lunged forward.

Drawing my katana, I threw myself between them.

"Stop this!"

I turned on Jackal with the sword, barring his path and at the same time grabbing the wrist that held the stake. Jackal halted inches from the blade, eyes gleaming, and Zeke stiffened in my grip, but didn't try to yank free. "We are not doing this now!" I hissed at both of them. Jackal growled, and Zeke tensed, ready to lunge, and I shoved them back. "Dammit, we have bigger problems to worry about, like the city tearing itself apart around us. If you haven't noticed, we're sort of in a bad way here. And I'm not going to stand by and watch you two tear each other's throats out." They both glared at me; I glared back and didn't relent. "I don't care about your personal vendettas. Kill each other later—right now, there are other things to deal with. So you boys are just going to have to suck it up and get over it!"

A brittle silence stretched between us. I could feel the violence pulsing on either side. I could feel Jackal's vicious intent and Zeke's pure, unfiltered rage, straining against the barrier that held them back. Me. I swallowed hard and waited, hoping they would not continue this fight. Because then I would be forced to take a side, and I didn't know what side I was going to choose.

Surprisingly, it was Jackal who finally smiled and stepped back, raising his hands. "Okay, bloodbag," he said, looking past me to Zeke. "Fine. I can be civil. For now. Observe." He made a great show of looking around the chamber. "Nice place you got here. Love what you've done with it. If I'd known, I would've brought a housewarming gift. A shag rug to go with the lovely piles of garbage."

I felt some of the tension diffuse and relaxed a bit, turning to Zeke. He yanked his wrist back, and I let him this time, dropping my hand. "Zeke—"

The look he gave me was withering. Anger, betrayal and a cold, appraising stare, as if he was seeing me again for the first time, and I wasn't the person he'd known before.

Zeke shoved the stake through his vest, where a number of wooden spikes hung, I noticed, and grabbed the crossbow off the floor. "What are you doing here, Allison?"

His voice was clipped, hard, and he wasn't looking at me. My heart sank, hurt and anger and frustration spreading through my insides. I watched him swing the weapon to his back and took stock of the rest of them. It was an impressive armory, different than the one he'd carried when we first met. Crossbow, stakes, heavy pistol, armored vest—he was ready for vampires this time. The only thing that was familiar was the machete, still strapped across his back beneath the vest and crossbow, and the small silver cross around his neck. He didn't look like a lost wanderer anymore. He looked like a soldier, more than he ever had with Jeb. He looked like someone who killed vampires for a living.

But why was he here at all? Why wasn't he back in Eden, where I'd left him?

"We're looking for someone," I said, searching his face for any hint of the boy I knew. His expression remained cold, closed-off, but I kept going. "He's in the Inner City, and the gates up top are sealed. We need to find a way inside through the tunnels."

Zeke shot a glare full of loathing at Jackal, as if wishing he could pull a stake from one of the many on his vest and bury it in the vampire's heart. Jackal watched him calmly, the hint of a smirk on his face. I pushed back my despair. Keeping these two from killing each other was going to be difficult. But I had to try. I knew Zeke was angry; maybe he despised me now. But we still needed his help, and I couldn't let this stop me. Kanin's life depended on it.

"Well, that's going to be difficult." Zeke finally turned to face me, though his face and voice remained cold, businesslike. "I don't know a way to the Inner City through the tunnels. If I did, do you think we'd still be here, in the Fringe? I'd take everyone into the Inner City if I could. But even if I knew the way, we'd have to get past the mole men."

"Are they threatening you?"

He nodded, once. "We've had several issues with them, and things are getting…nasty. One of my scouts told me they're amassing in huge numbers, something they haven't done in the past. They want us gone."

Great. Bleeders up top, testy mole men below…and Zeke. Who, though he seemed completely at home here, in his element as the one in charge, did not know the way into the Inner City, as I'd hoped. Finding Kanin was proving harder than I'd thought possible. And we still had Sarren to deal with.

Zeke continued to watch us, his gaze blank and mirror-like. "Zeke." I gave him a pleading look, hoping that our past friendship, the times we'd saved each other, fought side by side against rabids and raiders and vampires, still meant something to him. "We have to get into the Inner City. Please, is there something you can do? Anything you can think of? It's important."

He stared at me with hooded eyes. I could see the wheels turning in his brain, thinking things through, putting the pieces together. "Are you going to see the Prince?" he asked finally.

I blinked. That wasn't what I'd expected from him. "Yes," I replied. "Or, we're going to get as close to him as we can. We discovered something about the plague—we think we know who started it, and we're hoping Salazar can help us. It's his city. He has to be concerned that his food source is dying out."

Zeke's expression hardened, and I wanted to kick myself for bringing up that last little fact. *Damn, I think Jackal is rubbing off on me.* "If we can get to the Prince, then he can help us find the one responsible, who might know how to stop it." *And hopefully rescue Kanin, too.*

Zeke was quiet a moment longer, struggling with himself, before he sighed. "I don't know the way into the Inner City," he repeated. "I can't help you there. But there is a group that knows these tunnels better than anyone."

Who? I wanted to ask, but behind me, Jackal made a noise of disgust.

"Oh, piss. You're talking about the filthy cannibals, aren't you?"

"The mole men have a lair not far from here," Zeke continued, ignoring Jackal. "I can take you there, but you'll have to convince them to lead you past the Inner Wall. They won't listen to me. A couple vampires, though..." He shrugged. "But, if you do convince them to lead you to the Inner City, I'm coming with you."

That threw me. Zeke hated vampires, and the Inner City was crawling with them. "Why?"

He gestured back at the group. "Because nothing is happening to make this better. The food trucks have stopped coming, there are no resources down here, and no one can go topside without running into bleeders. If this continues, people will starve. I want to see what the vampires are doing to stop this, if they *are* doing something to stop this, or if they're just planning to let everyone die out here."

Zeke. I shook my head sadly. *You haven't changed. Still looking out for everyone, regardless of who they are. Even if they're a group of Unregistereds who would sell you out as soon as your back is turned.*

Behind me, Jackal chuckled. "You sure you want to do this, bloodbag?" he asked, smirking. "Go up past the wall, where all the scary vampires live? Maybe you want to pour some honey or barbeque sauce over yourself before we leave, too."

I turned on Jackal before Zeke had a chance to retaliate. "Will you, for once, stop being such an ass?" I snarled at him. "Stop antagonizing our only guide. Do you want to get to Salazar or not?"

"It's all right," Zeke said in a surprisingly calm voice. "He doesn't scare me. None of them do. Not anymore." He gave us both a hard look, then backed away. "Wait here. I have to tell everyone what's going on, make sure they know not to venture topside unless it's an emergency." His eyes lingered on Jackal, narrowing. "Can I trust you not to eat anyone while I'm gone?"

"Hey." Jackal raised both hands in a placating gesture. "Don't worry about me, meatsack. I'm being a good vampire tonight. I get the feeling the *other* murdering bloodsucker in the room wouldn't be too happy if I went and tore your pretty head off."

Zeke's dark expression didn't change. Without another word, he spun on a heel and left, calling to the rest of the group, gathering them along the far wall. I watched him go, my stomach in knots, wishing I could talk to him alone. I had so many questions. Why was he here? Why did he leave Eden? Where was the rest of our original group; were they still alive, were they safe? How did he even get here?

And why did he have to show up now, when I had brought Jackal with me, the vampire who'd killed his family?

My blood brother stepped up beside me, also watching Zeke talk to the group of humans, his low, calm voice rising above the confusion and fear. "Well, this has gotten a lot more interesting," he mused, crossing his arms. "So that's the stubborn old man's little whelp. Ezekiel. Tell me, sister, how much does he know about the cure?"

I eyed Jackal warily. "What makes you think he knows anything?"

"Oh, please. Don't play dumb, not with me." Jackal continued to watch Zeke, his gaze hungry now, intense. I didn't like it. "After you and that little bloodbag set my city on fire—destroying everything I worked so hard for, I might add—you led him and his little friends to Eden. You said as much yourself. And I'm betting the old man left him all his research, everything he knew about the cure and the experiments they ran on the vampires sixty years ago. So don't tell me the kid is innocent to all of this. He knows just as much as the old man."

"There is no cure, Jackal," I said, remembering what Zeke told me once, when I'd discovered the real reason they were looking for Eden. "He might be aware of the research, but there's nothing he can do about it, even if he wanted to."

"But he *has* come from Eden," Jackal went on in that same appraising, eerie voice, making me very nervous. "Look at him, sister. Armor, stakes, crossbow..." He snorted, shaking his head. "The kid left Eden with a purpose, and he knew he would run into vampires. He's not here by chance, that's for certain. What is he looking for, I wonder?"

I didn't know, but that wasn't important. What was important, and far more worrisome, was Jackal's sudden interest in Zeke and the cure. "Leave him alone," I warned, my voice low and threatening. "You already killed his family. He'll be looking for any chance to return the favor."

Wait, why was I warning Jackal about Zeke? Why was I even defending him at all? Before all this, I'd wanted the vampire to pay for what he'd done, and yet here I was, traveling with him. Stepping in front of a crossbow for him. Worse, the person on the other end of the crossbow had been Zeke, who had every reason in the world to want Jackal dead and who probably thought I'd turned on him now. But I couldn't let either of them die. For different reasons, I needed them both. Even if I had to keep them from killing each other.

Dammit, when had this all become so complicated?

Jackal only chuckled. "I know vengeance, sister," he said in an equally low voice, giving me an evil smile. "I know the boy will try to kill me someday. It's not like this is the first human I've pissed off." His smirk grew wider as I glared at him. "Don't worry, I'm not about to eat your little human pet, unless he tries to kill me, of course. This is more of a warning for you, my dear sister—if you want that kid to live, you'd better make sure he doesn't come after me. The second he does, I'll tear him in half."

"All right." Zeke walked back, unaware of the tension between me and Jackal. "I'm ready."

"Zeke, wait!" Roach crept out of the shadows, eyeing me and Jackal fearfully, but turning a desperate gaze on Zeke. "You can't go," the Unregistered kid pleaded. "You're the only reason the mole men are staying away. What if something happens? You said you'd take care of everyone."

"I know." Zeke raked a hand through his hair, clearly frustrated. "I'm sorry. I have to do this, but I'll come back as soon as I can." Roach's eyes hardened, flashing betrayal, and Zeke sighed. "Here," he said and pulled something from his belt, a small rectangular device with a short antenna poking up from the side. "Take this." He handed it to Roach. "It's a walkie-talkie. If there's any trouble, hold this button down and talk into the speaker. I'll be able to hear you if I'm not too far away." Roach took the device gingerly, brow furrowing as he turned it over in his hands. Zeke put a hand on his shoulder. "Only use it if there's an emergency, all right? The battery life is limited."

Without another word, Roach scurried off with his prize, vanishing into the shadows. Zeke shook his head and turned back to us, his eyes gone hard and cold again. "Let's go," he said briskly. "The mole man lair isn't far, but I'm assuming you'll want to reach it before sunrise."

"Oh, give the human a prize," Jackal said as Zeke swept by us, walking toward the exit where we'd come in with Roach. The vampire looked back at me and grinned. "Next thing you know, he'll be informing us that vampires might drink blood."

I stifled a groan, already dreading this trip, knowing I'd probably have to step between these two again to keep them from killing each other.

"How long have you been here, Zeke?"

He glanced at me warily. We'd been walking several minutes in tense, weighty silence, the only sounds the shuffle of our footsteps on the concrete and the occasional scuttle of a rat in the darkness. Around us, the Undercity—the labyrinth of tunnels, corridors and mazelike passageways—spread out in a tangled mess, hiding any number of secrets. Zeke held a flashlight, its thin white beam cutting through the shadows, illuminating the decay around us. He'd kept several paces ahead of me and Jackal, not looking back, and his cold silence had begun to eat at me.

So after several minutes of struggling with myself, wondering if I should try to reach out to him, I'd finally quickened my pace and caught up. He was going to have to talk to me sometime, and I had too many questions that I wanted answered.

I thought he was going to ignore me, and if that was the case, I would just keep pushing until he said something. But after that first suspicious glare, he sighed and looked down the tunnel again.

"About a month." His low voice echoed faintly as we stepped into a huge cement pipe, ducking slightly as we walked through. "Give or take a few days. I got here a couple weeks before the plague hit and the vampires sealed everything off. It was pretty crazy."

"How did you end up down here?"

"I got in through the tunnels, probably like you and Jackal did." He gave me a split-second glance. "Came up in Sector Four of the Fringe and met Kyle's gang, and they were pretty suspicious of me at first—I just sort of showed up out of nowhere one night, armed and definitely not from around here. They thought I was a pet or a guard or something. No one believed I came from outside the Wall.

"But then," Zeke went on, "people started getting sick, going crazy, and attacking each other. Just a few at first, isolated incidents here and there. But in a few days, it was an epidemic, spreading through all the sectors. I was there when Kyle went nuts and tried to kill Roach." His expression turned grim. "I ended up shooting him. There was nothing else I could do."

I winced in sympathy. Zeke hated killing, taking human life, even when it was necessary.

"After that," Zeke went on, "everyone started rallying around me, wanting me to take over, to tell them what to do. Maybe because Kyle was dead, and they were all freaking out. Or maybe it was just because I was armed. I couldn't say no—they needed help." He sighed. "I remembered this place from when I came through the tunnels, and it seemed safer than anywhere up top. That was before I knew it was right on the edge of mole man territory." His brow furrowed, and he shook his head. "But anyway, we came down here, and more people followed. It's sort of become a refugee camp now, for anyone trying to escape the craziness up top. But things are getting pretty bad. There's no food, and the mole men are getting bolder. Something has to be done, or everyone here is going to die."

And you can't let that happen, I thought. *Even if these aren't your people, even if they would turn on you the second something better comes along, you've never been able to walk away from those in need. You really haven't changed at all.*

But that still didn't answer the most important question. "Zeke," I began, and he tensed as if he knew what was coming. "*Why* are you here? Why aren't you back in Eden with everyone else? Why did you come to New Covington?"

He gave a short, bitter laugh. "It's obvious, isn't it?" he snapped, sounding angry again. I blinked, hearing the veiled hurt in his voice, not knowing where it was coming from. He stopped and turned, blue eyes glittering, facing me down. "Because of you, Allie," he said, almost an accusation. "I came here looking for you."

Oh.

Zeke spun and started walking again. Jackal snickered behind me. "Ahhh, young love," he mocked, making me want to turn and kick him. "Makes me feel all warm and fuzzy inside."

"Shut up, Jackal," I muttered, trailing after Zeke. I felt even worse now. Zeke was here…for me? Why? Not because…of what Jackal said, surely. That was crazy. He wouldn't trail me all the way across the country for *that*.

And anyway, it didn't matter. I'd said my goodbyes to Zeke when I was turned away from Eden. I hadn't thought I'd ever see him again, and I had almost come to terms with that. He'd worked so hard to get his people to Eden safely—why leave that all behind to go searching for a vampire who could be anywhere? Zeke had to know that anything between a vampire and a human wouldn't work. Even now, following him through the tunnels, watching his shoulders and the back of his neck, I couldn't help but want to bite him. To sink my fangs into his throat and draw his essence into myself. Worse, I knew what he tasted of—he'd given his blood to save my life once, and it was hot and powerful and intoxicating. I wanted more.

With a start, I realized my fangs had slid out, poking my bottom lip, and I retracted them with a shiver.

"You know…" Jackal mused as we walked down a narrow metal bridge over a crumbling levy. Water must've run through it at one point, but now it was mostly dry, covered in rubble, broken bottles and other hazardous things. "This reminds me of a certain puppy I saw one day. Cutest little thing—one of my raider's pets, I believe. This puppy was friendly with everyone, it didn't know a stranger. Until one day, it tried approaching a dog—a bitch—that was guarding another raider's bike, wagging its little tail, wanting to play. And that other dog ripped it to pieces."

"Thank you for that disturbing and completely pointless story," I said, ignoring the obvious reference. "Maybe you should stick to death threats and intimidation. Or better yet, don't talk at all."

We reached the end of the tunnel, where Zeke waited for us, clicking off his flashlight. If he'd heard Jackal's story, he didn't comment on it. "We have to be careful through here," he murmured, nodding into the shadows. "Up ahead is a big chamber where the mole men sleep. There's no way around, we have to go straight through."

"Oh, good." Jackal smiled. "I was getting awfully bored. Nothing like a good massacre to get the blood pumping."

"We're not here to fight them," Zeke reminded him, narrowing his eyes. "We need them to show us the way through the Inner City tunnels. Unless you would rather wander aimlessly around until the sun comes up?"

Jackal snorted. "Oh, right, because the murderous, flesh-eating cannibals are just going to give us what we want because we ask them nicely."

"They usually don't attack larger groups," Zeke insisted. "And they're terrified of vampires. This doesn't have to be a bloodbath."

"I know, little meatsack." Jackal bared his fangs in a savage grin. "I just hope it is."

We continued down the tunnel, a bit slower this time, as Zeke had turned the flashlight off and everything was pitch-black now. For Jackal and I, that wasn't a problem—our vampire senses allowed us to see in absolute darkness, but Zeke's human vision wasn't nearly as good. But we didn't want to alert the mole men to our presence and have them scurry off into the maze of tunnels before we could talk to them.

As we came out of the passage, the ceiling rose up into a large domed room, surrounded by tunnels on every side. The chamber was strewn with rubble and trash, piled unceremoniously into corners. Filthy, stained mattresses and piles of rags were scattered around a fire pit, the ashes cold and gray. There was no one else in the room.

"That's weird," Zeke muttered, sweeping his flashlight around the chamber again. The beam flickered over mounds of junk and glinted off stripped white bones, scattered throughout the rubble. Some were definitely animal bones, rats and dogs mostly, but a few were…questionable. "They were here a few days ago. I wonder what made them clear out?"

"Maybe they heard rumors of vampires in the sewers," Jackal suggested, and shrugged. "Pity. I was looking forward to a nice bloodbath. So…" He picked a yellow cat skull out of an alcove, turned it toward me, and moved the jaws up and down as he asked, "What do we do now?"

Ignoring him, I turned slowly, taking a deep, careful breath. I smelled the grime and filth of this place, the stench of human waste in the tunnels nearby, and caught a hint of rotten meat from the mole men's last feeding. But through all that, I discovered a trace of something else, something instantly familiar.

I followed the smell around a large, rusty pipe until I found the source. Crouching down, I studied one of the mattresses, where a dark stain blotted one corner, soaking the fabric. The scent of fresh blood was suddenly very strong in my nose and mouth, and the Hunger responded eagerly. I pushed it down, gazing at a line of drops spattering the floor, leading away from the mattress until they vanished into a pipe on the far wall.

Jackal peered over my shoulder. "Well now. Looks like someone left behind a trail. How very careless, not taking care of that properly, especially with vampires in the tunnels." He took a deep breath and chuckled. "It's fairly recent, too. We should probably try to catch up, before he bleeds out and dies. That would just be a waste, wouldn't it?"

I rose, moving away from Jackal, toward the pipe. "Where do you think they went, Zeke?"

"I don't know." Zeke stepped over a pile of rocks and scattered bones to join us. "From what I understand, and this is mostly hearsay, they're fairly nomadic, moving around the Undercity at will. But individual families do have permanent nests like this one, and they stay away from other clans. They don't trespass into other territories. I don't have any idea where they could've gone."

"Well..." I stepped to the entrance of the pipe. I could still catch the faint hint of blood, even through the mold and rust and other smells. "I guess we're going to find out."

I noticed Zeke's cold stare, directed at Jackal as he sauntered past, and I motioned the other vampire forward. "After you," I told Jackal. "Unless, of course, you're afraid the mole men are waiting for you."

Jackal gave me an evil, knowing smile, chuckling as he stepped into the pipe. He knew what I was doing: keeping a body between him and Zeke, separating them. I knew Zeke wouldn't stab his enemy in the back or shoot him from behind—he wasn't like that—but Jackal *was* sadistic enough to say something unforgivable just to set Zeke off. And then he would have "no choice" but to defend himself when Zeke attacked him.

I hoped they both would keep it together, at least until we found Kanin. I couldn't watch the two of them every second of every day.

The pipe was narrow and claustrophobic, and all three of us had to duck so our heads wouldn't scrape against the top as we went through. Jackal was in front, moving as lightly and as smoothly as a cat, the edge of his duster trailing behind him. I could feel Zeke at my back, hear his steady breathing. And, even though I knew he wouldn't, I kept imagining how easy it would be for him to take one of those stakes at his belt and drive it through my back, maybe clear into my heart. Then, with me out of the way, he would have a clear shot at the vampire who'd killed his father....

I shook myself. No, Zeke *wouldn't* do that. I knew him. He hated vampires with a passion, and he was a fierce, determined fighter when he had to be, but he was also one of the few truly good people left in the world. He wouldn't stab me in the back in cold blood.

Or...would he? I realized I was being naive. Just because Zeke had known me before, that was no reason to drop my guard around him. It had been months; he could have decided I was a murderous, soulless monster after all and what we'd shared, what we'd done, was evil and wrong. If he hadn't reached that conclusion before, my showing up with Jackal—the embodiment of everything humans feared in a vampire—certainly hadn't helped.

And Zeke didn't even know about our...family tie yet.

What would he say once he discovered Jackal was my brother? He might stake me on principle.

Enough, Allison. I pushed those thoughts from my head. *What's done is done. Either Zeke will accept it, or he won't, but you can't worry about him anymore. Finding Kanin is the important thing now.*

The tunnels went on, and so did the blood trail. Just when I'd think we'd lost it, Jackal would nod to a dark smear on the wall, or a single drop of blood on the stones. Whoever this was, he was obviously badly hurt, and I hoped we wouldn't stumble across a corpse in the center of this endless maze.

Jackal was never quiet, continuously spouting some cruel remark or observation as we followed him through the labyrinth of corridors and pipes. He spoke in whispers, and many of his comments were intended to needle the human in our party. Much to his credit, Zeke ignored the vampire, remaining calm and businesslike even when Jackal asked him an obvious, goading question. I finally kicked Jackal in the calf and growled at him to stop.

"Hey, I'm just making conversation." Jackal's grin made me want to slug him in his pointed teeth. "I'm curious what the little meatsack has been up to since he burned down my city and disappeared with my cure. Is it in Eden, bloodbag?" His voice was no longer mocking or curious; it now bordered on menacing. "Is a new team of scientists studying that research? The failed vampire experiments? How close are they to discovering a cure?"

"Why would I tell you any of that?" Zeke asked softly.

Jackal bared his fangs, but a noise up ahead caught my attention. For a second, I thought I heard the shuffle of feet over the stones, and the low murmur of voices. "Quiet," I whispered. "Someone is out there."

They fell silent, and we eased through the tunnels, being careful not to make a noise. The footsteps scuttled away, and the snatches of conversation vanished with them, but I knew we were getting close to something.

"This way," Zeke whispered, and turned down another pipe that cut through a brick wall, into the darkness. Low voices echoed down the tube, a lot of voices, growing stronger the farther we went. I took a breath and smelled blood and smoke and the scent of many, many humans, all mingled together.

The pipe abruptly ended, coming out of the wall nearly fifteen feet off the ground. A thin line of water flowed past our feet and trickled into the large open room beyond. The air here was damp and smelled of metal, smoke and stagnant water. Rusty pipes snaked over the walls and ceiling, and several steel drums smoldered with a thick, greasy smoke in the corners of the room.

The pale, hunched figures of several dozen mole men milled about the chamber, their low, raspy voices drifting into the pipe. Some huddled around smaller fires throughout the room, gnawing on unidentifiable chunks of meat. Some lay curled up in rags, tattered blankets or each other, sleeping or trying to stay warm. One woman, her hair falling out in patches, pulled a skewer of rats out of the fire and handed one to a skinny, wild-eyed boy, who took the charred rodent and darted off to an isolated corner. Crunching noises drifted up soon after.

Beside me, Zeke blew out a slow, quiet breath. "So many of them," he whispered as we drew back into the shadows of the pipe. "I've never seen so many in one place. Why are they gathering now...." He trailed off, his voice turning grim. "The base. They've been threatening to drive us off, back to the streets. If they all decide to attack the base, we won't be able to stop them, not with those numbers. They'll kill everyone there."

"Take it easy," I soothed, putting a hand on his knee. He glanced at it in surprise, and I pretended not to notice. "We'll talk to them. There has to be a way to make them listen without bloodshed."

Behind us, Jackal gave a disgusted snort. "Hope springs eternal," he muttered, but didn't say anything else as we backed out of the pipe and searched for the entrance to the lair.

We found it a few hundred feet from the pipe, a crumbled section of wall with firelight spilling out of the cracks, flickering over the stones and rubble. No one guarded the entrance; I guessed the mole men didn't have many intruders in their twisty, mazelike world, especially not vampires.

I glared at Jackal as the entrance loomed closer. "We're not here to kill anyone," I reminded him, and he rolled his eyes. "Try to remember that, okay? I don't want to have to fight the entire mole man population of New Covington, and if we kill them all, we won't have anyone to show us the way to the Inner City."

"You don't give me much credit, do you?" Jackal replied, shaking his head. "I ruled an entire raider city before you two ever came along. I know how to deal with large groups of killers. So don't worry, I won't threaten the bloodthirsty cannibals." He smirked. "But if you think we're going to get out of here without some kind of bloodshed, you're more naive than I thought."

I didn't answer, because we had crossed the rubble pile that led up to the crumbling wall and entered the lair of the mole men.

CHAPTER 9

We caught their attention immediately. As soon as we ducked through the entrance and stepped into the room, three mole men glanced up from one of the fire pits. For a second, they stared at us, blinking in shock. Jackal grinned back at them and nodded.

"Evening," he said cordially, and the mole men leaped upright with shrieks and hisses of outrage, drawing the attention of everyone in the room. Weapons flashed, and howls rose into the air, as the entire sea of mole men surged toward us with murderous intent.

"Now, now!" Jackal bellowed, his clear, confident voice ringing through the chamber. "Let's not be hasty! We're not here for a massacre! And you people don't want a fight with us, trust me!"

Whether it was the certainty in his voice, or the sudden flash of fangs, the entire group of mole men skidded to a halt a few yards away, glaring at us with wide, hate-filled eyes. I shot an amazed glance at my blood brother, who faced the hostile mob with a smile on his face, completely in his element.

"That's better," Jackal said, still with that easy grin. "Let's all calm down a little. You know what we are, and we'd rather not have to paint the walls in blood to get what we want. We can all be civilized here, right?"

Whispers were beginning to spread through the mob, growing louder and more restless. I tensed again, but suddenly the crowd parted and an old woman with stringy white hair stepped forward. Most of her teeth had rotted out of her skull, and her eyes were filmy blue, but she curled her lips back and pointed with a bony claw. Not at me or Jackal, but at Zeke.

"You!" she hissed as Zeke blinked at her. "Topsider! I know you! You're the outsider that brought the rest of them down here, filling our tunnels with light, attracting what doesn't belong. You are the cause of this. You scare the rats away with your endless noise, and now, you bring *them* down from the streets, just as we feared! Curse you!" She spat at Zeke. "Curse you, and your whole thieving race! You're like the plague, crowding places you don't belong, bringing death with you! The Undercity will never be safe now!"

"It isn't safe up top, either," Zeke answered in a steady voice. "We couldn't stay aboveground, not with the sickness spreading so fast. I'm sorry we invaded your territory, but it was the only place we could go." She spat at him again, unappeased, and he raised his hands. "We'll be out of here as soon as we can, I promise."

"Which brings us to our next order of business," Jackal broke in, sounding slightly annoyed that the attention had shifted away from him. He took a step forward, and the woman flinched back, making him smile. "We have to get into the Inner City. And since all the gates up top are sealed off, the only way through is to go beneath. That's where you come in."

The old woman glared at Jackal fearfully. "Vampire, you want us to show you the tunnels to the Inner City so you can return and tell your people of the humans living right below their feet?" She shook her withered head. "Never! Kill me if you want to, we would all rather die than bring the monsters down here."

"We aren't going to tell anyone about you," I said, before Jackal could say something like, *That can be arranged.* "We're not from the Inner City—we're not even from New Covington." *Well, Allie the Vampire can't call the city home, anyway.* "The vampires up top aren't our friends. Why do you think we're down here with a human?" I didn't look at Zeke when I said this, but I felt his eyes on me. "I know you have no reason to trust us, but we have to get to the Inner City, and we're not leaving the tunnels until we do."

More muttering and whispers. I could sense that a few of the mole men were considering our words, though most of them still looked terrified. This was their worst nightmare, vampires making their way below ground, into their territory. Fear of the monsters had driven them underground in the first place, and now we had invaded their safe haven. I could suddenly understand their reluctance.

"Your words mean nothing to us, vampire," the old woman said at last. "We have only the promise of your silence, and that is not enough. We cannot take the chance that you will stay topside. If more monsters follow you into the tunnels, we have nothing with which to defend ourselves."

"Then let me offer something." Zeke stepped forward and all eyes snapped to him. He faced them calmly, hands at his sides, raising his voice to speak to them all. "Do you know the easiest way to kill a vampire?" he asked the crowd.

The mole men shuffled and hissed, muttering among themselves. They were reluctant to speak, but at the same time, they were intrigued. Killing vampires appealed to them, it seemed. Finally, a voice in the crowd spoke up, and more followed.

"Burn it."

"Cut off its head."

"Drive a wooden spike through its heart."

I shifted uncomfortably. *No need to sound so eager.*

Zeke nodded. "But you'd have to get awfully close to do that, wouldn't you?" he asked in that same cool voice. "And no one wants to be that close to a vampire and risk having it see you, right? Better to take it out from a distance."

"What is your point, topsider?" the old woman hissed.

Zeke narrowed his eyes. In one smooth motion, he swung the crossbow from his shoulders, drew back the string, and fired a dart at the far wall. The spike hit a rusty steel drum with a ringing clang, embedded halfway through the metal, and the mole men gasped then burst into a storm of muttering.

"I'll give this to anyone who can guide us through the tunnels to the Inner City," Zeke said when the noise died down. When I glanced at him in surprise, he shrugged. "I can't take it with me, anyway," he whispered. "Not up there. The vamps would take one look at this and freak out."

"Kid's got a point," Jackal said begrudgingly. "You go waving something like that around the Inner City, you'll get your head torn off before you know what's happening. Still, I'm not too keen on a bunch of vampire-hating cannibals having it, either."

One human edged forward, eyeing us warily. Like the others, he was frightfully thin, his hands and face spotted with open sores, but he seemed even more wasted than the rest. One side of his face was nothing but a furrow of scars, part of his lip had been torn off, and his eye was a milky-white orb, unseeing and useless.

"I'll take you," he rasped, his fevered gaze on Zeke's crossbow. "For that weapon, I'll take you there."

"Amos," the old woman hissed, turning her filmy gaze on him. "Don't be a fool. They're vampires. They'll kill you and leave your body for the rats."

The mole man shrugged his bony shoulders and stepped forward, away from the crowd. "Why should I care about that?" he asked in a dull, flat voice. "I have nothing left. And I'm tired of living in fear." He stepped up to Zeke, bringing his scarred face very close to the other human. Zeke stood his ground. "Give me that weapon," the mole man said, "and you have a deal. I'll take you to the Inner City right now."

Zeke nodded. "All right," he said, swinging the crossbow to his back again. "But you get us there, first. I'll give you the weapon once we're past the walls, not before."

The mole man bared rotten teeth in a grim smile. "Follow me."

We left the lair of the mole men through a tunnel on the far wall, feeling the cold, suspicious, angry glares of the mob on either side of us. I could smell their fear, see the tension lining their wasted bodies, the tight grip on their weapons, and hoped we could get out of there before things exploded into violence. They didn't move, however, just watched us as we trailed our guide through the chamber, into the tunnel, and melted into the darkness.

The mole man, Amos, moved quickly through the passages, never looking back, never checking to see if we were still there. He carried no light and maneuvered the pitch blackness and shadow with no trouble at all, sliding into tunnels and crawling through pipes as easily as walking. This was his world, this maze of concrete and rust and mold and damp, like the streets and broken buildings up top had been mine. I had the strange realization that the mole men and Unregistereds were very similar. Despite their aversion to light and their disturbing tendency to eat human flesh, they were just scavengers, fighting for food, avoiding the vampires, struggling to survive.

We walked for a few hours, following our silent guide through endless tunnels and dark passageways. Rats fled from us, and once a huge snake slithered into the water out of sight, but we met no one else as we ventured farther into the belly of the city.

Dawn was less than an hour away, and I was beginning to get a little nervous, when Amos finally stopped. A rusty ladder led up to a dark hole in the ceiling, covered by a metal grate. Weeds, grass and bramble smothered the top and poked in through the spaces, dripping water on our heads.

"The Inner City is through here," Amos rasped, peering at the exit with a half fearful, half disgusted look on his face. "The grate is loose, but no one has used it for years, and the vampires don't know about it. We don't go topside, especially not up there. Now..." He turned on Zeke, his eyes narrowed hungrily. "You promised me that weapon if I led you to the Inner City. Hand it over, and let me go."

Zeke immediately swung the crossbow off his back. "Thank you," he told the mole man, holding it out. "Tell your people we won't let the vampires know that you're down here."

Amos snatched the weapon from his hands and backed away, glaring at us. "It's a little late now, topsider," he growled, looking at me and Jackal. "The vampires already know."

Before we could reply, he turned and fled into the tunnels clutching his prize, and the darkness swallowed him instantly.

Jackal made a face at the retreating mole man then glanced thoughtfully up at the grate. "Well," he mused, squinting through the metal slats as if he could see the city through the weeds and vegetation, "here we are. I don't think we'll be knocking on the Prince's door tonight, though."

"Yeah," I muttered. Dawn was close. It would be risky and dangerous to continue through unknown territory with the light threatening the horizon. "The sun's almost up. Looks like we're sleeping down here one more day." I gazed down the tunnel Amos had vanished into and frowned. "And there's a mole man running around with a crossbow now. Let's hope nothing comes creeping back while we're all asleep."

Jackal's voice was a soft growl. "It's not the mole men I'm worried about."

I blinked at him, confused for a moment. Until Zeke did something I'd never seen him do before.

He smiled. A cold, dangerous smile, his eyes glittering with dark promise. It sent a chill through me as I realized I *didn't* know him anymore. Before, I would've trusted Zeke with my life, and had, on more than one occasion, slept through the day with him nearby, guarding me. I'd been wary, especially at first, but I'd come to realize that Zeke wasn't the type to stab someone in cold blood, even if it was a vampire.

Now, I wasn't sure. This vengeful, hard-eyed Zeke worried me; I didn't know if he still considered me a friend, or if I was just another vampire who had turned on him. I was even less sure about Jackal.

"Does it worry you?" Zeke's voice was soft, menacing. "That the human you've been pushing all night will be guarding your dead body while the sun's up? Maybe you should've thought of that before you started talking about my father."

Jackal stared at Zeke, appraising. Zeke put a hand on one of his stakes and stared back. I tensed, ready to jump in if either of them went for the other.

After a moment, Jackal bared his fangs in a savage grin. "Well, color me shocked—the human actually has a pair. He might survive the Inner City, after all." Stepping back, he nodded at me. "Getting a little crowded in here for my taste. You two have fun, I'll be back when the sun goes down. Oh, and human..." His amber gaze flicked to Zeke. "Contrary to what you might think, I actually *can* wake up in the middle of the day. So if you have the notion to track me down and take my head for a trophy, I suggest you be ready for the fight of your life, because I won't hold back until one of us is smeared over the walls. Just a friendly warning."

He gave a too-bright smile that was anything but friendly, turned and sauntered off. His tall, lean form melted into the darkness of a nearby tunnel, and he was gone.

Silence fell, stretched awkwardly between me and Zeke, who watched me under the faint light coming through the metal grate. We were finally alone, and dawn was close but not imminent. I could finally ask him all the questions burning inside my head, but I found that I didn't know where to start. He wasn't the same person as before.

And neither was I.

Finally, Zeke sighed and leaned against the wall, pulling his gun as he did. His fingers deftly released the cartridge, checked the rounds inside and snapped it back again. "You should go," he said without looking at me. "Find a place to hole up for the day. I'll stay here, keep the tunnels clear of mole men or anything else that might come creeping back."

"Haven't you been up all night? Don't you need to sleep, too?"

"Don't worry about me." He slid the chamber back, making sure it was loaded, then released the slide with a click. "I've been taught to survive on zero hours' sleep if I have to. I'll be fine."

"Zeke—"

"Allison." He finally looked up at me. "I know you have a lot of questions," he said, sounding uncomfortable, "but I can't answer them, not now, anyway. Just know that the others are safe. They're still in Eden, and they have a good life now. I made sure everyone was taken care of before I left." A shadow of a smile finally crossed his face, and he shook his head. "Caleb ordered me to tell you 'hi,' and that he and Bethany named a goat after you."

I laughed, feeling a strange tightness in my throat. "I'm glad they're okay," I told him, and he nodded, a wistful look passing through his eyes. For just a moment, he looked like the boy I'd left in Eden, hopeful and determined, only wanting a home and a safe place for his family.

"All right," I muttered, drawing away. "If you've got this, then I'm going to find a place to sleep. If Jackal comes back before I do, try to ignore him, okay? I don't want to come back to a massacre."

"Wait." Zeke pushed himself off the wall, as if he couldn't hold back anymore. I turned back to find him watching me with hooded eyes, the gun held loosely in one hand. "Why, Allison?" he asked in a hard voice. "You never told me why Jackal is here. You know what he is, what he's done. Why are you here with him?"

My insides cringed. I'd known the question was coming, and I still didn't have a good answer for him. Not one that he could accept. *Why should I tell you?* I thought rebelliously. *You don't trust me with your secrets anymore; you can't even tell me the reason you're here. I don't have to explain anything to you, Zeke Crosse.*

But…if I told him that, it would only make him more suspicious. He would think I was hiding something. And I wasn't going to play that game. I knew what I was; I had nothing to hide, not anymore.

"I ran into Jackal while I was looking for someone else," I told him. "I thought I was following a lead, but I was wrong. I found Jackal instead—he was waiting for me."

"And he didn't try to kill you?"

"No." I shook my head, watched his brow arch in disbelief. "Jackal had been following the same lead when I met him. We came to New Covington together because we're looking for the same person. His name is Kanin, and he's being kept in the Inner City now. I want to get him out, and I need Jackal's help to do it."

Zeke pondered this, no expression on his face. "That's who

you were talking about before," he mused. "You said you had to find someone, that you owed him." I nodded, though it wasn't really a question. "Who is he?" Zeke asked in a low, serious voice.

I paused. How could I explain Kanin's importance to someone who hated vampires and—with the possible exception of one—thought they were all evil, soulless demons? Revealing who Kanin was, our relationship within vampire society, probably wasn't going to go over well with Zeke. I was once again choosing to help a vampire, and maybe I was turning my back on my once-fellow humans, but I would not abandon Kanin. Not for Zeke, not for Sarren, not for anyone. I owed the vampire far too much.

"He's my sire," I finally admitted, and Zeke's brow furrowed, not recognizing the vampiric term. "The one who Turned me," I elaborated. "The one who made me a vampire."

Zeke's face went blank with shock. "That's who we're looking for?" he whispered. "A vampire? The monster that killed you?"

"He gave me a choice," I reminded him firmly. "I *chose* to become a vampire, it wasn't forced on me. Kanin isn't like that." I'd told Zeke this before, that Kanin had saved me from a rabid attack and given me the choice to become a vampire, but he still stared at me, disbelieving and horrified. Maybe because, to Zeke, all vampires were monsters. At least, that's what he believed before I came into his life and, even now, I wasn't sure what he thought of me. I shook my head in frustration. "He taught me everything I know," I continued earnestly, wanting him to understand, to see that Kanin wasn't just another monster to be hated and feared. "He took me in, and showed me exactly what I needed to learn about being a vampire. He didn't have to, but he chose to stay, to teach me. I'd be dead now if it wasn't for him."

With a little shock, I realized that I really missed Kanin. I hadn't allowed myself to think of him much; beyond the knowledge that we had to find him and get him away from Sarren, I had tried not to imagine what my sire was going through. But I remembered his deep voice, his lessons about feeding and fighting and vampire culture, the annoyed look he gave me when I was being stubborn. I desperately hoped he was all right, or at least still alive and sane. The Master vampire had been cold, stern, and sometimes harsh, but his teachings had basically saved my life. If not for him, I really *would* be dead, or worse, a soulless predator consumed with her own blood-lust, who didn't know she could be anything but a monster.

Zeke struggled with this a moment longer. I could see him thinking, trying to come to terms with the fact that we were venturing into the Inner City to rescue not a human, but another vampire. "You don't have to come with us," I told him quietly. "You don't know Kanin, and you don't have any reason to be here. I won't hold it against you if you leave."

But Zeke immediately shook his head. "No," he murmured, as if that was the end of it. "No, I went through too much to find you. And the refugees are counting on me to help them. I'm not leaving now."

There was something more to that and I wanted to ask what it was, but Zeke quickly changed the subject. "This Kanin," he began, looking thoughtful. "You told me why *you* want to help him, and that makes sense, but why is Jackal here? He led a whole raider army and controlled an entire city, and he gave all of that up? Why is he so interested in one vampire? Who is Kanin to him?"

I stifled a groan. "Why do you have to ask such hard questions?" I muttered. Zeke's expression didn't change, and I sighed. "Kanin," I began slowly, hoping he wouldn't instantly jump to conclusions, "is Jackal's sire, too. He Turned him a long time ago, before I was even born. Which makes us, at least in vampire society…"

"Siblings," Zeke finished softly. "Jackal is…your brother."

I nodded. "My blood brother," I confirmed, watching to see how Zeke was taking this. No expression showed on his face, which I found disconcerting—I used to be able to read him so easily. "That doesn't mean I like him, or that I've forgotten what he's done," I added, facing Zeke's blank stare. "I fully expect him to turn on me as soon as he gets what he wants. But Kanin is our sire, and we're the only ones I know of who have a chance of finding him."

"Why?"

"Because…" I paused, preparing to explain another piece of vampire history I didn't want to reveal. "Sometimes, we can…sense those who share our bloodline, members of our particular family. We can feel where they are, what they're experiencing, usually in times of intense emotion or pain. Our blood ties us together. There's a stronger pull toward our sire, but the offspring of a Master vampire are always aware of each other, once they know the other exists. That's why a Prince's coven is usually made up of his own offspring—it's harder for them to turn on him if he always knows where they are."

Zeke's brow furrowed. "So, you can sense where Jackal is? Right now?"

"I couldn't give you detailed directions," I said, not liking this sudden interest. "It's more like I know he's *that* way—" I gestured toward a wall. "But I don't know exactly where. And I'd have to make a conscious effort to concentrate on him before I could sense anything. Not like Kanin. Kanin… is in pain right now. And he's calling for us."

Zeke was silent, but his eyes narrowed as he stared in the direction I'd pointed, his face hard. I shifted uneasily. "Zeke," I began, hating to ask him but knowing I had to. "You're not going to go looking for Jackal, are you? He'll be expecting it, and he probably didn't lie about waking up in the middle of the day. Some of the stronger vampires are able to do that. Promise you won't go after him."

He glared at me, definitely angry now. "Do you really have to ask me that?" he demanded, his voice harsh. "Do you really think so little of me, that I would murder someone while they're asleep?" He shook his head in disgust. "No, when I kill that vampire—and I *will,* Allison, make no mistake about that—I want him to be fully aware of it. I want him to see my face. I want him to know exactly who killed him, and why." He tore his gaze from me and stared down the tunnel, a flicker of torment crossing his face. "Jeb deserves it," he said in a softer voice. "So do Darren, and Ruth, and Dorothy. And everyone else he's murdered for his entertainment. Who knows how many he's killed, how many have suffered because of him?" He glanced back at me, and his eyes were hard again. "So, no, I'm not going to stab your brother while he's asleep. I'll wait until we rescue your sire and make sure the refugees are safe, and who knows how long that will be? But when this is over, I'm going to kill that vampire, Allison. For my family, for those back in Eden, I'm not going to leave him alive. The only question is..." He looked me right in the eye, a shadow of uncertainty crossing his face. "Will I have to fight *you,* as well as Jackal?"

I bit my lip, feeling pulled in two impossible directions. Jackal had been the enemy, once. As far as I knew, he still was. But, we had traveled together, fought side by side. He hadn't left me to the rabid horde in the Old D.C. tunnels. And, as much as I hated to admit it, he was my brother. We might not be siblings in the human sense, but in vampire society, we were family. Turning on Jackal once I had what I needed sounded like something *he* would do, and I wasn't like him. Unless he attacked me first, I could not accept his help today and then try to kill him tomorrow.

But I could no more fight Zeke than stab my brother in the back. He was the one thing I would try desperately to save, no matter the cost. Even from myself, the demon that still Hungered for his blood. That was urging me, even now, to pounce on him and drive my fangs into his throat. If Zeke went for Jackal with the full intent to kill, I really didn't know what I would do, but it would probably involve trying to stop them both.

"I don't know," I said at last, and watched Zeke's face go from hopeful to devastated before shutting down completely. It sent a pang through my stomach; in his eyes, I'd just chosen Jackal over him, but I would not lie and say I'd help him kill my brother. Even if Jackal deserved it. "Let's hope it never comes to that."

Zeke turned away and stared into the darkness, his expression closed off. I wanted to keep talking, to explain that I wasn't turning my back on humans in favor of vampires. But dawn was closer now, and as I drew back to look for a place to sleep, I couldn't help but think that maybe it was better this way. It was better that Zeke hated me. He was one of those "dangerous attachments" Kanin had warned me about. The most dangerous attachment, if I was being honest with myself. What we'd had before, what we'd shared, that was just a fantasy and a deadly one at that. There was no way a vampire and a human could be together, and my inner demon laughed at the thought. It would just take one slip on my part, one tiny error of judgment, and I would kill him. Better that he think me a monster now, just like Jackal, and keep his distance. It was best for both of us.

With a heavy heart, I walked toward a side tunnel, wondering when I had made all these impossible connections. Making decisions had been so much easier when I was just Allie the Fringer, when my only concern was keeping myself and Stick fed, when basic survival was all I cared about.

At the mouth of the tunnel, I stopped and glanced back at Zeke. He was leaning against the wall beneath the metal grate, head bowed and eyes closed. Rainwater dripped into his bright hair, making it shimmer as he stood outlined in hazy light. He looked…very alone then, a single human in a monster-infested world, a fading bright spot surrounded by shadow. And despite my best intentions, my determination not to be a monster, I was part of the world that he feared. Part of the darkness that would drag him down and tear him apart.

"I'm sorry, Zeke," I told him, and stepped into the shadows before he could reply.

CHAPTER 10

I am ravenous, starving, dangerously close to losing control. My mind is a jumble of fractured, barely coherent thoughts and pure, savage Hunger. It has been too long, far too long. My body burns, my entire being consumed with wanting food. The demon overtaking my mind roars and fights the chains at my wrists, straining them, needing to break free, to hunt and kill and feed. It senses movement on the other side of the bars, and screams in frustration, in defiance, the howl echoing off the empty stones.

And still, through the constant agony and raging Hunger, part of me realizes how close to the edge I am, a mere step from falling into madness, where the Hunger finally shatters the mind and turns the host into a vicious, irredeemable beast. A madness that, once crossed, cannot be reversed. I know of only one vampire who clawed his way up from the pit of insanity, but the creature who returned from that utter darkness was not the same.

I have to hang on, just a little longer. They are close, I can feel them. They will be my salvation, if I can cling to sanity long enough for them to reach me. I just hope that, when she *finally comes, there will be more than a mindless, savage beast waiting behind these iron bars.*

Allison. Hurry. We're both running out of time.

I woke up terrified…and Hungry.

Shivering, I pushed myself upright, bumping my head against the ceiling of the cement culvert I'd taken shelter in. Kanin. Kanin was slipping, the Hunger pushing him closer to the edge of madness. The torment he felt, the agony consuming him from the inside, the horrible drive to feed still lingered in my mind, like an oily taint. I couldn't imagine his suffering—no relief, no end in sight. It would've driven me crazy long ago.

Dammit. I will not *let that happen. I'm still coming, Kanin, just hang in there.*

We were out of time. We had to get to Kanin, *now.* But as I shook the last vestiges of sleep from my head, a new sensation hit me like a blow to the face. Blood. A *lot* of it.

I scrambled out of the pipe and hit a body sprawled in the mud at the entrance. A mole man's glazed, unseeing eyes stared up at me, a bullet hole clean through his heart. Another lay nearby, also shot through the chest, one hand clutching a rusty blade. My stomach clenched. The knife smelled of blood, *his* blood.

Zeke!

More bodies littered the tunnel, pale and skinny, most of them shot through the chest or the head. Clean, efficient kill shots. But at least a couple bled from deep, gaping slashes caused by a blade. Most had weapons: knives or lead pipes or nails driven through wooden boards. Crude yet still deadly. Worry twisted my dead heart, and I hurried onward.

Voices rang out ahead, and I felt my lips curl back from my fangs. Rounding a bend, I saw Zeke, pressed into the space between the corner wall and another huge pipe, protecting his back. He held the machete in one hand, raised in front of him, and his gun in the other. In the shadows, his eyes were hooded, and blood spattered his face and arms, making him look dangerous. Three mole men hovered at the entrance, hissing and waving their weapons, but reluctant to step forward into that narrow space and the machete that waited for them.

"Don't do this," Zeke pleaded, his voice low and harsh, echoing off the pipes. "You don't have to die today, and no one else has to be hurt. Go home."

"You brought vampires into the tunnels!" one man hissed, striking the pipe with a rusty iron bar. The hollow clang caused a rat to flee from its hole and dust to fall from the ceiling, but Zeke didn't flinch. "If we don't kill you here, you'll go topside and let them know where we are. We can't risk that. All trespassers have to die, starting with you!"

He hurled his pipe at Zeke. Zeke raised his arm, knocking it aside with his machete, and my vision went red.

I roared, baring fangs, and the men spun around, their eyes widening in terror. They bolted, but the corridor was narrow and I blocked the only way out. I lashed out with my katana and caught one across the throat as he went by, cutting his head from his shoulders. My follow-up blow hammered into the next one's back, slicing through flesh and muscles and severing the spine. He got four steps before his legs gave out and he pitched face-first onto the concrete. The last one, terrified beyond reason, came at me screaming, his knife raised high. I grabbed the wrist that slashed wildly at my face, yanked him forward and plunged my fangs into his throat. Hot, grimy blood filled my mouth, and the Hunger flared. I didn't stop drinking until the mole man shuddered and went limp in my arms, the knife hitting the pavement with a clink.

The Hunger faded to a low, barely noticeable throb, sated for now. Dropping the corpse, I wiped blood from my mouth and looked up at Zeke, watching me from the corner. His face was grim, but not horrified or fearful, making me slump with relief. Even though Zeke knew what I was, I'd never fed in front of him before. Except, of course, that one time where *he* had been the victim, and I'd barely stopped myself from draining him completely. He hadn't turned away from me then, and I didn't want to see fear, horror and disgust in his eyes now, because I was still a monster.

Wait, I thought that's exactly *what you wanted, vampire girl. Zeke* should *fear you—it's the only thing that will keep him safe, remember?*

I sheathed my sword, stepping farther into the narrow corridor. "You okay?"

"Yes." He eased out of the corner, wincing a bit. "They came out of nowhere," he muttered, his eyes dark as they scanned the bodies, scattered over the pavement. "I think someone followed us from the nest, then went back to alert the others. They wanted me to tell them where you and Jackal were sleeping so they could kill you, too. I tried explaining that it wasn't necessary, that we wouldn't reveal to anyone where they were, but they wouldn't listen. They just…kept coming. I didn't want to kill them." His face grew pained, eyes haunted, and he shook his head. "I didn't want this."

"Are you hurt?"

"Nothing serious." He slowly holstered his gun, the movement stiff and painful. "I'll have a couple nice bruises, and one of them snuck up from behind and stabbed me in the back. The vest took most of the damage, but he still got me." The machete followed the gun, with Zeke clenching his jaw as it slid into place. "They didn't really have a chance," he muttered darkly. "I had a gun, and they were coming at me with clubs and knives. They should've known. Why didn't they stop?"

The smell of his blood drifted to me again, and I frowned. "We'll need to clean that," I said, and he eyed me warily. "I can smell the blood on you, Zeke. You're wounded, and the other vampires will be able to smell it, too. We need to cover it. Unless, of course, you want to walk through a vampire city bleeding."

The color drained from his face. "Right," he muttered. "Point taken. Here." He bent to one of the many compartments on his vest and pulled out a roll of tape and a couple small white squares. He hesitated, clearly uncomfortable, then held the bandages out to me. "I don't think I can reach it myself," he said, not meeting my eyes. "Would you be able to..."

I nodded, taking the tape and the odd white squares. One was clearly a bandage of some kind, but the other was wrapped in paper and smelled of chemicals, making my eyes water. Zeke turned and silently shrugged off the vest, dropping it to the pavement. Then slowly, painfully, he reached up and pulled the shirt over his head, revealing his lean, muscular back and the vivid map of scars slashed across his skin.

Even though I'd been expecting it, I bit the inside of my cheek. I had witnessed his adopted father's punishment when Zeke didn't live up to his standards. It still made my throat burn with fury. Zeke had been raised with such a strict concept of obedience, it was a wonder he had defied or questioned Jeb at all.

I stepped up behind him, barely stopping myself from touching his back, tracing the scars on his skin. The knife wound, a small but deep-looking puncture, oozed crimson just below his shoulder blade. I stifled the urge to plunge my fangs into the side of his neck and bent to the task at hand.

"You're not asking the obvious question," Zeke murmured as I tore one of the white packets open, releasing a damp square cloth and the smell of disinfectant. At least, that's what I thought the strange packet was. Having never seen one before, I was just guessing here. "It doesn't bother me if you want to know how I got them. Everyone does."

"I know how you got them," I said quietly, pressing the damp square to Zeke's wound, dabbing gently. He stiffened, a short breath escaping him; whatever was on the strange cloth probably stung. "I was there, outside the church the night before Jackal's men attacked you. When Jeb…"

"You saw that?"

I nodded. Memories flickered; Jeb ordering Zeke to take off his shirt, the flash of metal as the old man whipped him repeatedly with a car antenna, Zeke braced against a gravestone, head bowed, saying nothing. Myself in the bushes several yards away, fighting the urge to leap out and tear Jebbadiah's head from his shoulders.

"I'd caught up from the Archer compound that night," I

told him, folding the cloth in half to wipe away the last of the blood. Hunger and something else, that strange twisty feeling whenever Zeke was around, warred through my insides. Touching him like this, feeling his warm skin under my fingers, only made it worse. "I'd been following you for a couple days, after we had our…falling out. I was in the cemetery when you and Jeb came through, and saw the whole thing." My hand hovered over a scar, slashed from his shoulder to nearly the center of his back, and I shivered. "I can't imagine what it was like for you."

"That's it?" Zeke challenged softly, though his voice lacked the bite I had been expecting. "Nothing to say about Jeb?"

"I have plenty to say about Jeb," I replied. "Though none of it is very nice and I figure it would be rude to talk about him right now. Besides, you know what Jeb thought of me." *He trained you to think the same.*

"I still miss him sometimes," Zeke said in a voice barely above a whisper. "I know you probably think it's crazy, but I respected him. Even though his principles were different than mine, and I never became the leader he wanted me to be, he still did everything he could to protect us."

I dropped the bloody square and unfolded the second one, pressing the dry cloth to the wound. Unwinding the tape he'd given me, I tore a strip off and smoothed it across the bandage, holding it in place. "You don't have to defend him to me, Zeke," I said, and my thoughts went to Kanin. "I know what it's like to miss someone. To feel like you're just…wandering around, lost. And how you wish they were there, if only for a moment, just to point you in the right direction."

Zeke was quiet while I finished bandaging the wound, tap-ing the edges down tightly. "This vampire," he said when I was nearly done. "Kanin. He's…important to you, isn't he? I mean…it sounds like he's more than just the vampire that Turned you."

"Kanin is…" I paused, thinking. It was hard to explain my relationship with the Master vampire. Yeah, he was my sire, but he was also my mentor, my teacher and…my friend. "It's complicated," I said at last, smoothing down the last piece of tape. "I wouldn't go so far as to say he's my adoptive father or anything like that but…I guess he is family."

"I can understand that," Zeke said, and turned so we were face-to-face.

His blue eyes met mine, softer now, conflicted. Like he was trying to see me, really see me, to find that person he knew. To look past the vampire and the monster, and the thing that had just ripped out a man's throat, to the girl beneath.

"Allie." His voice was still very soft, his brow furrowed as if he was in pain. "I will never forgive Jackal for what he did to my family," he said firmly, holding my gaze. "I know I should, that's what I've been taught, but…I can't. I keep seeing Jeb and Darren and Ruth and everyone who didn't make it, and all I want to do is put a stake through his heart and send him to hell where he belongs. Maybe that's messed up, and maybe it makes me just as bad as him, but that's the only way I'm going have any kind of peace with him around.

"But, you and me…" He paused, searching my face. "Maybe we can…start over. Put everything that's happened behind us, and try again. I don't want to fight you—I know you have your reasons for bringing Jackal here, and I will try to respect that. Even if I can't forgive him."

"I don't want to fight you, either," I muttered, looking down so I didn't have to see his shirtless, muscular upper body standing so close. I caught a glimpse of a few pale scars on his chest, not nearly the mess his back was, and it made my stomach squirm. "I'm still a vampire, Zeke. I'm still going to have to feed and drink blood and I might kill more people, you know that."

"I know." Zeke stepped closer, not touching, but I could feel the warmth coming from his skin, sense him trying to catch my gaze. "And I'm still going to hate everything the vampires have done to us. I'm going to do everything I can to help the people here, but…that doesn't mean that I hate you, Allie."

I raised my eyes, meeting his gaze. He gave a faint, rueful smile. "Everything used to be so black-and-white," he admitted with a tiny shrug. "Jeb's teachings didn't allow for much gray area, if any. But I understand vampires a lot more now. And I know that you, at least, still try to be different. To not be one of them. I believe that."

"How do you know?" I challenged. Part of me didn't know what I was doing. Zeke was finally saying the words I'd longed to hear him say—that I wasn't like the other vampires, that I was different. But my rational side knew this was dangerous ground, that Zeke should fear and hate me, that I was still a vampire that could lose control of herself at any moment, and then he would be dead. Jackal's words came back to taunt me: *You and me, sister, we're exactly the same. Fight it as long as you want—in the end, the monster always wins.*

"Maybe I am just using you," I continued, while my head continued its war with itself. I was torn between irrationally wanting to hug Zeke and wanting to scare him away for good. Away from the monster that still urged me to rip him apart. "Maybe Jeb was right the whole time. How do you know I'm not just like them?"

Zeke's voice didn't change. "Because," he said calmly, "if you were, I'd have been dead on top of Jackal's tower that night."

"Oh, please," came a new, unwelcome voice, breaking into our conversation. "I think I'm going to hurl."

We broke apart as Jackal sauntered into the tunnel, smirking and gazing around at the carnage. "Well, you two certainly left a nice trail," he commented, stepping over one of the men I'd killed earlier. "Made you easy to find, at least, though I feel a bit left out. Next time you two decide to go on a bloody killing spree, at least send me an invitation so I know that you care."

He grinned as Zeke retrieved his shirt and vest from the ground, shrugging into them quickly. "So, now that we're done making out in entrails-strewn sewer tunnels, are we ready to go see the Prince?"

I went up the ladder, shoving the grate aside and easing out of the sewers. As I straightened, a breeze whistled through the long grass, tossing my hair and sliding over my skin, unpleasantly cold, had I been alive to feel it. Flurries drifted on the air, swirling around us, and the ground was dusted in white.

I gazed around warily. Squat, ancient buildings surrounded us on three sides, crumbling to large rubble piles in the weeds. The area where we stood had been a parking lot once, but vegetation had completely taken over and now only a few spots of pavement showed through the grass and the light dusting of snow on the ground.

I turned and saw the gleaming lights of the vampire towers, looming impressively over the tops of other buildings, closer than I'd ever seen before. I half closed my eyes, and the pull was there, drawing me right toward them.

Kanin, I'm coming. Hang on.

"I scouted the area a bit," Zeke announced, coming up behind me. His gun and machete were in place, but he had ditched the stakes in the tunnels before going topside. Probably a smart move—the vamps, pets and guards would not look kindly on such an obvious vampire killer. "After you two went to sleep, before the mole men attacked. There's a patrol that comes by every thirty minutes or so, but not much traffic otherwise. It's different near the center, though. Lots of people, and I think there are several vampires, too. They've set up a security fence around those three buildings—" he pointed to the vampire towers "—where it looks like they're checking everyone who goes through the gates. I couldn't get too close—they have sentries with dogs surrounding the perimeter and I couldn't risk them scenting me."

"So," I mused to no one in particular, gazing at the vampire towers again. Here we were, past the wall and at the edge of the Prince's territory. "How are we going to get through?"

"We could check the perimeter," Zeke suggested. "See if there are any holes or lulls in the patrols. Maybe we can sneak past them."

Jackal snorted, kicking the grate into place again. "You won't be sneaking past anything," he mocked, turning to us. "Even if you get past the checkpoint, the guards and the pets, you're going into the lair of the *Prince of the city.* You think they just have weakling humans in any of those towers?" He shook his head. "Salazar's coven will be all over the place, the vampire Elite, his handpicked personal guard."

"Then how are we going to find Kanin?" I snapped, feeling his time was slipping further away. "We have to get in there somehow. What do you suggest, walk up and knock on the front door?"

"Actually," Jackal said, "that's exactly what we're going to do."

Zeke and I stared at him, equal parts speechless and horrified. "You're kidding," Zeke said at last. "There's no way they'll let us in. I'm not Registered here, and you both snuck in from outside the Wall. They'll know we're intruders."

"Not to mention, Salazar hates Kanin's entire line," I added. "He tried to kill me and Kanin both the last time I was here, in case you've forgotten. Guards, trucks, people shooting at us every fifty feet?"

Jackal chuckled. "Oh ye of little faith." He sighed, and started across the lot, motioning us to follow. "Thinking just like the humans. It's kind of sad. You forget, I've been at this vampire thing a long time. Just leave this to me, and try to keep your mouths shut."

Apprehensively, we trailed Jackal out of the lot and onto the cracked, broken sidewalks, moving steadily toward the center of the city. Streetlamps flickered, lighting the way, though more than a few were smashed and broken or sputtered erratically. The streets here were cleaner than those of the Fringe—fewer rubble piles, less vegetation growing everywhere, no dead cars clogging the roads. The buildings to either side of us were barren, decayed and empty, but the closer we got to the very center, the more lights we saw. I looked behind us once and, through a gap in the buildings, I caught a glimpse of the Inner Wall, dark and deserted. Beyond that wall was the Fringe. I wondered what madness was happening on the streets of my old home.

Jackal never stopped or slowed down. He walked the center of the road like he owned it, his duster billowing behind him, and didn't hesitate when a patrol of a half-dozen armed guards rounded a corner and came toward us.

I tensed, and Zeke's hand twitched for his gun, but the patrol, when they saw us, veered away and averted their eyes. Stunned, I watched them cross the road to avoid us, and realized how we must look; two vamps and an armed human, walking the streets of the Inner City like we were meant to be here. And I understood Jackal's mind-set, now. Of course the guards wouldn't question us—we were vampires. Skulking or sneaking around the Inner City was highly suspicious and would've drawn immediate attention, but when a fanged bloodsucker walked down the street in plain sight, *every* human—pet, guard or normal worker—gave them a wide berth.

I expected Jackal to let the humans pass while we continued our trek to the gate. But the vampire abruptly shifted directions and strode right toward them, his walk and everything about him aggressively confident. The patrol stopped, the guards immediately snapping to attention even as they avoided his eyes.

Jackal marched right up, grabbed the lead human by the collar and slammed him back into a wall, baring fangs in his face.

"Your Prince isn't being very friendly," Jackal growled, as the rest of the patrol cringed back, not knowing whether to draw weapons or flee. Zeke and I looked on, as shocked as the rest of them but trying not to show it. "Here we are, trying to be nice and polite and present ourselves to Salazar, but he's locked all the gates and shut down the Wall. We had to crawl up through the *sewers* to get here— Do you know how disgusting that is, human?" His lips curled back into a fearsome snarl, and the human turned white, looking like he might faint. "And what the hell is going on in the Fringe? The bloodbags have gone insane—they even tried to attack us! Has Salazar lost control of this place completely?"

"S-sir!" The human gave a feeble salute—difficult, as his arms were shaking so hard he could barely lift them. "I'm sorry, sir, we're experiencing a bit of a problem with the Fringe—"

"I can see that, human." Jackal bared his fangs again, making the guard jerk his head away, cracking the back of his skull against the wall. "I want to know why Salazar hasn't gotten it under control yet."

"Sir, I assure you—"

"Your assurances mean nothing to me." Jackal abruptly released the guard and stepped back, letting him slump to the wall. "I want to see Salazar. I demand an audience with your Prince. Take me to him, right now."

"Sir..." The guard looked absolutely miserable and terrified at the same time. "I don't have that kind of authority—"

"Incredible. How does this city even run?" Jackal growled, casting a disdainful look at me and Zeke. Turning back to the guards, he took a breath and made a great show of being patient. "Then, tell me, bloodbag, who has that authority?"

"The...the Prince's aide, sir. His pet. He's the one who admits visitors to the Prince's chamber."

"Well, then," Jackal said, taking a step forward, "I'd say you'd better get a hold of him soon, don't you think?"

"Yes, sir!" The guard leaped off the wall, looking relieved to pass this little problem on to someone else. "I'll contact him right now. Please, follow me."

Jackal grinned over his shoulder as we started down the road again, following the patrol toward the vampire towers. "See?" he said in a quiet voice, looking at me now. "When you act like a vampire, humans will treat you like one. None of this sneaking or skulking-around crap. They're the sheep, and we're the wolves, and they know it."

"So, this is what it's like in a vampire city," Zeke said in a cold voice.

Jackal snorted. "Did that upset you, bloodbag? Did I treat the human too rough for you?" He sneered. "Get used to it. This is our city, and we do what we want here. Every single human existing behind these walls belongs to us."

"Not all of them," Zeke said firmly.

Another time, I would've taken Zeke's side and argued with Jackal that there *were* humans in a vampire city who defied the bloodsuckers and lived free—I had been one of them—but I didn't want to start a fight in the middle of enemy territory. Not when we were rapidly approaching the fence that surrounded the Prince's towers. As we drew closer, my apprehension grew. If I'd still had a heartbeat, it would've been pounding against my ribs. This territory was the Prince's, the Master vampire that ruled the city with an iron fist. Not only that, the strongest vampires in the city, the Prince's coven, prowled the halls and corridors of those towers. So many bloodsuckers. If Jackal didn't know what he was doing, we were walking into a deathtrap.

"What do you expect to do in there?" I growled at Jackal, suddenly wanting to know the plan, if we had a plan, or if we were just flying in blind. "You know that if Salazar finds out who we are, he'll try to put our heads on his wall."

"Relax, sister." Jackal quirked an eyebrow. "Unless he's seen you personally, Salazar doesn't know you from Eve—you're just another wandering mongrel vampire to him. And he doesn't know me at all. Don't worry, I know how Princes think. We'll go in, feed him some story about passing through, make a little scene because we can't leave the city now, and he'll get annoyed but probably not enough to throw us out. There are rules for visiting vampires, after all, and these Princes are all such proud stick-up-the-asses. More likely, he'll apologize for the state of the city, offer to let us stay in the tower until the crisis is over, and we'll be free to look for Kanin as we please. Easy."

"Way too easy," Zeke muttered, and I agreed. Jackal rolled his eyes.

"Well, if you two have a better plan, I'd love to hear it."

We were very close to the fence now, passing more guards and humans waiting in line to get through the checkpoint. At the front of the line, a guard would ask the human to show his tattoo, usually located on the inner arm. A scanner was passed over the mark and scrutinized before the guard waved him through. I bit my lip to avoid curling it in disgust. Before I was Turned, *this* was what I had fought against my entire life—becoming a slave to the bloodsuckers. Taking the brand that would mark me as a bloodcow, an owned thing, the property of the Prince. Back then, I hadn't regretted it, even though it would've been easier to take the mark, to accept the promise of food and protection and an easier life. Now, looking back, I couldn't help but wonder. I was never truly "free" in New Covington. Sure, I hadn't given blood, but I'd still been trapped, at the mercy of the vampires, constantly living in fear. If I'd been Registered, the vampires would've won, but I wouldn't have been scavenging in the ruins the night the rabids attacked me. The night I died.

So, what was worse? Submitting to the bloodsuckers, letting them treat you as a slave and a bloodcow, or becoming that very same monster yourself?

Stop thinking about that, Allison. It doesn't matter now; you already made your choice.

"So, what are *we* supposed to do?" Zeke asked Jackal as a pair of big dogs growled at us from the ends of their leashes. Now only a few yards separated us from the gate, and the entrance to the vampire's lair. "They're going to know I'm human, Unregistered and armed. Isn't the punishment for that kind of thing death around here? Or is that what you're hoping for?"

"Kid, I got this. Trust me." Jackal gave us one last self-satisfied glance. "Just look dangerous."

Trust Jackal. That didn't sound like a good plan, but there was nothing we could do about it now. The patrol had stopped us at another checkpoint, and the lead soldier was speaking to another guard. The man in uniform looked up from the gatehouse, peering through a small window, and narrowed his eyes. I shifted uneasily, feeling a restless flicker of the Hunger stir to life. So many humans…

The man inside the gatehouse emerged and walked toward us, his pinched mouth drawn into a frown. Jackal glared, waiting imperiously as the human, flanked by two more soldiers with large guns, strode up.

"Sir," he greeted, with the obvious air of someone who thought they were important. "Welcome to New Covington. Please excuse the current state of the city. I understand you wish an audience with the Prince's aide?"

"No," Jackal said, giving the man a clear look of disdain. "I don't want an audience with the Prince's pet. I want to see Salazar himself. But since the sniveling little human is the only way to get to him, I'm being polite and following the rules. What I don't understand is why I'm standing here, talking to *you*."

This last must've been punctuated with a flash of fangs, for the man deflated a bit, looking paler then before.

"Well, you see, s-sir," he stammered, and gave Zeke a pointed look, "Unregistered humans are not allowed into the Inner City. If he came from the Fringe, I'm afraid we must quarantine him immediately. He could be infected, and we cannot risk the spread of disease within the city, certainly not inside the towers themselves. We must ask you to turn him over."

I tensed, a growl rising to my throat, barely stopping myself from stepping up and drawing my sword. Beside me, Zeke was frozen, his expression grim but not surprised. As if he'd been expecting this. The man gestured to his two guards, and they stepped around him toward Zeke. I did growl then, baring fangs, ready to jump between them, but Jackal's next words stopped everyone in their tracks.

"Lay one finger on him, and I'll tear your heads off."

Now everyone froze. Jackal's voice was calm, he hadn't even moved or turned around, but when a vampire made threats like that, you believed it. The two guards backed hastily away. The other human sputtered a protest, but Jackal stepped forward, looming over the man, and his objections fell silent.

"Tell me, human," the vampire said in a soft, dangerous voice. "What does the law say about seizing a vampire's pet?"

Zeke stiffened, though it went unnoticed by the other humans, who were still focused on Jackal. I saw anger flash across his face, but he remained silent as Jackal pressed closer, crowding the man.

"Well?"

The human swallowed hard. "Under pain of death, no one is allowed to lay a hand on a specifically branded aide without direct permission from his owner. Sir."

"And do you see Salazar's brand on him?"

"No, sir."

"Then get out of our way," Jackal continued, still in that soft, deadly voice. "Before I rip your heart out for your insolence and eat it in front of you. I've wasted enough time here already."

The human was in no mood to argue. His face was white, and his pompous attitude seemed to have fled with his courage. "T-take our guests to Mr. Stephen's office," he ordered, motioning to his guards. "Inform him of what is going on. He might be with the Prince now, so let him know it's important."

"Yes, sir!" The guards stepped forward, bowing slightly to Jackal. "Please, follow us, sir." And without any hesitation, they turned and marched through the checkpoint as the other human waved us through.

Incredible. We were past the gate without having to fight our way in. Without having to kill anyone for trying to take Zeke away. Jackal had pulled it off. I wouldn't have done it that way; I wasn't sure that I *could.* And I was still shocked that he had stood up for Zeke. He hadn't let the human be taken, though his insistence might've lessened our chances of getting in.

By Zeke's quiet, thoughtful expression, I knew he was stunned, as well.

The guards led us across the road, past several smaller buildings on the corner, and then up a sprawling flight of concrete steps to the wide double doors at the base of the first tower. Another guard opened the door for us, and we entered a massive lobby, green-and-black pillars lining the walls, and a huge wooden desk up front. Yet another security checkpoint waited for us beyond the door, where a couple humans arriving before us had to scan their tattoos to be allowed through.

How much security does the Prince need? I thought, as the guards on the other side of the desk eyed us warily. *Is he really that paranoid, to surround himself with so many guards, or is this because of the situation in the Fringe? You'd think the Master vampire of the city wouldn't be afraid of a few rogue humans wandering his tower, or even rogue vampires.*

A blonde woman in a business suit waited for us on the other side of the checkpoint, waving at the guards to let us through. She bowed as we came up, giving Jackal a bright smile as she straightened. I could hear her heart pounding in her chest and smelled the fear surrounding her, though she hid it well. In fact, all the humans in this place reeked of fear.

"Welcome to the Prince's tower, sir," the woman announced, as Jackal raked his gaze over her body and leered with appreciation. "I am Mr. Stephen's secretary, and if you will follow me, I will show you to his office. Mr. Stephen is in a meeting now, but he will be with you as soon as he is able."

"He'd better be," Jackal growled. The secretary didn't give any outward sign of emotion, though her heartbeat picked up and her shoes made anxious tapping sounds as she led us farther into the tower.

I shifted my focus, letting my consciousness flow outward, searching for something else.

There. I could feel it. I could feel *him,* very close, but… below us. Somewhere beneath the tower, just barely clinging to sanity.

Hang on, Kanin. We're almost there.

The woman led us from the brightly lit lobby into a maze of long, shadowy corridors, her heels clicking rhythmically over the tile. The halls were mostly empty. No light shone from beneath the doors or adjoining wings, and no humans walked the hallways except a single woman with a mop, scrubbing the floor. It was nearly as cold in the tower as it was outside. Zeke's breath hung in the air as we continued deeper into the maze, the shadows closing around us. The tower had a cold, stark, unfriendly feel to it, though it was far cleaner and well taken care of than any building I'd seen before.

A door opened ahead of us, and two men in business suits stepped out. Both were tall and pale, vampires, not a hair out of place or a speck of dirt on their clothes. I tensed as they spotted us. The secretary bowed her head to them as we went by, but they ignored her, watching us with glittering eyes, smiling faintly. I tensed, ready to draw my blade if they lunged, but they let us pass without incident and continued down the hall. I wondered if these were the Type-2 vampires Kanin had told me about, the nobles of vampire society. I also wondered what they did all night in this monstrous tower. Kanin had explained a little of vampire politics to me before we were separated, the constant backstabbing and maneuvering and climbing up the chain of command, trying to get closer to the Prince. I hadn't been very interested in hearing it at the time, having no desire to fit in with the city vamps. Now I wished I'd listened closer.

"In here, please." The woman opened a door that led to a large, well-tended office. "Mr. Stephen will be right with you."

Stepping through the frame, I gazed around, pushing back my distaste. The pets might be sellouts and traitors to their own race, but they were certainly well taken care of. The carpet beneath my feet was plush and soft, and heavy curtains draped the windows, keeping out the chill. A huge wooden desk, polished to a mahogany sheen, dominated one corner of the room, surrounded by shelves and files. It was warmer in this room, much warmer than it was in the halls, probably because of the fire flickering cheerfully in the marble fireplace on the far wall. I was shocked that the vamps allowed live flames within their buildings, even well caged as the fire was, but I supposed they couldn't have their prized humans freezing to death.

A leather sofa sat against the far wall, pillows and blankets folded neatly on the cushions, as if the pet slept here, and often. An object on the worn leather caught my attention. A book, open and upside down, straddling the armrest. Unable to help myself, I edged closer, leaning forward to read the title. *Of Mice and Men*. John Steinbeck. I glanced up, looking past the sofa, and saw another shelf standing in the corner by the window. This one was full of books, more then I'd ever seen in my life. And for just a moment, I felt a tiny prick of envy.

When I was Allie the Fringer, I used to collect books like this, from anywhere I could find them. Of course, in the Fringe, owning them was highly illegal. The vampire lords didn't want their cattle to be able to read—it might put ideas in our heads if we knew what life was like before. But one of my greatest secrets was that I *could* read. My mom had taught me when she was still alive, and I'd clung to that accomplishment fiercely. It was the one thing the vampires couldn't take from me.

When Kanin made me a vampire, however, I'd had to leave my collection behind, and it had been burned by the humans who'd moved into my old home. Years of effort, gone in a heartbeat.

But the pets could read without fear. They could have a book collection if they wanted, without having to hide it away from all prying eyes. They didn't have to scrounge and scrape just to get by, or huddle with a friend beneath a filthy blanket to avoid freezing to death. No, they had everything they could possibly want or need, for the low price of selling out their own kind.

Must be nice.

"I still don't think this is a good idea," Zeke was saying behind me. "Those were vampires in the hallway. If the Prince figures out who we are, we won't be able to fight our way out of the building, much less back to the Fringe."

"Stop being so twitchy," Jackal replied, and I heard him sit in one of the chairs near the desk, swinging his boots up. "I told you before, Salazar doesn't know us from Adam. No one here does. And it's better to act like you belong here than be caught sneaking around. So relax, *pet*." I heard the grin in his voice and could almost feel Zeke bristle. "We're vampires. What could happen?"

Something on the bookshelf caught my eye. A sliver of color among the darker, more subdued books. For some reason, I felt drawn to it. There was a nagging sensation in the back of my mind as I stepped around the sofa and approached the shelf. As I reached for the thin cover, the nagging turned into a sense of foreboding.

"Allie?" Zeke said, though I barely heard him as my fingers closed on the spine. "What are you doing?"

Pulling the book from the shelf, my mind went blank and a cold fist gripped my stomach. Bright animals danced across the cover of a children's picture book as familiar to me as the back of my hand. Unlike the other books on the shelf, it was dirty and torn, a mold stain eating one corner. I knew it instantly. This had been my mom's book, the one she'd read to me hundreds of times when I was a kid, the one I regretted losing the most. The cold spread from my stomach to my entire body. If it was here, that could only mean one thing….

The door creaked open, and several footsteps entered the room, followed by an instantly familiar voice.

"Thank you for waiting. I'm Mr. Stephen, Prince Salazar's aide. I understand you want an audience with the Prince?"

I turned slowly and met Stick's pale gaze across the room.

CHAPTER 11

He had changed.

The Stick I remembered had been tall and skinny, a ragged scarecrow with straw-colored hair and frightened, watery blue eyes. The person in the doorway, surrounded by four armed vampires and two humans, was still tall and thin, but he wore a business suit and carried a suitcase in one spidery hand. He wasn't nearly as skinny now, and his hair had been cut short and combed back, replacing the shaggy nest I remembered.

But the biggest change was in his eyes and the way he carried himself. Back in the Fringe, Stick had cringed and skulked his way through life, relying on me for survival. He was afraid of everyone and everything and often got picked on because he expected me to save him instead of standing up for himself.

Now, he carried himself tall, his tone and expression clear, almost arrogant. But maybe that was because of his entourage, the two humans and four vampires surrounding him with guns and crossbows, smaller versions of the one Zeke had given away. Seeing him, I felt the last piece of something inside me—hope, stubbornness, disbelief—shatter and die. I'd always wondered what had happened to Stick, if he really had sold me out to the Prince once he knew what I was. I'd been hoping, deep down, that it wasn't true.

But here he was. Salazar's personal aide, staring at me as if he'd just seen a ghost.

"A-Allie?" His voice was a choked, horrified whisper, and the guards stared at him, and us, in rising alarm. "No. No, it can't be you. You're supposed to be dead!"

"Stick," I said, taking a step forward. But Stick threw himself backward, into the hall, pointing wildly.

"Stop her!" he screeched to his guards, who immediately pulled their crossbows and aimed them at our hearts. Jackal cursed and shot out of the chair, and Zeke tensed, going for his gun. "Stop them all! She's here to kill me!"

"I'm not here to kill you!" I shouted, holding up my hands. Several wooden darts were leveled at my chest, making me cringe inside. Dammit, if I didn't get a handle on this, we'd all be skewered like rats. "Stick, wait!" I called desperately. "I didn't come for you. We want to see the Prince, that's all! I didn't even know you were here."

He peered into the room again, eyes cold and suspicious. "I don't believe you."

"Believe what you want. I'm telling you the truth." I kept my hands raised as he edged back into the room. "We're not here for you, or anyone. We just want to see the Prince."

He eyed Zeke and Jackal, then glared back at me. "You're not supposed to be here, Allie," he accused, sounding like his old sullen self. "Master Salazar said you were dead, he promised you had been killed. You're not supposed to be here."

Irritation, and something darker, flared. "Sorry to disappoint you. But I'm still alive."

Stick's gaze narrowed and an ugly look crossed his face as he turned to the guards. "Arrest them," he barked, and the guards straightened. "They want to see the Prince? We'll take them to see the Prince. I'm sure the Master will be *very* interested in meeting them."

I swallowed the growl as two vampires came forward, reaching for me while the others kept their weapons trained on us. *Dammit. What now?* We couldn't fight our way past the Prince's Elite, not with a whole tower of vampires between us and the exit. Even if Jackal and I got out, Zeke would be torn apart before we reached the front desk. And if we did manage to escape, we'd never be able to get back in. Stick knew I was here, and soon the Prince would, too. I glanced at Zeke and Jackal, wondering if they had any brilliant ideas to get us out of this, but they looked as grim as I felt. No way out. We were caught.

I clenched my fists as one guard grabbed my katana and drew the sheath over my head, barely stopping myself from breaking his nose as he took the blade away. I felt naked without it. The other guard pulled a pair of black metal cuffs from his belt and reached for my arms. "This isn't necessary, Stick," I said as the vampire yanked my arms behind my back and snapped the bands around my wrists. The weight of the chains dragged at me, thick and heavy, obviously designed for vampires.

"It's Stephen now," Stick corrected, his voice smug. "Mr.

Stephen. And I decide what's necessary around here, Allie." A faint smirk twisted his lips as he raised his chin. "No one tells me what to do, not anymore."

I could only watch as Zeke and Jackal were stripped of weapons and cuffed, as well. Jackal rolled his eyes and seemed annoyed with the entire event, but Zeke looked pale as his gun and machete were removed and the shackles were locked in place. He met my gaze, and I could see the resignation on his face, the expectancy that he wasn't going to make it out alive.

I'm sorry, Zeke. I didn't mean to drag you into this. I'll get us out somehow, I promise.

When we were restrained, Stick gave a self-satisfied nod, his pale eyes lingering on me. "This way," he stated grandly, as if he was announcing a tour. "Prince Salazar is expecting us."

A guard nudged me in the shoulder with the crossbow, and I went, following my former friend into the halls of the vampire tower.

Dammit, this was not the way I'd wanted to meet Salazar: arrested and in chains, unable to defend myself and those around me. Things had gone very wrong, but there was nothing I could do but try to bluff my way out when we met the Prince. I wondered if Jackal was already working on a plan, some kind of speech or con to get us out of this alive. He was the one who knew about vampire politics, not me. Of course, he was part of the reason we were in this mess to begin with.

I wanted to talk to him, and Zeke, too, but the guards to either side of us made that impossible.

We came to a pair of elevators, working ones, at the end of a hall, and Stick eyed us warily as the doors opened.

"Take them to the top floor," he told the four vampire guards, and stepped toward the other elevator across the hall. "I'll meet you there."

Coward, I thought, as Stick went into a box with his two human bodyguards, smiling and folding his hands before him as the doors slid shut. *Doesn't want to be in a tight space with the vampire he stabbed in the back, I guess.*

The guards drew their weapons and herded us into the elevator, standing at the corners as we huddled in the center. The doors glided shut, plunging the box into darkness, and the lift began to move.

I tensed, gritting my teeth. I'd been in an elevator before—a rickety, jerry-built one that had crackled and jerked and spit out sparks, making me afraid it would fall at any moment. I didn't like small, tight spaces with no way out—they made me very twitchy. The guards stared straight ahead, weapons drawn but not pointed at us, paying no attention. Experimentally I yanked at the chains around my wrists. If I could just get my hands free, I'd be prepared should an opportunity to escape arise. Unfortunately, the cuffs held. I wouldn't be going anywhere.

Jackal leaned in, his mouth close to my ear. "You didn't tell me about your little friend," he murmured, and if the guards heard him, they didn't care. "That would've been a nice tidbit to share, going into the Prince's tower."

"I didn't think I would see him here," I whispered back. "And it doesn't matter now. I hope you have something in that twisted head to stop the Prince from ripping it off."

"Working on it."

"Faster would be nice."

The guard closest to me gave the evil eye and curled a lip in warning, revealing fangs. I bared mine in return and faced forward, watching the numbers light up over the door—10... 12...14...16... How far up did this thing go? With every floor, we were getting farther away from the exit and closer to the lair of a Master vampire.

"Allie," Zeke murmured, barely audible even as close as we were. Despite our situation, and the vampires surrounding us on every side, his voice and expression were calm. Too calm. "If we don't make it...I'm glad that I found you. It was good to see you again."

I growled and bent toward him, lowering my voice. "Don't you even start with that, Zeke," I hissed, not knowing if I was angry or terrified at his words. "You have people waiting for you in Eden. You are not going to die here."

"It's all right." Zeke managed the tiniest of smiles. "I'm not afraid to die. I just wish..." He trailed off, a flicker of pain crossing his face, before he shook that off, too. "Never mind. It's not important now. I just... I want you to promise me one thing."

I didn't know how well I'd be able to keep any kind of promise now. I really hoped he wouldn't ask me to go to Eden and inform his family if he was killed. I wasn't sure I could do that, even if we made it out of here. But this was Zeke; it was hard to tell him no. "What do you want me to do?" I whispered.

He held my gaze, blue eyes solemn and intense. "Don't Turn me," he whispered, sending a spear of ice through my stomach. "Even if I'm dying, don't make me one of them. Just let me go."

"Zeke." My throat suddenly closed up. Zeke leaned forward, resting his forehead to mine, closing his eyes.

"Please," he whispered, his breath warm on my cold skin. "I don't… I can't spend eternity as a vampire. I can't. Promise me, if it comes to that, you'll let me go."

"Let you die?" I choked out. My first instinct was to refuse. The sudden thought that I could lose him tore a raw, gaping wound inside, which both shocked and terrified me. I'd distanced myself from everyone to avoid these kinds of attachments. In my world, people died. The only way to survive it was to numb yourself to loss and keep going. But Zeke… I couldn't lose him. If he was dying, and I could keep him here, if there was the barest chance to save him, I would take it. Even if I wasn't a Master vampire, and my attempt to Turn Zeke would likely spawn a rabid, there was still that chance. Or I would get another, stronger vampire to do it. Kanin, perhaps. Kanin was a Master, though he considered his immortality a curse and would likely be reluctant to Turn a complete stranger. I didn't care. I'd convince him, somehow. I couldn't let Zeke die without trying to save him.

Then I realized how selfish I was being.

You would really attempt to Turn Zeke, even though he hates and fears becoming a vampire more than anything? Kanin gave you *a choice. He respected you enough to allow you to make that decision.*

"Damn you, Zeke," I growled. "You're really going to ask me to stand there and watch you die?"

Zeke opened his eyes, his face just a breath away. In my mind the guards disappeared. Jackal vanished. It was just me and Zeke now, facing each other in the dark. "I'm sorry," he whispered. "I know it's selfish, but I'm not like you, Allie."

Hurt, I drew back and curled my lip, showing fangs. "You mean evil and soulless?"

"I mean, I'm not as strong as you are," Zeke went on earnestly. "I can't do what you do, what's required to be a vampire. Please." His gaze turned pleading. "If it comes to that, let me die as a human. Promise you'll let me go."

"You can't deny him that choice," Jackal muttered behind my shoulder, shocking me again. "It takes a certain mindset to be one of us. If you Turn someone who can't handle it, they end up destroying themselves, going out to meet the sun. I've seen it before. Better to let the little bloodsack die, if that's what he wants."

"Damn you both," I muttered, turning my face away. Zeke's gaze still hadn't left me, and I squeezed my eyes shut. "All right," I whispered. "If that's what you want, Zeke. I promise I won't Turn you. But that means you can't give up." Opening my eyes, I glared at him. "You can't roll over and die. Promise *me* you'll keep fighting, for as long as it takes. We're not dead yet."

Zeke gave the smallest of grins. "Technically, you are," he whispered, and if my hands were free, I might've smacked him. "But you have my promise, vampire girl. I don't intend to give up. I'll fight beside you for as long as I can."

The elevator stopped with a *ding,* and the doors slid open. Stick greeted us on the other side, smiling like a cat with a bird. His human bodyguards waited impassively behind him. "This way," he sang as the vampire Elite pushed us out. Zeke stumbled, barely catching himself, and I bared my fangs at the one who'd shoved him, my gaze flicking to the katana still looped around his shoulder. His face remained impassive as he jerked his crossbow down the hall, motioning us forward.

This hallway was more ornate than the ones on the previous floors. Thick red carpet lined the dim corridor, with electric lights set into alcoves on either side. Large paintings hung from the walls: a peaceful countryside, city streets filled with light and people, horses grazing within a fence. Scenes of a world I'd never known. The painting of a mountain range caught my eye, snowy peaks tipped with red and pink, a sunrise that I would never see again.

At the end of the hallway stood two massive double doors, a vampire guard on either side. As we approached, Stick held up a hand and turned to us with a smile.

"Wait here a moment," he said. "I will inform the Prince of your arrival." His watery gaze shifted to the guards at our backs. "Make sure our guests do not move from this spot. If they try anything, shoot them if you have to, but don't kill them." He smiled at me then, secure in his authority. "We don't want to deny the Prince his amusement."

At one time, I would've been angry, but right now I just felt numb. *What's happened to you, Stick?* I wondered as he strode away, snapping his finger at a guard, who pulled the door open for him. *Do you hate me that much for leaving? Or did you always despise me, even when we were Fringers together?*

"Well, he's a real charmer," Jackal muttered as the door closed. "You two must've been such great pals. I hope you don't mind when I say I'm going to rip his tongue out through his nose and make him eat it."

Zeke moved closer, brushing my shoulder with his. "You all right?" he asked softly, watching my face. I nodded. I couldn't think about Stick. I had to focus on Salazar, what I was going to say to him once we went through those doors. What would he want? What could I say that would appeal to the vampire Prince? His city was falling apart around him, so maybe he would be interested in what we knew about Sarren and the other lab. Did he know Kanin was so close, right below his tower? And if Kanin was somewhere beneath us, Sarren was probably here, too.

My skin crawled at the thought of Sarren being nearby. If he found us now…

Dammit, I wasn't going to die here. We'd come too far. Salazar was a Master and had us completely at his mercy, but I was not ready to stop living. I would not let Kanin or Zeke down, either. Whatever it took, we were all going to walk away from this.

The door creaked open, and Stick emerged, wearing his ever-present smile. "Bring the prisoners forward," he called, and I clenched my fists behind my back. "Prince Salazar will see them now."

Well, this is it.

As the guards prodded us through the doorway, Zeke's gaze met mine, solemn and grim. *Remember your promise,* he seemed to say, and I swallowed the lump in my throat. It wouldn't come to that. I wouldn't allow it.

The doors creaked shut behind us.

I didn't get a good feel for the room at first, only that it was very large and dim. Nearly the entire opposite wall was glass, showing the night sky and the other two vampire towers silhouetted against the black. A huge desk sat in front of that wall, dark and shiny, but the man standing before the desk, leaning against the wood, demanded all our attention.

Prince Salazar regarded us curiously as we came in, like we were some kind of strange new insect he'd found on his floor. Even leaning against the desk, he was well over six feet in a perfectly tailored black suit, his inky hair tumbling to his shoulders in waves, not a strand out of place.

"So," Prince Salazar said, gazing directly at me, "you are Kanin's daughter."

He knew who I was.

Prince Salazar, the Master vampire of New Covington, the one who hated Kanin so much he'd kept a citywide manhunt going for weeks when the vampire was in the city, knew who I was.

Things didn't look good for me.

"Don't bother to deny it," Salazar said, his voice rich and deep, with the faintest accent I couldn't place. "Your friend Stephen has already told me everything about you. Where you lived, where you slept, the other members of your small gang. Rat and Lucas, I believe their names were? All Unregistered. Not in my system."

I spared a quick glance at Stick, standing off to the side, his gaze solely on the master. His face was slack, almost adoring. My stomach turned, and I forced myself to face Salazar again, who still watched me with no hints as to what he was thinking.

"Nothing to say?" he asked, raising a thin, elegant eyebrow.

"What do you want me to say?" I challenged. "You seem to know everything about me."

Salazar smiled. Turning, he raised a hand and gestured to one of the guards standing rigid beside us. "Release them."

The guard snapped to attention, and Stick jerked, glancing at me and then Salazar, who watched everyone calmly. "Master, are you sure that's a good idea?"

I was stunned, too, and stared at the Prince as a guard moved up behind me, inserting a key into my shackles. Salazar plucked a wineglass of blood from where it sat on the corner of his desk and swirled it thoughtfully.

"They are newcomers to my city," he stated as the cuffs dropped away and my hands were freed. "I do not wish to appear rude. The law states that I meet visiting kindred as guests unless I deem them an obvious threat. And they are not a threat to me. I do not need them in chains if I wish to destroy them."

Still shocked, I watched as Jackal and Zeke were released as well, Zeke rubbing his arms as the shackles were taken away. My gaze strayed to my katana, still looped to a guard's back, tempting me to lunge forward and snatch it away from him. I desperately wanted my sword, but getting it would be hard. There were the four armed vampire guards to contend with and, worse, there was Salazar himself. I did not want a fight with the vampire Prince of the city, as Kanin had showed me just how powerful a Master could be.

"Mr. Stephen," the Prince said as Stick continued to look sullen. "Please inform the guards outside the room to wait in the elevator hall. Inform them that, unless there is a life-or-death situation, I do not wish to be disturbed by anyone. Is that clear?"

"Of course, Master."

Stick bowed and left the room, shooting me an unreadable glance as he left. His two human bodyguards followed him out. I heard him speaking to the sentries outside before the door creaked shut and they were gone. The four armed vampires in the room, however, stayed.

Salazar straightened and walked around his desk, dropping into the chair behind it. "Sit, please," he said politely, nodding to a trio of chairs. With nothing else to do, we sat, and the vampire Prince smiled. "I would offer you refreshments, but I'm afraid I have a bit of a situation here, and our blood supply has been…compromised. I do apologize for the state of my city. Rest assured we are doing all we can to bring it under control." His gaze went to Jackal, and then Zeke, sitting to either side of me. "I'm afraid you have me at a disadvantage," he said, turning to Jackal. "I know of the girl, but I don't yet have the pleasure of your name."

"Jackal." Jackal crossed his legs and leaned back in the chair, looking perfectly at ease. "Former King of Old Chicago."

"Ah." Salazar nodded, giving him an appraising stare. "Yes, I have heard the rumors of a vampire who ruled a city entirely of humans. They say he was raising an army to take out the other vampire lords, only it didn't work out the way he'd hoped." Jackal raised his eyebrows, and the Prince smiled. "I like to keep tabs on my competition," he explained, and his smile turned dangerous again. "Assess possible threats before they grow too big to ignore. You are welcome here, raider king, so long as you remember who the Prince is." His gaze flicked to Zeke on the opposite side, turning slightly predatory. "And who is this…human?"

I stiffened, but Jackal broke in before I could speak. "He's no one," the former raider king said dismissively. "One of mine. In case I get hungry, and because he's actually a pretty good shot. Not the sharpest tack in the bunch, but he's amusing, for a pet. So I let him follow me around."

I saw Zeke briefly clench his jaw, as if struggling not to say anything. Jackal caught my eye, one corner of his mouth twitching, and I bit my tongue. *You are such a bastard,* I thought, though I understood what Jackal was doing. *Ignore the human,* he was telling the Prince. *The human isn't important.* If Salazar knew who Zeke really was, where he really came from… No, it was better that the Prince think of Zeke as a nobody, unimportant. Jackal had been right to shift the Prince's focus away from him. Though he didn't have to look so damn smug about it.

"Hmm." The Prince nodded and, much to my relief, appeared to lose interest in Zeke. "Well, enough pleasantries," he went on, and his piercing stare centered on me once more. "You have come for Kanin."

I gripped the edges of my chair, feeling Zeke and Jackal tense. "What do you know about that?" I asked. The Prince's smile grew, showing fangs.

"Because he is being tortured in the lowest level of my tower," he continued, matter-of-fact, "and his pain calls out to you, his offspring. Because you dream of him, starving, going mad with Hunger, clawing at the chains around him like a beast. Because he is screaming for salvation, and you cannot resist your sire's call. It drew you here, to my city, and it compels you to find him. But you cannot save him now."

I swallowed hard. Salazar had Kanin. But how? How had he gotten him away from Sarren? Had he killed the psychotic vampire, or had Sarren simply lost interest and left Kanin for the Prince to find?

I shook myself. None of that mattered. Sarren was gone, and the Prince was the one we had to deal with now. "Why are you doing this to him?" I whispered. "He was trying to find the cure for Red Lung and Rabidism. He was trying to save everything."

"He betrayed all our kind when he went to the scientists." Salazar's voice was suddenly hard and terrifying, his eyes gleaming with hate. "He turned on his own kin, allowed the humans to experiment on those who would be their masters, and he is responsible for the abominations outside the city." Salazar sat back, composing himself, though his voice was no less scary. "What he allowed those humans to do to our former brethren is unforgivable. What he helped create has damned us all to the darkest pits of hell. Kanin will suffer for his crimes. I have all eternity to watch him writhe and scream and become that which he created. A fitting end, I believe." Salazar's gaze sharpened, cutting into me. "Perhaps you would care to join him."

I had to be careful. One wrong word or action, and we'd be down there with Kanin, chained to a wall and waiting for Hunger to drive us insane. "There has to be something we can agree on," I said cautiously. "Something we can offer for Kanin's life."

"Oh?" The Master vamp raised an eyebrow, amused. "Tell me, then, Kanin's daughter. What do you think his life, and the billions of humans and vampires he helped destroy, is worth?"

"How about your city?" Jackal broke in, and Salazar turned

to him in surprise. "How about the knowledge of what's really going on out there, and the name of someone who can stop it?"

Very slowly, the Prince sat back, regarding Jackal with intense black eyes. "I'm listening," he said in a low, controlled voice.

"It's not just a random plague," Jackal went on. "Someone created the virus inside your city and released it into the population. It's too similar to Red Lung to be a coincidence. We know who did it. He's the one you really want, because he's the only one who has the cure."

Cure? I wondered how much of that was truth and how much Jackal was making up. We really didn't know if Sarren had a cure or could create one. We didn't even know if he was still in the city. But Salazar stood, looming over us, his expression cold and terrible. "Let's say I believe you," he said. "What is the name of the person who unleashed hell upon my city? Who is this creature who will soon regret he was ever born?"

"If we give you his name," I said, "will you release Kanin?"

Salazar regarded me with blank, scary eyes. "You are in no position to bargain with me, Kanin's daughter," he warned in a quiet voice. "It is only my will and my own laws that have kept you alive this long. One word from me, and you will share your sire's fate. So perhaps it is your own life you should be bargaining for, not his.

"However," he went on, "the fate of my city is more important than the existence of one vampire. Even one as cursed as him. Give me the one responsible for this chaos, and I will… consider…releasing Kanin to you."

I looked at Jackal. He nodded. "Sarren," I told the Prince. "His name is Sarren. You might remember him—he came to your city several months ago, looking for Kanin. Tall, bald, scarred-up face, a little on the bat-shit-crazy side?"

"Sarren." The Prince's voice was flat. Turning, he walked to the window, gazing out on the city. I watched his reflection in the glass, serious and pondering, and waited impatiently for his response.

"Serious accusations," the Prince said, turning back. His voice was grim as he turned his head, facing the corner. "What do you have to say to this…Sarren?"

"I would say," a cold, terrifyingly familiar voice hissed out of the darkness, "that some little birdie is lying to you."

CHAPTER 12

He was here.

My blood turned to ice. I leaped to my feet, causing Zeke and Jackal to do the same, as a pale, thin form slid out of the shadows, smiling his awful smile. The guards, forgotten around us, closed in, hands on their weapons. From the corner of my eye, I saw the Prince watching intently, waiting to see what would happen. But I couldn't take my eyes off Sarren.

"It isn't wise to deceive the Prince, little bird," Sarren crooned as his grinning, hideously scarred face came into the light. One hollow black eye fixed on me, the other, covered in blue film, stared sightlessly. "What venomous lies you are spreading, just to save your sire."

"They're not lies," I shot back, really, *really* wishing I had my sword. Something, anything, between me and him. Screw the Prince and the vampire Elite. Sarren was the most dangerous thing in the room now, and I didn't trust even the guards and their crossbows to keep us safe. "We know you went to Old D.C., to the other lab. We found the room with the live virus samples, and know you took them before you came here."

"Do you now?" Sarren sidled closer, and I tensed. On either side of me, Jackal and Zeke were just as alert. Only the Prince watched us calmly, no change in his demeanor. I wondered if he would be so calm if he knew the true monster he'd invited into his tower. "I think you are grasping at straws, little bird," Sarren went on. "To weave your nest of deceit. Oh, what a tangled web we weave."

"You took something from the lab," I insisted, refusing to let his craziness draw me in. "You brought it here. And you turned it loose in the Fringe. That's why every Fringer is tearing his face off and puking blood in the streets. Why? Why would you risk another plague? We haven't recovered from the last one."

"Can you hear him?" Sarren whispered, either not hearing or ignoring the question. "Can you hear his screams? Do they haunt your sleep, his cries of anguish? Can you feel his pain, the exquisite torture? Oh, I envy you."

"Azura will vouch for me," Jackal said, speaking not to Sarren, but to the Prince. "The Prince of Old D.C. knows Sarren came to her city and went searching for the government's secret lab beneath the tunnels. If you ask her, she'll confirm what we just told you."

"Where is Kanin?" I demanded, glaring at the scarred madman in front of me. "What did you do to him?"

"There's nothing left of him," Sarren said dreamily, almost in a daze now. "Not anymore. His mind has broken. Just like mine." He chuckled, and it made my skin crawl. "Only he won't be coming back. Pity that. I've enjoyed our interactions so. But now, I have a greater purpose. I do miss his screams, though. Such a glorious song."

I bared my fangs. "You'd better hope that he's all right," I growled. "I swear, I'll take you apart if he's not." But Sarren seemed to be in a trance now. His eyes were closed, and he swayed slightly on his feet, his thin mouth still twisted in a smile.

"You can't save him, little bird," he whispered. "You can't save anyone now. The requiem has started, and when the last melody plays, the only applause will be sweet, eternal silence." He raised his arms, as if he could hear the applause, accepting it. "It draws ever closer now. I cannot wait until the final note."

The Prince shook his head. "I am still unsure what is going on," he admitted slowly, "or who I should believe, but in light of these events, I'm afraid I must ask all of you to remain in the tower. You will be guests here, but please do not try to leave the floor. I will get to the bottom of this, soon."

Damn. Not ideal, but better than being tossed in the dungeon.

"Guards." The Prince nodded to the vampires, still waiting at attention. "Please escort our guests to their rooms. Make sure they do not try to leave. If they do try to escape, you have permission to shoot them."

"Yes, sir."

The Prince turned away then, facing the window and his city below it, dismissing us.

Two of the guards stepped forward, weapons drawn, to escort us from the room. The others approached Sarren, still in a daze in the middle of the floor, swaying to some tune only he could hear. The crazy vampire ignored the guard's repeated attempts to get his attention, seemingly lost in his own head. Finally, the guard gave an exasperated huff and took his arm.

Sarren spun with blinding speed, his free hand whipping up faster than thought, slashing across the guard's neck. The vampire let out a startled gurgle, and then his head tumbled backward in a spray of blood, held in place by a single flap of skin. Still clutching his thin, bright dagger, Sarren grabbed the guard's crossbow arm and turned, pointing the weapon across the room. There was the snap of the bolt releasing, and the shaft buried itself in Salazar's chest just as the Prince was spinning around.

This all happened in the space of a blink. Salazar gave a strangled cry and collapsed, clutching his chest, clawing at the desk to keep himself upright. The other guards roared with fury and lunged to attack, drawing their blades as they rushed forward. The guard closest to Sarren pulled his sword and slashed at him in the same motion, but Sarren ducked the blow, stepped in close, and shoved his dagger under the guard's chin, into his brain. Yanking it out, he spun to face the remaining two guards, a maniacal grin on his face as they rushed forward.

With a howl, Jackal leaped into the fray, grabbing a dead guard's sword as he charged Sarren. I spun on Zeke. "Stay down!" I hissed at him, and lunged forward, too. But my goal wasn't Sarren, not yet. Dodging a blade that buzzed overhead, I threw myself at the first dead guard, my fingers closing around the handle of my katana.

A familiar cry made my blood run cold. I whirled just in

time to see Jackal fall, clutching the hilt of the blade in his chest as Sarren shoved him back. The other two guards lay nearby, one with a crossbow shaft protruding from his eye socket, the other missing a head.

So fast. It had happened so quickly. Drawing my sword, I rose to face Sarren alone.

The vampire smiled at me from the center of the massacre, blood painted across his face, seeping into his many scars. It covered his arms, his chest, running down his white skin and dripping to the carpet. "Hello, little bird," he whispered, stepping over a dead vampire, backing me toward the wall. I raised my sword and tried to calm the terror sweeping through me. "I believe we have unfinished business, you and I."

"Stay away from her."

Sarren turned. Zeke stood beside a dead vampire, a crossbow in hand, pointed unerringly at Sarren's heart.

"What's this?" Sarren watched Zeke in obvious amusement. "A human? Ready to die for a vampire? What a loyal little pet you are. But your master has no control over you now." He gestured to the carnage around him and smiled. "Run, little human," he crooned. "Run. The end draws nigh, and the sun will soon set for all your kind. How long can you evade the dark, I wonder?"

"Zeke!" I hissed, still keeping my gaze on Sarren, knowing how fast he could move, how he could suddenly be *right there* with no warning at all. "Listen to him! Get out of here!" Didn't he see what just happened, Sarren slaughtering four vampires and *the Prince* in the blink of an eye? He couldn't take on Sarren. Hell, I was pretty sure *I* couldn't take on Sarren. "Run!" I urged him. "Find Stick. Tell him what happened. Tell him to send help. Go!"

"Allie," Zeke said calmly, not moving an inch. "I'm not leaving you."

Sarren blinked, looking back and forth between us, and suddenly laughed. The raspy, dead voice sent chills up my spine as Sarren shook his head. "Ohhhh," he said, as if just figuring something out, "this *is* interesting. A little bird, making a nest with a rat. Are you a Prince then, little rat?" he asked Zeke, who frowned in wary confusion. But Sarren ignored him, turning back to me. "Well, this is quite the dilemma. Who shall I kill first? Shall I kill the prince's little bird in front of him?" His grin stretched wider as he stared at me, his voice dropping to a whisper. "Or shall I take apart the human, slowly? Peel the skin from his body, snap every bone, savor every scream, before I tear out his heart?" He chuckled and ran a tongue along his pale lips. "Would you like that, little bird? Or…perhaps you would like to watch?"

My fear vanished. The thought of Zeke at the mercy of this madman awoke a savage, almost desperate fury, and I acted without thinking. Baring my fangs, I lunged at Sarren with a roar, slashing at his neck. Sarren blocked the strike, reached in and grabbed my throat, spinning me around. Twisting my sword arm behind my back, he turned us toward Zeke, who had raised the crossbow and had it trained on us.

"Go on, little human," Sarren said over my shoulder. His bared fangs were inches from my neck, and the hand on my wrist was threatening to break my arm. I struggled, but he wrenched my arm up, and pain lanced through my shoulder. "You can probably hit me, if you shoot through us both."

"Let her go." Zeke's hand didn't waver, but his voice shook, just a little.

I felt something cold and wet touch my cheek—Sarren's tongue—and cringed in revulsion. "How do you taste?" Sarren whispered in my ear. "Shall we peel you open and see? Is your blood as dark and thick as Kanin's, little bird?"

"Get off me, you fucking psychopath!" I spat, nearly hysterical. He chuckled, and his fangs lightly scraped my skin.

"Hey."

A new voice, familiar and tight with pain, echoed behind us. Sarren glanced over, to find Jackal on his knees, one hand pressed to his bleeding chest, the other pointing a crossbow at us. "You missed," he rasped, and fired the weapon.

Sarren jerked back, throwing me to the floor. I hit the ground and rolled as a painful screech rang out behind me. Coming to my feet, I saw Sarren stagger backward, a wooden dart through his shoulder, his fangs bared in agony.

I grabbed my katana, but Sarren hissed like a furious snake, turned and flung himself toward the far wall. There was a deafening crash and glass exploded in all directions as the vampire hurled himself through the window and dropped from sight.

I shivered, gripping my katana so it didn't drop from my nerveless fingers. It didn't seem possible that we'd won, or at least, that we'd survived. The room reeked of blood, the carpet beneath my boots felt like a swamp, and the once-pristine office looked like a war zone.

"Allie." I turned as Zeke dropped the crossbow with a muffled thump, stepped forward and pulled me close, holding me tightly against him. He was shaking, his heart pounding against his ribs, loud and frantic. My eyes slipped shut, and my free arm reached around his waist to hug him back. The Hunger stirred, and my rational side prickled a warning that this was dangerous. I was getting too close, was already too close. I ignored it. Zeke felt warm and safe, and I had missed him, more than I thought I would ever miss anyone. I could allow myself this one moment.

"God, I thought I'd lost you," he whispered in a husky voice. "When Sarren grabbed you, my heart nearly stopped." Pulling back, he ran his thumb over my cheek, brushing the hair from my face. My senses buzzed from his touch. "Are you all right? I'm sorry…I couldn't get the shot off fast enough. Did he hurt you?"

"No." I reached up and wrapped my fingers around his wrist, feeling the pulse beneath my hand, assuring us both that we were okay. Hard to believe. I'd faced Sarren twice now when he was intent on killing me, and come out alive. How long would that luck last, I wondered. Especially since Psycho Vamp was still out there and hated us even more. "I'm fine, Zeke," I told him, squeezing his arm. "We're both still here."

He drew in a slow breath. "Allie…"

"Oh, don't mind me," came an extremely sarcastic voice near the wall. "You two go ahead and make out—I'll just sit here and bleed quietly."

Guiltily, we broke apart. Jackal sat against an overturned chair, surrounded by bodies, managing a smirk even through the horror around him. "That's okay," he said, gritting his teeth. "No need to thank the guy who just put a stake into Sarren and made him run away like a little girl. Though, I do feel that I'm missing something… What was it? Oh yeah, I just saved your lives, didn't I?"

Zeke started forward, but I grabbed his arm. "No," I told him urgently. "Don't go near him, he's lost a lot of blood. He might not be able to stop himself from biting you."

"I'm run through, not deaf," Jackal remarked from the floor. Honestly, he was the loudest mortally wounded vampire I'd ever heard. I figured that if he could make this much noise, he was in no danger of dying. "Although…" He grimaced, and his voice became lower, more like a growl. "You might want to get the meatsack out of here if you want his blood to stay on the inside. His inside, not mine."

"Go find Stick," I told Zeke. "Let him know what happened. Tell him Sarren is on the loose and that there's a wounded vampire who needs blood immediately." I glanced toward the wall where Salazar's body lay, motionless, behind the desk. "And that they're probably going to have to find a new Prince."

I winced, thinking how Stick would take that. Hell, how the entire vampire city would take that. "Actually," I continued, "it's probably best not to mention that quite yet."

Zeke nodded, though he looked reluctant to leave. "I'll be right back." He glanced at the dismembered corpses, the blood-spattered walls, the severed heads scattered around the room, and grimaced. "Will you be okay?"

"Yeah." I gave him a tired smile. "I'll be fine."

He brushed his fingers across my cheek, leaving a lingering trail of warmth, and turned away. Stepping around bodies, he wove his way through the blood-soaked room until he reached the doors and slipped through. They opened with a creak and groaned shut behind him, and the room seemed colder when he was gone.

Jackal grunted and shifted to a more comfortable position, leaning back against the chair. "You know you're playing a dangerous game," he said, watching me with glowing yellow eyes.

I started to snap that it was none of his business, then let my shoulders slump. "I know."

"When are you going to tell that kid that he doesn't have a chance? You'll have to let him know soon—looks like the poor sap has it bad." Jackal watched my reaction then raised his eyebrows. "You're not going to say anything, are you? You're going to let him tromp merrily down this road until the day the Hunger gets to be too much, and then the little bloodsack won't know what hit him." He chuckled, wincing, and shook his head. "And I thought I was a heartless bastard."

"It's not like that," I argued. Jackal snorted.

"What, then? Don't tell me *you* feel something for the little… Oh." The vampire blinked, then curled his lip back, disgust and pity crossing his sharp features. "Oh, sister. Really? That's just sad."

"Shut. Up. Jackal."

Jackal snickered again but fell silent. A few minutes later, the doors burst open and an armed regiment of vampires swept into the room. Most immediately surrounded me and Jackal, heavy crossbows pointed at us, while the rest searched the room, nudging the dead vampires and poking into dark corners.

"Little too late, chums," Jackal said from the floor. "If

you're looking for the psychotic murdering vampire, he already went out the window."

"Master Salazar!"

Stick swept through the doors, followed by two more guards, of the human variety this time. One of them carried a white cooler, the lid coiling with frost; the other held a gun to the back of an unresisting Zeke. I bristled, but Zeke met my worried gaze and gave a short nod, indicating he was all right.

"Oh, God." Stick gazed around the room in shock, his face draining of color. Looking at me, his eyes widened. "Allie!" he snarled, stabbing a thin finger at me. "Where is the Prince? What have you done to him?"

"We didn't do anything!" I protested. "Sarren did this. We were just trying to stay alive."

"Sarren?" Stick paled even more, one hand going to his mouth. "No. No, you're lying. Sarren wouldn't do this. That's…"

He trailed off, his gaze falling on the desk and the crumpled form behind it. "Master Salazar!" Stick cried, rushing over and kneeling beside the motionless body. I watched, bemused and, absurdly enough, a little hurt. Stick had never shown me that kind of concern.

"He's still alive," Stick whispered. "Master, can you hear me?"

A strained, choked whisper came from the body behind the desk, and I stared in shock. Salazar had taken a wooden quarrel right to the chest. A shot like that would've put me into hibernation. If I'd had any doubts before that the Master vampire was strong, they had vanished completely.

"You!" Stick stood and pointed at one of the human guards,

who straightened. Walking around the desk, Stick pointed back to the floor. "The stake needs to be removed. Take it out!"

"Sir!" Putting down the cooler, the guard rushed forward. Quickly, he hurried around the desk and dropped to his knees beside the Prince. Bending down, he vanished momentarily, and then stood a moment later, the bloody stick gripped triumphantly in one hand.

"I have it, sir," the guard said, looking at Stick. But Stick didn't move, didn't say anything. Just watched him with hooded, patient eyes. The guard frowned, confused, and opened his mouth to speak—when Salazar rose up from behind and plunged his fangs into the side of the man's neck.

I jumped. The guard let out a strangled gasp and went rigid, the stake dropping from nerveless fingers. Salazar tore at his throat, shredding flesh and muscle, blind in his Hunger, and the guard started to spasm. Stick and the vampire guards looked on impassively, their faces blank. But I glanced at Zeke, standing forgotten behind Stick and the other human, and his expression was grim, his fists clenched at his sides.

The Prince dropped the still-twitching guard to the floor with a hollow thud and turned blazing dark eyes on me. Blood smeared his lips, was spattered in vivid flecks across his face, and soaked his once-white collar. There was a crimson stain on the front of his shirt where the stake had been. I tensed, gripping the handle of my sword as the Prince stepped forward, over the corpse, his fury a terrifying storm that filled the whole room.

"Kanin's daughter!"

I winced as his booming voice shook the walls, making

the air tremble. Even the guards looked nervous, and a few backed away from me.

"You," the Prince snarled, baring his fangs in my direction. "A curse on you and all your line! If my city was not in such dire straits, I would hang you outside my window to meet the sun. As it is, Kanin's daughter, you will find Sarren, and you will bring him to me alive. I don't care what it takes or where you must go, if you have to scour the streets of the Fringe and fight your way through infected madmen until you reach him, that is what you are going to do. If Sarren knows how to stop this plague, he will tell me. If he knows of a cure, I will peel the truth from him, bit by bit. One way or another, I will get answers, and if you wish to leave my city alive, you will deliver him to me."

It's never a good idea to argue with a pissed-off Master vampire, but I still raised my chin, met his furious gaze, and said, "I'm not going anywhere without Kanin."

His glare grew even colder. "I am in no mood to play games, Kanin's daughter," Salazar said in a low, controlled voice. "You tread on dangerous ground right now, so think very carefully on your demands."

"Why do you need us to find Sarren?" I asked in a calm, reasonable voice. "You have a whole tower of minions—"

He cut me off. "Sending humans after Sarren is useless. I might as well tear their heads off myself. And with the chaos out in the Fringe, I find myself rather short staffed at the moment." He seemed to grow even more irritable, admitting that. "I do not have the resources needed for a full-scale manhunt, so I will have to be content with what is available. You claim to have dealt with Sarren before—bring him to me and I will let you live. Fail me and you will die, either at Sarren's hands or my own. Make your decision."

"Okay. Fine." I swallowed and kept my voice calm. "You want us to find Sarren and bring him back. He's the only one who might know of a cure. He's also completely insane, and he's already taken apart four vampires and nearly succeeded in killing us all. Besides that, we don't know where he's gone, and the more time we spend chasing him, the worse New Covington will get." I paused to gauge Salazar's reaction to this. His expression was cold, unimpressed, but he wasn't arguing with me or ordering his guards to kill us. That was something, at least.

"The one who knows Sarren," I went on, praying this would work, "the only one who might be able to tell us where he is, what his next move will be, is Kanin. And if we do run into Psycho Vamp again, Kanin is the only one who might be able to stop him. You want Sarren?" I took my last gamble. "Let Kanin go. He's your best chance to save this city."

Salazar's jaw tightened. The idea infuriated him, to have Kanin right where he wanted him, only to have him slip through his fingers. But his hatred for Sarren was stronger now. "Very well," he said with great dignity. "I will release the damned one to you, on the condition that he will help you bring Sarren to me. However, if he tries to escape, or if you attempt to flee New Covington, I will hunt you both down myself. And if that happens, you will wish I had chosen to leave Kanin chained to a wall."

I tried to contain my relief. Kanin was free. I would finally rescue my sire. If—and my stomach curled—if there was still anything left of him in that mind shattered from Hunger and torture.

Salazar seemed to read my mind. "Of course," he added, looking faintly pleased now, "let us hope that Kanin is sane enough to help you. We might go down to his cell and find nothing remains but a Lost One."

And that would just make your night, wouldn't it? I swallowed the anger and bit my tongue, stopping the words that would get me into trouble. *You'd love to see Kanin reduced to that. But it's not going to help you in the end, because if Kanin is gone, I'm not going to bring Sarren back. I'm going to kill him.*

"About time." Forgotten beside me, Jackal suddenly stirred and pulled himself to his feet, gritting his teeth. His fangs were out, and his eyes gleamed a little too brightly as he straightened. "Don't anyone get up, I wouldn't want my near death to inconvenience you." He eyed the cooler, still sitting on the floor, then stared at the remaining human guard standing beside it. His lips curled, making him look as if he was barely holding himself back, and the human gulped. "You gonna eat that, Prince, or should I find someone else?"

Salazar made a dismissive gesture. The guard quickly opened the cooler, pulled out a blood bag, and tossed it to Jackal, who caught it and, even though he was starving, took a moment to give the Prince a mocking salute before biting through the plastic. Blood spurted, ran through his fingers and dripped to the floor, and I saw Zeke look away.

"Maybe you should stay here," I told Jackal, who ignored me in favor of savaging the blood bag. Uneasiness flickered. I knew that one bag wouldn't completely heal him, and I didn't want another half-starved vampire at my back when

I went down to see Kanin. Plus, according to Jackal, he and Kanin hadn't parted on the best of terms. Our sire wasn't in the clearest state of mind right now; seeing Jackal might send him over the edge into violence. I couldn't afford that.

"Wait up here," I told Jackal again. "I'll be back with Kanin as soon as I can."

He tossed the empty bag to the floor and grinned at me through a wet smear of red. "You do that," he said, licking blood off his bottom lip. Turning to the guard still beside the cooler, he snapped fingers at him, and the human pulled out another bag. Jackal caught it with a grimace. "You go ahead and play with Kanin," he told me. "I'll be here. Oh, and the little bloodbag should probably wait this one out, too. If Kanin is that starved, one whiff of human will make him absolutely nuts."

Dammit, I hadn't thought of that. I did not want to leave Zeke with a bunch of hungry, sadistic vampires. I especially didn't want to leave him here with Jackal. But Jackal was right. It was hard enough to resist biting a human when I was a *little* hungry. I couldn't imagine the depth of torment Kanin was feeling, but I knew that the mere sight or scent of a human would probably drive him completely insane. Zeke couldn't be there.

Zeke crossed the room, coming to stand beside me. His voice was low and calm as he leaned in. "What do you need me to do, Allie?"

I swallowed. "Jackal is right." I looked up into his solemn blue eyes, hoping he would understand. "I need you to stay here."

He nodded. "I don't like it, but…I trust you know what

you're doing." He squeezed my hand, and I looked away. "Just promise me you'll be careful. I know we need him, and that he's important to you, but don't get yourself killed, okay?" He stepped closer, his voice dropping to a near whisper as he leaned in. "You're important to me, too, so remember that when you're down there."

"Zeke." I caught his gaze as he pulled back. His face was sincere, unguarded, no shadow of mistrust or suspicion lingering in his eyes. And something else in that open gaze made my stomach clench. I'd seen that look before, right before he had kissed me. I remembered his lips on mine, the warmth of his touch, the feelings he stirred. They were still there, rising up from the darkness, the part of me that refused to submit to the monster and the Hunger raging inside. The part that was still human.

I also caught Stick watching us from across the room, his mouth pulled into a thin line, his expression hooded and dark.

"If you are quite ready." Salazar's voice was coldly exasperated, and he turned hollow black eyes on me. "Wait for me in the hall. I must take care of a few things here, and then I will show you to the dungeon."

CHAPTER 13

I stood next to Salazar and two of his vampire guards on the long elevator ride down, trying hard not to fidget and glance at the numbers every half second. Every so often, the box would shudder or hit some kind of snag, making me clench my fists. I told myself that we were fine, that Salazar wouldn't use the elevator if it wasn't safe. Of course, Salazar had taken a crossbow dart right to the chest and survived, so a hundred-foot fall in a tiny metal box probably didn't worry him too much. He had changed into a new suit jacket, and he looked as pristine and perfectly groomed as ever. He had also warned me, in no uncertain terms, never to speak of the events in the office, and left Stick in charge of "cleaning up" when we left. I had no doubt that, when and if we returned, all traces of the carnage Sarren had left behind would be gone. Except maybe the broken window.

Where was Sarren now? I wondered. Was he still out there somewhere, lurking in the city? Or had he already left New

Covington, which would make finding him and bringing him back next to impossible?

I couldn't think about that. Kanin was my priority right now. One thing at a time. We'd worry about Sarren once I'd dealt with my sire.

Zeke and Jackal had been taken to separate rooms upstairs, so at least for now, they were safe. That was my only comfort as the lift shuddered and groaned, making me grit my teeth and wish, yet again, that there was another way down. Screw ancient technology or whatever old power made these things work—what was wrong with taking the stairs?

Finally, finally, the elevator squealed to a grinding, clanking halt and the doors swished open with an obscenely cheerful *ding.* I forced myself to walk out calmly and not leap through the doors as soon as they moved. Salazar and the guards followed, stepping into a narrow, dim hallway. The Prince's shoes echoed briskly against the tiled floor as he led us down the corridor to the door at the end. A guard stood beside the frame and straightened quickly as the Prince strode up.

"Sir!" He bowed, and the Prince nodded absently, gazing through the small square window in the door.

"Is Dr. Emerson inside?"

"Yes, sir. He's been with the patients all night."

"Any changes?"

The guard shook his head. "We had to put a couple down this evening. The screaming was getting to be too much. Sir."

"I see." No change in Salazar's expression, but his voice dropped several degrees. "Open the door."

"Yes, sir."

We swept through the door into a stark white room that

reeked of blood and chemicals. Curtained sections with individual beds lined one wall, and every one of them held a body, some covered with a thin sheet. Low cries and moans of anguish drifted through the air as the bodies thrashed weakly, held to their beds by thick leather straps. Several pale figures in white coats moved among the cots, checking on and tending to patients, which seemed odd to me. A hospital in the bowels of a vampire tower? Vampires taking care of human patients? Something was definitely wrong with this picture. Or were they experimenting on them, like the patients in the D.C. lab? My stomach churned at the thought.

Another vampire broke away from one of the cots and walked toward us, staring at a clipboard and shaking his head. He had been a young man at the time of his Turning, with short brown hair and a handsome, beardless face. But his dark eyes held a clinical impassiveness that belied his youthful appearance. Leafing through his clipboard, he didn't seem to notice us until he was just a few yards from the Prince and one of the guards cleared his throat.

"I know you're there," the vampire said without looking up. And though his voice was young, he sounded like an exasperated grandfather being prodded by a relentless family member. "No need to grunt and growl at me until I make eye contact."

The guards stiffened as if offended by this, but the Prince remained unruffled. "Dr. Emerson," Salazar greeted in his cool, low voice. "I hope we are not disturbing you."

"Not at all. At this point, I'm so disturbed that anything else will seem tame compared to the week I've had." The vampire finally lowered his clipboard and faced Salazar, his eyes dull and exhausted. "What can I do for you, my Prince?"

"What is the status of those infected?"

"At this point?" Dr. Emerson shook his head. "They're fucked. Sorry to put it so bluntly, but that's how it is. I'm probably going to need a whole new batch to study by the end of the week. I might start shooting this group in the head to get them to stop screeching and babbling at me nonstop."

I was suddenly glad that Zeke wasn't here. Salazar didn't seem amused, either. "I will not risk sending my people out into the Fringe to retrieve more test subjects for you, Dr. Emerson. You will have to make do with these." He stared hard at the other vampire, who dropped his gaze. "Have you made any progress at all?"

Emerson started to reply, but suddenly noticed me, waiting rather impatiently behind the Prince and trying not to say anything. I didn't know why we had stopped, and I really didn't care. I was only here for Kanin.

"Who's this?" Emerson asked in a tone that suggested I might get in his way or knock over something important. I narrowed my eyes and scowled back. "Are you sure it's wise to bring civilians down here, my Prince? If she forgets herself and bites one of the patients—"

"That will be my concern, not yours," Salazar interrupted. "And we are not staying long."

Thank goodness, I thought. *Get me out of this creepy place. I want to find Kanin.*

"I have but one request before we go," Salazar continued, and I bit down my impatience, tapping my heel against the floor. "Our 'volunteer.' Is he still alive?"

Emerson's face fell, making him look far older. "Yes," he murmured. "Barely. By now, I wonder if we shouldn't just take his head and put him out of his misery." He looked at the Prince for consent, but Salazar didn't give it, just continued to watch him with blank eyes. The doctor nodded slowly. "You want to see him? Follow me."

"I thought we were going to see Kanin," I told Salazar as we trailed the doctor down another hallway, the guards close at our back. "You gave your word you would release him, and I'm not going after Psycho Vamp without him."

The Prince gave me a cold smile.

"Patience, girl. I assure you, Kanin is not going anywhere. Before you meet your sire, I want you to see this."

We'd come to a door in the side of the hallway, marked with a strange yellow-and-black sign in the center. WARNING, it read in bulky letters, but before I could read the rest, Emerson unlocked the door and pushed it open.

Salazar motioned for me to go in. Cautiously, wary of things that might leap at me through the door, I stepped inside. The room was dark, lined with shelves of instruments that winked at me in the shadows. Nothing moved or made a sound, until I heard a low groan coming from the far corner. A curtain hung from the ceiling, obscuring whatever was there from view, but beyond the sheets, something was moving.

Resisting the urge to draw my sword, I stepped up and pushed back the curtain.

A rotting corpse lay there on a mattress, flesh decayed and blackened in areas, showing hints of bone beneath. I could see the chest cavity, where the skin had withered and shriveled away, and ribs poked up through disintegrating flesh. Some of its fingers were missing, either fallen off or lost as it had thrashed around in life, for leather cuffs still encircled the bony wrists, tying it to the bed. Its skull lay on the pillow, gazing sightlessly at the ceiling, much of the skin rotted away. I saw the curve of bone in its jaw, the outline of teeth through its wasted cheek. And just as I was wondering why Salazar would show me this, the corpse turned its head and stared at me with bright, glassy eyes, opening its mouth in a silent scream, and I nearly bolted from the room.

It was a *vampire,* or it had been, once. I could see its fangs, hear the click of teeth as it opened and closed its mouth, silently gaping at me. Like it was trying to speak, but was unable to make a sound. Horror twisted my stomach when I saw his eyes, glazed over with agony but conscious and alert. He knew what was happening to him.

"Disturbing, is it not?" Salazar said over my shoulder. The vampire Prince moved beside me, staring blankly down at the living, rotting corpse.

"What happened to him?" I asked.

The Prince put a hand on the bed railing. "He was volunteered for an experiment, and given the infected blood of the humans in the Fringe. This is what happens when we feed on the sick outside. Not only does the virus affect humans, it carries over to any vampire who bites one of the infected. We start to rot away from the inside, until our bodies are so damaged they cannot sustain us anymore."

A virus that attacked not only humans but vampires. No wonder the city vamps were freaking out. What had Sarren done? Salazar turned from the body and stared at me with hard black eyes, his expression grim and frightening.

"Now you understand why we must find this madman," he said. "If Sarren truly caused this, we must stop at nothing until we capture him and force him to give us a cure. Otherwise, New Covington will be lost." Without taking his eyes from me, he gestured to the vampire in the bed. "Remember what you have seen tonight, Kanin's daughter. If Sarren is not found, we could all end up like this."

I could only nod. Salazar studied me a moment longer, then turned away. I gazed at the horrific, rotting corpse one last time, seeing his mouth gape, pleading silently for death, before I shuddered and hurried after the Prince.

One of the other vamps met us at the door with a cooler, which he handed solemnly to a guard. Then we followed the Prince through another set of doors, another maze of hallways and, finally, down a long flight of steps that continued past several floors until it seemed we were miles below the surface.

Just as I was about to ask Salazar how deep this place went, the stairwell ended at a pair of massive steel doors, padlocked shut and barred from the outside. Salazar gestured, and we waited as the vampire guards removed the bar, unlocked the chains and pushed the doors open with an earsplitting groan.

The room beyond was dank and cold, carved from natural stone. Cement pillars marched down the aisle, and cells with thick iron bars lined either side. A bloated, hulking figure lumbered toward us, a vampire whose head nearly brushed the low ceiling, whose eyes were beady and cruel. His bottom jaw didn't quite fit the top half, and jagged teeth poked from his mouth like shards of bone. He loomed over the Prince and the guards, eyeing me curiously, until Salazar snapped his fingers.

"Take us to Kanin."

The huge jailor grunted then turned, lurching away down the corridor. We followed him, stepping over puddles and weaving around pillars, until we came to the last cell.

My skin felt tight, crawling with nerves. Through the bars, I could see a pale, ragged shape, shirtless and filthy, huddled against the far corner. Salazar and the guards didn't move, but I edged closer until I was touching the cell door, peering in. Heavy iron chains dangled from rings set into the wall, jangling softly as the figure shifted on the hard ground. I couldn't see his face, but I could suddenly feel him watching me.

"Kanin," I whispered. "I'm here."

He raised his head, and my insides shrank in fear and horror. The face was his: it *was* Kanin, but the man staring across the cell at me was a mere shadow of my mentor. His skin was chalky-white, stretched tightly across his bones, withered and gaunt. His eyes were hollow, sunken and stared at me with no spark of recognition, no sense of self, nothing but Hunger. His lips curled back, revealing deadly fangs, and he lunged at me with a roar.

I jerked back, even as the chains brought him up short, several feet from the bars. Kanin roared again, straining to reach us, his face a terrifying mask of Hunger and rage.

I felt sick, close to tears, and swallowed hard to control myself. I'd come so far, put everyone through so much, just to find my sire. And now that I'd finally found him…he was gone. Driven to madness by Sarren's cruelty and Salazar's hatred. I never thought I'd see him like this. Despite everything, I'd always thought Kanin was too strong, too wise and composed and stubborn to turn into the savage creature in the cell. A Lost One, like Salazar had said.

I clenched my fists. No. No, I wouldn't give up on him. There had to be something left. Kanin was starving and crazy with bloodlust, but that didn't mean he was gone. He was too strong for that.

The hiss of plastic drew my attention, and I turned to see one of the guards open the cooler and pull out two blood-bags. Their attention, and the attention of the monstrous jailor, was on Kanin, still hissing and snarling at the end of his chains. But Salazar was watching me, a small, pleased smile on his face.

"He can't hear you now, girl," the Prince said over the mad snarling coming from the cell. "He doesn't recognize you, or me, or anyone. All he knows at this moment is Hunger. Let us hope that his mind is still intact when he comes out of his blood frenzy."

Anger flickered, but I pushed it down. I watched the guards approach the cell, and stepped aside as they very cautiously reached through the bars, being careful not to lean too far in. I could see the fear in their eyes. Kanin hissed and snarled, fighting to get to them, a demon barely restrained.

They tossed the bags at his feet, and he fell on them instantly. I forced myself to watch, even though it was hard, seeing him like this. A mindless animal. He ripped the bags to shreds in seconds, gulping down the blood inside, until his lips and hands were dripping with red and the floor of his cell was splattered with it.

At last, the savage feeding came to an end. Growling softly in his throat, Kanin slowly rose, dropping the mangled plastic. For a moment, he just stood there, staring at the bloody floor of his cell, his expression blank. Then, without looking at us, he slowly backed away. Hitting the wall, he slid down until he was hunched over on the floor, staring straight ahead, at nothing.

Salazar turned to me.

"Now it is up to you," he said, dropping a small iron key into my palm. "If you think you can reach him, you may go into his cell and free him from his chains. But be warned—if he is truly Lost, he will attack you viciously, and if that happens, we will not open the cell door again. You will be trapped with a mindless, savage Master vampire, and he will tear you apart. So be very certain, Kanin's daughter. Are you sure you want to do this? Do you trust your sire that much?"

I closed my fist around the key. "Just open the door."

He nodded and motioned to the jailor. The massive vampire drew a ring of keys from somewhere beneath his bloated stomach, inserted one into the cell lock and pulled back the door with a rusty screech.

If I were alive, my heart would've been slamming against my ribs as I approached the cell and slipped through the frame, the key clenched tight in my fist. I took one step forward, and the door shut behind me with a clang, trapping me in the small space with a half-crazed Master vampire fully capable of taking me apart. I gazed at the huddled figure against the wall and shivered. If Kanin attacked me, I would have to defend myself with lethal force. Even if he was shackled and I was armed, he was still far stronger and far more deadly than anything I would ever face. Even if I got away from him, Salazar wouldn't open the door to let me escape, he'd made that very clear. If my sire was truly Lost, if he came at me with nothing on his mind but Hunger, the only way I'd leave this cell would be if I killed him.

Slowly but deliberately, I moved forward until I stood just shy of how far his chains would stretch. Kanin remained still, staring at the floor. But I felt his awareness shift, stirring to my presence. Even though he wasn't looking at me, he knew I was there.

"Kanin," I said very, very softly, ready to surge back if he lunged. "It's Allison. Can you hear me?"

Nothing. No movement or sound from Kanin's hunched figure, though I could still feel his cold stare, aware of my every move. "I'm going to try to set you free," I continued, slowly gathering the nerve to take that first, and perhaps final, step. "I don't know if you can understand what I'm saying right now," I went on, searching for any sign that he was at least listening, "but I'd appreciate it if you didn't try to kill me when I get close."

Again, there was nothing. Kanin shifted just the tiniest bit, making his chains clink against the wall, but he gave no indication that he'd heard. And, standing in that filthy cell, just a few feet from the man who had saved my life, Turned me into a vampire and taught me everything I needed to survive, I suddenly realized…that I was afraid. Of Kanin. Not because I could lose him, though there was that, too. I was afraid to step forward, because I didn't know him anymore, because I'd seen the true demon that lay beneath that smooth, unruffled facade, and it was terrifying. We were all like that, deep down. Stripped of our awareness, our presence of mind, our logic and reason, we were all just monsters waiting to feed.

This was what my demon looked like. What I could become. What Zeke could never see.

I shook myself. This was getting me nowhere. If Kanin was Lost, he was Lost, and nothing I did now would bring him back. The only thing left to do was to see if his mind was still intact, or if I was going to have to cut him down before he could kill me.

I clenched my fist…and stepped forward, into his reach.

Kanin didn't move. I took another step. And another. Until I was right beside him, gazing down at the top of his head. Relief hammered through me, but I didn't relax. Standing this close to Kanin felt like watching a rabid that hadn't quite noticed me yet. But once it did…

With slow, cautious movements, I knelt beside him. He stirred faintly, and I heard a low growl that made me freeze, but he still didn't attack.

My hands were shaking. I bit my cheek to steady myself then smoothly reached for his arm and the iron shackle on one wrist.

He let me take it without protest, without spinning around and lunging at me with bared fangs. My heart rose a bit higher, but we weren't out of here yet.

Still shaking, I put the key into the metal band at his wrist, turning slowly until it clicked under my fingers. The shackle loosened and dropped away with a clink.

And Kanin moved.

His head came up, turning to me. As if he'd just realized I was there, how close I was. For a split second, I met his blank, glassy stare, daring to hope.

Then his lips curled back from his fangs, and I knew I was dead.

I threw myself backward as Kanin lunged, snarling, his eyes bright with madness. Getting clear was the only thing on my mind now, putting distance between myself and this vicious demon who could easily rip me apart. I wasn't nearly fast enough. Kanin grabbed my leg and dragged me to him, hissing, and I howled in fear, kicking at his chest. He yanked me beneath him, and one hand clamped over my throat, squeezing hard. Thankfully, I didn't need to breathe, but my vision went red with pain—he was *so strong!*

"Kanin!" My fingers grabbed the hand on my throat, the other groped for my sword—hard to do while pinned on my back. "Dammit, get a hold of yourself! It's me—"

His grip tightened, crushing my windpipe, and I gagged on the words. Standing, Kanin yanked me upright, turned and slammed me into the wall. My head struck the stone with a sickening crack, but I barely felt that pain as Kanin brought his head down and sank his teeth into the side of my neck.

I went rigid, unable to move. For just a moment, I was there again, the night I was Turned, where I died, Kanin's fangs in my throat. It did not feel the same. My last night as a human, I remembered the pain, but also an intoxicating pleasure and warmth that had radiated from my core, soothing me to sleep, to death.

This was nothing like that. This was pure, blinding agony. With the exception of a wooden stake through the gut, it was the most painful thing I'd ever felt. I couldn't move, I couldn't even think. My mind emptied of all rational thought, except for one memory that flashed across my consciousness, clear as day.

"Vampires do not feed from each other," Kanin had told me once in the hidden lab. *"One, feeding from our kind does nothing for the Hunger. In some cases it can make it worse. Two, forcibly taking blood from a vampire will cause that vampire untold pain. It's one of*

the most violent, intrusive acts we can commit on another kindred, and is viewed as barbaric and needlessly cruel by most."

"Ew," I had responded, making a face. "Good to know. So, vampires don't bite each other? Ever?"

"I said we don't feed *from each other," my mentor replied in that infuriating way of his. "However, on rare occasions, two vampires who are attracted to one another will sometimes share blood. It becomes more of a sensual thing, the desire to offer a part of themselves, to feel close to another, rather than the need to sate the Hunger."*

"Ewww," I'd said again, with a little more emphasis. "Well, thanks so much for that lovely image. Let's just say I'm not going to let any vampire near my throat, now or ever. I can promise you that."

The memory flickered and was gone in an instant, leaving nothing but pain behind. And a savage regret that I hadn't heeded my own promise. "Kanin," I gritted out, my voice harsh and ragged. I tried to make my arms move, to push him off, but he growled and sank his fangs in deeper, making me gasp. I closed my eyes, clenching my jaw to keep from screaming. "Kanin, s-stop. Please."

Abruptly, Kanin froze. He still had me pinned to the wall, but the hand around my throat loosened the slightest bit, and his fangs *finally* slid from my neck. I shuddered, slumping in relief as the vampire paused for a long moment, his brow furrowed as if trying to remember something.

"You…" The voice was low and raspy, as if it hadn't been used in a long, long time. Kanin blinked, and his gaze shifted to me, still confused, tormented by indecision. But his eyes were clearer now, the glassiness fading into the black. "I… know you."

I nodded painfully. "It's me," I whispered, my own voice ragged and faint. My throat burned, raw from abuse, but I tried to keep my gaze steady. "That night in the rain, when you saved me from the rabids? Do you remember?"

He stared at me, frowning. I watched his face, watched him struggle to claw himself out of the dark pit of madness, back into the light. *Come on, Kanin,* I urged him. *You're stronger than this. You're almost there. Please, don't make me lose you again.*

Kanin closed his eyes, his face tormented. When he opened them, I saw the last of the madness fade away, and for a moment, his expression was a raw, gaping wound. Horror, shame, guilt and despair lay open on his face as he looked down at me, recognition breaking through at last.

"Allison."

I almost collapsed in relief. "Yeah," I whispered, forcing a pained smile as he stared at me as if I were a ghost. "It's me. Damn you, Kanin. You were a pain in the ass to find, you know that?"

Kanin didn't answer. Without warning, his hands rose, pressing to either side of my face as I went rigid. His stare was awed, hopeful, as if he couldn't quite believe I was real and had to touch me to make sure I wasn't a phantom.

"You're here." I barely caught the whisper, and Kanin's eyes closed again as he bowed his head. It was a broken sound, a man desperately grasping at the last thread of hope, when he had been in the darkness for so long. "You came."

And, as I stood, shocked, against the wall of the cell, Kanin sank to his knees in front of me, holding the backs of my legs. The top of his bowed head pressed against my thighs. "You came," he repeated, a chant holding him to sanity. I swallowed the lump in my throat and touched his broad shoulders, biting my lip to keep the tears in check, as the cell door opened with a creak, and the Prince beckoned us both to freedom.

CHAPTER 14

Zeke was waiting for me when the elevator doors opened with their annoying ding. Leaning against the wall with his arms crossed, he straightened quickly as I stepped into the hall with Salazar and the guards, relieved as ever to be on solid ground.

"Oh God, Allie," he said, worried blue eyes straying to my neck, the blood on my skin and collar. "Are you all right? What happened?"

"I'm fine." My fingers went self-consciously to my throat, feeling the slight punctures Kanin had left behind. "It's nothing. I've already fed, don't worry about it." Dr. Emerson had given me a blood bag when I emerged from the dungeon with Kanin and the Prince, and though it was cold and disgusting, I'd choked it down. The wounds hadn't closed completely, and even now, my neck still ached where Kanin had bitten me. The doctor insisted that was normal, that the pain would fade in a day or two, though the faint, tiny scars might remain forever. It was just the nature of a vampire biting one of his own.

Emerson had also insisted that Kanin remain under supervision for at least a night, claiming that, even with a vampire's remarkable healing, it would still be a few days for a vampire to fully recover after being starved for so long. My sire was down in the hospital wing now, being watched carefully by vampiric doctors and several guards, but he was no longer going mad in a lonely dungeon. I had felt a little apprehensive about leaving him, since I'd come so far to find him, but Salazar had assured me he would be well taken care of. That Kanin was a guest in his tower now, and all his needs would be met. That there was no need to worry about my sire; he would allow no harm to befall him, for any reason.

I believed him. After all, he needed Kanin alive and well to go after Sarren.

Salazar regarded me with blank eyes. "I have business to attend," he stated, bored and coldly polite once more. "If you have need of me, please inform a pet or a guard. I've told you where you can find your temporary quarters, and the servants can attend to your other needs. Feel free to wander about, but remember, you are not to leave the tower until you are ready to go after Sarren. I suggest you do that soon. Tomorrow, perhaps. As soon as the sun goes down."

"We'll leave when Kanin is well enough," I said flatly. The Prince's mouth twitched in a humorless smile.

"Trust me, girl. You do not have long. And neither does Kanin."

He strode away with his guards, leaving me to ponder

that ominous statement and hope he was just making empty threats.

Zeke stepped close and hesitantly put his hands on my waist, watching me intently. "Did you find Kanin?" he asked, drawing me against him. "Is he all right?"

"Yeah." I put my hands on his chest, splaying my fingers, feeling his heart beat under my palm. Funny how such a simple thing like a heartbeat could fascinate me now that I didn't have one. Or maybe it was just Zeke's heart that I was fascinated with. "I think he's going to be fine."

His hand rose to brush the hair off my shoulder, fingers gently skimming the dried blood on my neck. My stomach danced, even though the Hunger stirred at the contact, like a sleepy, sated beast. "I was worried about you," he whispered.

"What? Why?" I tried to ignore my fluttering insides, the fingers tracing soft patterns against my skin. "This is nothing, Zeke. Hell, I've been shot, stabbed, staked, bludgeoned, cut open and thrown out a window. Super vampire healing, remember? A couple little bite marks aren't going to slow me down."

"It's not the physical scars that are the most painful," Zeke said. "I know you can take care of yourself, probably better than anyone. Certainly better than me." He smiled a little, reminding me of how handsome he was when he smiled. How he could make my cold heart stutter when he did that. "But I know you, Allie. Even if Kanin was Lost, like Salazar said, you wouldn't have given up on him. You would have kept trying to save him, whether he could be saved or not. It's just how you are."

Since when? I thought, giving him a dubious look. He chuckled.

"You know it's true." He brushed a thumb across my cheek, his gaze intense. "I didn't see Jackal down there, risking his life. Just you." His voice went low and soft, tinted with a little regret. "I'd forgotten how incredible you really are."

The Hunger stirred again, and I tensed. *Getting too close, Allison. It doesn't matter what Zeke thinks of you—you're still a vampire and he's still human. This won't end well, and you're not helping either of you.*

"Speaking of which, where is Jackal?" I said, pulling back. Zeke let me go, looking disappointed but resigned. "I should tell him what happened—not that he cares, but he should at least know that Kanin is safe."

I also wanted to tell them both what I had discovered in that cold hospital room, the horrible truth about what Sarren had really unleashed. I remembered the dying vampire, the flesh slowly rotting away as it stared at me, pleading and hopeless, and felt ill. The Prince was right. Bargain or no, we had to find Sarren, force a cure from him. Before this new virus wiped out both our races.

First things first, though, and that was Kanin's recovery.

"Last I saw him," Zeke said, "he went upstairs with a few other vampires. They were having some sort of gathering, I think. I'm not really sure, I didn't want to stick around. A couple were starting to stare at me like I was the main course."

I bristled at the thought of Zeke in a crowded room of vampires, all eyeing him hungrily. He didn't have any weapons on him now and would make an easy target. Just another human to be fed upon and discarded.

"Come on," I told him, starting down the hall. "Let's go see if we can find the lazy bastard. We're here to do something, not sit around sipping blood from wineglasses and cozying up to the vamps of the Inner Court."

We wandered the many hallways and rooms for a while, searching for the raider king. The tower was like a maze of sterile tile floors and glass windows and, after a while, all the rooms began to look the same. We avoided the elevator and took the stairs between floors, passing well-dressed humans and even better dressed vampires on their way to whatever vampirey business took place around here. Many of the vamps, seeing me in my long black coat and scruffy boots, regarded me with disdain, like I was a mongrel dog come in off the streets. I ignored them, unless their attention shifted to Zeke. Then I would give them a hard stare and the hint of a curled lip, and they would either smirk or stare coldly back before continuing on.

"I wish I had my knife," Zeke muttered as we ducked into another stairwell, continuing toward the top. His voice echoed hollowly in the dark passageway. "Or a stake. Or something to defend myself with. Now I know what a rabbit feels every time a wolf passes by." He rubbed his arm, frowning. "I wonder how the humans working here can stand it."

"I'll make sure Salazar gives you back your weapons when we head out," I told him, stepping into yet another identical hallway. "Until then, you probably don't want to draw a lot of attention to yourself."

"Yeah." He stabbed his fingers through his hair, looking up and down the empty corridor. "It's just frustrating. I know

I'm deadweight right now. If anything happens, I won't be much use."

"You are *not* deadweight." Anyone who could face down Sarren with nothing but a crossbow and still come out of it alive was anything but useless.

He just smiled grimly.

I was about to protest again when a strange noise began to filter down the hall, making me blink and cock my head. It was faint, melodic and unlike anything I'd ever heard. I couldn't even describe it. The closest thing I could think of was someone using a pipe to bang a tune on another pipe, but that was just *noise.* This was haunting and eerie and full of emotion and sound, like sadness or longing given voice.

Unable to resist, I followed the strange tune down the corridor, past a pair of open doors, and into some kind of gathering place. This room was carpeted in red, with plush black couches and chairs surrounding low tables, and a glass wall showing the ruined cityscape beyond.

Vampires lounged in corners or on couches, looking elegant and bored, their pale skin a stark contrast to the red-and-black furniture. Uniformed humans slipped among them, carrying trays of wineglasses—blood, of course—and whisking away the empty cups. On the right, a black marble counter dominated the wall, with a couple vampires seated at the bar, a weary-faced human behind it. I frowned when I saw none other than Jackal seated at one of the stools, glass in hand, talking to a lithe vampire woman with long blond hair. But I wasn't focused on him at this point; my attention was on the large object sitting in the far corner.

The one making the strange, haunting noise. A human

sat in front of it, his hands moving over a black-and-white shelf set into the dark, polished wood. I stared, entranced. The sounds it was making, the eerie cacophony of emotion, pulled at my insides and made my throat feel tight. I closed my eyes, letting the sound flow through me, forgetting everything for the moment.

I heard Zeke's footsteps behind me, felt him gazing over my shoulder at the device making the strange, terrible, beautiful sounds.

"A piano," he said, his voice full of awe. "I haven't seen one since I was a kid. The old church used to have one, very out of tune, I remember. Of course, me banging on it every week probably didn't help."

"A piano?" I opened my eyes as I scoured my memory for the word, finding vague, half-forgotten stories. "This… is music?"

Zeke turned to me, blinking. "You've never heard music before?" He sounded stunned.

I shook my head, unable to tear my gaze from the strange instrument. The Fringe was full of ugly noises: screams, shouting, cries of terror and anger and pain. My mother used to hum to me when I was very little, and I used to think her voice was the most beautiful sound in the world. I had never heard anything…like this.

"Oh, Allie," Zeke whispered, and stepped up beside me. "Come here a second."

Taking my hand, he drew me aside, to the back of the room where the shadows were the thickest, away from the vampires near the bar. I gave a puzzled frown, tensing, as he put my hands on his shoulders and drew me close, wrapping an arm around my waist.

"What are we doing?"

He smiled sadly and put a hand over mine, his eyes asking me to trust him. "Just follow my lead," he murmured, and began swaying back and forth, a slow, easy rhythm.

I resisted a moment, unsure of what to do. Gradually, though, I began to feel what he was doing, moving in time to the…music, and started to follow. It was strange, this slow, unhurried motion, our bodies mirroring each other as we swayed and circled, but somehow it felt right. We didn't stray from that corner, remaining in the shadows, but Zeke pulled me against him and I closed my eyes, and for just a few heartbeats, with the music and darkness swirling around us, we were lost in our own world.

"I missed you, you know," Zeke murmured, bending his head to mine. I clenched my fingers in his shirt and listened to his pounding heart. "The whole time I was in Eden, I couldn't stop thinking of you. When I woke up and they told me you had gone…" He shook his head, and his heartbeat sped up. "I wanted to come after you right then, but I knew I had to take care of the others, that they were my first, my most important, responsibility. And I did. They're safe, every single one of them, even though I had to let them go."

"Let them go?"

He swallowed hard, and his grip on me tightened. "Caleb, Matthew and Bethany were adopted by a great couple who always wanted kids. They have chickens and cats and goats, and everything they could ever want. Jake actually married one of the nurses at the checkpoint clinic, and Silas and Teresa moved into a little cottage by the lake's edge. They're happy. They're finally home." His eyes glimmered, even as he gave a faint smile. "They don't need me anymore."

"Zeke..."

He gazed at me, his expression so tender I felt my heart constrict. "There was just one person missing," Zeke whispered, his hand framing my face. "One person I couldn't bring home."

I gave him a sad smile. "Eden isn't my home."

"It could be."

I shook my head. "How?" I whispered. "That is the one place in the whole world where there are no vampires or rabids, the one place where humans are free, and you're saying they'd let a vampire just walk in? With no consequences whatsoever?" I gave a rueful, not-quite smile. "They already kicked me out once, Zeke. I told you before, Eden isn't for me."

Zeke ran his fingers through my hair. "You're not like the others," he murmured. "I know you. I've seen you." He drew me closer. "You're the one vampire in the world they might let in. When this is all over, you could come back with me. We could go to Eden together—"

"Stop," I whispered, putting my hands on his chest. This was getting dangerous. Again. The Hunger emerged once more, making want to step close, pull him to me and sink my fangs into his neck. Zeke gazed down at me, pleading, and I kept my voice firm. "I can't, Zeke. I'm still a vampire. That won't ever change. You don't know me as well as you think."

Kanin's face swam across my mind, vicious and snarling, a demon fueled only by Hunger and rage. If the Hunger could overtake even one like Kanin, what hope did I have to keep it contained? The bite marks at my neck suddenly throbbed, making me wince. If I reverted to that while in Eden, if Zeke or Bethany were nearby…

No, that would never happen, because I would not get that close. The others were safe in Eden, far from the madness surrounding the rest of the world. They were safe from vampires and rabids and monsters and demons. Safe from me.

Except for this one stubborn human who kept playing with my heart.

Zeke looked like he was about to say something, but I pushed harder on his chest and stepped back, freeing myself from his arms. "Why didn't you stay in Eden?" I asked roughly, glaring at him. "You were *home,* Zeke. It was what you were looking for, what you always wanted. Why did you leave?"

He met my gaze, unwavering. "It wasn't home without you."

I swallowed hard, and suddenly noticed that the piano music had stopped and most of the vampires in the room were gone. Glancing out the window, I gave a start. The sky over the crumbling buildings had faded from black to midnight-blue, and many of the stars had disappeared.

Dawn was coming. I'd been so distracted with Zeke, Kanin, Salazar and everything else, I hadn't even noticed. It had been a long night.

Zeke glanced at the window, too, and sighed. "You have to go, don't you?"

Too late, I remembered the reason I'd wanted to come here was to find Jackal and tell him what had happened with Kanin. He was gone now, as was his female companion. Guilt flickered, along with a little anger.

He didn't even bother to ask about Kanin when I came in. I guess I'm the only one who really cares if he lives or dies.

Maybe that was the reason I was such a lousy vampire, why I would never fit in with Salazar or his city vamps. Not that I wanted to in the first place, but beyond being stabbed in the back or destroying a rival, they didn't seem to worry about their kin. Their Prince had nearly been assassinated tonight, and I could just imagine many of them flocked together like vultures, planning, scheming, calculating. I couldn't be like that. No matter how much my demon insisted it was right. That this was what we were.

"Allie," Zeke said quietly, stepping forward. And suddenly, the price of holding on to my humanity, my determination not to be like all the other monsters, was almost too much. In that moment, I'd never wanted to be human more, just so I could be with Ezekiel Crosse. Zeke, who was brave and loyal and selfless, who hated vampires but was still here, surrounded by them, because of me. Who had left Eden and traveled across the country, to New Covington, because he wanted to bring me home.

And I could never go with him.

I backed away, increasing the distance between us. He watched sadly, making no move to follow, but the yearning in his eyes made my throat ache. I had to get away from him now, or I'd be tempted to do something we'd both regret.

"Wait," Zeke whispered as I drew back. "Allison, please. Don't run off again."

I shook my head. "Good night, Zeke," I told him simply, and walked away, out of the room and into the hall, leaving him alone.

There was a guard, a human one, outside the door to the guest room Salazar had assigned me that night, standing there calmly with his hands clasped behind him. I gave him a wary frown as I approached, but he didn't acknowledge me until I stood right in front of him. And still, he stared over my shoulder, blocking the doorway, and didn't look like he was going to move. I was tired, both in body and spirit, the encounters with Kanin, Salazar and Zeke all tugging at different parts of my mind. I did not want a fight with a nameless guard in the middle of the corridor.

"Are you going to let me in?" I asked, feeling the approach of the sun outside the building and just wanting to crawl beneath the covers of a bed to pass out. "This *is* my room, right? I didn't get Jackal's quarters by mistake?"

He ignored me but lifted a hand and rapped twice on the door. "She's here, sir," he called through the wood. There was a muffled reply from within, and the guard stepped aside, nodding for me to go on. Puzzled, I pushed the door open and stepped warily through.

Say what you would about Salazar, he certainly knew how to live, if this guest suite was any indication. It was a pretty impressive room, much grander than what I was used to. The lighting was muted, orange lamps throwing shadows across the floor and rose-colored walls. Real lamps. Not flickering candles or oil lanterns, or the rarer battery-powered flashlight. A massive bed stood against the far wall, long black curtains draping the frame to ensure total darkness while you slept. Even thicker curtains hung from a pair of glass doors at the back, which I assumed led onto a balcony and a view of the city below.

Standing in front of those doors, arms crossed over his thin chest and watery gaze meeting mine across the room, was Stick.

Inwardly, I groaned. I was tired. Dawn was almost here. I did not want to deal with him right now. Stick wasn't alone, either. Another guard stood in the corner, eyes blank, gazing straight ahead. But his hands held a crossbow, already strung, ready to unleash it on me if I tried anything.

"What do you want, Stick?" I asked, coming slowly into the room, keeping a wary eye on the guard with the crossbow. Strangely enough, I wasn't even that angry. Disappointed, perhaps. Disgusted with his choice, that he had become a pet in the vampire regime I despised, a fawning lapdog to the Prince himself. But I was more weary than angry, and not even remotely surprised. I'd always known, deep down, that Stick had betrayed me. And it seemed he'd taken to this new role like a fish to water. I couldn't even muster the energy to care.

His pale eyes narrowed. "It's Mr. Stephen, now," he reminded me in a sharp tone. "And I want to know what you're doing here, Allie. Why you're really in New Covington. Is it revenge? Come to get even for what happened?" His lips thinned. "I'm warning you, I'm not the same pathetic Fringer you knew before. My word carries power around here. I can get you thrown into the dungeon if I wanted. Remember that, if you're thinking of sneaking into my room one night."

"I didn't come here for you," I told him disdainfully. "Trust me, you were the farthest thing from my mind when I entered New Covington. I'm here for Kanin, nothing else."

That didn't please him at all. His nostrils flared, and he stiffened, as if offended. You'd think he'd *wanted* me to have come back for revenge. "Liar," he accused. "You always hated me. You wanted to see me gone, just like Lucas and Rat. And now that you're a vampire, you've come back to punish me for…" He trailed off.

"For what?" I challenged. "Selling me out? Giving the Prince the location of your friend, so you could come live in the tower as a pet?"

"You were a vampire." Stick glared back, remorseless. "You showed up in the middle of the night after disappearing for weeks, and you were a monster. What was I supposed to think? What was I supposed to do?"

"I don't know, Stick." My voice came out soft, resigned. "Maybe talk to me? Let me explain my side of the story? You could have given me that much, at least. I think…" I hesitated, to see if the words were true, if they were real. They were. "I would have done the same for you."

"Well, it's too late for that now." There might've been a hint of regret in Stick's voice, or I might've imagined it. "What's done is done, and we both chose our paths. Because you *did* choose this, right, Allison?" His watery gaze sharpened. "There's no way you became a vampire by accident. You chose to become a monster."

Now, I felt a hot stab of anger. And something entirely unexpected. Hurt. "You want to know how I became a monster?" I snapped, making Stick flinch and the guard raise his crossbow threateningly. "Remember the night outside the Wall, where Rat and Lucas died? Remember the rabids that were chasing us, the ones that I led away from *you?* They killed me. Ran me down and tore me apart. And then Kanin showed up as I was dying and gave me the choice. Die for real, or become undead. So yes, I took the deal to become a vampire. And you took the deal to become a pet. I guess that makes both of us monsters, doesn't it?"

Stick's jaw tightened. He nodded slowly, as if he had just confirmed something he'd known all along. "I knew you blamed me," he muttered, and I clenched my fists to keep myself from flying at him and slamming his skinny frame into the glass. *It's not about you,* I wanted to scream at him. *It was never about you. I never blamed you that I became a monster—that was my choice. But you betrayed me to the Prince without a second thought. Vampire or no, I thought our friendship meant more than that. I thought...I meant more.*

Unclenching my fingers, I composed myself, forcing my fangs back into my gums. The rage flickered and died, and cold numbness spread out to take its place. I hadn't known him, not at all. The realization was a bitter lump in my stomach, acrid and poisonous. "Stick," I said dully, feeling as if a part of me had died. Or worse, that it just didn't care anymore. "I'm tired, and it's nearly dawn. If there's nothing you want, please go away so that I can sleep."

Stick shook his head, his expression curling in disgust. "You always thought you were so superior," he said, as if he were the one betrayed. "You never thought I could be more than I was. That I was just some poor, pathetic kid you let hang around. You never thought I could have dreams beyond trailing in your shadow, did you?"

"Are you done?" I asked flatly. He sneered.

"You haven't changed," he stated, determined, I supposed, to get a rise out of me. I wondered if he knew what a risky game he was playing. Favored pet or no, you could only push a vampire so far. "You might be a bloodsucker now, but you're still the same ignorant street urchin you always were. Who's this new kid you have following you around like a lost puppy? Does he know what you really are?"

"Leave Zeke out of this," I snapped, shooting him a warning glare. Fear rose up, and I stifled it, keeping my voice steady. "This has nothing to do with him. He's no threat to you or anyone."

"That remains to be seen," Stick replied, smirking faintly. He'd gotten what he wanted—a way to raise my hackles—and wasn't about to let it go. He didn't know how very, very dangerous this newest game was, especially when it came to Zeke. "As far as I'm concerned, he might've been the one to shoot that crossbow at the Prince." Stick met my gaze, mean and challenging. "Better be careful, Allison. He's only human, and around here, humans go missing sometimes. If you want to ensure his safety, I suggest you start treating me with respect."

I took a deep, calming breath, trying to dissolve the sudden fury, the urge to stalk forward, grab my former friend and snap his skinny little neck.

"Stick," I said very softly but making certain he heard every syllable. My voice trembled, but it was from an icy rage, from holding myself back. My fangs flashed in the dim light as I faced him. "Listen to me very carefully. If you lay one finger on Zeke, if he is harmed, for any reason, all the guards in the world won't be enough to protect you from me."

Stick went pale, but he still raised his chin, eyes flashing. "You…you can't talk to me like that anymore, Allie," he stammered. "I'm in charge here, and you're supposed to listen to me now. I could order your human thrown in the dungeon, and the Prince wouldn't care. I could have him tortured, drained until he's nothing but skin and bones, and no one would raise a hand to stop it." He was feverish now, staring at me with a mix of superior defiance and fear. I'd never seen him like this, and I didn't care. All I knew was that he was threatening Zeke, who had never raised a hand to him or even spoken to him. And if he didn't leave my room right now, things were going to get ugly.

I snarled, baring fangs, and he jumped, skittering backward. The guard raised the crossbow, pointing it at me, but I didn't move. "Get out!" I told Stick, barely holding on to my rage. The Hunger had emerged full force with my anger and was goading me to attack, to rip out hearts and snap bones and sink my fangs into soft fleshy throats. "Get out of here, Stick," I hissed through my fangs. "Right now, before I tear off your stupid head and throw it through the window."

Stick still looked defiant, like he didn't believe I would really hurt him. Thankfully, his guard was a bit more sensible. "Sir," he said tightly, easing forward with his crossbow raised. "Sir, we should go. The Prince will be upset if you're harmed by one of his guests. Sir, we need to leave now."

Gently but firmly, the guard took his elbow, pulling him away. Stick resisted a moment then relented with an irritated huff.

"Get your hands off me." Stick yanked his arm loose, but continued to walk toward the door, glaring back even as the guard continued to herd him out. "Remember what I said, Allie," he threw over his shoulder. "I'm in charge around here. You're not the important one anymore."

I stood there seething long after the door closed. And, for the first time since that night in the rain, I wondered what would've happened if I'd just let Stick…die. If I hadn't led them away, straight to my death. If the rabids had taken him, instead of me.

CHAPTER 15

I didn't expect to dream, but I did.

A flash, a brief stab of confusion. My eyes open to a strange room, one I haven't seen before. It is different than what I'd become used to: darkness, stone, iron bars, anguish. Pain has been my world for so long; I had forgotten an existence without it. And now, just like that, I am free. Because of her.

Except…there is still something wrong. Something inside me, a dark coiling intruder that I can barely feel, spreading through my veins. What happened to me, in the time I was gone? And where is he *in all of this mess?*

I opened my eyes, Kanin's suspicion ebbing away into reality. I lay at the edge of the enormous bed with my sword clutched to my chest, gazing at the ceiling. The room was very dark; the thick curtains across the balcony doors shut out all light, but by my internal clock, the sun had just gone down.

I swung my feet off the mattress and stood, still in my black coat and original clothes. I'd locked my door, even considered dragging the dresser in front of it, as I did not trust the vampires in this tower, or even the humans. Worse, I did not want Stick to come creeping back into my room. Just the thought of him sent curls of anger and loathing through my stomach. He was my enemy now, or he thought he was, anyway. I remembered the sullen contempt in his eyes, the resentment, as if I was offending him by being here, by still being alive. I still didn't fully understand it. Maybe we'd never been friends at all.

Still holding my sword by the sheath, I wandered into the bathroom. A mirror ran the length of the counter, and my reflection gazed back at me over the sink. I snorted. No wonder the city vamps looked down their noses at me—I was filthy and dirt streaked, dried blood still clinging to my collar and skin. I pulled the collar of my shirt aside, peering at the place Kanin had bitten me. Two raised white bumps, no larger than pinpricks, grazed my skin right above the collarbone. Mementos from Kanin that I'd probably have forever.

Kanin. I'd have to go down and check on him soon, but for now, at least, he seemed to be fine. Maybe I should make myself a bit more presentable, not that I cared what the city vamps thought of me, but there was no reason not to take advantage of Salazar's hospitality when I had the chance.

Experimentally, I twisted the faucet above the sink, only half expecting it to work. To my surprise, it did, shooting a stream of warm water into the basin. I started to splash my face and neck, wiping away the dried blood, then stopped.

Pushing aside the shower curtain, I reached down and spun

the handle. A burst of hot water erupted from the showerhead, sending up tendrils of steam and fogging the mirror behind me, and I grinned with delight.

Stripping out of my clothes, I stepped beneath a gadget I'd only heard about in the Fringe and doubted its existence. Hot, clean water hit my cold skin, soaking my hair, the heat seeping into my bones, and I closed my eyes. Bliss. I stayed under the pounding stream for a long time, letting it sluice the dirt from my skin, letting the lather of real soap slide down my body. So this was what life was like in the Inner City, at least for vampires. And probably even their humans. A huge bed and electricity and hot water, and food whenever you wanted it. I could see how tempting it was. How some people would betray and kill for it. If I was a city vampire, this could be my life.

All I had to do was give up my humanity.

Frowning, I turned off the water and dried myself with the thick red towels that hung beside the shower. And though it was mildly repulsive, I dressed in my old clothes, having no clean ones and no time to wash them. Swirling the coat around my shoulders, I left the bathroom just as loud banging came from the door.

Warily, I buckled the katana to my back before heading toward it. If it was the Prince come to tell me about Kanin, I wanted to hear what he had to say. If it was Jackal, I would tolerate him long enough to explain what had happened the night before with our sire. And if it was Stick, come to taunt me again, I was going to slam the door in his face and hope I broke his nose in the process.

However, when I opened the door, it wasn't Stick or Jackal or the Prince facing me across the threshold.

It was Zeke.

"Hey," he said quietly, hesitantly, as if afraid I *would* slam the door in his face. He looked tired, as if he hadn't gotten any sleep, and his blond hair was tousled. "Can I come in?"

Wordlessly, I stepped back, letting him cross the threshold into my room before locking the door behind us. I noticed the large blade across his back, strapped over the combat vest, the gun at his hip, and blinked. "You found your weapons."

"Yeah." He took in the room with a practiced sweep then turned to me with a shrug. "Well, I didn't find them, exactly. Someone gave them to me early this evening, said Jackal ordered them returned to me."

"Jackal?" I gaped in shock. "Are you sure it was him?"

One corner of his lip quirked. "Positive. In fact, this came with them." He fished in his jeans pocket and handed me a note. I opened the crumpled paper, seeing the messy black slashes of Jackal's handwriting.

"Try not to lose these again, minion."

I snorted. "He's such a bastard, even when he's being helpful." Crumpling the note, I looked back at Zeke, expecting him to smile and agree with me.

His small grin had faded, and he was watching me with solemn blue eyes, his face tormented with unspoken words. My mind stirred uneasily. Was he angry at my rejection the night before? Maybe he had come to say goodbye, that he'd made a mistake coming here, and he was going back to Eden without me.

"Are you leaving?" I tried to keep the bitterness from my

voice, the sudden desperation. "The Prince isn't keeping us here. Are you headed back to Eden tonight?"

His brow furrowed. "Of course not," he said in a quiet voice. "I wouldn't just leave like that."

"Then why are you here?"

Zeke gave a short, frustrated huff. "I don't know. Talk with me a second?" Looking faintly embarrassed, he went to the balcony doors, slid them open and stepped out onto the ledge. I followed, leaving the door partially open behind us. The wind whipped at our hair and clothes, tiny flurries dancing on the breeze.

Resting his elbows on the ice-covered railing, Zeke peered out over the city, his face dark. I followed his example, seeing the lights of the Inner City wink up at me and, beyond them, the looming darkness of the Fringe.

"It looks different from up here," I ventured. I didn't know why I was telling him, but the words flowed out of my mouth and swept away with the flurries. "When I lived in the Fringe, I used to stare up at these towers and think, what are they doing up there, right now? What kind of twisted life do they live? And now, here I am, staring down at the city, and there's probably some kid, some Fringer down there, thinking the exact same thing."

"Dreaming of a life in a vampire tower." Zeke's voice was low but not accusing, though he still didn't look at me. "Did you ever think about it? What it could be like?"

"Sometimes," I admitted. "Not very often." I remembered one frigid night, staring up at the vampire towers, hating the humans who were warm and fed and spoiled for betraying their own kind. But jealousy and hatred didn't keep you warm, and expending energy on wishing was useless. You might wish your mom was still alive, that she could still hold you and read to you every night, but it wouldn't bring her back. You could wish your friends wouldn't die in front of you, starving or bleeding or frozen, or that, just once, you didn't have to worry about finding food to keep yourself alive for one more day, but people still died, and you still went hungry many, many times.

Or you could wish that there was a way for a human and a vampire to be together without fear.

I swallowed and flicked a sideways glance at Zeke, still silent as he leaned against the railing, gazing into the darkness. Snowflakes perched in his pale hair and dusted his shoulders, making me want to brush them away. It was suddenly painful not to touch him, to feel his hands on mine, his lips, warm and strong. But, of course, with the desire came the savage ache of the Hunger. I remembered the sweetness of his blood, the hot strength flowing through me, the intoxicating power. I wanted him, badly, but I didn't know which was stronger. And I was afraid to find out.

I took a gulp of frosty air to clear my thoughts. My breath, I noted, did not billow out in front of me. "Why are you here, Zeke?" I asked, trying not to look at him again. "You came to tell me something. What is it?"

Zeke hesitated, idly brushing bits of ice off the railing, then took a deep breath himself. A small white cloud writhed into the wind as he exhaled. "Okay," he murmured, more to himself. "I can do this." Another pause, where he seemed fascinated by the lights of the city below, then, without looking at me, he asked, "Remember…remember what I said about wanting to start over?"

His voice was soft, nearly carried away on the wind, on the breath that twisted into the air and disappeared. I nodded warily.

He swallowed, turned to face me. "I lied. I don't want us to start over."

If he'd shoved a stake through my heart, I doubt it would've hurt more than what I felt right then. My throat closed up, but I kept my voice and expression neutral. "Oh?"

"No." He moved closer, and now we were almost touching. "I want things to be like they were…before," he whispered. "Before Jeb died, before Eden…before all of this. Do you remember those days? What it was like…between the two of us?"

I'd never forgotten. I recalled everything, from our first meeting in the abandoned town, to the hardness in his eyes when he'd discovered I was a vampire, to our first kiss in absolute darkness. He was a preacher's son, and I was the monster he'd been taught to hate, to destroy, but very gradually, we'd come to see each other as something more. And by the time we'd reached Eden and I'd said goodbye for the last time, something had grown between us that terrified us both.

"I remember," I whispered. "I wish things were the same, too."

Zeke reached out, and suddenly his warm hands were on my arms, drawing me close. "So stop running away from me," he whispered, sounding pained. "Please. I care for you, Allie. I…" He broke off, pausing, then continued in a soft, clear voice. "I want us to be together. I don't care what it takes."

One hand rose to gently brush my cheek. "Let me prove it to you. Give me another chance."

"Zeke..." I closed my eyes against the softness of his touch, the sweet ache stifling the Hunger for just a moment. "You know what I am," I said, not able to look at him. "You know it could never...that a vampire and a human..."

"I'm not afraid." His breath fluttered across my skin. I heard his heart, pounding in his chest, and the Hunger stirred restlessly, never still. "I know what I'm getting into," Zeke continued softly. "I have both eyes open this time. You're a vampire and I'm human, and I don't care anymore. Unless... you don't feel the same."

He paused, waiting for me, but I couldn't answer, couldn't even look at him. Then, his forehead touched mine, and his thumbs were brushing my cheeks, palms gently cupping the back of my head. "Allie," he murmured, very softly, "if you don't feel anything, if this is all one-sided, tell me now and I won't ever bring it up again. But I'm betting one last time that I...mean something to you, and despite everything that's happened between us, we can make this work. I want to try. Allison..." He stroked my skin, his eyes boring into me. "I trust you."

No. I put my hands between us, not pushing him off, but stopping him from coming any closer. His words burned into my heart. He trusted me, a vampire, a monster. It was maybe the most precious thing he could offer, and something that I would never deserve.

He waited. His heartbeat pulsed against my fingers, rapid. Anxious. I felt its thrum vibrating all the way to the silent place in my own chest. Zeke's heart, in the palm of my hand.

He was offering it to a monster who could so easily crush it, both literally and figuratively. I should. I should crush it figuratively now, so there'd be no chance I would literally rip the heart from his chest in the future.

But the thought made me ill. I didn't want to hurt him. And this thing we shared, these feelings swirling inside whenever he was close, they belonged to my other half. The part that was still human, however small it was, the one struggling with the demon and the Hunger every second of every day. That side wanted this, needed this. Zeke was a brilliant light that cut through the evil and darkness and bloodlust, down to that tiny part struggling to stay alive. I'd been clinging to his memory, that small piece of hope, ever since I left Eden, and I couldn't let it go. I just prayed I wouldn't drag him into the darkness with me.

"You don't feel the same, do you?"

Zeke stepped back, the warmth leaving my hands, his heartbeat vanishing from under my fingers. I felt hollow without it, empty. His voice and expression were flat as he looked away. "Sorry. I shouldn't have expected… I'll leave you alone, now."

"No! I mean—" I grabbed his arm before he could leave, and his gaze rose to mine, desolate and heartbroken. I spoke quickly to reassure him. "It's not that. Zeke, I…" I slumped against the railing, then finally came out with it. "I want this, too," I whispered. "I just can't trust *myself.*"

He blinked, and his eyes were gentle again, hopeful, as he eased closer. "You didn't kill me that time in Jackal's tower. You could have. I basically gave you the chance, and you didn't."

"You don't know how close I was," I answered. His expression didn't change.

"I'm still here."

"I've *killed* people."

"Do you think my hands are clean?"

"Zeke." I gave him a desperate look, needing him to understand. "I will always be a threat to the people I'm around. I'm not just saying that. Not a day goes by that I don't think about biting you. Yes, I try to control myself, but that doesn't mean I'm always successful. And the last thing I want…" I faltered, not wanting to tell him, knowing I had to. "The last thing I want is to come out of a blood frenzy and find that I've killed someone. Someone I know. Like Caleb. Or Teresa. Or you."

"Allie." Zeke's eyes were intense now; I could see my reflection in those glittering blue orbs as he took my hand. "I've watched you. From the time we met, to the day I discovered what you really were, to now. You have always been the same fierce, stubborn girl who refuses to give in to anything. I've seen you fight so hard not to hurt people, to keep your distance so you're not a danger to anyone." He closed his eyes briefly. "And I'm ashamed that I thought the worst of you when you showed up with Jackal that night, but I know better now. You haven't changed. You're still beautiful and dangerous and incredible, and I'll keep telling you that for as long as it takes you to believe it. But right now, all I want to do is kiss you, except I'm terrified that if I try you might throw me off this balcony."

My laugh had a little sob in it. I remembered the first time Zeke had tried to kiss me, he'd ended up on his back in the dirt, a katana pointed at his heart. "This is not going to work," I warned him, meeting his gaze. "A vampire and a human? This is crazy, Zeke."

He gave me that heartrending smile.

"Well, like you said before. Maybe we're both a little… *mmm*."

He got no further, because I had pushed myself off the railing, wrapped my arms around his neck and kissed him.

His arms slid around my waist, holding me tight, pressing me against his body. His lips moved with mine, soft and warm and just as I remembered. I felt the Hunger rise up, always there, but I tamped it down. I could do this. I could be a vampire and still be with Zeke. He was willing to try, to offer his heart to a demon, and I would not betray that trust. No matter what it took or how hard I had to fight it, I would not become a monster.

The wind picked up, whipping at our hair and clothes, as Zeke pulled back to look at me. Snow eddies swirled around us, clinging to my cold skin, melting away on Zeke's. I blinked at him, meeting those intense sapphire eyes, cocking my head. "What?" I asked, a faint murmur between us, blown away by the wind. Zeke smiled.

"You," he replied just as softly, and held me tighter. "I never really thought I would be here like this. With you. In all the world, in all the places we could end up, we came here at the same time and ran into each other. Like it was meant to be."

"Meant to be?" I couldn't help but scoff, though I scoffed very quietly. "Extremely lucky coincidence is more like it. I don't believe in fate."

"I don't, either." He smoothed a strand of hair from my face. "But someone was listening, I think. Someone wanted us to find each other. How else would you explain it?"

"I was under the impression that God hated vampires," I said, keeping my voice light and my hands locked around the small of his back. "Evil, soulless spawn of the devil, right?"

"You're not evil," Zeke said with absolute conviction. "I might have believed that once, but not now." His hand framed my cheek, brushing my skin. "No one who fights so hard to do the right thing is evil."

Unexpectedly, that simple, sincere statement was enough to unravel me. My throat closed up, and my eyes stung with hot tears. I ducked my head, not wanting him to see me cry, to be revolted by the red tracks oozing down my cheeks. Zeke cupped my chin and gently tilted my face up. I resisted a moment, then gazed at him defiantly, feeling the blood trickle from my eye, expecting him to recoil. But he smiled and lightly touched my face, wiping the tear away.

"Both eyes open," he whispered, and brought his lips down on mine.

I made a tiny sound in the back of my throat and relaxed into him, clutching the back of his shirt. I couldn't think. I could barely move. I just clung to him, reeling with a storm of emotion that buffeted me from the inside, making me want to hide and embrace it all at once. I didn't know how this would work, if it could work. I was just aware of one thing: I could *not* lose him. Zeke had seen the monster at its worst and was still here. He dared to get close to the demon, knowing it still Hungered for him, craved his blood and his life, and he wasn't afraid. For the rest of my existence, if I lived to see the end of this world, there would never be another Ezekiel Crosse. There would never be another soul as bright as his. And that both terrified me and made me savagely—and maybe selfishly—determined to keep him. Zeke was mine now. Forever.

A pounding came at the front door. We broke apart, Zeke reluctantly letting me go, his warm hand lingering on my skin. My senses buzzed, Hunger and passion like twin hurricanes, fighting each other, but I walked calmly back into the room with Zeke trailing behind me and opened the door.

"Morning, sunshine," Jackal drawled. His gold eyes peered past my shoulder at Zeke, and an eyebrow arched sardonically. "Am I interrupting anything?"

"Always," I muttered, watching him smirk. "What do you want, Jackal?"

"Salazar has called for us," the other vampire said with mock grandeur. "He's waiting for us down in the hospital wing with Kanin. Looks like we've worn out our welcome."

We rode the elevator down together, me in the center, Jackal and Zeke flanking me on either side. There was no vampire Elite to escort us this time; there weren't even any human guards at the doors or in the halls. I did see the female vamp Jackal had been talking to the night before, and she gave him a sultry smile as we passed, her eyes gleaming. Jackal winked at her as we turned the corner.

In the creaking metal box, Zeke stood close beside me while Jackal leaned against the wall, looking bored. I still clenched my teeth every time the lift shook or trembled, and perhaps Zeke picked up on my discomfort, for halfway through the ride, his fingers curled around mine. My body uncoiled, if just slightly, and I squeezed his hand. I thought I heard Jackal snort, but I didn't look at him.

Zeke. I was still getting used to this new, crazy idea: a human and a vampire. Maybe I was being naive. Maybe I was being deliberately blind. Most likely I was being incredibly stupid and endangering his life. What would Kanin say if—when—he found out? Would he scold? Would he shake his head and give me that familiar look of exasperation? Or would he be angry, disgusted, that I was ignoring one of his most primary rules: *don't get attached to human beings.*

The elevator shuddered, rather violently this time, and gave a rusty screech that made my skin crawl. I closed my eyes, squeezing Zeke's hand in a death grip, before I realized I might be hurting him. Guiltily, I tried pulling back, but he only laced our fingers together and tightened his grip.

You know what? Screw it, I told myself. *I'm not Kanin's protégé anymore. I've been on my own for a long time. I'm the one who trekked halfway across the country to find him. He has no say in what I do with my life or who I decide to spend it with.*

The elevator dinged, and Zeke released my hand as the doors opened. Salazar and several Elites waited for us at the end of the hallway, their cold faces giving nothing away.

"He is awake," the Prince informed me as we walked through the room of moaning, writhing humans, keeping well back from the wall of beds. I saw Zeke's eyes linger on the human "patients," saw his hands clench as he realized what was really happening, but he didn't say anything. Jackal, giving the humans a cursory glance, just wrinkled his nose.

"He is waiting for you," Salazar finished as we came to

a room much like the one from last night that held the rotting, dying vampire. Except this one was guarded by a pair of armed vampire Elite. The Prince continued, "You will go to Kanin and inform him of what needs to be done. Afterward, you will all leave my tower, and you will not return unless you have found Sarren or a cure for this madness. Is this clear?"

I nodded, staring at the closed door, feeling my sire's unmistakable presence on the other side. Now that I was moments from seeing him, I was nervous. So much had happened. What would he say to me? What would I say to him? Neither of us was the same as before.

"You go ahead," Jackal told me, giving a dismissive wave. "I have no burning desire to see the old bastard just yet. I'm sure he's much more inclined to talk to you, anyway."

I gave him a sharp look. "For someone who's come all this way to find Kanin, you're certainly keeping your distance." I frowned. "You didn't seem to care about him last night, either. It's almost like you're avoiding him."

"What can I say?" Jackal leaned back against the wall. "I'm not the fair-haired son."

"What the hell is that supposed to mean?"

"Go," said the Prince again. "I care not who retrieves Kanin and gets him out of this tower, I only want him gone. I want you all gone."

"Prince Salazar." Zeke spoke up quietly, startling us all. I blinked and stared at Zeke as the vampire Prince turned to the human, a bemused look crossing his face, no doubt wondering why the lowly mortal dared to speak to him. "Sir," Zeke went on, his voice calmly polite. "Before we go, I have to inform you that there are still uninfected people out in the

Fringe. If…" He paused, taking a breath, as if what he was about to say next was difficult for him to get out. "If you are concerned about your blood supply, maybe you should consider bringing them to the Inner City. Or at least sending them food and supplies. I know where they are, and it seems to me that you need all the healthy humans you can find. Will you consider letting them into the city? They need to get out of the Fringe as soon as they can."

The Prince raised an eyebrow. "I am not unreasonable," he stated, sounding suspiciously amused with this mortal who wasn't afraid to speak to a Prince. "If there *are* uninfected humans out there, I would ideally rather have them behind the Inner Wall. However, I will not risk my people's safety by sending them into the Fringe. So I am afraid there is nothing I am willing to do for them. I'd rather a few more humans die than bring that sickness into my city." Zeke clenched his fists, and the Prince narrowed his eyes, not missing his anger. "Find Sarren and a cure," he told Zeke. "That is how you can help the rest of the population. I cannot offer more than that, human.

"Now," he continued, turning away from Zeke, dismissing him easily. I gave him an apologetic look, and he crossed his arms, looking grim. "Kanin's daughter," Salazar said, drawing my attention. "We are wasting time. Are you going to speak to your sire, or shall I send someone in there to drag him out?"

Biting my lip, I stepped forward, between the guards, and placed a hand on the cold metal of the doorknob. A pause, then I quickly turned the handle and stepped through, shutting the door behind me.

The small room was dark, the only light coming from the

sliver that filtered beneath the door and the tiny window in its center. Everything else was shadowy gray to my vampire sight, washed out and colorless. For a second, I wondered if I should maybe flip the switch beside the door frame. I knew the room had power, same as the rest of the floor. But that seemed rude and intrusive and even cruel, to force my sire into the light. For as long as I'd known him, Kanin had preferred the darkness.

I could see him now, sitting in a chair in the far corner, fingers laced together beneath his chin. Already, he looked better. His skin was still pale, but not the chalky, wasted flesh of the previous night. He was dressed in black, his usual color, and, except for his face and powerful arms, he was a featureless shadow sitting against the wall. He didn't look at me at first, staring intently at the floor, deep in thought. But as the door clicked shut, plunging the room into darkness, he raised piercing black eyes and met my gaze across the room.

"Allison."

The soft, deep voice shivered into me. His tone wasn't welcoming or angry or relieved or anything. It was just my name, giving away nothing, no hint to his thoughts or feelings. And, quite suddenly, I didn't know what to say. I hadn't really imagined getting this far, this point where I finally stood before my sire, face-to-face, and I was a completely different person than the one he saw last.

I opted for the safe, noncommittal response. "Hey."

Nothing. No eye twitch, no movement, nothing to show he had heard. I swallowed and stayed where I was. "I'm… uh…glad you're okay."

Kanin bowed his head. "Yes," he murmured, and his voice now sounded faintly uncomfortable. "Although…"

He lowered his hands and rose, startling me with the sudden, smooth motion. I didn't move as he crossed the room, coming to stand before me. He was still immensely powerful, his presence overwhelming. I had to tilt my head up to meet his gaze, which was dark and searching, flickers of pain showing through his calm mask as he stared at me.

Slowly, his hand rose, brushing the hair off my shoulder, his movements deliberate yet gentle. I shivered as his fingers took my collar and eased it aside, away from my neck, revealing the scar he'd left behind.

His eyes closed, and now the pain and guilt on his face was unmistakable.

"It wasn't you," I told him softly, my voice nearly lost between us. "I don't blame you, Kanin. You weren't yourself."

"No," he agreed, his voice choked. "But it does not excuse what I did. You haven't been a vampire long enough to understand. To think that I…" He released me and turned away, hunching his broad shoulders. I again remembered his words to me in the hospital, explaining vampire history and customs. *Vampires do not feed from each other. It's one of the most violent, intrusive acts we can commit on another kindred, and is viewed as barbaric and needlessly cruel by most.*

"And yet, you're still here." His voice was a little stronger now, and he straightened, though he still didn't look at me. "You found your way. I hardly dared to hope."

"Of course I did." I frowned at him, stung. "Kanin, I wouldn't leave you like that. Not with Psycho Vamp. Not after everything you did for me. What, did you think I could just ignore the dreams, knowing what Sarren was doing? You think I'd just abandon you?"

"You would not be the first," Kanin said, and finally turned. His eyes, so dark, hooded and full of shadows, met mine and did not shy away. "I don't find myself in this position very often," he admitted with a hint of his old confidence. "But…thank you. Out of all my offspring, you are the only one with which I have no regrets."

I couldn't handle that piercing gaze, the way he was staring at me. Embarrassed, needing to break the tension, I half smiled. "Don't go soft on me," I told him, and Kanin's eyebrows rose, making me smile wider. "We're not out of here yet," I said, watching his face. "We still need you to help us find Sarren."

"Sarren." He narrowed his eyes, probably remembering those long, awful nights where Sarren had tortured him ruthlessly. His voice was dangerously calm as he ordered, "Tell me everything that's happened."

So, I did, beginning with those first dreams, following his trail to Old D.C., finding Jackal instead, discovering the other lab and finally tracking him to New Covington, where Sarren had revealed his treachery in a spectacular bloodbath and fled. "We don't even know if he's still in the city," I finished, making a helpless gesture. "But we're supposed to find him and either beat a cure from him or bring him back for the Prince to deal with."

"He hasn't left yet," Kanin said. I blinked, and the vampire shook his head, frowning. "Whatever he's planned, he'll want to stay to see how it ends. That's how his mind works. He won't leave without knowing the final results, not when he's gone through all the trouble of setting this up." Kanin looked at the door. "He's in the city, somewhere."

"Excellent," said a new voice as the door creaked and Prince Salazar came into the room. "That will make it easier for you, won't it? As it is, you do not have a lot of time."

I spun around, placing myself between Kanin and the Prince, and very deliberately on Kanin's side of the room. I imagined the temperature dropped several degrees as the two Master vampires stared at each other, fury and hatred smoothly hidden beneath their icy facades.

"You should be quite proud of your protégé, Kanin." Salazar's voice was a thin veneer of calm over his utter loathing. "No one else would have done what she has, the effort she put forth to save you, when all others would have let you rot down here. I would have let you rot down here." His lip twitched, his eyes cold and cruel. "Of course, that might still be an option."

"What have you done to me?" Kanin's voice was calm, but something in Salazar's triumphant gaze made my stomach clench in fear. "You wouldn't just let me go, not without a safeguard. What's to stop me from leaving New Covington and never coming back?"

He wouldn't, and I knew he wouldn't. Kanin wasn't like that. The question pandered to Salazar's way of thinking, and by the slow, evil smile spreading across the Prince's face, I suddenly knew, and my blood turned to ice. Kanin had felt sick when he'd woken this evening. I should've known not to trust the Prince, who hated Kanin and wanted to see him suffer, even if he was free.

A dark, coiling thing inside me, spreading through my veins.

"You bastard," I whispered, glaring at Salazar, and the Prince arched an eyebrow at me. "You gave him infected blood last night!"

Salazar regarded me without remorse. "Are you surprised, Kanin's daughter?" he asked mildly. "I promised I would set him free, but I needed something to insure you would all go after Sarren and not vanish into the night." He smiled again, showing fangs. "This will give you that motivation."

I thought of the dying vampire, the flesh peeling from its bones, turning black and rancid while its eyes pleaded for me to end its life. Enraged and suddenly terrified, I bared my fangs at the Prince of the city and snarled, "Damn you, Salazar! There was no need! You knew we would go after Sarren, regardless!"

"Allison." Kanin's cool voice stopped me from doing something monumentally stupid, something that probably would have gotten my head torn off. I almost didn't care. Salazar knew Kanin wouldn't try to leave the city. He knew that we were invested in stopping Sarren and finding a cure. Hell, how could we *not* be, with a plague that threatened both species? This was just cruel, evil spite. I had come so far to rescue him; I had watched Kanin drag himself out of madness, endured the awful dreams and visions of torture, and now… now he would probably…

"How long do I have?" Kanin asked, his voice still unnaturally calm. The Prince, watching me with cold, dangerous eyes, turned his attention back to the other vampire.

"About seventy-two hours," he replied casually, "from the time the first symptoms appear. Give or take a few. After that, the virus reaches the brain and begins to shut it down.

Of course, by that time, your body might be too damaged to continue sustaining itself."

Three days. Three days to find Sarren, discover a cure—if one even existed—and make it back to the Prince, before the virus ravaging Kanin's body destroyed him. "That's not enough time!" I protested, and the Prince turned a pitiless glare on me.

"It will have to be enough time. You do not have another choice."

No, we didn't. Numbly, I listened as Kanin and Salazar discussed the situation in the Fringe, what we could expect when we left the tower, and our plans to get through the Inner City. Like it was a perfectly normal conversation. Like one of them wasn't dying from the treachery and betrayal of the other.

"Where do you intend to search first?" Salazar asked.

"The Fringe," Kanin replied immediately. The vampire Prince raised an eyebrow.

"You don't believe Sarren is in the Inner City anymore? You think he is hiding among the infected, unable to feed himself?"

Kanin smiled coldly. "It won't matter where he is now. He will come to us. Because I know where all his research is. I know where he went to unleash this madness."

"Do you?" Salazar said mildly as I stared at Kanin, frowning. Did he? I sure didn't, and I had followed Sarren all the way from Old D.C., from the ruined city and the tunnels and the hidden lab…

Oh. Oh, of course. Kanin *did* know where Sarren had created the virus. I did, too. It was so obvious—why hadn't

I thought of that before? I'd been there. I'd spent my first weeks as a vampire there.

The laboratory beneath the old hospital, where Kanin had taught me how to be an immortal.

"Very well. Then you leave tonight." Salazar gave me a brief glance as he opened the door. "When you are prepared, I'll have my guards escort you to the gates." A faint smile crossed his face as the door began to swing shut. "I truly hope I see you again."

And we were alone.

I seethed at the closed door for a moment, then turned to the vampire behind me. "Kanin, I had no idea. I didn't think Salazar would—"

He cut me off with a gesture. "It's fine, Allison. It's done." For just a moment, his face grew dark, and I saw regret pass through his eyes before he shook it off. "We have work to do. Let's find Sarren and try to stop this insanity in the time I have left."

Salazar wasn't in the hall when we emerged, which was a good thing, because I still burned with fury toward the vampire Prince and might've said or done something that would've gotten me in trouble if he was there. Zeke and Jackal were, however, one leaning casually against the wall, the other standing a few feet away with his arms crossed, wary blue eyes taking everything in. They both straightened when the door opened and I stepped into the hall, followed by Kanin.

"I'm sure you two know each other," I said, moving aside to watch Jackal and Kanin, wondering if I would see a hint of their past, a clue to what had happened between them.

"Yes," Kanin said in a toneless voice, staring at Jackal, his face unreadable. "We do." Jackal stared back, a dangerous smirk on his face, and Kanin smiled faintly. "Hello, James."

Jackal's eyes closed, and mine nearly bulged out of the sockets. *"James?"* I said in disbelief, an evil grin spreading over my face as I turned on him. "Your real name is James?"

Jackal sighed, giving Kanin a disgusted look. "Nice one, old man. Well played. You would have to bring that up, wouldn't you?"

"I believe I also said I would kill you if I ever saw you again."

"Yeah, well…" Jackal shrugged and nodded to Zeke. "Get in line behind the little bloodsack over there. Although, really, *you* should be the one at the top of his list. It's kind of amusing, really. That he has no idea who you are, what you've done."

Kanin's eyes flicked to the human, silently watching this exchange a few yards away. "Kanin," I said, stepping in before Jackal could do any more damage, "this is Zeke. He came to help us find you. He's coming with us to look for Sarren, as well."

I thought he would ask questions, but Kanin just nodded acceptance. I was relieved, but it seemed Jackal wasn't done yet.

"Oh, and here's an interesting tidbit for you, Kanin," the raider king added, his voice low and his eyes gleaming dangerously. "Remember those scientists, the ones working on a cure sixty years ago? The ones you hunted for, handed over our kin to? What was the head guy's name again? Oh yeah, Malachi. Malachi Crosse."

Zeke jerked, and Kanin tensed at the name. I turned to

Jackal, fangs bared, ready to tell him to shut up, but it was too late.

"Say hello," the vampire continued, jerking his head at Zeke, "to his great-grandson. Ezekiel Crosse."

Kanin went rigid. Slowly, he turned, staring at Zeke as if seeing him for the first time, then started toward him. Zeke stiffened but held his ground as the vampire approached, the dark eyes frighteningly intense.

"Kanin," I began, stepping forward.

My sire ignored me, his entire focus on the human in front of him. "Your father," he rasped in a low, husky voice, "is Jebbadiah Crosse?"

"Was," Zeke answered calmly. Briefly, his gaze flicked to Jackal, who was watching this little scene with a smile on his face. Anger rippled over Zeke's features, making his eyes flash, before they were composed once more. "He died. A few months ago."

"I am sorry," Kanin said, and by his tone, he did not miss that brief look between Jackal and Zeke, and could guess what had happened. "But, the research," he continued, almost desperately, making me blink. I'd never seen him so anxious before. "The vampire experiments. Do you know about them? Do you have the data?"

Zeke shook his head. "Not anymore," he replied, and Kanin's shoulders slumped. In that moment, he looked like he'd lost everything, that the terrible burden he carried had finally broken him, and he didn't have the strength or the will to fight any longer. Zeke shot me a questioning look and I nodded, telling him to go on. "I don't have it," Zeke continued softly. "But, it's safe. It's in Eden now."

"Eden." Kanin's voice was a whisper, and he raised his head. "Then it's real. It exists."

"Don't ask me to tell you where it is," Zeke said firmly. "I won't do that."

"I would not ask." Kanin backed away, almost in a fog. "You have no reason to trust me," he continued, speaking to Zeke though his eyes were distant now, far away. "But, to know that it is safe. That there is still hope..."

He trailed off, but the look on his face made my stomach tighten in sympathy. I was about to say something, but footsteps down the hall announced the approach of Dr. Emerson and a squad of four vampire Elite. The doctor looked bored as he came up, a knapsack in one hand, a small cooler in the other.

"The Prince has decreed that you be resupplied before heading out into the Fringe," he said flatly, as if this was some unnecessary detail he had to take care of before going back to work. "Here. Supplies for pets..." He tossed the knapsack at Zeke, who caught it with a frown and held out the cooler. "Supplies for vampires. Though I'd suggest you use these soon. They will not keep very long."

"Forget it," I growled, eyeing the cooler with suspicion. I remembered the blood bag I had choked down the night before, and my stomach curled. Had it been poisoned, as well? Would I be feeling sick right now if it had? Kanin had known something was wrong, but Kanin was a Master and had been a vampire far longer. Would my body start to rot away in a few hours, the virus consuming it from the inside? I bared my fangs at the thought. "We're not touching any blood you offer us, ever. Especially after..."

I trailed off as Kanin gave me a sharp look, warning me not to say anything. The glare was obvious: he didn't want anyone to know he was sick. Frustrated, I fell silent, but no one disagreed with me, though Jackal gave me a bemused look, as if he thought I was being irrational.

The doctor shrugged. "Suit yourself. You should know by now not to feed from any humans out in the Fringe. If their blood is infected, the virus they carry will destroy you."

"We know that," I said icily. "Your Prince made it very clear."

"Good. Then the guards will escort you out."

And they did, riding the elevator up to the first floor with us, seven vampires and one human packed into one small metal box. I had an odd sense of surrealism as I thought about it—me, my sire, my blood brother and Zeke. Four very different people who, under normal circumstances, would never be together. Who would probably be enemies. But here we were.

There were two vehicles sitting in the street right outside the tower, boxy-looking things with large tires and headlights across the hood. A uniformed human nodded at us as we approached.

"The Prince has ordered that you be taken to the Sector Two gate," he told us, and nodded at Kanin and Jackal. Another soldier, standing beside the humming vehicles, opened the back door as the guard motioned them inside. "Two to a car, if you would. The girl and the human can take the second one."

"Why can't we all go together?" I asked.

"I'm sorry, ma'am." The soldier's voice was polite but firm. "But we must escort you there like this."

I could've argued, but Kanin and Jackal didn't seem to care, beyond Jackal giving Kanin a smug look, which Kanin ignored. I guessed if the Prince wanted us dead, he would've killed us by now. "Fine," I muttered, turning toward the second car. "Let's go, Zeke."

One we were inside, however, I realized why we'd been separated. It wasn't on the Prince's command after all.

Stick and his ever-present bodyguards sat across from us, their crossbows already drawn and angled at my heart. I felt Zeke tense, but the doors closed behind us, the locks clicking into place. Stick smiled, crossing his legs, gesturing to the seats across from him. "Sit down, Allie."

Warily, we sat. The vehicle rumbled and began to move.

The lights of the city cast moving shadows across Stick's face as he stared at me, fingers steepled under his chin. If he was trying to impress or intimidate me, I was so not having it. "What do you want, Stick?" I asked before he could say a word. His eyes narrowed, as if I'd stolen the first line from him, as if this was some kind of stupid game.

"My name," he said, glaring at me, "is Stephen. Mr. Stephen, first aide to Prince Salazar himself. Stick was my worthless Fringer name, the name everyone thought I deserved. The name you and Lucas started calling me, because that's all I was to you. Something that could be broken and easily thrown away." His gaze slid to Zeke, who watched us in confusion, and his eyes glittered. "I used to be her best friend, you know. Did she tell you that? Back when we were both street rats, living in the Fringe? Did she ever mention us?"

"No," said Zeke calmly. He sat with his arms crossed, regarding Stick warily. He had to feel the obvious tension rising between us, but his voice remained neutral. "I never asked."

"Maybe you should someday," Stick went on, ignoring my warning growl. "Maybe you should ask her about Lucas and how he died. Our old gang leader, you know. She cared for him, too, even though she tried to hide it. Poor Lucas." Stick shook his head. "He thought he loved her, and got left to the rabids because of it."

"Stick!" I bared my fangs, and the guards next to him raised their crossbows, stopping me. I seethed, furious and desperate to shut Stick up. My demon, of course, was urging me to silence him by ripping out his throat, and it had never been more tempting than it was at that moment.

But Zeke's cool, soothing voice broke through the rising anger, stilling it for now. "Why are you telling me this?" he asked quietly, and I heard the disapproval in his tone. "I thought you two were friends."

"Friends." Stick gave a bitter smile. "Maybe once. I thought she was my friend. But she was just pretending. They all were. She's good at that, you know." Stick turned a wounded gaze on me, a flash of real hurt crossing his face. "She pretends to care about you, she pretends she wants you around, but it's all an act. Nothing she shows you is real, isn't that right, Allie?" He held my gaze, and to my shock, I saw the glimmer of tears before he blinked and they disappeared, almost too fast to be seen. "I wanted you to trust me, I wanted to show you that I could be more, but you never gave me the chance. You always thought I was worthless. Well, I'm not worthless now, am I?"

"I never thought of you like that," I whispered through

clenched teeth. "And if I closed myself off, it was because I couldn't bear to see you die. I couldn't bear to see any of you die."

Stick laughed then. It was an ugly sound. "For all the good it did." He turned to Zeke again, one corner of his mouth twisted and sneering. "Fair warning," he said, glaring contemptuously at the other human. "Don't get too close. She doesn't trust anyone, and she'll never let you in. Besides, everyone who gets close to her tends to disappear."

"Thanks for the warning," Zeke said. And, in full view of Stick, the guards and everyone, he very deliberately reached over and took my hand, lacing our fingers together. "But I think I'll be fine."

I'd never really seen Stick livid before, but the look he turned on Zeke could've peeled paint from the wall. Pure hate, anger and…jealousy?…darkened Stick's expression, but Zeke stared back, unruffled, stroking my hand with his thumb and sending shivers up my arm. I sat rigid, watching Stick, seeing his face turn a dangerous red, his jaw clenching as he glared at the boy across from him.

Abruptly, Stick turned, snatched the gun from his guard's belt and raised it, point-blank, at Zeke.

"Don't move, Allie!" Stick cried as I jerked up, his glare wide and feverish. "If you move, all I have to do is pull the trigger, and his brains will be all over the back window. Keep going!" he yelled to the soldier up front, who cursed but continued to drive. "You see?" Stick went on, panting and grinning savagely. "You see how they listen? Everyone listens to me, except you! But now, you'll listen to me, because I have the power. I can kill him—" He stabbed a glare at Zeke, raising the gun. "I can kill him now, and the Prince won't care. He won't care about one human. So you'll start listening to me now, Allie, or I swear I'll shoot him!"

"All right!" I held up a hand, trying to calm him down. Zeke was tense, both arms raised, his gaze never leaving the gun. I was quick, but I didn't know if I could reach Stick before the gun went off. And at such a close range, Zeke would definitely die. "I'm listening, Stick," I told him. "What the hell do you want from me?"

Stick grinned, eyes bright. "I want you to tell him—" he jerked the gun at Zeke again, who stiffened "—what happened to Lucas that night. And Rat. Go on, Allie, tell him. Tell him what happened to everyone else."

"They died," I answered, not really knowing where this was going. All I wanted was to get that gun out of his hands, but the muzzle was so close to Zeke's face I wasn't going to risk it.

"Why?" Stick demanded.

"They were killed by rabids."

"Why?" Stick asked again, and I scowled. What did he want me to say? What the hell was he trying to prove? "Why were we there in the first place?" Stick asked, keeping his gaze on Zeke. "Why were we outside the Wall?"

I suddenly knew what he wanted. My shoulders slumped, not wanting to say it, to remember that night. But I had to. "We were outside the Wall," I answered in a flat voice, "because I led us there."

"And why did Lucas die?"

Lucas. I glared at Stick, and he raised the gun a fraction, aiming for Zeke's face. His eyes were hard. I clenched my fists and muttered, "Because…I left him."

"To die," Stick repeated.

Damn you, Stick. "Yes."

Anger, sorrow and guilt burned. I tried not to think about that night, to remember the horror and terror when the rabids had surrounded me, when they'd yanked Rat into the tall grass, when they'd dragged Lucas over a fence. But the memories were still painfully clear, as if it had happened yesterday. I remembered the way Lucas had stared at me, his eyes begging me to save him, right before the rabids pulled him into the darkness. Stick didn't need to remind me. I already knew. It was my fault they had died, my fault we had all died.

I felt Zeke trying to catch my gaze, and glanced at him quickly. His face was grim, his eyes staring at me, trying to tell me something. *Be ready,* they seemed to say. I spared a quick glance at the guards. They seemed uncomfortable, still keeping the crossbows trained on me but also shooting Stick looks of anger and disgust. Obviously, their boss's erratic behavior was making them uneasy, too.

Oblivious, Stick waggled the gun at Zeke, making me tense. "You see?" he asked the other boy. "She doesn't care. She lets others die to save herself. Isn't that right, Allie? Tell him. Tell him that you don't care, that you're just using him, just like Lucas."

"I…" The words caught in my throat. Swallowing, I forced them out, making myself talk, to let Stick think I was playing his sick little game. "I don't care about you, Zeke. Stick's right. I'd leave you to the rabids if I had to, same as Lucas."

My eyes narrowed. "In fact, I'm about ready to let you die, just so I can get to Stick and rip his arms out of their sockets."

Stick jerked, his attention flashing to me, and Zeke moved.

He ducked to the side, lunged forward, and grabbed the other boy's wrist with both hands. Stick let out a yelp, fighting him, the gun flashing in a deadly arc between them. The guards gave shouts of their own, turning to the boys, and I hit one of them hard, slamming my fist into his nose, snapping his head back. The second was on the other side of Zeke and Stick, still grappling for the gun. He grabbed for the weapon, but a shot rang out, and the guard fell back, the side of his face covered in blood, his crossbow dropping to the floor.

All of this happened in the space of a heartbeat. As the gunshot boomed behind him, the driver swerved, lost control of the vehicle and smashed into the hulk of another car sitting on the sidewalk. The force jerked us all sideways, one of the guard's bodies slamming into me as we hit the wall, his skull cracking against mine. As the car rocked to a halt, I pushed the body off to see Stick, dazed and still holding the gun, wrench open the door and stagger into the road. Zeke was right behind him, though, shoving away the second body and lunging out of the car.

I followed, reaching back to draw my sword, but it was clear Zeke didn't need any help. As Stick stumbled away, raising the gun, Zeke leaped forward and smashed his fist across Stick's jaw. Stick's head snapped sideways, his body jerking as if an invisible string had been cut, and he sprawled limply on the pavement.

Panting, Zeke bent down and took the gun from Stick's numb fingers. Releasing the clip with practiced ease, he stuffed it into a vest pocket, racking the slide to get the last round of the chamber. That also got tucked neatly away before he tossed the gun aside with a revolted look. As I came up, he held out an arm to me, and I stepped into him without hesitation, feeling his heart race through his vest as he hugged me close.

"You okay?" he murmured as we drew back. I nodded, then looked down at Stick's limp body, lying on the cement, the snow falling around him. Rage flared, and I had to fight the overwhelming urge to pounce on him, drive my fist through his rib cage and tear the heart from his chest. Maybe Zeke knew what I was thinking, for his grip on my arms tightened.

"I'm fine, Allie," he whispered. "It's over."

The first car with Kanin and Jackal had pulled around and was now speeding back toward us, the headlights blinding through the snow. I raised an arm, shielding my face as it skidded to a halt and the guards leaped out, pointing guns and crossbows in our direction.

"What's going on here?"

Kanin and Jackal stepped out, too, regarding the body in the snow with looks of detached curiosity and amusement. No one, I noticed, went forward to see if Stick was all right, if he was even still alive. As the guard shouted at me again, demanding to know what had happened, Stick groaned and stirred weakly. I smelled the blood that streamed from his cut lip, spotting the snow, and felt a vindictive stab of pleasure. I hoped it hurt. I hoped he'd have a swollen jaw for weeks. He'd gotten off easy this time.

"Ask him," I told the guard as the body in the snow struggled to rise. "He's the one who tried to kill us."

All eyes went to Stick, who clawed himself upright and stood there panting, glaring at me and Zeke. His face twisted into a mask of rage and hate.

"Kill him!" he spat, stabbing a finger in Zeke's direction. I snarled and tensed, baring fangs, as Zeke put a warning hand on my arm. No one moved. "Well? What are you waiting for?" Stick snapped, staring at the guard captain. "Shoot him, now!"

The guard shifted uncomfortably. "Sir, that's not really an option."

"What?" Stick narrowed his eyes. "What did you say, Captain?"

"The Prince ordered us to escort them to the gate, sir." The captain's voice was stiff, flat. "All of them. We cannot countermand his orders, even for you."

"He's just a human!" Stick burst out. His eyes were bright and glassy, and a vein pulsed in his temple. "Not a vampire. The Prince won't care about one human. Do as I say!"

"I would think very carefully about that," came a low, deep voice. Kanin's, from the edge of the circle. He stood in front of the car, while Jackal leaned casually against the hood, watching in amusement. Though both vampires were stationary, they stared at the humans with unmistakable menace, and Jackal's eyes glowed in the shadows. "I would think very carefully on where you are standing, right now," Kanin went on. "Alone, far from the Prince's tower, surrounded by three vampires. If violence erupts, what do you think is going to happen here?"

The guards were pale now, as if they'd just realized their position and the danger from all sides. "Sir," the captain said, turning back to Stick, his voice low and deliberately calm. "We need to go, now. Let's get you back to the tower and inform the Prince of what has happened." He motioned at Stick with his gun, his voice polite but brooking no argument. "Go, sir. Now."

"And where do you think you're going, exactly?" Jackal crooned, sliding off the hood of the car. An edge had crept into his voice, and his eyes glittered. "Running back to the Prince, are we? I don't think so, bloodbags."

Stick's eyes widened, fear finally piercing the madness as he realized his guards were dead and the ones remaining could not protect him. Not from three angry vampires, far from the safety of the Prince's tower.

I glanced at Kanin, expecting him to step in, but he said nothing, his face expressionless as he stood there, unmoving. The guards raised their weapons and shuffled hastily away, keeping Stick behind them. But between me and the other two vampires, there was nowhere for them to run.

Jackal's gold eyes slid to mine, and he grinned, vicious and eager. "Come on then, sister. Let's do this, you and me. I'll even leave you the little parasite. You can rip his heart out and eat it in front of him if you like."

I growled and turned on the humans, curling my lip back. It *was* tempting. I could kill Stick. Right here. No one would miss him. The Prince wouldn't care, so long as we found Sarren and a cure. Stick, for all his delusions of grandeur, was still just one human in a world dominated by vampires. A pet. And pets could be replaced.

"Allie, no!" Stick's voice came from behind the guards.

"Don't let him hurt me," he pleaded. "We were friends, once. That means something, right? You're better than this."

I snarled at him, and the demon roared up full force, releasing all the anger, hurt, rage and grief that I'd kept locked away for so long. "You have no right to bring that up!" I shouted, and he shrank back, looking like the Stick I'd known. I took a step forward, baring my fangs, hating him now. "Don't you dare, not after what you've done! I can live with your hate, your anger, your crazy vendetta to prove that you're better than me now. I could even live with the fact that you sold me out to the Prince in exchange for an easy life. That's fine. You always had it in you, I knew that. I always knew..." Unexpectedly, my throat closed up, and I swallowed hard to open it.

"But don't try to appeal to my humanity now," I rasped, my voice low and cold, unfamiliar, "not when you forced me to admit that I'm a monster. Not when you tried to take away the only good thing I'll ever know. If he had died, I would've shown you a *real* monster."

"Yes," Jackal encouraged, grinning as he stalked forward. "That's right, sister. Let it go. This is what we are. And it's been ages since I've had a decent kill. Let's send the Prince a message, that this is what happens to pets who don't fear vampires like they should."

My demon agreed. I was losing myself to the monster, and I didn't care. Reaching back, I pulled my sword, drawing it with a metallic screech. The guards angled their weapons at us, but they were insignificant, a fragile wall of meat and blood. They would fall, and then there would be nothing between myself and my enemy. "You want to see what I am now?" I told Stick, who looked about ready to faint.

"What saving your life turned me into? Fine! I'll show you what I really am!"

Gripping my sword, I tensed to lunge.

"Allison, no!"

Something grabbed my arm from behind, jerking me to a halt. Snarling, fangs bared, I whirled on Zeke, barely stopping myself from springing forward and plunging my teeth into his neck. Zeke met my gaze, unflinching, even though I could see myself in his eyes, furious and demonic, lips curled back to show the full length of my fangs.

"Don't do it," he whispered, keeping a tight grip on my arm, though he had to know I could shove him off with little effort. "Allie, it's not worth it."

I hissed at him, not really myself. The monster was raging inside, and the Hunger was a bright flame in my stomach. "Why not?" I demanded.

He raised a hand, sliding his fingers into my hair, his gaze imploring. The contact shocked me, how close he was willing to get to a raging, snarling vampire. "Because, I know you," he said gently. "Because, when it's over, you'll regret it for the rest of your life." His fingers found the side of my neck, the palm brushing my skin. "That's forever, Allison."

I closed my eyes. The demon still howled within, wanting blood, eager for violence. But...Zeke was standing there, begging me not to do it, not to give in to the monster. I could feel his eyes on me, pleading for the life of the one who'd tried to kill him.

My anger wavered and I slumped, retracting my fangs. "Get out of here, Stick," I spat without turning around. "I don't want to see you again. I don't want to talk to you again. Go back to your Prince and forget I ever existed."

Jackal gave a disgusted snort. "You're kidding," he muttered, and sighed. "Well, bloodbags, you heard her. Guess it's your lucky night. Better hurry—I'm not as squeamish as my dear sister. You have five seconds to be gone, or the first human I see when I'm done counting won't make it to the end of the street."

I heard the humans walk swiftly away, as fast as they could without fleeing outright. The vampire in me still roared a protest, urging me to run them down and tear them open. To spill their hot blood into the snow, to watch the light dim from their eyes. From *his* eyes. I kept a tight hold on it, concentrating on the sound of Zeke's heart, his touch, until the footsteps faded into silence and the scent of fear blew away into the night.

Zeke stepped closer, his forehead resting against mine. "You did the right thing," he whispered, and I nodded, still trying to clamp down on my raging emotions. "Are you okay?"

"Give me a second," I said stiffly, and he didn't move, his hands resting lightly on my skin, as my muscles slowly uncoiled and the Hunger settled reluctantly, like a sullen, angry beast.

When I was fully in control, I pulled away, and Zeke released me. Jackal was shaking his head at us, pity and disgust written clearly on his sharp features, but it was Kanin's presence I sought. He stood beside the vehicle, his dark figure hazy through the glare of the headlights, his face impassive. Hollow black eyes regarded me without expression as I walked up, frowning.

"Why didn't you stop us?" I asked, not angry with him, just surprised. "I almost killed those men. If Zeke wasn't here, Jackal and I would've torn them apart. Why didn't you say anything?"

Kanin peered down at me, his impassive gaze softening just a touch. "I am no longer your teacher, Allison," he said quietly. "You have been one of us for a while now. You have hunted, and you have killed. It is not my responsibility to curb your demon." He glanced past me to the place Stick and the men had stood moments before. "And I wanted to see what type of monster you had become."

"Oh," I muttered as the last of the anger flickered and died and the sharp edge of regret sliced in to take its place. I suddenly felt like a new vampire again, back with my mentor, having just failed one of Kanin's tests. Defiance colored my voice. "Well, I hope you liked what you saw, because it's not going to change."

Kanin's words were so soft I might've imagined them. "I hope not."

"Great," Jackal said, sauntering up. He eyed the abandoned car, the smashed one a few yards away, and sighed. "Looks like we're walking to the Fringe."

Part III

ARDENT

CHAPTER 16

We didn't use the Sector Two gate. The guards escorting us were supposed to open it so that we could go through, but we weren't going to stand around waiting for them to return. Not when they could come back with an angry Prince and a squadron of vampire Elite, having been fed some crazy story by Stick on how we'd tried to kill him.

Instead, Kanin took us into the tunnels, somehow finding a sewer entrance beneath the hulk of a crumbled building, and we dropped into the Undercity once more.

"Well, it's official," Jackal said, his voice echoing down the long corridor. "This is the most I have ever been in the sewers in one place. If someone had said to me a month ago, *'Hey, Jackal, guess where you'll be spending most of your time in New Covington? Ankle-deep in shit!'* I would've ripped their lips off."

"This way," Kanin said, ignoring him. "It's a long walk to the old hospital, and we'll probably have to use the streets once or twice. Let's not waste any time."

He started off down the tunnel, and we followed, heading deeper into the sewers. No one spoke, which gave me plenty of time to remember what had just nearly happened. What I'd almost done.

I almost killed Stick tonight. The realization sent a cold shiver through me, as well as a bitter flood of anger and regret. I really had been about to kill him. Stick, the boy I'd looked after nearly half my human life, who had relied on me for everything. Who was weak, frightened, unable to fend for himself. I'd almost killed the boy I'd once considered my only friend. If Zeke hadn't stopped me…

Wonder what he thinks of you now.

Zeke walked behind me, making very little sound even through the puddles and scattered debris, the narrow pipe forcing us to stay single file. He didn't say anything about the incident with Stick, and I wondered what he was thinking. Did he regret being with me now, kissing me, putting such blind trust in a vampire? Did he realize the implications of tonight, that if I could kill *Stick,* someone I'd known far longer, what would stop me from turning on him, as well?

I warned you that I would always be a demon, I thought, skirting a trickle of water seeping down from above. Zeke followed, his presence close at my back, and I closed my eyes. *I should have heeded my own advice. Who am I trying to fool?*

Ahead of us, Kanin came to a stop at a rusted ladder that led to a sealed hole above. "The tunnel ahead is collapsed," he stated, turning back to face us. "This leads into the Fringe, very close to the Inner Wall. We can reach the hospital by going through the Undercity most of the way there, but we'll have to travel aboveground for a few blocks, so be ready."

"What if we run into bleeders?" Zeke asked. "They're sick and crazy, but they're still alive. Still human."

"Try to avoid them if possible," Kanin replied. "If the situation is as dire as the Prince says, we don't want to attract a crowd. But if you must, do not hesitate to cut them down, cripple them, whatever you must do to stay alive. That is the first priority. We won't be helping anyone if we get ourselves killed, is that clear?"

Zeke nodded reluctantly. Kanin went up the ladder, shoved back the opening and climbed out of the hole. Jackal followed, then Zeke, and finally me, emerging onto the deserted streets of the Fringe.

Even though it wasn't my old sector, the Fringe still looked familiar, with its cracked streets, crumbling buildings and frost-covered weeds pushing through everything. A layer of snow dusted the rusty hulks of cars scattered about, and the puddles in the road had iced over, making the ground slick and treacherous. Back when I was human, this was the most dangerous time of year, when everything was hard and frozen, and food was virtually nonexistent. Every winter, someone in the Fringe would die, frozen in some lonely back alley or dead of hunger in their beds. I remembered many mornings that I'd woken up shivering under my quilt, dreading the task of venturing outside in the freezing cold to scavenge for food. But if I didn't, I would starve, and so would Stick, curled against me for body warmth, refusing to leave the room.

I didn't have to worry about that anymore. And neither did Stick.

Movement on the street corner caught my attention. A body lurched out of a distant house, shambling and awkward, walking barefoot across the icy ground. I caught the gleam of red covering its face, the wet strips raked down its arms, as it mumbled and chuckled to itself, not watching where it was going.

"Quietly," Kanin told us, and glided into the shadows, becoming part of the night. We hurried after as silently as we could.

As we moved swiftly through the Fringe, we caught sight of several more bleeders, laughing or talking to themselves, sometimes shrieking at nothing, clawing at their faces. As we ventured farther from the Inner Wall, we began stumbling across bodies sprawled in the street, stains of dried blood around their lips or spattered on the ground beneath them. Some were frozen, covered in snow, having lain there a few days. Others were more recent, having died that very night or the day before, their self-inflicted wounds still fresh and seeping. There were more bodies this time, a lot more than when Jackal and I had first come through. The final stage of the virus was emerging full force.

"This city is screwed," Jackal remarked as we ducked through an old grocery store, roof blown off, windows shattered. Narrow aisles lined with rubble and glass now bulged with corpses, pale and bloody in the sickly light coming through the ceiling. We picked our way over sprawled limbs and sightless, staring faces, wary in case one leaped up and came at us, howling. "If I was Salazar, I'd let the virus run its course, wipe everyone out and start over again with the humans he has left. He's got enough bloodbags in the Inner City to feed himself and the rest of them. But noooooo, he has to send us on a wild-goose chase to find a madman and a nonexistent cure."

"He doesn't," Kanin said quietly from up ahead. "Not if he wants to keep the city alive. There aren't enough humans to feed all the vampires in New Covington, not without severely limiting the blood supply. Some of them would go mad and have to be destroyed. The humans in the Fringe are their greatest source of food. If they all die, New Covington will be threatened with extinction."

"Oh, well, my bad," Jackal said, stepping over a body lying facedown in the aisle. "Thanks for clearing that up, old man. I just have one more question for you. Why the hell do we care?"

"Because there are still people who can be saved," Zeke replied in a voice of cool contempt, deliberately not looking at Jackal. "Because there are still people in the Fringe who aren't infected, who are locked out of the Inner City and don't have any way of protecting themselves."

"Right, okay, let me revise that question," Jackal said, giving the human a disgusted look. "Why the hell should the *vampires* in this party care if the Prince's city goes up in flames? The plague isn't going anywhere. New Covington is as isolated as they come. Look, we can turn around, go back through the sewers, slip under the Wall and be outside the city by midnight."

For a second, I felt a blaze of anger at Jackal's callousness. Not just his complete disregard for the humans in the city, or even his fellow vampires—that was expected. Now he was willing to let Kanin die, knowing he didn't have a lot of time, knowing we had only a few days before our sire was so far gone nothing would save him.

But then, I remembered that Jackal *didn't* know about Kanin's sickness. Because Kanin hadn't told him. Or Zeke, either. I was the only one who knew about Salazar's betrayal, and the infected blood killing him from the inside. I didn't know why Kanin was keeping it a secret, but I guessed he had his reasons. And knowing Kanin, this was something he would reveal himself, if it came to that. I didn't like it, but if he didn't want them to know, I wasn't going to tell them.

"Come on then, old man," Jackal urged as the other vampire continued through the aisles, ignoring us all. "Let's get out of here, what do you say? Wasn't it you who taught me not to fight battles we can't win? Forget Salazar. Forget this hellhole. Let Sarren come to us."

I snorted. "Your compassion continues to astound me. *James*."

He shot me an evil glare. "Oh sorry, I should've been more clear. I'm only interested in the opinions of *real* vampires."

"Well, if that's the case, why don't you go find Sarren without us? I'm sure you two have a lot to talk about."

Kanin finally turned then, giving us both a weary look that said, *Are you two quite finished?* "We can't stop," he stated calmly. "We keep moving. Hopefully Sarren will have left something in the lab that we can use."

"And if he hasn't?" Jackal asked.

Then Kanin is dead, I thought numbly. *Because there won't be enough time to develop a cure, not for him. He'll rot away until he looks like that vampire in the hospital room.* Sickened, I clenched my fists, not knowing how Kanin could be so calm about it.

"Then we find another way," Kanin replied, still talking to Jackal. "We hunt down Sarren, if we must. But I am not leaving the city until this is over. You, however, are free to go." He nodded back the way we came. "I'm not keeping you here, I never have. If you want to leave, I'm not stopping you."

"You'd love that, wouldn't you?" Jackal's grin turned vicious. "What's the matter, Kanin? Don't want your newest spawn to hear about your greatest disappointment? What you created and then tried to kill?"

Kanin didn't answer, though I saw a flicker of regret pass through his eyes. Regret that he'd tried to destroy Jackal, or that he hadn't been able to? "Is there anyone you haven't pissed off so much they want to kill you?" I asked Jackal, who sneered at me.

"Hmm, lemme think. Well, there was this one chick who... No, wait, never mind. That didn't end well, either."

A shot rang out behind us.

I spun around, ready to draw my sword or attack. Zeke stood with his gun drawn, pointed down the aisle behind us. Several yards away, a human screeched and collapsed, pitching forward from an all-out charge, crashing to the ground. Another human leaped over the body and came rushing down the aisle, shrieking and waving a hammer, and Zeke's pistol barked once more. The body slammed into the shelves, laughing, twitching, clawing at its face, before it slumped and finally stopped moving.

Zeke holstered the weapon, his face grim, and I forced my nerves to calm down. "I know I'm the only human here," he said in a low, even voice, glancing back at us, "but maybe we can move the vampire family discussion to a later time? Maybe when we're off the streets and out of the open?"

I blinked at him, and even Kanin raised an eyebrow, a flicker of amusement crossing his face. But he only nodded and turned away. "Come, then. We're not far from the next stretch of tunnels."

Leaving the store, we walked swiftly through the ruins of the Fringe, wary this time of bleeders who might've been drawn to the noise. Kanin led, with Jackal close behind him. Zeke and I brought up the rear, hanging back a few paces.

"What's the story with Jackal and Kanin?" Zeke asked after a few minutes, his voice soft. "Kanin Turned him, right? What happened between them that made him change his mind?"

"I have no idea," I replied. "In fact, I was wondering that myself, but good luck getting a straight answer from either of them. Kanin has never spoken about his past, and Jackal will be a bastard just on principle. Why?" I glanced at Zeke, forgetting for a moment that I was trying to remain aloof. "You've never been curious about them before. What brought that on?"

"Nothing." He looked away, sounding evasive. "I was just wondering."

It hit me then, and my eyes widened. "Because you want to know if Kanin is planning to kill Jackal before you have the chance to," I guessed, and Zeke winced. "You're still planning to fight him when this is over."

"He killed my father, Allison." Zeke's eyes met mine, angry and hard. "Jebbadiah and Darren and Dorothy, even Ruth—they're all dead because of him. And I'm sorry, but I can't let that go. Yes, he's helping us now, but what happens after that? It doesn't change the past. My family is still dead."

"Killing him won't bring them back," I said softly.

"I know." Zeke looked away again, his face tightening. "I just…I need to find some kind of peace. If I can send him to hell where he belongs…"

My stomach clenched. "Jeb thought he would bring a vampire back to hell with him," I said, not really knowing why I was telling him this. "That was me."

He glanced back sharply, but at that moment, a sudden crackle buzzed in the silence, making us both jump.

"Zeke?" came a faint voice, and Zeke's hand went to his belt, pulling out that strange rectangular box. The voice came from the device, broken and hissing with static. "…there? Mole men…coming…you gotta…"

"Roach!" Zeke put the device to his mouth, his face intense. "Can you hear me? What's happening? Where are you?"

"…help us!" the box spat back. "Everyone is…sealed the entrance…mole men…will kill us!"

The device buzzed, then faded into an unbroken string of static, despite Zeke's attempts to contact the voice on the other end.

"Dammit," Zeke muttered, and I blinked. I couldn't remember ever hearing him swear before. He looked back at me, guilty but determined. "I have to go."

"Go?" Jackal repeated, having circled back with Kanin. His yellow eyes regarded Zeke curiously. "Where exactly are you going, bloodbag?"

"The refugees are in trouble," Zeke continued as Kanin stepped up, his dark gaze searching. "The mole men are moving on the base and will kill them if they get in. I have to help them."

Kanin frowned. "Refugees?"

"A bunch of noninfected humans living in the tunnels," I answered, watching Zeke eye the road behind us, like he could barely keep himself from rushing off. "It's on the edge of mole man territory, though, and they don't want them there anymore. They were threatening to drive them out when we came to find you."

"How many?" Kanin asked Zeke.

"Close to two dozen or, at least, that's how many there were when I left." Zeke raked a hand through his hair, looking distressed. "I can't leave them. They've locked the gate and sealed themselves in, but the mole men are waiting for them outside and they don't have any food. I promised I would come back if there was trouble, especially now that Salazar isn't sending any help."

"Have fun with that," Jackal said, crossing his arms. "They'll probably be dead by the time we get there. But don't let us stop you. We don't have time to play with bloodthirsty cannibals."

He was more right than he knew. Time was our enemy now, more than ever. Kanin's seconds were ticking away, even as we stood here and argued. But I also knew Zeke would never abandon those he'd sworn to help. "You go on," he told us all, backing away. "Keep looking for the lab. I'll catch up when I can."

"Zeke, no." I stepped forward, stopping him from running off. "There are too many. You're going to get yourself killed." And, knowing that he didn't fear death like he should, like all sane people did, I added, "If you die, you won't be able to help anyone."

Zeke hesitated. Stared at me, as if he was about to say something then thought better of it. Then, in a very quiet voice, he murmured, "Come with me, Allie?"

It was a question. Not a demand, or even a request. He was giving me a choice: human or vampire. Help the refugees, or continue on with Jackal and Kanin. I didn't know what to do. I wanted, desperately, to go with Zeke. I couldn't let him rush off to face an army of mole men by himself. He would be killed, and I'd never forgive myself.

But…Kanin was dying. He literally had hours left. If we couldn't find Sarren and a cure, Kanin was doomed. I couldn't leave him, either. If I returned to find my sire dead, killed by Sarren or the insidious virus working its way inside him…

Dammit. How could I choose between them? This was impossible.

I could feel the eyes of all three on me, waiting for a decision. Frustration and despair rose up, and I stifled the urge to snarl and drive my fist through a wall. "Zeke," I began, not really knowing what I would say next. "I…"

"Where are they?" Kanin suddenly asked.

Surprised, we all looked at the Master vampire, who waited calmly for Zeke's answer, no emotion crossing his face. "Sector Four," Zeke replied, and glanced at me. "Allison's old district."

"That isn't far," Kanin murmured, sounding tired and resigned. He closed his eyes, as if preparing himself, or coming to a decision, then sighed. "All right. Let's go."

"What?" I gaped at him as he stepped forward, brushing

by us. "Kanin…are you sure? What about…" I trailed off, certain he knew what I was talking about.

My sire looked back and gave me a weary nod. "Don't worry about that, Allison. This is important, a debt I must pay. I…" He hesitated, briefly closing his eyes. "I have an obligation to fulfill," he almost whispered. "Yours and his both. You came to New Covington for me, and I owe you several lives for that. Let this be the start of my compensation." He shook himself and gestured at Zeke then, motioning him forward. "Come. If we hurry, we can be there in a couple hours. Let's hope your people can hold out that long."

"Wait, I'm confused," Jackal said as we began walking back the way we came. "Did the entire world just get turned on its head? Now we're going to save a bunch of dirty meatsacks from a bunch of dirty cannibals? Why don't we rescue some orphaned kittens and put food out for stray puppies while we're at it?"

It took longer than we'd hoped to get to the tunnel that would lead to Sector Four. Bleeders roamed the streets between buildings, forcing us to hide, sneak around or wait for them to pass. This irritated Jackal to no end. They were only human, we should just carve a path right through and let God sort them out. But the rest of our party, Zeke especially, were opposed to needless killing, besides the fact that we didn't know how many of them were out there. The last thing we needed was a huge mob to come rushing down on us.

The last stretch to the tunnel was eerily silent. Kanin took us through an abandoned lot overgrown with frosted weeds and grass, crumbling buildings lining either side. I didn't like how exposed we were, even less so when I tripped over something large in the weeds and discovered it was a corpse, eyeless face turned to the sky.

Wrinkling my nose, I hurried on. It was too quiet. The houses sitting on the edge of the lot seemed to watch us with silent intensity. I could feel eyes on me, and though everything was deathly still, the air was thick with the smell of blood and open wounds.

"Kanin," I whispered, catching up to him, "I don't like this. Are we almost there?"

He nodded, and I could see that he was tense, too. "Very close. The entrance to the sewers is about another hundred yards from—"

And the screaming began.

Figures appeared in the doorways of the buildings, dozens of them, a huge ragged swarm. Bleeding, wailing, reeking of blood and pain, they burst through frames and windows and came shrieking at us, catching us in the center of the field.

Snarling, I drew my sword as the roar of Zeke's pistol joined the screeching chaos closing in from all sides. Spinning toward him, I saw him shoot two more bleeders, draw his machete as one came leaping at him and slash it across the human's throat. The man gurgled a wild laugh and pitched forward into the weeds, still clawing at him. Zeke stepped away, nearly bumping into me as I lunged in to help, and I spun around to guard his back.

A woman sprang at me, shrieking something about burning her laundry, swinging a chair leg at my face. I cut the weapon in two and plunged my sword between her breasts, yanking it out as she laughed at me and fell. A man with a bloody hole where his nose had been grabbed for my arm, insisting I give him a kiss as he raised a knife in the other hand. A flash of my katana, and his head toppled into the weeds.

"Keep going!" Kanin's roar rose above the shouts and laughter of the mob. Through a split-second break in the mob, I saw him and Jackal, fighting side by side. Kanin had his thin, short blade in hand, and he moved so quickly he was a blur: quick, lethal strikes that wasted no motion or effort. Every single cut or stab was a fatal blow, and he would move on to the next attacker before the previous one even knew they were dead.

At his side, Jackal bared his fangs in an evil smile as his attackers rushed forward, swinging his steel ax with lethal force. His blows knocked the humans off their feet, and they didn't get up again. One time, a human lunged in, grappling for the weapon, and Jackal simply drove his other fist into the man's chest, snapping bones as his hand vanished into the body and emerged wet to the forearm.

"Allison," Kanin called to me. "This way! The sewer entrance is about a hundred yards straight ahead!"

I slashed a bleeder through the ribs, ducked a wrench swung at my skull and cut the legs out from under him. "Got it! Zeke!" I glanced at him, my blood going cold as a bleeder rushed him from the side, slamming into him. Clinging to Zeke's arm, it howled in his ear and sank its teeth into his shoulder, growling like an enraged dog. I started forward, but Zeke planted his feet, shoved the man away and raised his gun as the human sprang at him again. His pistol barked, catching the bleeder right between the eyes, and it collapsed without a sound.

"Zeke!" I cut my way through two more humans to get to him, grabbing his arm as he retreated, his gun still raised and firing into the mob. "You all right?"

"I'm fine." Blood seeped through the collar of his shirt where the human had bitten him, two red splotches right below his neck. His jaw was set, eyes grim as he fired twice more, emptying the clip, and swung his blade up in front of him. "Get going, I'll be right behind you."

The bleeders screamed at us, insane and senseless. Slowly, we fought our way through the crowd to where Jackal and Kanin stood in the center of the lot. A square cement tube lay open at Kanin's feet, metal doors folded back, rusty ladder descending into darkness, but the bleeders, pressing in from all sides, prevented us from going down.

Jackal snarled, bashing the ax hilt into a woman's face, sending her reeling back with a wail. "Bloody persistent bastards," he growled, swiping at another who instantly crowded in, knocking it aside. "We move now, they're just going to follow us down."

"No, they won't," Zeke muttered, and pulled something from his vest. It was a green, cylindrical-shaped object with a handle and a metal ring attached to the top. I had no idea what it was, but Jackal looked back at it and swore.

"You've been carrying around grenades all this time?" He blocked a bleeder's stab to the head and back-fisted the ax across its face. "That would've been nice to know."

"This is the last one." Zeke looked at Kanin, standing at the edge of the sewer entrance. "Flashbang. We only get one shot at this." The vampire gave a short nod.

"Everyone, get down there, now," he ordered, pointing at me. "Jackal, Allison, move!"

Jackal responded instantly. Grabbing a human, he hurled it back into the crowd, turned and dropped through the hole, vanishing into darkness. Cursing, I slashed through one more bleeder and followed, landing on hard cement and instantly looking back for Kanin and Zeke.

Through the hole, I saw Zeke fend off a human, kicking it away, then draw back his arm and throw something into the crowd. Kanin snapped at him to go, and Zeke ducked into the opening, scrambling down the ladder and joining us at the bottom.

"What about Kanin?" I asked as soon as Zeke hit the ground and immediately backed away from the ladder. "How—"

A blinding flash of light, and a monstrous boom rocked the ground up top. The explosion echoed down the tunnel and caused dirt to rain from the ceiling, showering us with filth and bits of ice. I swore and looked desperately back for Kanin, but the Master vampire was already descending the ladder, closing the metal doors behind him.

"That should keep them distracted for a goodly while," he murmured, looking back up the ladder. He glanced at Zeke, a hint of approval crossing his impassive face. "You can keep your head in a fight," he said. "Well done. Are you injured?"

Zeke's hand went to his neck, his face tightening. "It's nothing," he said, dropping his arm. "I'm all right. We should get going."

Kanin nodded and turned away without a word, and we slipped into the darkness of the tunnels.

CHAPTER 17

Zeke began coughing a few hours later.

The first time it happened, no one really noticed. The sewers, while they were mostly dry and frozen over, not having been used for decades, were still sewers. I didn't have to take a breath to know it reeked down here of mold and fungi and rot and…other things. And the tunnels were filled with rodents and insects, crawling over everything, leaving things behind. So when Zeke first started coughing, I blamed it on the cold and damp and nasty odors, and kept going.

The second time was worse.

We were traveling through a narrow stretch of pipe, the two taller vampires having to duck to clear the low ceiling, when Zeke's harsh explosions caused ice to form in my stomach. I turned to see him bent over, one hand against the wall to steady himself, his whole frame racked with shuddering coughs. Panting, he straightened, dropping the hand covering his mouth, and I saw a splash of blood between his fingers.

"Zeke," I whispered, staring at him in growing fear as I finally realized what was happening. *No. Not him. Please.*

"I'm fine." He met my gaze, and his eyes were dull. Seeing my face, he offered a tired, resigned smile. "It's all right. There's nothing you can do, Allie. Let's keep moving."

Ahead of us, Jackal gave a soft curse, staring at Zeke with a dangerous expression. "Yeah, you say that now," he said, and his fangs glinted in the shadows, "but don't expect me to hold back when you start clawing your eyes out."

"If that happens…" Zeke kept his gaze on me, steady and composed. "You know what to do, right? Don't…don't let me suffer, or become a danger to anyone else. Just…make it quick."

I resisted the urge to snarl at him. It was too much. I couldn't pretend any longer. All Kanin's warnings about getting too close, all of my *own* sensibilities, keeping my distance, hardening my feelings—all collapsed beneath the undeniable truth: I cared for Zeke, it was useless to tell myself otherwise. I cared for him more than I'd cared for anyone in my life save my mom. It would destroy me if I lost him now.

"You don't ask for much, do you, Ezekiel?" I asked, my voice breaking a little. He had started forward but now paused, staring at me in surprise. "First you make me promise to let you die, now you're asking me to kill you? Do you think I'm just some soulless machine, that it would be so easy, just because I'm a vampire? It's not enough that Kanin is dying, now you want me to kill you, too?"

"Allison." Kanin's voice was weary, disapproving. Both Zeke and Jackal straightened, glancing at the older vampire in shock. I ignored their surprise, clenching my fists in sudden rage. I didn't know where this was coming from, but I was tired of losing people. I'd lost so many in my short life, even before I became a vampire. The cynical street rat in me sneered in disgust. Loss was just a part of life, I knew that. Nothing lasted in this world. The harder you held on to something, the more it would kill you when it was gone, so it was best not to get attached to anything.

But, dammit, I wanted to try. I wanted to fight to keep what was important to me. *Who* was important to me. And it pissed me off that they weren't willing to do the same.

"We are not giving up," I said, glaring at them all. There was a stinging sensation in the corner of my eyes, but I forced it back. "The rest of you can be fine and accepting and fatalistic if you want, but I refuse to let this thing win. I plan on tracking Sarren down and beating a cure out of him if I have to. And I'm sure as hell not giving up until I am certain, beyond a shred of doubt, that there is no hope left. So you—" I pointed at Zeke "—can stop asking me to kill you, and you—" I whirled on Kanin "—can stop hiding from the rest of us the fact that you're dying. We're fighting this thing together, and I am not going to lose anyone else."

For a few seconds after my rant, there was silence. I could sense they were all a little stunned; even Kanin appeared to have been left speechless. That, or he was too annoyed to say anything. I didn't care. He could be angry with me all he wanted, as long as he was still alive.

"Well," Jackal remarked, "that was quite the speech. Almost as good as the one you delivered on my tower that night with the old man. You do have a certain flare for the dramatic, don't you, sister?"

I scowled at him, but before I could say anything, he turned on Kanin with a dangerous glare. "You never told us you were dying, old man," he said softly, narrowing his eyes. "Let me guess—Salazar wanted to make sure you wouldn't leave the city, so he made sure you couldn't run out on him. Cunning old bastard. How long?"

"Does it matter?" Kanin's voice was emotionless. "Would it change anything?"

"See, that's the funny thing," Jackal shot back. "If it were anyone else, it should! Any sane vampire would be looking for Sarren right now, not trying to save a bunch of worthless meatsacks who are probably already dead. But that's always been your problem, hasn't it? You always sided with the humans. And now look where it's gotten you."

I stared at him. I'd never seen Jackal like this, not truly, seriously angry. His irritation always took the form of some obnoxious comment or jab to get under a person's skin. He looked furious now, glaring at Kanin in utter contempt, lips curled in a silent snarl. I couldn't tell if he was angry at Kanin for wanting to save a bunch of humans, or because Kanin was dying and hadn't told him.

"What do you think is going to happen when we find Sarren?" Jackal demanded of Kanin, who watched him calmly. "You think you can take him now, falling apart like you are? Your compassion for these worthless humans is going to get us all killed!"

"I've made my choice," Kanin said, unruffled as always. "You don't have to stand with it."

Jackal shook his head in disgust and took a step back. "You know what? You're right," he said softly, eyeing each of us.

"This isn't worth it. I thought the old bloodsucker would have information on the Rabidism cure, maybe lead us right to it. But if he's going to throw away his life for a bunch of worthless mortals, I'm better off finding it myself."

"Where do you think you'll go?" I demanded, wondering why I should care if Jackal left. *Let him go, you always knew he would leave or turn on you if he got the chance.* I didn't know why I felt so angry. A part of me said we needed Jackal's help against Sarren, that he was a good fighter and another body between me and Sarren: that was why I didn't want him to go.

But that was a lie. Jackal was my brother, and, as selfish and monstrous as he was, I was hoping he would prove me wrong. "You can't take on Sarren alone," I argued. "He's too strong for just one person, you said so yourself."

"Who said anything about fighting him?" Jackal crossed his arms, smirking. "I'm not that stupid, sister. Way I see it, Sarren is the closest one to discovering a cure now. If I ever cross paths with our disturbed friend, it'll be to ask a few friendly questions, and then I'll be on my way. I'm not crazy enough to try to stop him. But I'm certainly not going to hang around here with the lot of you, wasting time. You have fun with the sickies and the psychos. I'll be leaving now."

A metallic shiver echoed through the pipe as Zeke drew his machete, the raspy sound making my stomach clench.

"What makes you think I'm going to just let you go?" Zeke said in cold voice. His eyes glittered with anger and hate as he stared Jackal down. "You have crimes to answer for," he went on, the light glimmering down the length of his blade as he raised it toward Jackal. "People you murdered. I haven't forgotten any of them, and you're still going to pay for what you did."

Oh no. Zeke was serious—he was ready for this fight. The confrontation he'd hinted at since arriving in New Covington had finally come. *"For my family,"* he'd said in the tunnels. *"For everyone back in Eden, I'm going to kill that vampire, Allison. The only question is...will I have to fight you, as well?"*

I had to make a decision. I couldn't fight them both. As if sensing my thoughts, Zeke flicked a glance at me, his blue eyes suddenly remorseful. "I'm sorry, Allison," he said quietly. "You don't have to help me. Walk away if you have to. But I can't just let him go."

Jackal turned a purely sadistic smile on Zeke, and I tensed, ready to leap in if either attacked. "You don't have time for this, bloodbag," he crooned. "Shouldn't you be saving your pathetic little human tribe? You think you can take me on alone? How are you going to help them if you're dead?"

It was probably the hardest thing I'd done in a long time, but I made my choice. Drawing my sword, I stepped up beside Zeke, facing Jackal down. "He won't be alone," I said.

I could feel Zeke's relief and gratitude even without looking at him. Jackal, however, stared at me, eyes narrowing to yellow slits. "Well," he muttered, and all his arrogance disappeared, leaving cold rage in its place. "So that's how it is, huh, sister? You would choose a human over your own blood kin. You really are like Kanin, a traitor to your whole race."

I bared my fangs. "From where I'm standing, you're walking out on us. So don't expect any tears from me, *brother.*"

"Allison. Ezekiel." Kanin's voice cut through the tension, the rising fury. I paused and glanced at the other vampire, who hadn't moved from his spot beneath the drain. "Let him go," he ordered softly.

Zeke didn't move, but his jaw tightened stubbornly. "Kanin—"

"We don't have time for this."

I slumped. Kanin was right. We didn't have time to fight Jackal now. The seconds were rapidly ticking away, for all of us. For the refugees and Kanin, and now…now Zeke. What would happen, I thought numbly, if that time ran out? There'd be no one left. Everyone would die.

Except me. I would be alone again.

Sheathing my blade, I turned to the human beside me. "Zeke," I said, and put a hand on his arm. It was tight beneath my fingers, muscles coiled into steel bands. "Let's go. Come on, we need to find the refugees." His arm shook, tightening his grip on the weapon, and I lowered my voice. "Please."

He resisted me a moment, then finally lowered his blade, the tension leaving his back and shoulders. "This isn't over," Zeke warned in a low voice, still glaring at Jackal. "I'll find you. The next time we meet, vampire, I'll kill you."

Jackal chuckled. "The next time I see you, bloodbag, you'll be a stinking, eyeless corpse. So forgive me if I'm not too terribly concerned."

Zeke didn't reply. My blood brother stepped away, the evil grin back on his face. "Well, I can't say it hasn't been fun," he said, giving us a mocking salute as he turned to leave. "But I have other things to do now—vampires to find, armies to raise, that sort of thing." He glanced at me, and his smirk faded a bit. "Sister, if you ever get tired of these walking bloodbags, come find me. We could still do great things, you and I."

And, with a final sneer, he turned his back on us and walked away, disappearing into the shadows of the pipe.

I stared after him, still half thinking he would come stalking back, laughing at us for falling for such an obvious trick. It didn't happen. The darkness behind us remained silent, still and empty. I closed my eyes once, searching for him, and felt his presence through our blood tie. Though it was very faint, pulling farther and farther away. Jackal was gone.

"Come on," Kanin said, when it was clear he wasn't coming back. "Let's keep moving. We're almost there."

"Did you know?" I asked Kanin a few minutes later when the pipe ended and we came to the main stretch of sewer again. We hurried down the tunnel, knowing we were racing the clock, but questions still hounded me, refusing to leave me alone.

The vampire glanced me, puzzled, and I elaborated. "Jackal," I said. "Did you know he would leave if he found out you were…sick? Is that why you didn't tell him?"

"One of the reasons." Kanin's brow furrowed slightly. "Jackal has always been…pragmatic. If he suspects he is on the losing end of a bargain, he'll get out of it somehow and come at it from a different angle. In his eyes, I could no longer give him what he wanted, so he decided to find another way. He's always been like that."

"I screwed up," I muttered, angrily kicking a rock into the water. "I'm sorry, Kanin."

He shook his head. "Don't apologize for Jackal's shortcomings, Allison. We all made our choices."

That didn't make me feel much better. Jackal was still gone, and Kanin was still sick. And Zeke, walking quietly behind us, was starting to cough more and more. He tried to hide it, and he never complained, but I could hear the raspy, painful breaths, caught the faint scent of the blood he would cough up sometimes, and worry gnawed at my insides.

"Kanin?" I asked again, and heard him sigh, as if steeling himself for more questions. For a second, I almost didn't ask, but then hardened myself. I wanted to know. "Why did you Turn Jackal?"

He didn't answer for a long time, and I thought he was going to ignore me. "Why do you want to know?" he finally asked in a quiet, almost sorrowful voice.

I shrugged. "Because I'm curious? Because I want to know, how do you choose? If there's a criteria for Turning someone into a vampire? Because..." *Because I want to know if he was ever like me, once. And if I...could ever become like him.*

Kanin, in that knowing, inscrutable way of his, seemed to guess what I was thinking. "I found James a few decades ago," he began slowly, as if resigning himself to the tale. "When I returned to this country again. I'd been gone for many years."

"Why?"

"What do you mean, why?"

"Why were you gone?"

He closed his eyes. "You're not going to make this easy for me, are you?" he murmured, and I felt a tiny stab of guilt. But it was overshadowed by determination and a burning desire to finally know all his secrets. Kanin had kept almost everything from me for so long, but I was no longer his student. I wanted to know who my sire really was.

I paused then said, very carefully, "I think I have a right to know, Kanin."

"Yes," he murmured, running a hand over his eyes. "Yes, I suppose you do." Dropping his arm, he continued walking down the tunnel, his face dark. "To answer your question," he began, his tone flat, deliberately emotionless, "I was forced to go on the run. After the other Masters discovered what I had done, what I created, they all wanted my head. For the first time in countless centuries, they were united under one goal—destroying one of their own. It became almost a competition, to see who could kill me first. And, of course, there was Sarren...." His expression darkened. "So, I fled the country, spent many years on the run, never staying in one place for long. Eventually, the other Masters stopped sending people to kill me, and things finally calmed down. Except for one."

I shivered, knowing who he meant. Kanin shook his head. "Sarren never stopped. Wherever I went, he wasn't far behind. I knew that, one day, he would catch up with me. And I knew that, when he did, his revenge would be terrible. But I hoped to atone for my mistakes before that happened. So, I returned to this country after many years, to find the research the scientists left behind. I knew there was at least one scientist who had survived the carnage the night the rabids escaped, but I knew nothing of where he was, if his ancestors still lived. After years of searching and getting nowhere, I finally decided to investigate the very place the rabids were created. Though it was a vampire city now, and its Prince still wanted me dead, I had to try." He gave me a sideways look, a faint, rueful smile crossing his lips. "You know the rest."

I listened in rapt amazement. This was the most I'd ever heard Kanin speak of his past, as shameful and horror filled as it was. "Where does Jackal fit in?" I asked, remembering my original question.

"Jackal." Kanin's eyes narrowed. "When I returned, the world was not the same. The vampire cities were in full power, and everything outside the cities was chaos. That first year, I stumbled upon the burning remains of a small homestead in the middle of the wilderness. It seemed that bandits or raiders had killed everyone, or so I first thought. But, later that night, I found James lying in the road several miles away. He'd been shot in the leg, but had dragged himself as far as he could before his strength gave out."

"He was dying," I guessed. "Like me."

"Yes. Though his death was not quite as imminent as yours." Kanin's brow furrowed. "Rather, I had no food, no water or medicine or bandages, and we were many miles from civilization. He would have died of blood loss and exposure, and he knew it. We had a rather interesting conversation." Kanin almost smiled again, though his voice was grave. "Him lying there, and me standing over him, trying to determine what kind of person he was. I thought I knew what I was creating when I offered him the choice. I thought..." Kanin laughed softly, a sound completely without humor. "I thought I'd found someone who would help me bring an end to what I had caused. I didn't see what he truly wanted until much later."

"What happened?"

Kanin looked reluctant to continue, but he did. "I taught him how to be a vampire, same as you. We traveled for several months, the two of us. He seemed fascinated with the idea of curing Rabidism and would ask me questions about the research, the scientists, the hidden labs. We argued about a lot of things, but I was still too blind to see what I'd created.

"Then, one night, he tracked down those men who killed his family, and tried Turning them. To this day, I don't know what he told them. Perhaps he offered them immortal life, perhaps it was only revenge after all. But all those men he attempted to Turn became rabid, every single one of them. And he didn't stop trying. I found him with the last of the humans, dead rabids everywhere, still trying to create his own offspring. And I finally realized what kind of vampire I'd brought into the world.

"James wanted to bring an end to Rabidism," Kanin finished, his eyes hard, "but only to create his own army, his own kingdom, and to fill the world with our kind. Vampires should rule, he told me. Why should humans take over the world, when we were so vastly superior? Only numbers had stopped us before, and if vampires could produce offspring again, the humans would never rise up against us."

"Jackal said you tried to kill him."

"I did." Kanin's voice was remorseless. "He was the only vampire I've ever Turned and then tried to destroy. Before James, I didn't care what my few offspring did when we parted ways. I could only teach them how to be an immortal, and then let them carve their own path through eternity. But the world that James envisioned was something I could not allow.

Unfortunately, he managed to escape, though I told him if our paths crossed again, I would end his life."

"And that's the last you saw of him?"

"He took the name Jackal and vanished into the mountains with the last of the humans who'd slaughtered his family. I suppose they became the first of his so-called raider army. So…" Kanin looked down at me. "Now you know all my secrets, all my regrets." He raised his head, frowning. "You and Ezekiel, who I know has been listening to every word we've said."

"Sorry," Zeke said from behind us. "I wasn't trying to."

Kanin's lips twitched in a bitter smile. "Perhaps it is better," he mused, "that someone knows who Jackal really is. I swore that I would never create another after James, but…" He paused, his next words nearly lost in the shadows. "I am glad that I broke that promise."

"Kanin…"

Zeke quickened his pace, catching up to us. "Now I have a question," he said, and Kanin sighed once more. He didn't protest, however, and Zeke went on ruthlessly. "So…you *are* the vampire that was helping the scientists, aren't you?" he asked, and there was a hint of awe in his voice. "The one who helped the original team looking for a cure."

"They spoke of me?" Kanin sounded surprised.

Zeke nodded. "The scientists in Eden told me everything," he said. "Everything about the vampire experiments, and how the rabids were created. They said you vanished the night the lab caught fire and the rabids escaped." His voice took on a faint edge. "The common belief…was that you started it."

"No." Kanin's voice was low, remorseful, and a hint of

pain glimmered through his calm expression. "Since you both seem determined to drag my entire past into the light… no, it was not I who set fire to the lab. I told them the rabids needed to be destroyed, but most of the scientists disagreed. There was a split among them, those who wanted the rabids put down, and those who thought they could still be used. Finally, a decision was made to kick several of the scientists off the team—the ones who wanted the rabids destroyed." Kanin paused, then said, very softly, "One of them was the head scientist, Malachi Crosse."

Zeke drew in a sharp breath. "Jebbadiah's grandfather."

"I went to the lab that night to stop him," Kanin said darkly. "I knew what he was planning, but by the time I got there, it was too late. The lab was in flames, the scientists were dead, and the rabids were gone. I had failed."

For a moment after this revelation, we were all silent, the only sounds being our footsteps echoing on the cement and Zeke's ragged breathing. "Did you know about the other lab?" I questioned at last. "The one in Old D.C.?"

Kanin shook his head. "Not at the time. Though I did find out about it later. They were giving human patients the experimental 'cure,' weren't they? Foolish."

"There was a massive rabid outbreak in that area," I said. "Thousands of people, tens of thousands, maybe more, died and Turned because of it. So, you might not be responsible for the spread of Rabidism, Kanin. It might have started in D.C., not New Covington."

"Even if that were true…" Kanin glanced at me, his eyes shadowed. "I was the one who exposed our race, who offered the lives of other kindred to find a cure. I appreciate the thought, Allison, but this is still on my head. Now..." His attention shifted to Zeke, who was listening to this in somber silence. "I have told you everything about my past, and we are still a few minutes away from Sector Four. I wish to know about the scientists in Eden. Have they been given the research? Are they working on a cure?"

But before Zeke could answer, scuttling sounded up ahead, and two skinny, pale figures darted out of a nearby tunnel. The mole men slid to a halt when they saw us, hissing and raising their crude blades.

"More topsiders!" one rasped, baring rotted black teeth. "Get out! Get out of our territory. You'll find no safety down here. The topsider camp is destroyed. The intruders will be dead soon! You will join them if you do not leave, now!"

Zeke stepped forward, pistol in hand, his face and voice icy. "What did you do to them?"

The mole men hissed again, eyes widening. "The topsider chief!" the second man snarled. "He's returned! With...with *vampires!* Run, warn the others!"

They took off, but Zeke was already bringing up his gun, and I was lunging forward. The pistol boomed, striking a mole man in the back, and my katana sliced down, beheading the other.

"Quickly." Kanin came forward, hurrying into the dark. "It sounds like we don't have much time."

The smell of blood hit me soon after, soaking the air and making my stomach turn with Hunger. As we drew closer to the underground camp, voices began to echo out of the tunnels: cries, shouts, angry hisses and snarls. A desperate scream cut through the clamor ahead, and we began to run, weapons already drawn.

A mole man emerged from a familiar tunnel, shrieking in alarm as he saw us. With a chill, I recognized the tunnel as the entrance to the camp, the one that had been barred when Roach first brought us here. The gate had been torn off and lay in a rusty heap in the water.

Zeke didn't slow down. As the mole man lunged forward, Zeke ducked beneath the wild swing and brought his machete flashing up, striking the man in the chest and ripping the blade out through his side. Screeching, the mole man crumpled behind us, and Zeke led us through the gate.

A body lay in the entrance, the young guard Roach had spoken to on our first trip here. Stab wounds covered his chest and stomach, and he gazed unseeing at the roof. Another body sprawled nearby, a mole man, bloody and still. Stone-faced, Zeke rushed past them to the staircase that led to the floor above, and began taking them two at a time.

Kanin and I followed. We emerged from the stairwell into chaos. Fires burned erratically through the boiler room, steel drums knocked over and spilling hot coals onto the cement. Bodies darted through the flames and shadows, pale mole men and terrified refugees, scurrying about in panicked confusion. A pair of mole men had trapped a woman against a corner and closed in, stabbing and punching, and Zeke sprang forward with a furious yell.

I went to help him, but Kanin stepped out of the shadows, into the sickly red light, and roared. The chilling sound echoed through the room, making my hair stand on end and causing everyone to spin around. As Zeke slashed his blade across one mole man's neck and clubbed the other with his gun, everyone else in the room, both attackers and refugees, screamed as they realized what had come into their midst, and scattered into the darkness.

Goaded by the scent of fear and violence, I roared a challenge as well and leaped into the room. Several mole men came at me, slashing and flailing, screeching their hate. I cut them down, my demon reveling in the blood that coated the walls and spattered the floor, arching in ribbons across my face. A few yards away, Zeke fought his way through the center, blade flashing, the occasional bark of gunfire ringing off the boilers. Kanin swept into the room, a dark shadow of death, and every person he passed crumpled to the ground a second later, bleeding and lifeless.

In seconds, the room emptied. Most of the attackers opted not to stay and fight, but fled toward the ladder when they realized vampires had joined the fray. I let them go, though it was hard not to chase them into the tunnels, to run them into the darkness and rip out their throats. Keeping a firm hold on my bloodlust, I sheathed my katana, willed my demon to settle down and looked around for Kanin and Zeke.

Zeke stood in the center of the room, panting, his gun and machete dangling at his sides as he watched the last of the mole men leave. His blue eyes gleamed dangerously in the dim light, as if he was holding himself back, forcing himself not to fire on the pale, retreating forms. Kanin stood nearby, all but hidden in the corner shadows.

"Zeke!"

A young man rushed up to him, panicked, grabbing at his shirt. Zeke flinched as the other boy yanked on him desperately. "Where were you? We've been trying to contact you for hours!"

"I came as soon as I could." Zeke freed himself and took a step back, surveying the room grimly. Bodies lay scattered about, some moaning, most deathly still. The refugee came at him again, and Zeke jerked away. "Don't come near me!" he snapped, and the boy froze, gazing at him in shock. Zeke backed away, his arm to his mouth. "Stay away from me, all of you. I don't..." He swallowed hard. "I'm sick," he told him, and the refugee's face went white. "I don't want you getting what I have. Keep your distance."

The boy fled to a corner of the room. Zeke watched him go, then gazed around at the other survivors, now eyeing him with nearly the same amount of fear as they were the vampires. A pained look crossed his face, and he turned to me.

"Allie. Will you help me figure out how many are still alive?"

We took a head count of the survivors. The results were sobering. Of the two dozen or so refugees Zeke had left behind, only nine had survived the sudden attack. Many of them had been badly wounded, and at least a couple of them wouldn't survive the night.

Zeke took the news stoically then began the slow process of organizing the chaos; helping the injured, directing people to bind wounds, posting a guard at the entrance in case the mole men returned. But he kept his distance from everyone and, more than once had to back away when harsh coughing racked his lean frame, pressing an old cloth to his nose and mouth. The refugees cringed back when he did this, glancing between him and the vampires, clearly not knowing which was worse.

"They're vulnerable here," Kanin told me when I joined him in the corner. I'd tried to help Zeke manage the confusion in the aftermath, but it was hard when everyone was terrified of the blood-drenched vampire girl. Kanin, more intelligently, had taken a spot along the far wall, and was simply watching with cool detachment.

I glanced at him. "What do you mean?"

"The mole men know where they are. Their defenses are gone. If they attack again, they'll likely succeed in killing everyone." He watched a refugee limp across the room, and shook his head. "We won't be around to protect them much longer."

"They can't stay here then," I muttered. "They have to find another camp. Where, though? Another place in the tunnels?"

"You would risk running into more mole men," Kanin pointed out. "If they are this incensed about topsiders invading their territory, perhaps it is best that they leave it altogether."

"Yeah, but where?" I asked again. "Up top isn't any safer, with the bleeders and the crazies running around. Where could they possibly go that's remotely safe?"

"This was your old sector, was it not?"

"Yes, but…" I stopped, thinking. I did know of one place. *It's not far,* I mused to myself. *And it's fairly isolated. The basement is a good spot to hole up if things go bad. Not ideal, but better than here.* "Right," I muttered, pushing myself off the wall. "I know where we can go."

I found Zeke standing among the huge rusted boilers at the back of the room. His back was to me, and his head was bowed as he gazed at something near his feet. Curious, I walked up behind him, peered down and winced.

Roach sat against one of the columns, his young face turned sightlessly to the ceiling, the hilt of a dagger shoved through his chest. The walkie-talkie was still clutched in one hand.

Knowing Zeke, knowing he was blaming himself, I put a hand on his arm. It was so hot, burning under my fingertips. "This isn't your fault," I said softly.

He didn't answer. Stepping forward, he bent down and gently took the walkie-talkie from Roach's limp grasp, a heavy, broken sigh escaping him as he rose.

"Zeke," I ventured as he turned around, his face frozen into a stoic mask. "The other refugees. They can't stay here."

"I know." He replaced the walkie-talkie, sliding it onto his belt, and became businesslike again. "I was trying to come up with a way to tell you and Kanin. I'm taking them topside. You don't…have to stick around. You should go after Sarren. I'll be fine."

He wasn't looking at me. Anger flickered, but I kept my voice calm, reasonable. "You don't know this sector as well as I do. Where will you go?"

"We'll find a place." His eyes strayed back to Roach, and he turned away, walking slowly back toward the group. "Dawn is about two hours from now," he said, passing me without looking up. "It'll take that long to get topside and find a place to hide from the bleeders. You and Kanin can still get a good head start back to Sector Two before morning. Don't worry about me. I'll catch up when I can."

A growl rose to my throat. Reaching out, I grabbed his elbow, spun him around and pushed him back into a pillar.

He gave a startled *whoof,* eyes widening in shock, before I stepped up and kissed him, hard.

He froze for a second, before his arms came up to pull me closer. I leaned into him, feeling the Hunger rise up, feeling his lips on mine, his hands sliding over my back. I let myself feel all these things, including the urge to drop my head to his neck and plunge my fangs into his throat. I could control it, I *would* control it. Because there was no way I was letting Zeke go now.

"I have a better idea," I whispered when we finally pulled back. My face was inches from his, and I could feel the heat radiating from him, hot and feverish. "Why don't you let us help you?"

His chest heaved beneath my palms. "What about Sarren?"

"We'll find Sarren." I slipped my fingers into his hair, brushing it back, and he closed his eyes. "We can get these people to safety *and* find Sarren in time. It doesn't have to be one or the other, Zeke." He didn't answer, and I dropped my hands, resting them on his shoulders, the backs of my fingers lightly touching his neck. "I have a place we can go topside—the old school, where I used to live. It's isolated, there's plenty of space and it's fairly secure. They'll be safe there, as safe as they can be anywhere in the Fringe. We just have to get them out of here, now."

"I don't want to slow you down."

I gave him a challenging half smirk. "You were the one who traveled halfway across the country to find me, Zeke Crosse. Now that you have, and now that you insist that something brought us together, I'm afraid you're not getting rid of me that easily. Or, maybe I should say, I'm not letting *you* go. Vampires are possessive like that."

A tiny snort, and his eyes finally lightened a shade. "So, you're saying I'm a pet now, vampire girl?"

It really wasn't the place, or the time, to be thinking of this. Sarren was out there, Jackal was gone, and we still had the refugees to deal with tonight. Kanin and Zeke were both living on borrowed time, and every second was crucial. But all I could think of now was how much I wanted this. I wanted to take this risk, despite all the years of self-preservation telling me to hide, to pull back, protect myself. Zeke had not protected himself. He'd come to New Covington knowing exactly who I was, what I was, and he was the reason I could take a chance. The reason I could, for once, put my heart on the line, open myself up and let someone in.

My arms slipped around his neck. I looked up at his face, into those clear sapphire eyes and whispered, "Kiss me, Zeke."

He did. His eyes closed, he lowered his head and his lips closed over my own, gentle and soft. This one lasted several long moments, and when Zeke drew back again, his eyes were dark with passion. But they were a little wary now, too.

"Kanin is watching us," he murmured.

My head cleared instantly. I felt a tiny stab of fear, wondering what my mentor would say, if he would scold, or shake his head in disgust. Certainly, he wouldn't be pleased. I couldn't see his face very well, as he was still across the room in his dark corner, but I could feel the weight of his stare, boring into me.

Zeke gently pushed me back, stepping off the pillar. "I'll

get the others ready to move," he said. "It shouldn't take long. How far to this school of yours?"

"We'll be there before dawn," I told him, still feeling Kanin's eyes on us. *You knew he would find out about you and Zeke sometime, Allison. He probably suspected everything even before this. Question is, do you care what he thinks about a vampire and a human?*

"All right." Zeke nodded. "Let me explain what's going on to everyone. We'll be ready to head out in a few minutes."

"Zeke?"

He turned back, eyes questioning. And before I lost my nerve, in full view of my sire, I stepped up to him, put my hands on the sides of his face and kissed him one more time.

I know you're watching, Kanin. And yes, this is my answer.

Zeke drew back, looking a little dazed. Gazing down at me, he gave a wry smile, licking his lips. "That...didn't have anything to do with him over there, did it?" he asked, sounding suspiciously amused, and a little breathless. I bit my lip.

"Does that bother you?"

"If it involves kissing you? Please, use me to prove a point anytime." With a faint smile, he squeezed my arm and stepped back, and I let him this time. "I'll get everyone together. Give me ten minutes and we'll be ready to go."

I watched him depart, steeled myself and then walked over to Kanin, who hadn't moved from his place in the corner.

"That was interesting." he mused in a toneless voice as I joined him along the wall. "I assume that last display was solely for my benefit?"

"Kanin—"

"Allison." My sire looked at me, solemn and grave. "I am

not in any position to tell you what to do, or how to live your life," he said, surprising me. "You already know my thoughts, and, as I've discovered before, you will either heed my advice, or you won't. I don't need to remind you. You're not the same girl I left outside New Covington, and I am no longer your teacher.

"However," he continued, just as I'd started to relax, "I will issue this one warning. I will not Turn that boy for you, if it comes down to that. He is…too human to make it as a vampire. It would destroy him very quickly."

"I know," I muttered, watching Zeke move among the refugees, keeping his distance in order not to infect them. "He already made me promise the same thing. That if he was dying, to just…let him go."

Kanin's eyes searched the side of my face. "And could you?" he asked softly. "Let him go?"

I didn't answer, and Kanin didn't push the question. We watched the humans in silence, two vampires standing in the darkness on the outskirts of humanity, always looking in.

CHAPTER 18

We took the remaining refugees through the tunnels, very nearly the whole way. This soon after the attack, we weren't worried about a mole man ambush. Now that they knew vampires had invaded their home, they were likely fleeing to scattered corners of the sewers, to hide and wait for the monsters to return to the surface. The bigger danger would come from the bleeders up top. Despite the emptiness of the tunnels, progress was slow. Most of the refugees had been hurt, and a couple were severely wounded, slowing our hike to a near crawl. I bit down my impatience and ignored the demon inside telling me to eat a few, to kill off the weak and sick. Dawn wasn't far, and at this rate, we'd barely have enough time to get off the streets and out of the light.

The sky was an ominous gray as we finally made our painstaking way across the empty lot, ignoring the few frozen corpses lying in the weeds. The snow had stopped, and the old school looked like a sullen beast huddled against the cold.

I led everyone through the doors, down the shadowy, rubble-strewn halls, to the basement at the bottom of the stairs. It was pitch-black down there and probably freezing, but the room had cement walls, no windows, and a single thick door that barred from the inside. It was the most secure place I knew, in the Fringe, anyway. If the bleeders could get this far, there was no hope for the uninfected humans.

Zeke watched the refugees set up the new camp, waited until blankets had been passed out, fires had been lit, and people had settled in, before turning to me.

"They'll be all right now," he muttered. He'd been coughing the whole way here, and had wrapped a strip of cloth around his nose and mouth to keep the sickness contained. Sweat glistened on his brow, even through the cold, and the fabric below his lips was spattered with red.

I nodded. "At least they'll be safe from the bleeders here." Food was still going to be a problem, but food was always a problem in the Fringe. Zeke suddenly winced and pressed a palm to his forehead, making my stomach clench in worry. "You all right?"

"Yeah, I'm fine. Headache." He dropped his hand, smiling to ease my fear. "Where did Kanin go?"

"He said he was going to find a place to sleep." Kanin had vanished soon after we had showed everyone to the basement, slipping into the darkness without a sound. And in this big, crumbling building with its countless rooms and dark corridors, I'd probably never find him. I would have to follow him soon. The sun was up now, and sluggishness pulled at my eyelids. "I need to get going, too."

"Allie." Zeke sounded uncomfortable, raking a hand

through his damp bangs. "Can I…come with you?" he asked, making me blink in surprise. "I don't want to stay down there," he continued, nodding toward the basement door. "Not when I could put the others at risk. I don't want this thing to spread."

I nodded. "Sure."

"Thanks. Hold on just a second." Zeke turned and shrugged out of his pack, placing it down inside the door. "There's food and supplies in there for anyone who needs it," I heard him say to the people in the room. "Try to make it last as long as you can."

I gave him a chiding look as we stepped into the hall again, shaking my head. "You could've used that, too, Zeke."

"They need it more," he replied without hesitation. "Better that it doesn't go to waste. I'm…" He stopped, dropping his gaze, but we both knew the words he was about to say next. *I'm not going to be around much longer.*

Fear squeezed my insides again, but I didn't say anything as I led him back down the hall, through a door I'd used thousands of times, and into a familiar room.

It was light outside now; the sun would just be peeking its head above the rooftops, but the black bags over the windows did a good job in darkening the room. I didn't need the artificial light to see most everything was how I'd left it. When I was living with Kanin in the old hospital, I had defied his wishes and returned to my old room one night, only to find that two strangers had moved in. Though they'd been killed by Psycho Vamp before they had the chance to really change anything, they had managed to burn my entire book collection to keep themselves warm. That was the last I'd seen of this place before Kanin and I were forced to flee New Covington and go on the run. I didn't know what had become of the two corpses that had been here the night I first met Sarren, but they weren't here now.

Zeke shone the flashlight around curiously, taking everything in. When the beam swept over the mattress and blanket in the corner, he paused, frowning. Scanning the room once more, glimpsing the subtle signs of inhabitation, understanding suddenly dawned on his face. "This…was your room?"

I nodded wearily. "I lived here with my gang, back when I was still human." Picking up an overturned chair, I set it back beneath the table. "It's not much, but it was better than some people had."

I took a candle off the shelf, burned down to just a stump, and turned it in my fingers. Could it be that I'd been human just a few short months ago? It didn't seem possible. "Anyway," I said, replacing it, "go ahead and take the mattress. You look like you could use the sleep. Just keep to the left side—the right edge is kind of pokey."

"What about you?"

"Don't worry about me." I gave him a half smile and moved toward a far corner, away from the windows. "I can sleep on anything now, as long as it's out of the sun. But, I really do have to get to sleep, Ezekiel. I can barely keep my eyes open as it is."

It felt strange, admitting that. At one point, I would never have let anyone but Stick stay in my room. And now, my vampire instincts warned me never to let anyone see where I slept during the day. I knew the older, stronger vampires like Kanin and Salazar could force themselves awake if they had to, and Jackal claimed he could do it as well, but, while I could force myself to stay awake after the sun rose, I had yet to develop the talent of waking up once I'd already gone to sleep. If it were anyone but Zeke, I would've done what Kanin had this evening and slipped away to find a safe, hidden spot to retire, away from fearful humans.

I was still leery of the refugees. I hoped they would stay down in that basement and not go wandering the halls. But there was nothing I could do about them now, and at least my door was locked from the inside.

"Allison." Zeke's voice stopped me as I began to look around for a spot where I could lie back against the wall. "You don't have to… I mean…" He raked a hand through his hair, suddenly embarrassed. "We could share," he finally admitted, not meeting my eyes. "The mattress is big enough."

I stared at him, my stomach doing a little cartwheel. I'd shared the mattress before with Stick, but only for body heat, so that we wouldn't freeze to death on frigid winter nights. This…would be something completely different.

Zeke peered up at my silence, and spots of color tinted his pale cheeks. "That is…if you wanted to. Just to sleep. I wasn't implying that we…" He colored even more fiercely. "Ah, that came out all wrong. I wouldn't do anything, Allie, you know that, right?"

"I know," I said, easing his humiliation. "And, it's not that, Zeke. It's just…" *You would be right there, lying next to me. Can I control myself? Would it be too much of a temptation for the monster?* I spoke slowly, needing him to understand. "Sleeping next to a vampire might not be the safest thing for you."

Zeke actually chuckled at that, though it turned to a painful cough that made me wince. "I think it's a little late to worry about what's safe now," he rasped. "But, it's your decision, of course. Whatever you want to do."

I wanted to lie down. Fatigue pulled at me, making my thoughts sluggish, my reactions muted. The sun was fully up, and my vampire instincts, the ones screaming at me to go to sleep, were getting too strong to ignore. The thought of being pressed against Zeke, feeling his warmth and his heartbeat as we lay together, was suddenly very, very tempting.

"All right," I murmured, and Zeke's eyebrows rose. "I still don't know if this is a good idea, but..." I walked forward, pulling my sheath over my head and setting it down beside the mattress. If I didn't lie down soon, I was going to fall over. This was as good a place as any.

I didn't look at him as I sank to my knees on the bed. It was thin and threadbare, but instantly familiar. Behind me, I felt Zeke hesitate, then shrug out of his combat vest, dropping it at the corner along with his weapons. The mattress groaned as he settled atop it, his movements stiff and uncomfortable.

"Are you sure you're all right with this?" he asked.

Without answering, I grabbed the blanket and lay back, tossing it over myself before I could change my mind. Zeke paused, then lay down, too, sliding beneath the cover. Though he kept his body from touching mine, his heat filled the space instantly, a cocoon of warmth spreading between us under the blanket. It felt sick, however. Feverish.

Zeke turned to his side, shifting to face the wall, away from me. I felt the mattress shake as he coughed, trying to muffle it in the blanket, and a stab of fear pierced my exhaustion. What if I woke up tomorrow night and there was a corpse lying beside me? What if Zeke died, slipping away from me during the day? I'd never know until the sun went down and it was too late.

I turned toward him, gazing at his lean shoulders. He lay with his head cradled on one arm, his breaths labored and raspy. The back of his neck was bared to me, and I felt my fangs slide out, the Hunger urging me to ease forward and sink my teeth into his flesh. It cared nothing for the fact that biting Zeke would be fatal to me now; all it saw was a sick, vulnerable, unsuspecting human, and the perfect opportunity to strike.

I forced my fangs to retract, and reached out for him, brushing his arm.

He let out a ragged, shaky breath, and his shoulders hunched at my touch. "Allison…?"

"Turn around," I whispered.

He hesitated then shifted to his other side, facing me in the darkness. For a moment, we gazed at each other, our faces an arm's length apart. Zeke's head lay in the crook of his elbow, solemn blue eyes watching me. I could see my own reflection in them, but also the pain that creased his forehead, the sickly heat pouring off him.

"What's wrong?" he whispered after a moment.

I can't lose you. I'm terrified I'm going to watch you die. "I hate this," I finally muttered, my voice just a whisper between us. "I hate being so helpless. I wish this was something I could fight, something I could face one-on-one. I'd have a chance, then."

Zeke, I noticed, was being careful not to move, careful not to reach out and touch me. I caught hints of the longing on his face; it was clear he wanted to, but restrained himself. "I don't believe in fate," he said carefully, "but…I do believe everything happens for a reason. That there is some plan, some meaning to this darkness we live in." He sighed, wrinkling his forehead, his eyes going distant. "Maybe I'm wrong, but it's gotten me this far. It's the reason I fight, the reason I can keep going, despite everything. And it…it led me to you."

The room was much lighter, now. I knew the sun's rays were sliding across the windows behind me, clawing at the barrier. My eyes were heavy; my body felt like it was made of stone. With the last of my strength, I reached out and hooked Zeke's shirt, tugging him forward. He blinked then scooted close so that we were pressed together beneath the covers, his arms wrapped around me and mine around him. His heart pounded against my chest, my nose and jaw were nestled in the hollow of his throat. Temptation and Hunger tried to flare up, to take advantage of this perfect opportunity, but I was half-asleep now, too tired to listen. Not even the sweet blood coursing right below my lips could tempt me at this moment.

"Stay," I whispered, as my eyes flickered shut. "I'm not… letting you go."

I felt him shift in my arms, holding me tighter, tucking my head under his chin. "Only death will take me away from you, vampire girl," he whispered. "And even then, I'll watch over you from wherever I end up."

That was the last thing I heard before sleep pulled me under.

No nightmares. My sleep was blissfully free of the visions, dreams and emotions of my creator. Whether Kanin had finally found some sort of peace or he could control himself now that he wasn't being tortured, the next time I woke, the room was dark, and my thoughts were my own.

But the space beside me was empty.

Zeke? I stood, gazing quickly around the room. The flashlight was gone, as were his combat vest and weapons, and the room was empty save for me. Alarmed, I opened the door and stepped into the halls, searching for him. He wasn't in the dark corridors, or in the room with the refugees, though the door was still shut and locked from the inside. I didn't think he would risk going into the room with them.

So where *was* he?

I finally caught sight of a lean, blond figure in the open doors that led outside, gazing at the empty lot. It was snowing again, and thick flakes fell softly around him, landing in his hair and spotting his shoulders. Relieved, I strode forward, joining him at the entrance to the school, though he didn't turn to me immediately.

"Zeke, what are you doing?" I asked, scanning the lot for bleeders. It was empty, and the city beyond seemed still. Too quiet.

"I couldn't sleep," Zeke muttered, his voice low and tense. "It was too hot and…" His hand went to his face. "My head is killing me."

Chilled, I took his arm and turned him to face me. His eyes were bloodshot, his skin gaunt and wasted, and his hair was drenched with sweat. Heat poured off him like an ember, that intense, sickly heat that made my stomach turn. We were almost out of time. We had to find Sarren, now.

"Where's Kanin?" I demanded, releasing him and stepping away. "We're leaving. There's no more time to wait. Where is he?"

"I saw him this evening," Zeke said as we ducked back inside. "On the steps to the second floor." He hesitated, his face grim. "Allie…it's not pretty. Prepare yourself."

My dread grew. We hurried through the building, past the door to my room and the hall to the basement, to a flight of crumbling cement stairs leading to the second floor. I'd been up there before when I'd been human, but the gang didn't use it much. The third floor had collapsed on top of it, and most of the rooms were filled with rubble and stone, making it hazardous to navigate.

A dark figure sat on the top steps of the flight, elbows resting on knees and head bowed. Just seeing him like that made me uneasy. He looked like he was in pain—Kanin, the vampire who'd taken three bullets to the chest once and pulled them out again without flinching. Then Kanin raised his head, and I had to bite my lip to keep from crying out in horror.

The skin on his cheeks, forehead and jaw had blackened and was beginning to peel away, showing hints of bone through the wasted flesh. His dark eyes had sunk into his head, leaving black circles beneath them, and were glazed over with pain. The skin along his arms and the backs of his hands had darkened, too, ominous patches getting ready to crack and rot away, as the virus ravaging his body from the inside finally started to break through.

"Oh, Kanin…" The words came out choked. I didn't even know what to say—it was too horrible. And terrifying. *One day. One day for the virus to spread this far. What will he look like in another twenty-four hours?*

"Are we ready to leave?" His voice was as deep and as calm as ever. You would never guess he was in terrible pain unless you noticed the glassy look in his eyes, the tight set of his jaw. I nodded, and Kanin pushed himself upright, glancing at Zeke behind me. "Will you be able to travel?"

"I can make it."

He didn't argue, only nodded and started down the stairs. "Then let's go. It will take us several hours to reach Sector Two on foot."

The door to the basement hall was open as we walked by, and one of the refugees hovered in the frame, watching us pass. His face was hard as he stared at us, eyes narrowed in suspicion and fear. When Zeke glanced at him, his lips thinned, and he vanished through the frame without a word, the door clicking shut behind him.

Back in the sewers, we moved quickly, feeling the night slipping away from us. Neither Kanin nor Zeke spoke much, saving their strength for walking. Zeke's coughs seemed to have slowed, but he would often press a hand to his eyes or temple, gritting his teeth, and a few times he stumbled, as if he couldn't quite see what was on the ground in front of him. It made me sick with worry, for both him and Kanin. Kanin, of course, didn't make a sound, marching on with grim determination, his jaw set. But the one time he stopped to get his bearings, leaning heavily against a wall with his shoulders hunched, I could tell how awful he was feeling.

They're dying, was the thought in my head, constantly tormenting me with every step, every labored breath from Zeke or look of pain from my sire. *They're dying, and I can't help them. I can't do anything for them. Dammit, what good is immortality if I can't help the ones I care about? If I have to spend eternity alone?*

Overhead, the bleeders roamed the streets, muttering and laughing to themselves. Or they would scream at nothing, beat at cars, walls and each other, claw at their faces. And though I didn't want to, I wondered when Zeke would start showing signs of that insanity. The screaming and blind rage, the tearing at eyes and skin until the face was a mangled, bloody mess. What would I do if he started that?

Just make it quick. Don't let me suffer, or become a danger to anyone else.

Ice formed in my veins, chilling me to the bone, as the realization hit all at once. I might have to kill them. Both of them. If we couldn't get to Sarren in time, Zeke would turn on us, and Kanin would be in so much agony he'd be better off dead. I hadn't let myself think we could fail until now, but if Sarren didn't have a cure, I would have to…

I veered away from those thoughts, my throat dangerously tight. There was no one else. It would have to be me. It wasn't a question of whether I could do it. I would not let Kanin suffer like that vampire in the hospital room, his eyes begging me to kill him. If it came down to that choice, I would take his head and put him out of his misery at last. I knew my sire well enough to know he would want it that way.

But Zeke. I could barely stand to think about it. It didn't seem right that we had just found each other, that I had just let myself think that we could make this work, and he might have to die. By my hand.

But the world wasn't fair, and I'd known that for a while. If I had to kill Kanin and Zeke, so be it. I would mourn and scream and grieve their loss, and I would never get that close to anyone again, but I would not let them suffer needless agony because I couldn't let them go.

Someone, however, would pay for their deaths. Sarren and Salazar would pay, and now I could add Jackal to that list, as well. If we couldn't find a cure in time, not even the Prince himself would be safe from my retribution. If either of them died, there would be hell to pay.

But I wasn't giving up yet.

After a few hours of walking, Zeke began to stumble badly, and Kanin stopped, turning to give him an appraising look.

"Take a break," he said, nodding to a section of wall that had crumbled—large, flat stones providing a few places to sit. I was struck by how awful he looked, the blackened wounds on his cheeks and forehead spreading a bit more each time I looked at him. "We're going topside soon, and we'll need to hurry to get out of the open. Rest a few minutes."

"I'm fine," Zeke said stubbornly, though his voice was ragged. "I can keep going."

"It's not negotiable." Kanin's eyes narrowed and he gestured more firmly to the rocks. "Sit."

Zeke complied, dropping onto a stone block, rubbing his eyes. Kanin leaned against a wall, wincing slightly, as if the pressure of the cement against his back was painful. I hoped more wounds had not opened up beneath his clothes.

"How far are we from the hospital?" I asked Kanin. "I don't remember going this way the last time we were here."

"A couple more hours, depending how crowded the streets

are." Kanin closed his eyes for a moment, a tiny flicker of pain crossing his features. "This way is a bit longer, but we've stayed belowground nearly the whole way there. I would rather avoid the infected for as long as we can."

"What if Sarren isn't there?"

Kanin smiled humorlessly. "I think the more pressing question would be, what if he *is?*"

I shivered. Then we'd probably have to fight him. He certainly wouldn't just give us the cure, even if he had one. I hoped I was up for it. I hoped Kanin and Zeke were up for it. Sarren was certainly no pushover when it came to violence.

"Sarren." Dropping his hands, Zeke leaned forward, resting his forearms on his knees. For a moment, he appeared deep in thought. "I remember Jeb telling me something," he muttered at last, staring into the darkness, "about the vampire who killed his family. He was sixteen when it happened, and I only got the story out of him one time. He never spoke of it again, ever."

I blinked. Jebbadiah as a kid, a teenager like me. I tried to picture it and failed. The dour, unsmiling old man with the steely eyes was all I could see.

"What happened?" I asked.

Zeke's brow furrowed. "I don't remember the whole story. But, the way Jeb told it—his father came home one night, frantic, saying they had to leave town, that Malachi had done something horrible, and that something was coming for them. So they loaded everyone into the car, Jeb and his younger sister in the back, and left without taking anything."

Another shock. Jebbadiah had had a sister. How old would she be now? I wondered. And would Jeb be the same bitter, angry old man if she had lived? I didn't know anything about him, I realized. Even Zeke, his adopted son, barely knew his father at all.

I wondered how many more secrets Jebbadiah had taken with him to the grave.

"They thought they had gotten away," Zeke continued, oblivious to my thoughts about his father. "But, a few miles out of town, a tall, pale man suddenly appeared in the middle of the road, smiling at them. Jeb's father swerved, and the car went into a gully, rolling down to the bottom. Jeb was thrown clear, but when he crawled back to the car, his sister was dead, his mom was lying against a rock with her head split open and his father was bleeding all over the place. Jeb tried to pull him free, but his father pressed something into his hand, said it must be protected at all costs and told him to run. He wouldn't have listened, except the pale man was coming. So he ran."

Kanin stood silent, unmoving, while I still tried to wrap my head around the thought of Jeb as a teen and a brother, watching his family die. "That was Sarren, wasn't it?" Zeke asked, looking up at Kanin. "Taking revenge by killing the scientists and their families. When you were talking about the lab burning down and the rabids escaping, everything sort of clicked." When Kanin still didn't answer, he gave a humorless chuckle, shaking his head. "It all comes back to you, doesn't it?" he murmured. "The rabids, Sarren, Jackal. Everything."

"If you want vengeance for your father," Kanin finally said, his tone low and weary, "I would ask you to wait until we solve this crises. Afterward, if I am still alive, feel free to join the ranks of every vampire and human who wishes to remove my head, though I fear it is a very, very long line."

"I don't want revenge," Zeke told him before I could speak up. "Not on you, anyway. And not just because of Allison, either." He leveled a piercing stare at Kanin, who regarded him blankly. "You tried to help the scientists before," he said. "Do you still feel the same way? Do you still want to save the human race?" When Kanin frowned, Zeke paused, as if debating with himself whether or not to continue. Finally, he sighed. "If there was a possible cure for Rabidism," he went on slowly, "what would you do to find it, to protect it?"

"Zeke." I stared at him as Kanin straightened, giving him his full attention. "What are you saying?"

He gave me a guilty look. "I wanted to tell you earlier," he began. "But I didn't want to mention it around Jackal or the other vampires. The scientists in Eden...have something. At least, that's what they hope."

I gaped, feeling my stomach drop. "There's a cure?"

"Maybe. It's too soon to tell." He looked at me and Kanin in turn. "With Jeb's research, they've been able to get closer than they ever have before. But they've hit a block. They're missing something crucial. Something that isn't in Eden."

I frowned in confusion, but Kanin closed his eyes. "Vampire blood," he murmured, and my insides went cold.

Vampire blood. The thing that had started it all, that had birthed the rabids and turned the whole world into hell on earth.

And then the real reason Zeke was here, the reason he had tracked me across the country, begged me to go with him to Eden, hit me like a slap in the face. "That's...that's why you wanted me to come with you to Eden?" I asked faintly, looking at Zeke in horror. "You want to hand me over to the scientists, to use as their damn lab rat? So they can stick me in a cage and poke me with needles, like the vampires in the old hospital? Like the humans in the Old D.C. lab, tied to their beds and screaming while they were being experimented on?" My voice was growing louder, the vampire within howling at this betrayal, urging me to attack. My fangs slid out, and I bared them at the human before me. "Is that why you came, Ezekiel?"

"Of course not!" Zeke rose quickly, wincing as he steadied himself. I snarled and backed away from him, and he held out a hand, his voice gentle. "Allie," he pleaded, "you know me better than that. I would never do anything that would hurt or imprison or put you in danger. If that was my only reason for coming, I wouldn't be down here trying to stop Sarren. I would've gotten the blood some other way and gone back to Eden by now." His brow furrowed, and he rubbed his forehead before focusing on me again. "You…you are the only reason I'm here, the only reason I came."

"Are you sure about that?" I asked, forcing my voice not to shake. Against the wall, Kanin watched us, unmoving, but I barely noticed him. "Jeb knew how important the research was, that's why he gave everything he had to get it to Eden. He knew how desperately we need that cure. He would've done anything to find it. What's one vampire to save the entire world?"

"I'm not my father," Zeke said evenly. "And I was going to come looking for you, anyway. Even if there was no cure, I would've still come. If you believe anything at all, believe that. But, Allie, the scientists heard about you from the guards at the gate—they heard the stories about a vampire who didn't immediately slaughter everyone at the clinic. And they asked me a lot of questions about you, and Jeb, and our travels together. When they found out I was planning to leave the island, they asked if I was willing to bring you back to Eden. Not as an experiment or a lab rat—I would never agree to that. But they need vampire blood to continue working on the cure." He sighed, raking a hand down his face. "I know how it sounds," he admitted. "Even I was suspicious at first. But the Eden scientists know what happened at the other lab, how the rabids were created. They're not going to make the same mistakes twice."

"How do you know?" I demanded. "They could be using you, Zeke. They could be lying, just to get you to bring them a vampire. And if that's the case, you won't be able to stop them from turning me into an experiment. I'm not going to Eden just so they can do to me what they did to the vampires sixty years ago."

"I'll go," Kanin said softly.

We turned to stare at him. He shrugged, looking mostly at Zeke. "If I survive this, if we somehow manage to stop Sarren and end the plague, I'll go with you to Eden. And your scientists can use me however they want."

"Kanin," I whispered, appalled. "You can't be serious. You, of all people, should know what could happen. What they created last time. They're doing the same thing!"

Kanin just smiled. "What could they possibly do to make it worse?" he asked. I started to protest, and he cut me off. "I was wrong before," he said, his voice hard. "I allowed the blood of others to be shed, when the sacrifice should have been mine. I've spent a lifetime atoning for that mistake." Pain lit his eyes, the guilt of countless decades weighing him down. "But Ezekiel is right. I cannot let the fear of the past color the future. If a cure is to be found, if the humans still require vampires to create one, at least, this time, the blood on their hands will be mine. It is only fitting. But we must find Sarren first."

"We should get going then," Zeke muttered, and took a staggering step forward. "Because honestly, I don't know how much longer I can keep walking." He pressed the heels of his palms into his eye sockets. "God, it feels like my eyes are going to burst out of my skull."

My anger with him vanished. Stepping forward, I reached up and gently pulled the hands from his burning face, keeping his wrists trapped in my fingers. His eyes, glazed and bloodshot, met mine, and I squeezed his hands.

"We're almost there," I whispered, willing him to keep going, to not give up. "Stay with us, Zeke. You promised me you wouldn't stop."

He gazed at me, not making any move to free himself. "I'll remember my promise, vampire girl," he whispered back, forcing the words out through the agony. "If you remember yours."

CHAPTER 19

Two hours later, Zeke was no longer with us.

He hadn't said anything since our short break in the tunnels, marching on with a set jaw and glassy, pain-filled eyes. The heat pouring from his skin intensified, instantly melting the snow that settled on him when we finally went aboveground, as we hurried from shadow to shadow to avoid the bleeders.

And then, as we crossed a snow-covered parking lot, weaving between rusty hulks of cars, there was a thump behind me, the sound of something hitting the pavement. I whirled and saw Zeke lying in the snow beside a van, as if his body had finally given up.

No. I hurried over to him and knelt, turning him to his back. He groaned, half-opening his eyes, peering at me through glazed blue orbs.

"Zeke," I said, taking his arm. It was so hot. "Come on, get up. We have to keep going."

He tried. Gritting his teeth, he leaned against me as I pulled him upright, but as soon as we tried taking a step, he collapsed again. Panting, he sank back into the snow, ignoring my attempts to keep him on his feet.

"Zeke, don't do this," I said, watching helplessly as he slumped to the ground again. "Get up. We're almost there." I knelt and reached for his arm, but his hand clamped over mine, stopping it.

"Leave me." The words were so soft I scarcely caught them. But my stomach, heart, mind, everything, recoiled in absolute horror, and I stared at him in anguish. "I can't go any farther," Zeke whispered, his voice strained. "Go on without me."

I snarled, furious and defiant. "Dammit, Ezekiel! Don't you dare pull this self-sacrificing crap now. If you think I'm leaving you…" My throat unexpectedly closed up, and I swallowed my despair. "Forget it. There's no way I'm going on without you—"

"Allie." Zeke squeezed my arm, and the words faltered to a stop. "I can't," he murmured, making my throat clench. His hand rose, weakly, to his face. "I can feel the sickness… burning, and it's making me crazy. You have to go on without me. I can't even see straight, much less fight."

"No," I whispered, frantically shaking my head. "I'm not doing this. We can carry you, if it comes to that."

He closed his eyes, the snow falling around him, melting on his forehead and cheeks. "You can't stop Sarren…if you're constantly worried about me," he said, breathing hard between phrases. "He'll use me against you…that's what he does. When you face him again, you can't have…any distractions."

"You are not a distraction," I choked out. He didn't answer or open his eyes, and I clenched my fist against the snow. "Dammit, Zeke! Don't ask me to do this."

Kanin's footsteps crunched behind me, coming to a stop at my back. The Master vampire loomed over us, his gaze solemn as he stared down at the human. *Say something,* I begged silently. *Don't let him do this, Kanin.*

"This is your choice," Kanin said, even as I wanted to scream at him. "Are you certain?"

Zeke nodded painfully, opening his eyes. "I know what I have to do," he whispered. "Having me along, when we're so close to Sarren, is dangerous now. I can't go any farther. Allie," he said, looking up at me. "Leave me here. Go on without me."

"Leave you here in the snow?" I demanded. "With the bleeders? You'll be dead before we get back, Zeke. They'll tear you apart."

A scraping of metal, as Kanin turned and wrenched open the side door of the van, revealing a darkened interior and an empty space. "In here," he told me, unconcerned with the glare I turned on him. "Get him out of the open. Hurry. We don't have much time."

"Kanin, you can't expect..."

His hard stare made me trail off. "What happens if we take him with us and Sarren sees him?" he demanded. "What do you think he will do? Or if we are ambushed by the infected again and have to run?" His gaze softened, his forehead wrinkling with sudden pain. "I...am not at my best, Allison. I'm not sure that I will be much help against Sarren when we find him. If we must fight, and Sarren will almost certainly push it that way, then it will be up to you to stop him."

Fear spread through my insides, turning them cold. I didn't want to face Sarren alone. I had thought Kanin would be the one to deal with crazy Psycho Vamp, but it was obvious now that he was barely functioning. It would be me. I would have to fight Sarren. I remembered his tongue on my skin, his face close to mine, taunting Zeke over my shoulder. If Sarren turned on me, if he saw Zeke, sick and unable to defend himself…

Swallowing the lump in my throat, I put Zeke's arm around my neck, lifted him upright, and half pulled, half dragged him into the van. He clenched his jaw, his breath hissing painfully through his teeth as I settled him against the wall opposite the door, kneeling beside him. He panted, squeezing his eyes shut, sweat beading on his forehead and running down his skin. That blazing, sickly heat filled the small interior of the van, driving away the cold.

"Allie," Zeke whispered, dropping his arm, "can you… reach my gun?"

Silently, I reached around his side holster and pulled out the pistol. Zeke eyed it wearily.

"How many bullets?"

With shaking fingers, I checked the clip. "One," I said quietly. "Just one left." Zeke nodded.

"Good. If it comes to that, one shot…is all I'll need."

Dread gripped me. I watched, numb, as Zeke took the gun from my limp grasp and set it down, close to his leg. I had the sudden image of myself walking away from the van, and a shot ringing out behind me. Or returning with Sarren's cure, sliding the door back, and finding a frozen corpse sitting here, the van cold and lifeless. It made me want to scream.

Zeke finally looked at me, warmth breaking through the glassy pain in his eyes. "I'll be all right," he assured me, his voice faint. "I'm not going to do anything stupid, Allison, I just…need to rest. If you find Sarren and get a cure in time, I'll be here. If not…then it won't matter, anyway."

Leaning forward, I touched my forehead to his, closing my eyes. "I'll find him," I promised softly. "Try to hang on. I'm coming back, Zeke, I swear."

Zeke cupped the side of my face, his palm searing hot, as he raised his head and kissed me. Just a slight brush of his lips over mine. "I'll wait, vampire girl," he whispered, tracing my skin with his thumb. "For as long as I can. But, if I don't make it…" He hesitated, as if he wanted to say something, but thought better of it. His heart, already pounding, sped up, thumping in his chest. "Allie, I…"

"Allison." Kanin's voice echoed from outside, gentle but firm. "We need to go. Now."

Zeke slumped. "Go on," he whispered, pulling back. "Go stop Sarren. Don't worry about me. I'll be here."

Hot tears stung the corners of my eyes. I wanted to stay, to argue more, but words caught in my throat, and there was nothing left to say. Furiously blinking back tears, I drew away from Zeke and stepped out into the snow.

For maybe the last time, I glanced through the frame, at the human watching me from the interior of the van. He offered a faint smile and nodded before I wrenched the door shut, sliding it along the track until it clicked into place. Hiding him from view.

Kanin didn't give me time to second-guess my decision. "Let's go," he said, and spun, continuing through the aisles of cars. I gave the van one last look and followed, feeling Zeke's presence become smaller and smaller behind me.

We walked in silence for a bit, me trailing behind the other vampire, my thoughts on Zeke and how I had likely killed him by leaving him there. Alone, sick and dying in that van. If I'd only insisted he come…but then, that would likely get him killed, too.

"There are no good choices, Allison," Kanin offered in a quiet voice. "There are only those you can live with, and those you can work to change."

My throat felt tight. "I killed him," I whispered, voicing the dread I couldn't allow myself to face a few minutes ago. "He's going to die in there."

"You don't know that," Kanin said. "You're not giving him enough credit. He's fighting it, Allison. At this stage, he should be insensible, mad from the sickness. That he still retains his sense of self is little short of amazing. He might be able to stave it off a little longer."

"Enough to get him the cure?"

"If Sarren has one." Kanin sounded weary. "Though I find that difficult to believe—he's never been one to undo what he has started."

Despair rose up, threatening to crush me. "Why are we doing this, then?"

"Because we must." Kanin's voice and expression remained the same. "Because there is nothing else we can do. Because there is no one else." His voice dropped, becoming nearly inaudible. "I will put my trust in hope once more, and perhaps this time, it will be enough."

Hope. Hope that Sarren had a cure. That it would be enough

to save Kanin, Zeke and New Covington. Allie the Fringer would've seen it as foolish—hope was a luxury that could very easily get you killed. But that was what had kept Kanin going all this time, wasn't it? The hope for an end to Rabidism, that he could undo what he had helped cause. It was what had kept Zeke and the others searching for Eden, too. They'd made it only on the strength of their beliefs. And…it was what *I* held on to with Zeke. The hope that a vampire and a human could defy every instinct and fear, to fight the monster and the bloodlust and the desire to kill, and find a way to be together.

All right, then. I wouldn't give up. I would see this through to the end. For Zeke and Kanin and the city that had been my home for seventeen years, I would also put my trust in that tiny sliver of hope, and cling to it until I was certain everything was lost.

Kanin suddenly stopped at the edge of the street, then quickly backed behind a corner. Wary, I edged up beside him and peeked past the brick.

I recognized the lot across the street, the surrounding buildings, the weed-choked field with its skeletal trees and cement blocks poking out of the grass. The last I'd seen of this place, I'd been fleeing the Prince's coven with Kanin, trying to get out of the city before we were both killed. I couldn't see the ruined, blackened remains of the building across the street, through the grass and twisted old trees, but I knew it was there.

The old hospital. The hidden lab. We'd made it.

"It's too quiet," I remarked as we stood at the edge of the lot, peering across frozen grass, weeds and the leftovers of old buildings. "Do you think Sarren is really here?"

"We'll know soon enough," Kanin muttered.

His voice was tight. I looked at him and tried not to let my worry get the best of me, but it was hard. The entire length of one arm was cracked and peeling, and a hint of bone glimmered through the wasted flesh of one cheek. I knew he was in pain, that just walking was agony for him, no matter how stoic he tried to appear.

"Can you do this?" I whispered. The thought of facing Sarren was terrifying, even more so that I might have to do it alone. I thought of Zeke, dying in the van, alone in a snowy parking lot. It was killing me that I had to leave him behind, but Kanin had been right: Sarren would use him against us. He would do the same to Kanin if he could.

"You should stay here," I told Kanin when he didn't answer. "I can find Sarren alone, Kanin. You don't have to come."

My sire looked at me, and I gave him a brave smile. If I had to face Psycho Vamp by myself to save Zeke and Kanin, I'd do it. It scared the crap out of me, but I would do it.

An almost affectionate look entered his eyes. "No," Kanin murmured, turning to the lot. "Sarren and I… We've been at this for a long time. This war ends tonight. I will not let you face him alone."

"Are you sure?"

His smile turned dangerous, and his dark eyes gleamed. And for a moment, I was reminded that Kanin was a Master vampire, that he was far stronger than I, and that he still had that terrifying demon inside him.

"Let's go," Kanin said quietly, and together we started across the lot toward the distant hospital ruins, walking side by side. Just the two of us, me and my sire, against the most frightening vampire I'd ever known. Whatever came of this night would determine the fate of everything.

As we approached the first of the skeletal buildings, my skin prickled a warning. I could hear movement, shuffling footsteps to either side of us in the dark, the low murmur of voices. Something giggled softly, just as I caught a glint of metal in the weeds that hadn't been there before, and stopped.

Cages. There were *cages* surrounding the old hospital building, wire kennels built for dogs. Except, these were filled with humans. Humans that bled from self-inflicted wounds, who muttered and giggled to themselves, heedless of the snow falling on them.

Looked like Sarren was here…and expecting us.

"Can we sneak around?" I whispered to Kanin.

But, at that moment, whether from a timed latch or some kind of wire that I couldn't see, all the cage doors opened with a bang, and the bleeders leaped up, howling. Lurching into the open, one man spotted us over the grass and gave a scream that alerted the whole pack.

So much for sneaking in.

With shrieks and wails, the bleeders flung themselves across the snowy ground, rushing us in a chaotic swarm. I roared my hatred, for them, for Sarren, for this whole stupid mess, and lunged forward with Kanin right beside me.

The first human didn't know what hit him, as my sword passed through his middle in a crimson spray and out the other side. I ripped the blade free and slashed at the pair of attackers filling my vision, carving through one and into another. Tendrils of blood filled the air, and I kept my mouth shut in case any hit me in the face. A huge man with one eye swung a rusty chair at me with both hands. I rolled beneath it, cutting at his leg as I passed, hearing him crash to the ground behind me.

"Allison!"

Kanin stepped in front of me as I was lunging to my feet, blocking a club with his arm. The wood splintered against his forearm, and he roared with pain, driving his blade beneath the man's chin. A woman wielding a steel bar leaped at his back, coming from nowhere, and met my katana slashing down between them, splitting her open.

Another bleeder rushed me, screaming. I snarled and started to meet him, raising my katana to take his head off, but Kanin spun, grabbed my collar and yanked me backward. As I was jerked away, a flash and a sudden boom erupted at the human's feet, the stench of explosives, smoke and charred flesh searing the air.

"Watch out for mines," Kanin warned, setting me beside him. "Sarren likely has this whole place trapped." Another explosion rang out ahead of us, accompanied by a painful screech.

Wary now, I pressed close to Kanin as we faced the last of the bleeders, rushing us from different sides. I dodged the coil of chain whipped at my head and plunged my sword between the man's ribs, while Kanin simply grabbed the face of the human trying to stab him, lifted him off his feet and calmly slit his throat.

As the last of the bleeders crumpled into the snow, I gazed around the trampled, blood-laced field, now eerily silent once more. "Think Sarren knows we're here?" I asked Kanin.

He snorted. "Let's be careful."

Very cautiously, we made our way through the lot, wary of mines, traps, trip wires and other nasty things Sarren might have planted. I trailed behind Kanin, who had an uncanny sense of knowing where hidden dangers lurked in the snow and long grass, sidestepping them with ease. I literally followed in his footsteps, matching my strides to his, stepping where he stepped, until we were past the field and had ducked into the charred, crumbling remains of the old hospital.

Still wary of traps and mines, we picked our way through the ruins. Near a collapsed wall, a yawning, narrow hole plunged straight down into darkness, bringing with it a storm of memories. Me and Kanin, our lessons that had taken place down that dark tube, our hasty retreat from New Covington. I met Kanin's eyes over the gap and wondered if he was thinking of the same.

Or was his mind solely on what waited for us, deep in the bowels of the hospital?

"I'll go first," he said softly. "Stay here. Wait for my signal to come down."

I nodded. Kanin stepped up to the edge and, without hesitation, dropped into the black.

I crossed my arms and listened, trying not to be impatient, trying not to imagine all the things that could happen to Kanin when I wasn't there. Sarren might be lying in ambush. He could've placed mines at the bottom of the elevator shaft. He could have another wave of bleeders waiting in the hospital foyer, ready to attack. I fidgeted and shuffled my feet, stifling the impulse to leap down after him, until Kanin's voice drifted up from the darkness again.

"It's clear."

I dropped into the shaft, not bothering to grab the cables, falling maybe thirty feet to the ground floor. I landed with a grunt and a cloud of plaster dust, and Kanin turned with a look warning me be to be quiet. Ducking a beam, I stepped into a familiar room.

It seemed everything was as we'd left it the night that we fled New Covington. There was the huge desk on the back wall, its tarnished gold letters hanging skewed on the wood. The space in front of the desk where Kanin had taught me to use my katana was clear—no rubble, no debris. The room had a hollow, desiccated feel, the air here not having been disturbed in years.

But, somewhere in this dark, empty tomb, our enemy waited for us.

Kanin jerked his head at me, and we began walking, gliding, across the tiles, making no sound as we moved, two vampires on the hunt for their prey. We didn't bother with the countless rooms down the narrow hallways, Kanin's office and my old room, where I'd slept on the lumpy cot in the corner. Sarren wouldn't be in any of them. There was only one place he would be.

The room past the red door at the end of the stairs.

And once we reached the top of the stairs, it became grimly apparent that Sarren was waiting for us.

Blood coated the steps down to the red door, smeared in thick swaths over the walls, wet and black. Hands and feet had been strung by wire to the ceiling, and a severed head seemed to float in the air among them, lips pulled back in a crazy grin. Above the red door, written in large bloody letters, was: *Revelations 21.*

"Ready for this?" Kanin asked softly.

Reaching over my shoulder, I pulled my katana, gripping the hilt tightly. "As ready as I'll ever be, I guess." The severed head suddenly dropped from the ceiling, landing with a wet thump that made me flinch. "Let's get this over with."

We descended the stairwell, stepping over discarded limbs and congealing puddles of blood, making our way to the red door. It was unlocked, the handle turning easily in my palm, the door swinging back with a creak. Beyond the frame, the hall was smeared with more red, the word *Revelations* written over and over again with different numbers beside it. Kanin put a hand on my shoulder and nodded to the top corner. The broken security camera blinked a tiny red light at us, the lens trained on me like a staring black eye. I shivered, knowing Sarren could be on the other end, watching us right now.

The round door at the end of this hall was also slightly open. Exceedingly wary of traps and ambushes, I edged forward and pushed it back. It groaned as it swung open, and we stepped through the opening, into the room where, six decades ago, monsters were born.

The cells lining the walls were empty, which was a relief. I'd been half expecting them to be full of bleeders that would burst out and attack us. But everything about the room was silent and still. Sarren, unless he was hiding in one of the cages, wasn't in the room.

"Not here," Kanin said in a low, barely audible voice. "We have to go through the last door at the end."

I'd never been through the last door. The farthest I'd gotten was this room, where Sarren had found me after he'd tracked

Kanin to the city, and I'd jammed a pocketknife into his eye. I doubted he'd forgotten that.

Kanin's blade was suddenly in his hand. No turning back now. For Kanin, for Zeke, for all of New Covington, we had to face the madman. We moved steadily toward the last door, finding it unlocked, of course, and pushed it open.

For a moment, Kanin didn't move, and neither did I, staring into the darkness beyond the frame. From where I stood, I could make out a few old cots, covered in mold and dust, scattered around the room. Thick leather straps and cuffs dangled from the edges, just like the ones in Old D.C., making my skin crawl. Against the wall, an ancient computer, its screen cracked and distorted, sat beside an odd device with a long tube poking into the air. More cells lined the other wall, with thick steel bars running vertically across the windows and metal doors barred from the outside. Cold, stale air wafted through the door fame, laced with the faintest hint of blood.

A hissing chuckle slithered out of the dark. "Ah, there you are," purred a soft, sibilant voice, somewhere in the shadows of the room. "Step into my parlor, said the spider to the fly. We have a lot to talk about."

A chill crept up my spine. Gripping my sword, I started forward, but Kanin put a hand out, holding me back. "After me," he muttered, in a voice only I could hear. "If this is a trap, at least you'll be in the clear."

I swallowed. "Be careful, Kanin."

He lowered his arm and stepped through the frame into the room. Nothing happened immediately: no explosion, no sudden projectiles, and the door didn't slam shut behind him.

Kanin gazed around calmly and raised his voice. "Sarren. You've obviously been waiting for me. Here I am."

Another evil chuckle. "Oh, Kanin," the voice purred, and *he* appeared, melting out of the dark to stand before us in the center of the room. My skin crawled as his hideous, scarred face lifted to meet ours. "I have enjoyed our games, old friend," he said, folding his hands before him. "You were a most compelling quarry, and I shall miss our time together. But you have already played your part in this symphony. Your voice, your music, is dying and will soon fade to nothing." His hollow, mad eyes flickered to me, and a smile stretched his face. "I am more interested in the songs the little bird can sing."

I wanted to recoil. Instead, I stepped through the door to stand beside Kanin, giving Psycho Vamp my best challenging glare. "You want me? Here I am."

"Yes," Sarren agreed, clasping his bony hands. "Here you are, little bird. Here you are, and here we are, and the world spins and dies around us." He cocked his head at me, appraising. "But where is your prince? I would think he'd want to be here, to see the end of this symphony."

"He's gone," I snapped, baring my fangs. I was suddenly glad Zeke wasn't here, standing in this creepy room with this insane vampire who would use every weakness to his advantage. "Your virus took him," I went on, not needing to fake the fury and hatred in my voice as I faced Sarren, who raised his eyebrows. "And you are going to give us a cure, right now, or we're going to beat it out of you."

"A cure?" Sarren feigned surprise. "What makes you think I have a cure, little bird?"

I growled, bringing up my sword even as I felt Kanin's warning hand on my arm. I was tired of talking to crazy Psycho Vamp, and I was *not* in the mood for his sick games. "Do you have one, or not?"

"Oh, let me think. A cure, a cure..." Holding up his empty hands, Sarren took two steps to the edge of the counter. "Do you mean...this cure?"

I should've known not to trust him. I should've been more wary, more on guard, but in the split second I realized he was up to something, his hand flipped a switch over the counter and a brilliant light erupted right in front of us, pinning us in the glare. Blinded, I hissed and turned away, shielding my eyes, hearing Kanin do the same. And in that moment, something grabbed me from behind, clamping my sword arm beneath it, and a sharp wooden point was shoved under my breastbone, angled up toward my heart.

"Hello, sister," a familiar voice whispered in my ear. "Bet you didn't expect to see me again."

CHAPTER 20

I went rigid. As the light faded, I became aware of my surroundings all at once. My attacker stood behind me, pinning my arm, a wooden point shoved into my chest. It dug painfully into my skin, making me stiffen and arch to get away from it, but I couldn't escape.

"I'd drop the sword, if I were you," the cool, smug voice said into my ear, punctuated with a sudden jab of the stake, making me wince. "Don't make me use this, sister. Drop it. Now."

I cursed, and my katana hit the ground with a clang. "Dammit, Jackal," I muttered, craning my head back to look at him, smirking at me. "You two-timing bastard!"

"Oh, come on," Jackal said mildly, pulling me a few steps away from Kanin, who stared at him with eyes that had gone cold and terrifying. "You act like this is such a stretch. Don't move, old man," he warned Kanin, maneuvering me into a corner. "One little slip, and I might just impale your favorite little spawn here. Wouldn't want that."

Sarren suddenly moved across my vision in a blur, striking Kanin with a vicious snarl, sending him reeling back. Kanin recovered and lashed out with a kick as Sarren came at him again, flinging him back several yards to crash into one of the cots. I tensed, but Jackal growled and twisted the stake into my flesh, making me gasp. Kanin froze.

A chilling laugh made my stomach curl, and Sarren staggered to his feet, eyes blazing. His tongue licked out, dabbing a corner of his cut lip, and he smiled. "For every drop of blood I lose," he promised, stalking forward again, "I will make your little bird scream for an hour. Her song will seep into the very walls and will remain here forever, and everyone who hears it will know how much she wanted to die. The longer this goes on, the longer her music will last, until she is begging for it to end. But it will not end, as long as you are still alive."

"Then let me take her place." Kanin lowered his blade, facing Sarren across the room, his voice resigned. "I'm the one who did this to you. I'm the one you want to hurt. You spent your days in this hellhole because of me. I deceived you, promised a better life. I betrayed you, Sarren, and I'm still here. The pain you want to inflict belongs to me alone."

"Kanin, no," I whispered, but it was too late.

Sarren came at Kanin again, striking savagely with a metal pipe he'd snatched off the floor, and this time, Kanin didn't move. The weapon hit his collarbone with a sickening crack, dropping him to his knees, and Sarren instantly smashed the pipe against the side of his head. I cried out as Kanin sprawled to the floor, only to have his enemy ruthlessly kick him in the ribs, sending him crashing into the wall.

"Ouch." I felt Jackal wince behind me, though his grip never loosened. "You know, this is when you wish you had a working camera, just to remember these moments always." I tensed, and he immediately tightened his grip on my arm, digging in the stake so that I felt blood well up from the tip. "Don't even think about it, sister. I have no problem shoving this thing right into your heart if you get too rowdy, and it won't be pleasant, trust me."

"How could you do this to him?" I whispered through clenched teeth. The stake in my flesh throbbed, making me desperate to get away from it. I kept trying to arch back, but only succeeded in pushing myself harder against Jackal, who never relented in his grip on me or the stake. "He saved you. You would've died if he wasn't there."

Jackal chuckled. "Look at you, actually trying to tweak my conscience. Isn't that cute." He eased up the tiniest bit, though not enough for me to relax. Sickened, I watched Sarren stalk back to Kanin, haul him upright and backhand him with the pipe. And still, Kanin barely defended himself, raising an arm to shield the side of his head, and the blow knocked him off his feet.

"You made this pretty easy, did you know that, sister?" Jackal remarked, watching the hopeless, one-sided fight with casual disinterest. "Didn't even think to use our blood tie to check up on me. I knew exactly where *you* were, and Kanin was in too much pain to do much of anything, but I'm rather disappointed in you. I keep telling you, you're just too trusting."

"Jackal," I pleaded, "don't do this. Kanin is—"

"What? Family?" Jackal snorted. "We're all demons, my

dear little sister. And in our world, only the strong and the smart, survive. You and Kanin were on the losing team, and I'm a sore loser. Don't take it personally—it's what any true vampire would do."

Sarren yanked Kanin to his feet again and slammed him into the wall, pressing a forearm to his neck. His face was viciously inhuman. Kanin stared back, unwavering, the open wounds on his face glimmering black against his pale skin. I cried out, bracing myself, certain that I was going to watch my sire be killed right in front of me.

But then, Sarren smiled his blank, terrible smile, dragged Kanin off the wall and hurled him through one of the open cell doors. Kanin hit the ground, rolling against the wall, and Sarren shut the metal door with a ringing clang that echoed through the room.

"No, old friend," he mused, throwing down the heavy bar as Kanin staggered to his feet. "Your pain is still coming. I want you to see this. I want you to see what they did to us, every night, in these rooms. And your little bird will be the perfect demonstration."

"No." Kanin's voice was a rasp. He limped to the bars and grasped them tightly as I stiffened against Jackal. "This is our war. You have the opportunity to end it, right now. She has nothing to do with it. Sarren!"

Sarren turned and walked to the center of the room, picking up the cot he'd overturned. His face was calm as he spoke, not looking back. "Our war is over, old friend. You are but a rotted soul trapped in a decaying body. There is nothing I can do to your flesh that will surpass the coming agony. You will simply rot away in that cell, and my only regret is that I will not be here to see it. By the time you succumb to your decaying prison and depart this world for hell, I will be long gone." He turned, beckoning to Jackal with a pale, bony hand.

I snarled and tried to fight him, but he jammed the stake farther into my body so that I arched in pain, and he started dragging me to where Sarren waited beside the cot.

"Never...took you for a mindless crony," I gritted out, trying desperately to stop this procession while fighting the pain stabbing through me. "When did you become...Sarren's lapdog?"

"Hey, I'm a team player," Jackal replied as Sarren loomed terrifyingly near. "Provided I'm on the winning team. Just give it up, sister. You lose. Try to have some dignity when he's peeling your skin off."

Despair and fear threatened to drown me as Jackal dragged me over to where Sarren waited, his hollow eyes and soulless grin reminding me of a skull. I shook violently, but swallowed my terror, raised my chin and met his demonic smile head-on.

"Hello again, love." Sarren reached out to caress my face, making me cringe in revulsion. "We just keep running into each other, don't we?"

Abruptly, his hand slid to my neck, grabbed my throat and lifted me off my feet. Before I even had a chance to gasp, he turned and slammed me to the cot, pinning me down. I realized what was happening and snarled, fighting wildly to get up, to resist. But I was no match for both Sarren and Jackal; they held me down and fastened the leather cuffs around my wrists, tying me to the bed. More straps were drawn across my chest, legs and neck and buckled down, holding me immobile.

I bared my fangs at them and howled, struggling with all my might, straining at the cuffs and straps, but I couldn't move.

I caught a glimpse of Kanin through the bars of the cell. His face was calm, but his eyes were anguished as they met my gaze. Then Sarren leaned over me, smiling, and I forgot everything else as his horrible, scarred face hovered inches from mine.

"Do you know how many times I woke up like this?" he whispered as my terrified reflection stared back at me from his one good eye. "How many nights I awoke, tied to this bed, starving and insensible, while the humans milled around and stuck me with their needles and their poison? Cut me and bled me, sometimes to the point where I had but a few drops of blood left in my body? I screamed at them to stop, pleaded for them to stop. But they never did. All because of your sire." He straightened, casting a glance back at Kanin. "So you can thank him for whatever I do to you, tonight."

"Sarren." I barely recognized Kanin's voice, so full of despair and desperation was the low rasp that came from the cell. "This isn't what you want. Take your vengeance on me. The girl has no part in this."

Sarren shook his head. "It is no longer about vengeance," he said, turning away. I watched as he went to a corner and returned with a metal cart. It had been draped with a towel, and several needles, scalpels and other sharp instruments glinted on top. Fear lanced through me, and I struggled hard against my restraints, to no avail. "It has become far more than that. This is about redemption. Salvation." He gave me a creepily affectionate smile as he returned, eyes gleaming hungrily. "And you, little bird, you will be the first to taste it."

I bared my fangs defiantly, though my voice trembled when I spoke. "What are you talking about, you psychopath?"

"Do you want to know a secret, little bird?" Without waiting for a reply, Sarren leaned down, his cold lips brushing my ear. "There is no cure," he whispered, making my stomach drop. "There was never a cure. The sickness has spread too far, and is too deep, to be cured now, but it is not what you or Kanin or that fool Salazar thinks. The virus *is* the cure, and it will heal the entire world."

I felt cold. "What…what do you mean?"

Sarren drew back, looking almost sorrowful. "You will see," he said, and took a needle from the metal cart, regarding it impassively. "New Covington was only a test, little bird. A place to work out the kinks, to perfect the virus. Now that I know what it can do, the next time I release it, it will be unstoppable."

"The next time?" I asked, appalled. "This wasn't enough for you? Killing a whole city of vampires and humans wasn't enough? If you release that virus again, you could wipe out the entire population—"

I stopped. Stared at him. *Redemption. Salvation. Heal the entire world.* No, he couldn't be that crazy…

Sarren peered down at me, his eyes and face completely blank, and my stomach went cold. He was.

"Oh, God," I whispered as a horror unlike anything I'd ever felt crept over me. "That's what you want. You want to kill *everyone.* Not just humans. Vampires, too. You want to wipe out everything."

Sarren jammed the needle into my arm, and I clenched my jaw, tensing until he pulled it out again, full of blood. "The corruption has spread too far, little bird," he said, holding the syringe up to the light. "It is time to start over. Wipe the slate clean, and let the world finally heal itself. A new beginning, with no humans, or vampires, or rabids. There was just one unknown variable to the equation, and that was you."

I couldn't answer, still staggered by his revelation. It was absurd, unthinkable. A real end of everything? There was no way he could pull it off. Or could he? I had to keep him talking, keep his attention on me, though I didn't know what I could do now. I just knew I needed answers. "Why me?" I forced out, and he looked at me in surprise.

"Because, little bird." Sarren lowered his arm and smiled down at me. "I have heard the most interesting story about you and a place called Eden. Rumors are, the scientists in Eden possess the same research that I took from the other lab. You can imagine how that would make me a bit nervous."

My insides trembled. I thought of Zeke, and deliberately did not look at Jackal, leaning casually against a wall with his arms crossed. "I don't know what you're talking about," I lied. Sarren shook his head.

"Oh, little bird. Your song is far too honest to deceive me with untruths." He reached down and stroked my cheek, his nails scraping across my skin, making my flesh crawl. "No matter. You will sing, soon enough. Oh yes, you will sing for us all."

He turned, then, holding the syringe of blood, and walked to the machines on the counter. I didn't know what he was doing, but he squeezed a drop of blood onto a tiny glass square, covered it with another and slid it beneath the strange tubelike machine next to the computer. Bending down, he peered into the top of the tube.

As soon as his back was turned, I wrenched at the cuffs one more time, knowing this would be my last chance. Before Sarren came back and… I didn't want to think about what he would do. The metal instruments on the cart glinted at me from the corner of my eye, and I yanked harder, desperate to get loose, to free myself before Sarren began carving the skin from my body, or whatever horrible thing he had in mind.

Jackal suddenly pushed himself off the wall, and I froze. He could see me struggling with the restraints, and would either make some snide comment to draw Sarren's attention, or stop me himself. I curled my lips back, hating him for his betrayal, for turning us over to this madman who literally wanted to destroy everything. I opened my mouth to tell him so, when he suddenly put a finger to his lips, silencing me.

Stepping casually to my side, he lowered his arm, and I saw the glint of a scalpel in his hand. With a quick jerk of his wrist, he sliced halfway through one of the cuffs tying my wrist to the bed. Not enough to free it completely, but making a visible tear in the leather strap. I stared at him in astonishment, and he winked.

"Well, little bird." Sarren straightened, and Jackal stepped away, the scalpel vanishing as quickly as it appeared. "I must say, I'm a tad disappointed. Your blood is not tainted or altered in any way. It appears you are quite unremarkable." He stalked back, smiling as he loomed over me, his gaze searching. I tensed as, for a split second, his eyes seemed to pause at my cuff, and the half-torn strap attaching it to the bed. But the hollow stare slid past it to rest on my face. "So, what does Kanin see in you?" he asked, more to himself than me. "What lies beneath this envelope of flesh and bone and blood, hmm? Is it something special? Perhaps, when I peel it open, I will be able to see. Perhaps your screams will tell me everything I need to know."

His face was hungry now, eager, as if the thought of inflicting pain brought him joy. I shuddered and tried to control my terror as he turned and plucked a knife from the cart beside him, letting it flash in the light. I wouldn't beg. And I would not tell him what he wanted to hear. I might scream and cry and wish I was dead before this was over, but I would not tell him about Eden, or Zeke, or anything about the cure.

"I know what you're thinking, love," Sarren whispered, before running the knife blade along his tongue, making me cringe. "You're thinking, *I won't sing. I won't tell him anything.* But pain has a way of loosening the strongest lips. There's only so much a body can take, with all those lovely nerve endings, millions of them, sending screaming messages of agony up to the brain. It's amazing how trivial the world becomes when you begin to long for death."

"I won't tell you anything," I choked out. "So you might as well kill me now."

"Everyone has a limit, little bird." He placed the flat of the blade against my cheek, the edges biting into my skin. I wanted to close my eyes, but I kept them open, glaring at Sarren defiantly, though my jaw hurt from clenching it so hard. "Let's see if we can find yours."

I braced myself, trying to disconnect my mind from the pain I knew was coming. And for a frozen second, it was as if I could see the whole room and everything that was happening around me. Kanin turning from the bars, hunching his shoulders as if he, too, was steeling himself. Sarren's muscles tightening as he prepared to slice the blade across my flesh. And Jackal, looming behind Sarren, his eyes hard and cold.

A stake gripped in one hand, raising it over his head.

A stinging pain sliced across my cheek, making me gasp, as the world blinked into motion again. As Sarren ripped the knife from my face, spun and plunged the blade into Jackal's stomach.

Jackal gaped, baring his fangs in a snarl, though only a choked sound escaped him. The arm that held the stake was now gripped in Sarren's other hand, bony fingers locked around Jackal's wrist.

"You almost fooled me," Sarren said, smiling at Jackal's stunned expression. "I believed you would betray your companions without a second thought—that was all true. But you don't want redemption, do you? No, you are far too attached to life."

He yanked the knife up, slicing him open, and Jackal howled. Sarren thrust him away, sending him crashing into the counter, the sound of breaking glass and clattering metal nearly deafening.

Amazingly, Jackal staggered to his feet, holding his stomach with one hand, the stake still clenched in the other. "You're a fucking insane bastard, you know that?" he snarled at Sarren, who calmly picked up a pipe and advanced on him. "So the whole time you were sitting on that research, you decided, 'Hey, instead of curing Rabidism, I'm just going to make a superplague and wipe everything out! That'll show them!'" He sneered, curling his lips back in a painful grimace. "But you'll have to pardon me for not jumping on your little Destroy the World train. I happen to like this world, thanks."

Sarren lunged. Jackal dodged his first swing, lashing out with the stake, but Sarren blocked his arm, stepped in and brought the pipe smashing across his jaw. Reeling away, Jackal snarled defiantly and punched Sarren in the face as he stepped in, rocking him back a step. *Dammit, don't just stare at them, Allison! Get out of there!* Tearing my gaze from the fight, I yanked on the weakened leather cuff, trying to tear it away completely. It held stubbornly, and I yanked again. It took three tries, but on the third, the cuff finally snapped, ripping in two and freeing my wrist from the bed. Frantically, I clawed at the straps across my neck and chest, tearing them away, then reached over to free my other wrist.

Scrambling off the cot, I turned to see Sarren slam Jackal against one of the cell doors, one where the window had been smashed, a couple of the iron bars rusted and snapped in two. As I paused, torn between helping Jackal and going for my katana, Sarren yanked Jackal from the door, lifted him up and slammed him onto one of the broken iron bars. The rusty pole punched straight through his stomach, impaling him on the spike, and Jackal screamed.

Fear shot through me. *Katana, it is.* I bolted for my weapon, lying on the floor, but just as my hand closed on the hilt, something grabbed my hair from behind. I was swung off my feet and hurled back into the room, striking a cot on the way down. I scrambled upright, clutching my weapon with shaking fingers. Sarren prowled toward me, pipe in hand, Jackal's blood streaked over his arms and face, almost like war paint. Behind me, my brother cried out in agony, and Kanin watched from his prison, helpless. It was just me and Sarren now, and he looked like he was enjoying himself.

"Oh, don't leave now, little bird," Sarren crooned, licking blood from one long bony finger. "It was just getting interesting. You can't fly away just yet."

"I wasn't leaving," I snarled. "I'm not about to let you spread your superplague or virus or whatever you want to call it. You might have given up on this world, but I am not ready to die yet. I don't need your brand of salvation." The katana shook as I raised it in front of me, but I gripped the hilt and forced my arms to be steady. "So, come on, you psychopath. Let's do this. I'm not tied to a table anymore."

Sarren's grin widened, making him even more frightening. "I still owe you for this, love," he said, gesturing to his left eye, cloudy and blind. "An eye for an eye, a tooth for a tooth. Perhaps, I will pluck out both your eyes, then remove all your teeth, and make a necklace from them. Or maybe a wind chime. I do love wind chimes, don't you, little bird?"

Before I could answer, he lunged, coming in fast. I just managed to dodge his first swing, feeling the pipe miss my head by centimeters, and slashed upward with my katana. I felt the very tip bite something, saw Sarren jerk back and stumble to a halt, one hand going to his face.

I retreated, raising my weapon, waiting for his next move. Sarren pulled his hand down, looking at the blood on his fingers in amused surprise. More blood welled from a deep gash across his cheek and ran down his chin, and I blinked in shock.

I...I hit him.

"Well done, little bird." Sarren nodded at me, almost proud. "I see you have gotten stronger since our last meeting. I think I am beginning to realize what Kanin sees in you. Very well, then." He stalked toward me again, the smile fading, the true madness rising to the surface. My gut clenched as even his voice changed, becoming low and demonic. "I shall not toy with you a moment longer."

I didn't even see it this time. I had a vague, split-second impression of him coming at me, but that was all I saw before something hit the side of my head, and it felt like my skull imploded. I found myself on the ground, dazed, my only coherent thought to keep hold of my weapon. Something struck me again, in the back this time. I felt my body leave the floor, the world spinning wildly, before striking the wall and crumpling to the ground in a heap. And still, my fingers remained clenched around my sword. I would not let it go. Though everything blazed with pain, and it was difficult to tell which way was up at the moment, I had to keep hold of it.

Footsteps, and then something grabbed the back of my neck, hauling me to my feet. Sarren's arms wrapped around me from behind, bony fingers clamped around my wrist, the one that still clutched the katana. His cold, dry lips brushed against my cheek as his other hand gripped my throat.

"Now, little bird," he whispered, scraping his fangs over my skin, "how would like to die?"

"Sarren."

A clear, impossible voice echoed behind us. Sarren froze for just an instant before he whirled, dragging me with him, to face the door.

Zeke stood in the frame, his gun out, angled at us both. His blue eyes flashed, hard and angry.

"Not this time," he growled, and pulled the trigger.

The boom of the heavy pistol rocked the room, echoing off walls and flaring orange and white in the darkness. I felt the wind of something small whip at my hair as it passed inches from my face, and slammed into the vampire behind me. Sarren roared, reeling back, blood exploding from his shoulder and neck.

I spun, bringing up my katana, slashing with all my might. Sarren saw the deadly blade coming and threw up his hand, trying to block my swing. This time, he wasn't fast enough. The katana edge sliced into his arm, right above the elbow, cutting through flesh, tendons and bone. The pale, bony forearm flew through the air in a spray of blood, hitting the ground several yards away, and Sarren's scream shook the walls.

Cradling his arm, he fled, rushing toward the door and Zeke, who stood in front of it. I tensed, but Zeke wasn't about to take on a pain-maddened vampire and quickly jumped aside. Sarren hit the frame and paused for just a moment to stare at the human, his lips curled back in a grimace of pain and hate. A puzzled look crossed his face, and then he was gone, vanishing into the hall, leaving a blood-drenched war zone behind him.

"Zeke."

I crossed the room in a blur, not stopping to think about anything—how Zeke was still alive, how he could be here, how *I* was still alive. I shoved all of that to the back of my mind, promising to deal with it later, as I hurried across the floor, dropping my weapon as I did, and lunged into Zeke's arms.

He crushed me to him, his breath warm on my skin. I felt his heart racing in his chest, felt the hard muscles shifting below his vest, and, for a moment, I let myself relax against him. He was alive. How, I didn't know, but he was alive.

"Allie." Pulling back, Zeke peered at me, blue eyes intense. "Are you all right? Where's Kanin?"

Kanin. Jackal! "In there," I said, nodding to the cell that held Kanin. I couldn't see him anymore, and hoped he was all right. "And Jackal," I added, feeling Zeke tense. "Jackal is here, too."

"What?"

"It's all right. He wasn't really working with Sarren. He's… back on our side again. I think." I pulled away. So many questions, but they would have to wait. "Go check on Kanin," I told Zeke, reaching down to grab my katana. "Make sure he's okay. I'll deal with Jackal."

He nodded, though his eyes were still hard at the mention of the hated vampire. As he walked toward the cell, I turned and picked my way across the room, to where Jackal had fallen.

Even now, it was hard not to cringe when I saw him, impaled on the rusty metal spike, dangling off the edge of the sill, his face tight with agony. His hands clutched the pole in his middle, and blood bubbled up from his lips as he looked back at me.

"If you're…wondering…this is…so much more…uncomfortable than…it looks."

I shook my head. Mortally wounded, and still running his mouth. "How do you want to do this?" I asked.

Jackal grimaced. "Back…right corner," he gritted out. "Cooler. Blood bags."

I found the cooler, which was half-full of bags like Jackal said. Obviously Sarren had been stocking up for a while. Grabbing three, I returned to the impaled vampire, who was barely holding himself up by clinging to the pole through his stomach. He eyed me as I approached, his gaze falling hungrily to the plastic bags I carried.

I stopped just out of reach, still holding my katana in the other hand. "Why did you do it?" I asked, as he gave me a look of disbelief. "How much of that was a lie, or were you really planning to double-cross Sarren all along?"

"Sorry, sis. Hard to think…right now. Slight…stomachache."

"Yeah, well—" I narrowed my eyes, my voice ruthless "—you're not going anywhere without my help, so I'd say you'd better start talking."

He bared his fangs. "Fine…damn you." He panted, clenching his teeth through the pain. "I had to…make it seem…real. Sarren would've known…otherwise. Had to…make you think…I switched sides. Wouldn't have worked…without that hate."

I slumped. "So you really didn't double-cross us."

He barked a strangled laugh. "Don't…be so sure. I would've

done anything…for that cure. If Sarren…really had one… you'd still be…tied to that table."

"Why should I help you?" I raised my katana, letting the edge hover very close to his bared throat. "How do I know you won't turn on us in the future?"

Jackal tried to shrug. "Guess…you'll have to…take your chances," he gasped, and squeezed his eyes shut, desperately trying to keep himself upright. "Damn you, sister! Either… help me…or kill me now! But make…some sort of decision."

I set my jaw. Pulling back my sword, I slashed it across the cage bar, my vampire strength and the impossibly keen edge of the katana slicing through the rotted iron, cutting it in half, so only a few inches poked through Jackal's stomach. I held out a hand. He grabbed it, and I pulled him from the spike. Jackal let out a howl of pain as the bar slid from his stomach, and he slumped to his hands and knees in front of the cell, shuddering, but he was free.

I dropped the bags in front of him and stepped back, knowing he had to be starving now, very close to losing control. "I have to check on Kanin," I said, not sure if he heard me or not. "Stay put. I'll be back in a few minutes."

"Hey."

I looked back. Jackal was still kneeling in front of the cell, one arm curled around his mangled stomach. He held one of the bags, but hadn't started in on it yet; his golden eyes were fixed on me. "I won't…forget this," he said, making me stare in astonishment, wondering if the blood loss had affected his brain. "Thanks."

"Uh. Sure."

"Allison."

I turned. Zeke stood a few paces from Kanin's now open cell, his blue eyes solemn as he beckoned me forward. "I think you need to be here, now."

Dread twisted my stomach. I hurried forward, past Zeke, and into the small room. Kanin sat in the corner beneath the window, slumped against the wall, his head bowed to his chest. The fist clutching my insides squeezed painfully, and I slipped into the cell, dropping down in front of him.

"Kanin?"

He raised his head, and it seemed like that tiny motion was excruciatingly difficult. I bit my lip. The black wounds on his face had spread; I could see new ones on his neck, creeping down his chest, and spread across his arms. His dark eyes were glazed with pain, though he still tried to speak calmly.

"Where…is Sarren?"

"Gone," I told him. "I don't think he's coming back." He nodded and closed his eyes, tilting his head back to the wall. "Kanin…?"

"I think," Kanin said very slowly, "that I am in the final stages of the sickness." His face tightened. "I have not had a migraine in centuries. I'd forgotten how unpleasant they are."

"Wait here," I continued, starting to get up. "I'll look around. Maybe Sarren left information on a cure somewhere—"

"Allison." Kanin's voice was weary as he looked back. "There is no cure," he said simply. "There never was a cure. Sarren doesn't want this to end. You heard what he said."

"There has to be something," I argued, refusing to accept

what I knew was true. Sarren was gone. There was no cure. No hope for New Covington, for the sick humans and vampires, for Kanin. My eyes started to burn, and I blinked them angrily. "I'm not giving up," I told him. "Dammit, Kanin! You're not going to die."

"Death." Kanin closed his eyes again. "I've lived so long," he whispered. "Maybe it has been long enough. Maybe…I've atoned for my sins by now. Surely by now I can be forgiven."

"No." My voice came out choked, because hot, angry tears were starting to run down my cheeks. "There has to be a way. We've come so far, beaten Sarren and everything. You can't die now."

Vaguely, I was aware of Zeke, hovering just inside the door, looking grim. Kanin's tortured eyes strayed past me, to the human, and a puzzled look filtered through the agony. "Ezekiel. You're here." He sounded surprised. "You…did not succumb to the illness."

That's right! Zeke is still here.

I gasped and spun around, clutching at a tiny, wild hope, a ray of light in this darkness. "Zeke, *you* survived," I whispered, making him blink at me. Striding forward, I grabbed his arms and pulled him forward, into the cell. "You survived," I said again, peering intently at his face. It was pale, a little gaunt, but his skin was dry; the sickly heat pouring from him had vanished. "You fought it off. How?"

"I don't know." His brow furrowed. "After you and Kanin left, I think I passed out for a while. When I woke up, I felt fine, so I came looking for you again. I don't know how…"

He frowned suddenly then shook his head. "It…it might be connected to what they did to me in Eden."

I stared at him in alarm. "What did they do to you?"

He raked a hand through his hair. "I spent a lot of time with the scientists on Eden, talking about Jeb's research. They needed a test subject, so…I agreed to be their lab rat for a little while."

"Why?"

He sighed. "I figured, better me than anyone else. And it was all to find a cure, so…yeah." He shrugged. "Don't look so horrified, Allie. They explained everything they were doing, and always gave me the option to refuse. They weren't going to turn me into a rabid."

"You didn't know that!"

"Someone had to take the chance." His voice was firm. "I won't say it didn't terrify me at times, but someone had to volunteer. Right before I left to find you, they inoculated me with a couple 'experimental vaccines' based on their research up until then. They weren't certain it would help with the rabids, but it was better than sending me out with no protection at all. It might've not helped with anything but…" He made a helpless gesture. "I'm still here."

Yes, he was. And the inkling of an idea was beginning to creep through my brain, taunting me with possibilities, with hope. "Zeke," I said, talking his hand, "if you survived, then…then maybe the cure…is in *you*. In your blood."

He frowned slightly, but I took his arm again and pulled him out of the cell, back into the main room. He didn't protest and let me drag him to the cot where Sarren had tied me down, and the cart of metal instruments still beside it. Ignoring the blades and scalpels and the other awful tools, I picked up a syringe and turned back to Zeke, who was still watching me with a bemused look on his face.

I paused, excitement warring with a desperate hope, my last gamble. If this didn't work…

I pushed the thought away. "Zeke," I began, holding up the syringe. "You…might be the only one who can help Kanin now. If you survived Sarren's plague, then whatever is in your blood might be the key to a cure, to saving everyone. If… if you're willing…to help a vampire, to give your blood…"

"You don't have to ask me, Allie." Zeke stepped closer and held out his arm, wrist up. "Kanin is important to you, and he's saved my life, as well. If this will help, if this might cure him, I'm willing to give it a shot."

I wanted to hug him in gratitude, but there was no time for that. Instead, I gingerly took his offered wrist, staring down at the smooth, warm skin. I'd seen Sarren draw blood, when he'd done it to me, but…how did you do it, exactly? Was there a specific place to put the needle, or did you just poke and draw?

"Allie? You okay?"

"I…um…don't really know how to do this," I finally admitted, embarrassed.

Zeke didn't laugh. Reaching out, he gently took the syringe from my hand, flipped the needle around and, clenching his fist so that the veins suddenly rose to the surface, sank it beneath his skin. "Had to do this a lot back at the lab," he muttered, lips tight in concentration. I watched, fascinated, as he used his thumb to push back the top of the syringe, and the vial slowly filled with dark red blood. Annoyingly, the Hunger perked at this, and I shoved it back. "It takes a few times to get the hang of it."

Pulling the needle from his skin, he solemnly handed the syringe to me. "I hope this works," he whispered, and the honest concern in his voice made my throat close up. Clutching the syringe, I hurried back to Kanin's cell.

He still sat in the corner, legs crossed, head bowed, arms resting on his knees. I walked up to him and dropped down, peering into his face. His eyes were closed, and he did not open them when I whispered his name. My alarm grew, and I put a hand on his knee.

"Kanin."

"I hear you, Allison." He did not move or open his eyes as he said this, his voice low and strained. I swallowed hard and held up the syringe, even though he wouldn't see it.

"I'm...going to inject you with something," I told him. "Zeke's blood." I hoped he wouldn't refuse, because I wasn't going to take no for an answer. "It might help, Kanin. It might be enough...to save you."

Kanin didn't reply. Without a word, he raised an arm to me and turned it palm up, a silent acceptance. I wondered if he really believed it would help, or if he figured nothing I did could hurt, now. Regardless, I inched closer and took his wrist, his skin cold beneath my fingers. His arm looked ravaged, blackened and peeling, and by the tight press of his lips, I knew moving it even this much was painful. Remembering what Zeke had done, I found a pale blue vein and, before I thought too much about it, sank the needle into his flesh, sliding it beneath the skin.

I slowly injected the blood into Kanin, rose and backed away, staring down at him. Zeke entered the cell and stood beside me, watching the vampire, as well.

"That's it," I whispered, feeling Zeke gently take my hand. "That's all we can do. I hope it works."

Zeke pulled me to him, wrapping his arms around me. "He's strong," he murmured into my hair. "If anyone can pull through this, it will be him."

"You two do realize I can hear you, right?"

I felt like laughing and crying at the same time. Pulling myself together, I let Zeke lead us out of the cell, keeping his fingers laced with mine. "Where's Jackal?" he asked as we left the room.

"Right here, bloodbag."

Jackal leaned against the wall beside the frame, arms crossed, watching us as we came out. His shirt was a mess of blood, especially around his stomach, but the vampire seemed fine now. Zeke went rigid, his hand clenching around my fingers, but he did not pull his weapons.

"He gonna make it?" Jackal nodded through the door to the hunched form in the corner.

"I hope so."

"Huh." Jackal pushed himself off the wall, stretching long limbs. "Well, dawn's almost here," he announced, as if nothing had happened between us. "And it's been sort of a rough night. If we don't have anything else to do, I'm going to get some sleep. Unless either of you objects, of course."

His tone was mocking, and Zeke glared at him. "You expect a whole lot of trust from us, after you just stabbed us in the back."

"Tactical maneuver, kid." Jackal looked at him and smirked. "We wouldn't have beaten Sarren if someone hadn't taken that hit. Not with you and Kanin shambling around like drunk sleepwalkers. Sarren had to think he was winning. Ask your girlfriend."

"We didn't exactly beat Sarren," I reminded him. "He's still out there."

"And probably very pissed at you," Jackal added unhelpfully. "But I don't think he'll be back tonight. With that wound, he'll have to feed soon, and he's made it slightly difficult for himself with all the crazies outside. And even Sarren can't move around in broad daylight. So don't worry—he's not going to return for his missing arm tonight."

I glanced over to where the pale, dismembered limb lay in a spatter of blood on the floor, and shuddered. And, just as I had the image of it creeping across the floor on long bony fingers, Jackal bent down and whispered, "Try not to imagine it crawling up to strangle you in your sleep."

"I'll take watch," Zeke said before I could kick Jackal in the shin. "If anything comes through that door, they'll have to get past me. I'm fine, Allie," he added as I glanced at him, worried. "Go ahead and sleep. I'll be close. I'll keep an eye on Kanin, too."

I could feel the sun's approach, creeping closer, and knew I wouldn't be able to resist forever. But I hated the thought of going to sleep, not knowing what I'd wake up to. "I'll stay with Kanin," I muttered, turning back into the room. Pausing in the frame, I glanced back at Zeke and Jackal, narrowing my eyes. "I also don't want to wake up to find either of you dead. Just remember that."

"Perish the thought, sister." Jackal smirked. Zeke didn't say anything, just nodded. I continued into Kanin's cell and sank down into the corner opposite him, pulling my sword to my side and leaning against the wall.

You're not going to die, I thought at him. *This will work. It has to work.*

The seconds ticked away, turning into minutes, as outside, the sun began its ascent into the sky. I kept my eyes open as long as I could, struggling against the heaviness pulling at my lids. Inevitably, though, I lost my battle and sank into darkness.

CHAPTER 21

Dread assaulted me as soon as I opened my eyes.

There had been no nightmares, no visions, nothing in my dreams to indicate Kanin was still alive. I woke, slumped against the wall in the dank little cell, and instantly looked to the corner where his dark, hunched form had been the night before.

It was empty.

"Don't panic, Allison," soothed a low, quiet voice, stopping me from doing just that. I jerked my gaze to the door... and there he was, standing beside the frame, watching me. "I'm right here."

Relief, swift and sudden, coursed through me. I leaped upright and hurried toward him, studying his face as I drew close. The black wounds were still there, but they were smaller now, less severe. I could see pink flesh around the edges, where new skin was forming, beginning to regrow, to heal.

"It worked!" I whispered. Kanin gave me a small smile.

"It appears I am going to live awhile longer."

"Allie." Zeke appeared in the doorway, glanced at Kanin, back at me, and grinned. "Hey, vampire girl," he said, walking up to me, and I collapsed against him in relief. "You did it."

Kanin watched us, his dark eyes lingering on Zeke, appraising. "I believe," he murmured, sounding hopeful and awed himself, "that we have found our cure."

We drew two more vials of Zeke's blood, injecting me with one and giving the other to Kanin, just in case something happened to us on the way back. Zeke offered more, but I didn't want to take too much and weaken him for the trip back, especially after he'd just recovered from Sarren's virus. Jackal complained when he didn't get one, and I told him that the only way he would get any of Zeke's blood was over my dead body. Shockingly, he didn't follow up with the obvious threat, and we made our way back to the foyer and the elevator shaft. Back topside and to the Fringe. Back to the Prince.

"Don't tell Salazar how we got the cure," Kanin warned us as we all converged aboveground again. The snow had stopped, and overhead the moon was a huge silver disk in the sky. "If he asks, we found the blood in the lab. If he discovers the source of the cure, Ezekiel will never be allowed to leave the city. Is that clear?"

He looked at Jackal as he said this, but I felt cold at the thought of Zeke being taken away, down to the vampire hospital, where they'd probably drain every drop of blood from his veins. Or keep him imprisoned forever, in case there was another outbreak.

"Don't have to glare at me, old man," Jackal said. "I wouldn't allow anything to happen to our dear Ezekiel now."

He sounded serious, which made me very nervous in turn. I could tell Zeke didn't like it, either, but he didn't say anything as we followed Kanin across the trampled field, being careful to step only where he stepped. Was it because Jackal had started to respect Zeke as a human and an individual? I nearly snorted out loud at the thought. Or, as I suspected, was it because Zeke's blood was one step closer to the larger cure we all sought? The end to Rabidism?

We had one more run-in with bleeders, a small group on the outskirts between sectors, before we could drop into the Undercity. I tried not to kill them, knowing that, if we could just get to Salazar in time, they might be saved. But it was hard, since they ignored pain and refused to stay down, and I ended up cutting through several in self-defense. I wanted to help, but I wasn't going to die for them.

Finally, hours later, Kanin led us up a ladder, pushed back a manhole cover, and the gleaming trio of vampire towers rose before us into the sky. We walked down the center of the road until we met a patrol, who immediately took us into the tower, up the elevator—I still hated it—and to the Prince.

Salazar met us in a different office this time, probably because his old one was still demolished. As we walked up to the doors, they opened, and Stick emerged with his ever-present bodyguards. His eyes went wide as he saw us, mouth dropping open, before his face darkened and he gave me a look of pure loathing. I held his gaze as we passed, wondering if he would try to stop us, to give me an excuse to drive a fist into his sullen mouth once and for all. But he stepped aside, though I felt his glare on my back even after the door had closed.

Kanin swept into the office without preamble or explanation, the rest of us trailing behind. The Prince of New Covington stood at the back window, gazing out at the city when we came in, and turned as Kanin approached, raising an eyebrow. Kanin stopped, and something glinted in the dim light as it arced toward the Prince, who caught it easily.

"There's your cure," Kanin said as Salazar glanced at the syringe in his hand, brows drawing together. "I trust you have ways to synthesize it for the rest of the population."

The Prince looked up at Kanin, his gaze searching. I saw him putting the pieces together. Kanin, terminally sick when we left the Inner City. Who should be dead by now, or at least, a rotted corpse. "And you are certain this will work on both human and vampire?" he asked.

"Yes," Kanin said without hesitation.

"And Sarren?"

"Gone." Kanin didn't give any explanation. "The old hospital in Sector Two is where he made his lair, and the virus. If you care to search it, that is. Now…" He narrowed his gaze, staring the Prince down. "We've done what you asked, and found a cure for your city. Will you honor your end of the bargain and let us go?"

Salazar didn't answer right away. Walking to his desk, he scribbled a quick note on a piece of paper, then pressed a buzzer on the surface of the wood. A few moments later a guard entered the room and hurried to his side.

"Take this to Dr. Emerson in the subhospital," Salazar said, handing the note and the syringe full of blood to the guard.

"Tell him it is *vitally* important that he start work on this right away. That it takes precedence over every one of his other projects. And if that somehow becomes lost between this office and the basement, you will spend the rest of your short life wishing you were never born."

The guard paled. Clutching the syringe and the note in a death grip, he jerked a hasty bow and immediately left the room. Salazar watched the door click behind him, and turned back to us.

"Kanin." The look the Prince gave the other Master was not friendly. "This will not atone for your crimes. Nothing you do will ever erase what you have caused. I should kill you where you stand, and make your offspring watch, so that she will fully appreciate the depth of your treachery."

I tensed, my hand itching to draw my weapon. Kanin didn't move, so I forced myself to relax. But if Salazar decided to double-cross us again, I hoped he was prepared for a fight. I was certainly not going to stand there and watch Kanin be killed in front of me. What Sarren did to Salazar's last office would be nothing compared to what I would do to this one.

The Prince and Kanin stared at each other for another long, brittle moment, before Salazar turned away with a sigh. "However," he said, as though the very word was poison to him, "I am a man of my word, and you have done what I have requested. Therefore, I will honor my agreement. You are free to go…as soon as I am certain the cure will work."

"And when will that be?" Kanin asked softly.

"Soon." The Prince made a vague gesture. "Tomorrow night, if we are lucky. Until then, you will remain here as my guests. If you need anything, my pets will attend you.

Now, if you'll excuse me." The Prince turned his back on us in blatant dismissal, walking to the window again. "I have a city to put back together."

"Well," I ventured as we left Salazar's office, stepping back into the long hallway. I glanced over at Kanin, Zeke and Jackal, and shrugged. "What now?"

Jackal rolled his eyes and stepped away from us. "What now is that I am going to relax for a few hours without listening to the lot of you whine at me. 'Ohhh, don't hurt the humans, ohhh, we have to save refugees from mole men, ohhh, Kanin is dying.' Ugh." He made a disgusted gesture with both hands. "It's enough to make me puke. I am going to the bar to get this taste out of my mouth. You all can do whatever you want."

And with that, the former raider king spun on a heel and marched off down the hall. Kanin watched him leave and shook his head.

"Kanin? What about you?"

My sire gave me a tired smile. "I will be in my room, taking advantage of the Prince's hospitality, behind a locked door."

"Avoiding the other vampires, you mean."

"Precisely. And I would encourage the both of you to do the same. The Prince might have granted us amnesty, but the other vampires will not look kindly on your association with me. It is best that we lie low until we can leave New Covington for good."

Leave New Covington. Where would we go now? I wondered as the three of us wandered back down to the guest floor. I hadn't really thought about it until now. Before, my whole focus had been on finding Kanin, and then the whole mess with Sarren. Now that I'd found him, where did we go from here?

"Ezekiel," Kanin said, surprising me. We'd stopped in front of a door much like the one to my guest suite; this room was either Kanin's or Zeke's, I guessed. Zeke glanced back at the vampire, questioning, and Kanin lowered his voice.

"May I speak with you a moment? Alone?"

Zeke blinked, frowning a bit. "Uh, sure. Allie?" He looked at me. "Do you mind?"

Stung, I glanced at Kanin. Why would he want to talk to Zeke and not me? Wasn't I his "offspring"? Wasn't I the one who'd come all this way to find him? "Why?" I challenged. "Are you two going to talk about me, is that it?"

"Allison." Kanin had reverted to his annoyed-mentor voice, which only made me bristle.

"Fine." I stepped back, glaring at them both. Hurt and irritation made me want to stubbornly stay put, but I knew it was useless with Kanin. "You two have fun with your boy talk. I'll be in my room."

"Allie," Zeke said, but I turned and walked down the hall, and didn't stop until I'd reached my door.

Inside the suite, a middle-aged human woman was stocking the fridge with fresh blood bags from a cooler. She jerked up when I came in. "Oh, excuse me, ma'am!" she exclaimed, grabbing the cooler and hurrying out of the kitchen. "I've restocked your fridge, per the Prince's orders, and if you leave any dirty clothes on the floor, I'll be sure to wash and return them before tomorrow evening. There are extra outfits in the closet and the dresser by the bed."

"Um…thank you," I replied warily, and she bobbed as she backed toward the exit, keeping her gaze on the floor. More perks of living in a vampire tower, I supposed. I bet it was pretty easy to get used to this, if you didn't mind keeping slaves and ruling through fear. And that your hired help got eaten once in a while.

"Oh, and Mr. Stephen said to make sure you got your book," the human said in the door frame, making me jerk around, narrowing my eyes. She pointed to the nightstand by the bed. "He said to tell you not to forget it."

I strode to the nightstand, ignoring the human as she quickly shut the door. My mom's book sat beneath the lamp, the simple children's story she'd read to me countless times. Why would Stick leave it here? He hated me. I saw a slip of paper sticking out of the top and pulled it out, recognizing Stick's thin, loopy handwriting immediately.

Allie,
This is yours. I was going to burn it, but I want you to have it instead, because if it wasn't for you, I wouldn't be here now.
—Stephen

I crumpled the note in my fist, tossing it to the floor. I knew Stick well enough to know that he hadn't left this here to be nice or to apologize for the way things had turned out. It was just another jab in this stupid, imaginary war he thought we were in. He was able to become the Prince's aide because he could read. Because I had taught him.

Whatever. I wasn't going to let him ruin the memory of my mom. And I would be gone from this place soon enough, never to see him again. Shrugging off my coat, I folded it and placed it and the book on the dresser so I wouldn't forget them. Stripping out of my torn, dirty shirt and jeans, I headed into the bathroom.

After a long shower, I left my filthy clothes in a heap on the floor, changed into the dark pants and shirt in the closet—did every vampire in this place wear black?—and poured a bag of cold blood into a mug on the counter. There was probably a way the city vamps warmed up their blood—surely the Prince didn't drink it cold every night—but I had no idea how they did it, so I forced it down as it was. I wasn't worried about it being poisoned this time. With Zeke's blood, I was effectively vaccinated against Sarren's plague.

I sobered a little, thinking of Zeke. What were he and Kanin discussing? Why the big secret? There had to be a reason Kanin didn't want me to hear what they were talking about. Maybe it was about me. Maybe he was trying to convince Zeke of the foolishness of being with a vampire, since he'd written me off as a stubborn lost cause who didn't listen or follow his rules.

Dammit, now I had to know. There was no reason either of them should be talking about something without me, not after everything we'd been through. Unless it *was* about me, of course, which made me even more determined to find out what they were saying. Kanin wouldn't tell me, but I'd bet I could get Zeke to talk. And if he and Kanin were still in the room, they would just have to let me in on the secret, because I wasn't leaving until they did.

There were still a few hours till dawn. Finishing the last of the cold blood, I rose, grabbed my katana from where it lay on a chair and went looking for Zeke.

The hallways were empty of vampires as I made my way to the room where I'd left them. A couple humans scurried around, carrying mops and cleaning supplies. I didn't see anyone else until I neared the room and a furtive movement caught my attention.

It was Stick, without his guards for once. He hovered in the shadows, trying to be inconspicuous, looking like he couldn't decide whether he wanted to walk up and knock on the door.

My suspicion flared. I stalked forward with a growl, but Stick spotted me, went pale and fled down the corridor. Sprinting around a corner, he vanished from sight. I considered going after him, forcing him to talk, but he'd probably run straight to the Prince or his guards, and it wasn't worth the hassle.

Instead, I went to the door and knocked firmly on the wood, listening for familiar voices. If they were still talking, too bad. I wasn't leaving. They would just have to tell me what was going on.

But when Zeke opened the door a few seconds later, there was no sign of Kanin in the room beyond. For a moment, I was disappointed—I wanted to know what they were talking about.

But then, I realized it was just me and Zeke. Alone. And suddenly, I was glad Kanin wasn't around.

"Allie." Zeke seemed surprised to see me, though not unhappy about it. He had showered, too, judging from his damp blond hair and clean clothes. He looked good in black, I thought, noting the way his shirt clung to his chest and biceps. The vest had concealed how muscular he really was. "I didn't expect to see you again tonight," he continued, stepping back to let me in. "Is something wrong?"

I shook my head, moving past him into the room. It was much like mine: a single bed, a bathroom, a small kitchenette. A plate sat on a small round table, the remains of real food scattered around it, vegetables, bread, the skin of a potato. I was amazed. Salazar's luxuries extended even to our sole human.

"No, nothing's wrong," I told him, turning back. "I...just had a question, that's all."

Zeke smiled. "Let me guess." He shut and locked the door behind us, then turned back with a half amused, half resigned look. "You want to know what Kanin and I were talking about earlier, without you."

I shrugged. "Well?" I asked, not bothering to deny it. "What *were* you talking about?"

Zeke walked across the floor, coming to stand just a few feet away. "And, what would you do if I said I couldn't tell you right now?"

"That's easy." I grinned at him, setting my katana sheath on the table. "I'll just have to beat it out of you."

His eyebrows arched, and a challenging gleam entered his eyes. "Is that so, vampire girl?" he asked, smiling and crossing his arms. "I'd like to see you try."

"Okay, but you asked for it."

I lunged. He caught me around the waist as I crashed

into him, wrapped my arms around his neck and kissed him fiercely. No barriers anymore, no doubts, no Kanin or Jackal nearby, watching and judging. It was just us, alone, both knowing what we wanted. I slid my hands into his damp hair, pressing myself to him, and he hugged me close, his lips warm on mine. I felt the hard muscles through his shirt as we locked ourselves together, the beat of his heart against my chest. The Hunger roared up, even though it had been fed just minutes before, a now-familiar ache.

His scent and warmth surrounded me, heady and intoxicating. Unable to stop myself, my fangs lengthened, sliding out of my gum, as he bent to kiss my neck, murmuring my name. I wanted him. I wanted to feel that rush of heat and life flowing through my veins. I wanted to taste him again, drink in that essence, stifle the monster raging inside.

Dropping my head, I pressed my lips to the hollow at Zeke's throat, feeling heat and pulse and life beat there, right below the skin. So close. All I'd have to do was part my lips just slightly, bite down just a little, and that warmth would fill me again.

Zeke's arms tightened around my waist, and a shiver went through him. But before I could draw away, before I could feel horrified with myself, he very deliberately tilted his head back, baring his throat. And my world froze.

He would let me, I realized. Zeke would let me bite him, feed from him. Even now, with my fangs so close to his neck, my lips at his throat, he was calm. Waiting. My eyes stung with the understanding. He had truly accepted what being with a vampire meant. Everything.

My fangs slid back, retracting once more, and I gently

kissed the pulse at his neck…before reaching up and bringing his face down to mine again. I could feel his surprise as our lips touched. He had been expecting me to bite him, bracing for it. But, as I was slowly discovering, I could be more human around Zeke. He somehow reached that tiny sliver of humanity buried within the monster, and it had reached out for him, as well.

We kissed for several intense minutes, until Zeke drew back, his gaze fervent. I watched him, loving the rings of silver around his pupils when he was this close, the way his hair fell over his forehead. "Come with me to Eden," he whispered, never taking his eyes from my face. I gave him an exasperated smile.

"You're going to keep asking me until I say yes, aren't you?"

"Please," Zeke added quietly, holding me tighter. "Say yes. Kanin and I already talked about it—he's going, as well. That's what we were discussing earlier. He just didn't want his decision to affect yours in any way. But you're coming too, right?" His hand slipped into my hair, running it through his fingers. "I can't… I won't go without you, Allie. Please. Come to Eden with us."

"All right." I sighed, admitting defeat. "Yes. Of course I'm coming to Eden. Was there really any doubt with both you and Kanin going?" I shook my head at him, smirking. "So, yes, Ezekiel. I will come to Eden with you, and hopefully your scientists won't throw me in a cage and stick me full of tubes."

Zeke pressed his lips to mine, quick and sweet. "They won't," he said as he drew back. "I promise. They already know about you, what you did for me and the others. And

Kanin…" He shrugged. "I see now what you meant about him. He's not like the other vampires, either." His expression grew teasing. "I can see where you get it from."

"Don't make me bite you, preacher boy." I frowned then, remembering something. "Wait, what about Jackal?"

"Jackal." His eyes went solemn. "That was another reason Kanin and I wanted to talk in private. Tomorrow evening, we're leaving the city, without the Prince's knowledge. Jackal won't be coming with us."

"We're leaving him behind?"

"More like Kanin will make it clear that Jackal is no longer welcome to travel with us," Zeke said. "And that if he follows us or tracks us down, he'll kill him."

I blinked. "That's a little extreme."

"I'm not bringing him to Eden, Allie." Zeke's voice was grave. "Can you imagine someone like Jackal around Caleb? Or Bethany?"

I made a face. "Right. I can see your point."

"I'm taking a huge risk by bringing you and Kanin back," Zeke admitted. "Letting even a single vampire through the gates is one thing, but two?" He shook his head. "If I brought in Jackal, and he hurt someone, I could never forgive myself. Plus, the Eden officials would never trust *any* vampire again. They'd kill you, and Kanin, and probably me. Jackal could put us all at risk. He has to stay away."

"And if he ignores the warning and tracks us down using our blood tie?"

"Then I'll get the chance to make good on my promise," Zeke said darkly, his eyes going cold for a moment. "But I think Jackal will be smart enough to stay away from us, especially if Kanin warns him to."

I nodded. I didn't really like it, and Jackal wouldn't like it, but we certainly couldn't take him with us. Zeke was right. The raider king was far too volatile to trust in Eden, especially since the cure would be right there. Knowing him, he'd grab it and run as soon as he got the opportunity.

"So." I looped my arms around his neck, feeling mischievous and strangely wicked. "When are we putting this daring plan into action?"

"Just after sundown." His eyes half closed as I leaned in and brushed my lips across his jaw. "We'll come get you. Be ready to move fast."

"I can do that." I smiled at him lazily. "Or, I could just stay here tonight."

Zeke's breathing hitched. "Allie," he said, sounding breathless. His heart pounded as if he'd run several miles, fast and frantic. "I…I want you to. But…I want this to be right for us." His palm cupped my cheek, warm and smooth, stroking with his thumb. "We just found each other again. I don't want to do anything we'll regret later. If you stay, I don't think I could… I mean…" He sighed, squeezing his eyes shut. "You have no idea how hard this is for me, but…maybe, this isn't the right time. Not now, in a vampire tower…with *them* all around." He opened his eyes, giving me a pleading look. "Do you understand…what I'm trying to say?"

I smiled. "You're turning red, did you know that?"

"Allie!" Zeke blew out his breath in a huff. I laughed, released him and stepped back.

"All right," I said, picking up my katana sheath. "I'll go

back to my room then, preacher boy." He looked both relieved and disappointed, but oddly enough, I wasn't upset. Kanin was alive. Zeke was alive. We, against all hope, had found a cure for New Covington. Tomorrow, the three of us would leave the city to go to Eden. Zeke and I had time. He wasn't going anywhere, and neither was I.

He followed me to the door, pausing as I unlocked it and stepped into the hall. "Good night, Zeke." But as I started to leave, he reached out and took my wrist, stopping me.

"Allison, wait."

I turned. Zeke stood there, holding my hand, a conflicted look on his face, as if he was trying to find the right words. My skin prickled, blood singing, as he raised his eyes to mine. "I… What I'm trying to say is…"

A movement off to the side made him turn his head. I glanced in that direction and saw Stick once more, watching us from around a corner, his eyes dark.

Zeke faltered, then let me go, drawing back through the frame. "Never mind," he said, smiling to ease the embarrassment. And even though I was furious with Stick for his damned interruption, my skin prickled under that look. "It's not important. Well, it *is,* but…I'll tell you later. When we're out of New Covington. I promise."

When his door closed, I thought of going to find Kanin, just to confirm the plan. But then I thought I might run into Jackal, Stick or the Prince, all of whom I didn't want to see right then. So I wandered back to my room, flipped through my mom's book for a while and replayed my conversation with Zeke until I had it memorized. I almost went back to his room several times, despite what he'd said, until dawn threatened the horizon and the decision was made for me.

But something still nagged at my brain as I crawled atop the sheets of the huge bed, drawing the curtains against the light. Something dark and ominous, making it hard to relax, even in a place like this.

It hit me, then. Sarren. Sarren was still out there, somewhere in the dark. Where was he now? I wondered, lying back against the sheets. Had he left New Covington? Or was he still hanging around, waiting for us, eager for revenge?

The thought was troubling, but I put it from my mind as sleep began to draw me under. Even if Sarren was still in the city, he couldn't get into the Prince's tower, not without alerting every human and vampire in the place. This was the most secure place in all New Covington. Not even Sarren could take on an entire army. As long as we stayed in the tower, we were safe from crazy vampires and their plans for revenge. And between me, Zeke and Kanin, Sarren would have his work cut out for him if we faced him together.

Let him try something, I thought as my eyes closed and I slipped further into the darkness. I had already taken his eye, his arm, and Kanin and Zeke were alive and well. I wasn't afraid of him anymore.

I awoke the next night right at sundown, changed into my old clothes—which had been washed and laid out for me as promised—and waited for Kanin and Zeke.

After several minutes, my uneasiness grew. They weren't here yet. Where were they? Had the Prince reneged on his promise, and Kanin was down in the dungeon again, being tortured and starved? Had Jackal discovered the plan to leave him behind and decided to take matters into his own hands? I tried not to fidget, to imagine the worst possible outcomes, but as the minutes ticked by, my apprehension and anger grew more and more.

"Screw it," I finally muttered after nearly a half hour had passed and neither of them had showed. "I'm not waiting around here. I'll find them myself."

Making sure I had everything—my sword and my mom's book—I stalked across the room, threw the door open and nearly ran into Kanin on the other side.

"Dammit, Kanin!" I staggered back, glaring at him. "Where were you? I was just about to go looking for..."

I trailed off at the look on his face. "Come with me," he said in a low, strained voice, and immediately started walking away. I scrambled to catch up.

"Kanin? Where are we going? What's going on?" I frowned up at him. "Where's Zeke, and Jackal?" He didn't answer, and I jogged to keep pace with him. "Hey, you're kind of scaring me."

"I'm sorry," Kanin almost whispered, and a cold fist grabbed my insides. "I can't say more, Allison. You'll see when we get there."

Numb with terror, I followed him into the elevators, watching the numbers descend, one by one, until we hit the basement.

Prince Salazar glared at me as we entered the hospital, his dark eyes glittering with anger. Not for Kanin this time. Me. I ignored the Prince, though, when I saw Jackal, Dr. Emerson and several guards surrounding a single cot in the middle of the room. A body lay atop it, lean and tall, though I couldn't see it clearly through the crowd. The sheets beneath it were soaked in blood, and my mind started screaming a protest.

No! No, it can't be him! Dammit, it cannot *be him!*

"He was found outside the towers, early this morning," Salazar said, his voice tight with bridled rage. "We brought him in, but there is nothing more to be done. It is a miracle he has survived this long. He has been asking for you, Kanin's daughter."

No, I moaned silently, incapable of speech right then. But Salazar stepped aside, as did Emerson and the guards, and I saw who lay atop the bed.

Stick's glassy, pain-filled eyes met mine across the room, and widened when they saw me. "Allie?" he whispered, and my relief that it wasn't *Zeke* quickly turned to horror as I studied him. Blood soaked his middle, stained through his business suit, and his skin was the color of chalk. His expression was filled with pain and fear, and all the bitterness, rage and hurt toward him melted away as he held out a pale, blood-spattered hand. "Allie…"

I took it, stepping to his side. "What happened?" I whispered, looking over his wounds in despair. I'd seen this before. Stabbed through the gut, a wound that was painful and lingering. He didn't have long. "Who did this to you?"

"I'm sorry," Stick whispered, his voice choked. "I'm sorry, Allie. I didn't know. I'm sorry."

"Sorry for what?" I murmured as he shuddered and began coughing. Blood ran from his mouth, streaming down his neck, and I glared over the cot at Salazar. "Do something!"

I snapped at the Prince. "You have a doctor here! Don't just stand there and watch!"

The Prince's eyes narrowed. "I do not make a habit of aiding those who betray me," he said, and I stared at him in utter confusion.

"What? Betrayed you? How?"

"Allie," Stick whispered again, clutching at my arm. "S-Sarren," he gasped. "It was Sarren. He came back."

My blood turned to ice. "Sarren did this to you? How? When?"

"I…led him there," Stick went on. "I led him to Sarren. He was waiting for us. Promised to…take him away. Didn't know…he would stab me. I'm…so sorry, Allie."

Took him away? "Who?" I whispered, but Stick gasped and his hand dropped from my arm, his eyes rolling back. "Stick!" I growled, grasping him by the collar, my entire insides twisting like sharpened wire. "Who? Who did Sarren take? Who did you lead outside? *Who?*"

"Zeke," Stick whispered, and my world shattered around me. "It was Zeke. Sarren…has him now."

"Son of a bitch," someone growled behind me, Jackal perhaps, but I wasn't thinking straight anymore. I stared at this… *thing* below me, this creature who I thought had been human, once.

"He said…you would know…where to find them." I was barely listening, now. Sarren had Zeke. Zeke had been with him, all night. "He said…they would be in the place where you left him…in pieces."

The hospital. Sarren would be at the old hospital. And Zeke would be there, as well. Alive. He had to be alive.

"I just...wanted to get you to see me," the thing continued, pleading. "I...wanted you to know...that I wasn't useless. That I...could be strong, like you. I wanted you to see me, that's all. Just...me."

"I do." Numb, I slid off the bed. "I see you now."

"Allie..."

"Go to hell, Stick," I whispered, and turned away. He made a choking sound, clutching at my arm, but I ripped it out of his grasp. I kept walking until Kanin stopped me at the door, his face grave, and I glanced over my shoulder. The body had fallen back against the pillows, watery blue eyes gazing sightlessly at the ceiling. One pale hand dangled over the edge.

I felt nothing. The body didn't register as a friend, or even an acquaintance. It was a stranger. Turning away, I walked past Kanin and swept through the doors, leaving behind the corpse of someone I used to know.

CHAPTER 22

"Allison!"

Kanin's booming voice jerked me to a halt just before I hit the elevator doors. My sire almost never raised his voice, but when he did, it could either knock you over or freeze you in place. I turned, watching him stride up, his face impassive.

"You cannot rush off to confront him alone," he said in a low voice, joining me at the elevators. "If you wait, Jackal and I will come with you."

"Wait?" I snarled, glaring at the numbered lights above the metal doors, cursing them to move faster. "There's no time to wait! We have to find them, now!

The elevator dinged, and I started forward, but Kanin grabbed both my shoulders, holding me back.

"Listen to me," he said, giving me a little shake. "You need to hear this. Ezekiel has been with Sarren for hours. Alone. He knows where Eden is. He knows the scientists are working on a cure, and Sarren will want that information. Allison..." Kanin squeezed my shoulders. "You have to prepare yourself for what we may find. You can't let it destroy you."

I shook my head frantically. "No. No, Zeke will be there. He'll be all right."

"This is Sarren," Kanin reminded me, his voice uncharacteristically gentle. "You saw what he did to me. You know what he's capable of. Your human is strong. But...he's only human. And Sarren is the best at what he does." His voice softened even more. "This is our world, Allison. It's pain and blood and death, and this is the reason I wanted you to keep your distance. To not get attached." He let me go and straightened, though his dark eyes still bored into me. "Whatever we find," he said quietly. "Whatever you see or hear, you must be prepared, because it will be worse than you could ever imagine. Do you understand?"

"Yes," I hissed, hot tears stinging my eyes. Because he was, as always, right. He was right about Sarren, and he was right about his very first rule of vampirism. But it was far too late now. I was attached. And if Zeke was gone, I didn't know what I would do.

"Well," Jackal muttered, finally joining us at the doors. "I guess saying 'I told you so' is kind of pointless now. I knew I should've ripped that skinny bastard's head off when I had the chance. Back to the Fringe again, huh?" He groaned and gave me an almost pitying look. "Fine. Let's go see if there's anything left to rescue."

The hospital grounds were quiet as we slipped across the field: no bleeders, no mobs of infected humans, nothing. It was snowing heavily, and the flakes had covered up all traces of previous passings, ours and Sarren's. There was no blood, and no sign of a struggle at the entrance to the hospital or in the ruined foyer. I didn't know if that was a good or bad sign, but I was hopeful.

But then, we opened the door to the last room, and that all changed.

The scent of Zeke's blood was everywhere, slamming me in the face as soon as the door swung back. My stomach turned, and my legs nearly gave out, but I forced myself into the room, gazing around in terror. Where was he? Had Sarren locked him in a cell? Strung his body up? Where…? And then, I saw.

The table where I had lain the night before, the bed with the straps and thick leather cuffs, sat in the center of the room, a spotlight trained on it. It was covered in blood, as were the tools on the cart beside it, and the floor surrounding it was streaked with red. There was no body. The straps were empty, and the surface was clear, except for a strange flat square in the very center of the bed. Something glimmered in the light, something small and shiny, and vaguely familiar.

Numbly, I walked to the table, staring down at what lay in the middle. One of those strange, portable computers from the time before the plague. But it wasn't the ancient computer that caught my attention, but what lay on top of it.

Zeke's silver cross, covered in blood.

I picked it up in a daze, not really acknowledging what it meant. It was his; his scent clung to it, reminding me of him. He'd been wearing it the last time I saw him. He'd been fine, then, just last night. Alive, smiling, kissing me.

My hand moved on its own, seeming to belong to someone else, reaching out to push up the lid on the computer. As the screen rose, there was a soft click, and a faint whirring sound from within.

"Hello, little bird," came Sarren's faint, disembodied voice, small and tinny sounding, under the screen. *"The camera on this computer is shot to hell, I'm afraid, so we'll just have to be content with audio. Pity. I really wanted to show you what I've been doing. But, perhaps a song is worth a thousand pictures, hmm? Show her what I mean, Ezekiel. Sing for us."*

And a scream, a horrible, gut-wrenching scream rose from the computer, making me clench my fist so hard Zeke's cross pierced the skin of my palm. I almost reached out and slammed the lid shut, but I forced myself not to move, to listen to Zeke's agony, until the scream finally died away and the sound of tortured breathing took its place.

"You should be very proud, little bird." Sarren's voice slithered out of the computer, cruel and soulless. *"He's held out remarkably well. Better than I ever thought a human capable of. But I suspect he's reaching his limit. I wanted you to be here for his final moments, to realize just how much you've lost. It's only fair—you did take my arm, after all. A man can get very attached to his arm. Well, shall we get on with it, then?"* There was a faint metallic clink, as if Sarren picked up something small and shiny. *"Ezekiel,"* he crooned, his voice farther away now, moving around the table, *"I have asked you this before, but perhaps now you are more inclined to talk to me, yes? How did you survive the virus? Where did you find a cure?"*

"I…don't know."

I bit my lip so hard I tasted blood. Zeke's voice was a choked whisper through gritted teeth. The smell of him surrounded me, seeping into my mind, and I saw him strapped to the table, eyes bright with pain, as Sarren loomed over him with something that glittered in the spotlight.

"You don't know?" Sarren repeated, his voice mockingly surprised. *"Jackal gave me the impression that you were at death's door. Are you certain you don't remember?"*

Behind me, Jackal swore. But before I could register what that meant, it was drowned out in the scream of anguish that came through the machine in front of me. I froze, my blood turning to ice, as I waited for it to stop. It didn't stop. For several long minutes, it ebbed and flowed, sometimes fading to breathless, gasping sobs, sometimes rising to piercing heights of agony. For a second, I was vaguely aware of Kanin standing rigid beside me, eyes closed as if he was remembering his own misery. But after a while, everything shrank down to the soul-destroying noise coming from the computer, the sounds of someone wanting to die.

Oh, God, Zeke. Tears streamed down my face; my hands were clenched so hard I could feel blood dripping from my palm. *Please, just tell him. Just give him what he wants.*

Finally, finally, it stopped. And Zeke's shuddering, gasping breaths were all that could be heard for a few moments.

"Now, Ezekiel," Sarren whispered, his voice dangerously calm. *"One last time. Where did you find that cure? And if you lie to me, we can continue this all night. And the next. And the next. I have all the time in the world."*

Zeke took several more ragged, panting breaths, and then,

in a voice of utter pain and defeat, whispered, *"Eden. The cure…is in Eden."*

"Ahhhh," Sarren rasped. *"Now we are getting somewhere. So, little prince, we are nearing the finish point at last. One more question, and then I will end your misery, and send you on to your reward. Would you like that? Would you like the hurting to stop?"*

Zeke coughed, the sound bloody and painful. *"Just…kill me,"* he whispered in a strangled voice. "*Get it over with already."*

"Soon, little prince. Soon. One question more." Sarren put down the tool with a clink. I could see him bending over Zeke, bringing his face very close as he whispered in a slow, deliberate voice, *"Where is Eden?"*

Zeke sucked in a breath, and didn't make any noise. Sarren waited several heartbeats, then chuckled.

"Oh, Ezekiel. You were doing so well. Don't stop now." Zeke still didn't say anything, and Sarren's voice turned ugly and terrifying. *"Three seconds, little human. Before I make you wish you were never born. Before the pain you experienced up until this point will seem like a pleasant, half-remembered dream compared to what I am about to do. Be very certain this is what you want. One."*

"Allison." Kanin's voice was low, tight. "Close the laptop. You don't want to hear this."

"Two."

I started to reach for it, then stopped, shaking my head. "No," I whispered, drawing back, clutching Zeke's cross tightly. "I owe it to him, to remember."

"Three."

I braced myself for the worst.

It was worse. Far, far worse.

This one seemed to last forever, and Zeke's screams began to falter simply because his throat was too raw to continue. I wanted to close my eyes and cover my ears. I was tempted to slam the lid shut and stop the shrieks and sobs and cries that tore into my mind, imprinting themselves in my consciousness. I didn't. I stood there, hot bloody tears streaming down my face as the storm of anguish whipped around me like a hurricane, relentless and unending. My throat began to ache, and I couldn't stop shaking as the boy I cared for more than anything screamed and bled and begged for death, far beyond my reach.

When it stopped, I was exhausted, numb. I wasn't aware of anything but the words coming out of the computer, Sarren's voice, flat and merciless. And Zeke, gasping for breath, choking on blood. *"This is not the end, little human. Oh, no. This is just a reminder that you can stop this at any time. But it makes no difference to me. We have many more hours to go, and I am just getting started."*

"Stop!" Zeke gasped. *"For the love of God, enough!"* He sobbed, panting, his voice broken and empty. *"I'll tell you. God forgive me…I'll tell you. Just…no more."*

I nearly collapsed, so grateful that it was over. Sarren's voice came again, full of quiet triumph. *"Where?"*

"An island," Zeke whispered. *"Eden…is on an island, in the middle of Lake Eerie."*

"You're lying, little human." Sarren's voice hissed from the computer, and Zeke made a choked sound of fear and dread.

"Tell me where it really is, or we will go through this whole thing again from the top."

"No!" Zeke's voice cracked. *"Please. I can't give you another answer, that's where it really is. Oh, God..."* I heard the self-loathing in his voice, the absolute despair. *"I've betrayed everyone. Just kill me already. Let me die."*

I heard Sarren's smile. *"Yes, little human. Soon, you will feel nothing. Sweet oblivion. But, before I send you into the eternal night, would you like to say goodbye? Your friends will be arriving soon, I expect. The little bird, especially, might want to hear your voice, one last time. Is there anything you would like to tell her, before we say good-night?"*

"Allie," Zeke breathed, sounding horrified. I wanted to reach for him, to grab his hand and never let go, but of course, he wasn't here. This was just an echo, his final words. *"I'm sorry,"* he whispered, and I heard the tears in his voice. *"I'm so sorry. I wasn't strong enough. I couldn't..."* He took a ragged breath, and spoke with grim desperation. *"You have to stop him. Stop him from getting to Eden. He's planning to— Aaaagh!"* His voice dissolved into another scream, as if Sarren had interrupted him by jamming something sharp into his flesh. I wasn't expecting it, and cringed, squeezing his cross in a death grip.

"Now, now," Sarren said mildly as the cry died away. *"Let's not spoil the surprise. Is there anything else you'd like to add before I kill you, little prince?"*

"Allison," Zeke panted, his voice growing faint. *"I don't regret...anything...between us. I just wish...we had more time...that you could've seen Eden with me. I should've told you earlier..."* He

paused, gasping for breath, but continued in a soft, steady voice. *"Allie, I…I love you."*

No, Zeke. I dropped my head into my hands, feeling Zeke's cross press against my skin, and sobbed. For myself, for Zeke, for this stupid, screwed-up world we were born into. For lost chances and unsaid words, and for the hope that seemed so bright and certain one moment, but so easily snuffed out the next.

"Take care of everyone in Eden," Zeke whispered as I stood there, shaking, trying to stop the flood of tears. *"Tell them… I'm sorry I couldn't come back. But I…I'll be with my father soon. Tell Caleb and Bethany not to cry. We'll…see each other again someday. And then…it'll be forever."*

"Magnificent," Sarren said. *"Truly touching. A fine requiem. But it is time to say goodbye, little prince. Are you ready?"*

Zeke's voice was calm, now. Unafraid. *"I'm ready."*

"Then, let me release you from this mortal coil, and send you gently into the eternal night."

I didn't hear the exact moment Sarren ended Zeke's life. I was just aware of his breathing, ragged at first, then seizing up, as if he could no longer gasp for air. And then, a long, agonizingly slow exhale, the last gulp departing his lungs, as Ezekiel's tortured breaths finally, irreversibly, stopped altogether.

"Good night, sweet prince," Sarren crooned, a velvet whisper.

The recording clicked off.

EPILOGUE

I stood at the edge of a deserted road, gazing back at the Outer Wall of New Covington, the snow whipping at my hair and clothes. From this vantage, you could barely see the distant vampire towers through the snow and darkness. They glimmered weakly in the storm, looking small and insignificant against the vast wilderness beyond. At my feet, the road snaked off into the old suburbs, where rabids lurked, waiting to pounce on the unwary. It vanished around a corner, nearly invisible in the snow, but it didn't matter. I knew where we were going.

The wind picked up, yanking at my coat, spitting ice shards into my face. It didn't affect me. I was numb, inside and out. As if something had reached in and smothered that small bit of hope and warmth I was desperately clinging to, snuffing it completely. I hadn't cried since we left the lab that evening, following the deserted tunnels until we came out past the kill zone, free of New Covington at last. My tears, along with my emotions, my memories and my hope, had been swallowed by the darkness, until I couldn't feel anything at all.

Footsteps crunched over the snow, and Kanin came to stand beside me, a silent, unmoving shadow. We hadn't spoken since the lab. Immediately following Zeke's death, I had fallen to my knees, clutching the cross, and had screamed and beaten my fists against the floor until I felt the bones in my fingers snap, and the two vampires had silently drawn back and left me alone. A craziness had overcome me, and I'd taken my katana and destroyed the room, smashing glass, ripping things apart, slicing and tearing and shrieking my rage.

When it was over, I'd stood in the middle of the destruction, shaking with hatred, needing to kill. And the monster rose up, embracing my pain, turning it to vengeance. *This is what we are,* it whispered, easing the despair threatening to crush me. *We are vampires. We are not human, we do not need human emotion, we do not get attached to human beings. You knew that from the beginning.*

I did. Allie the Fringer knew that, even before she was Turned. She'd tried to warn me to keep my distance, to guard my heart.

Lesson learned. I was a monster. I would never forget that again.

"You were right, you know," I told Kanin as we both gazed at New Covington, the place where I'd been born, and died and left the last of my humanity behind. My voice came out flat and cold, unfamiliar to me. "We're monsters. Humans are nothing but food. I was stupid to fight it for so long."

Kanin was silent for a moment. Then he said very softly, "Do you think you will honor his memory by reverting to that?"

"What do you want from me?" I turned on the Master vampire, narrowing my eyes. "You were the one who told me not to get close, not to form attachments."

"I did," Kanin agreed, not meeting my gaze. "But I also said it was up to you to decide what kind of monster you wanted to become. And what I saw that night in the dungeon, at the refugee camp, facing down Sarren…it gave me something I have not felt in a long time. It gave me hope."

I stared at him. Kanin still didn't look at me, choosing to face the darkness, gazing toward New Covington. "Those of us who live this long so often become jaded," he murmured. "It is hard to hold on to what made us human. It is easier to simply let go, to become the demon everyone sees in us. I thought I was done being surprised. But you have managed to surprise me at every turn." He paused, his next words quiet, almost hesitant. "I cannot tell you how to live," he said. "But…it would a pity if you became just another monster. If you abandoned everything you've fought for until now."

"I can't," I whispered, shaking my head. "I can't do it, Kanin. I won't go through that again. It's too hard, losing someone like that, hearing Zeke—" My throat threatened to close, but the darkness, the monster, rose up, cold and impassive, shielding me. "I will not do that again," I said calmly. "And if I have to be a monster to survive, then I'll be what everyone expects. I don't care about Eden, or the scientists, or their damned cure. Right now, all I care about is finding Sarren and making him pay."

Kanin didn't answer, and we stood like that in silence, watching the city. A minute later, Jackal prowled out of the darkness from between two houses, smirking at us. "Well, I have good news and bad news," he announced. "The good news is that the jeep is still where we left it, and I got the damned thing working again."

"What's the bad news?" I asked.

"Something took my fuzzy dice."

I rolled my eyes, and Kanin started forward, brushing past him. "Come," he ordered, not looking back. "Sarren is moving fast, and he has a head start on us. We can't waste time if we're going to make it to Eden before him."

My hand rose to my neck, touching the small silver cross beneath my shirt. *Zeke,* I thought, smelling his blood on the chain, even now. *I'll avenge you, I swear. Sarren will scream for mercy before I'm done; I'll make sure he remembers your name as he dies. But I will not, ever, get close to anyone again. You were the last. I hope that, wherever you are, you're happy. And if you can see me now, I'm sorry for what I've turned into.*

Kanin turned, waiting for me at the edge of the shadows. Jackal watched me, too, his eyes glowing inhumanly yellow in the darkness. Monsters in the night, just like me.

This is what I am, I thought, walking forward to join them. *This is where I belong, in the darkness. We're vampires. That's all we'll ever be.*

The storm picked up, the snow falling heavily on the road, as the three of us—myself, my sire, and my blood brother—turned an old back jeep toward the northeast and roared off in the direction of Eden.

They are coming.

Leaning against the side of an ancient van, the lean, bony figure with the horribly scarred face smiled.

They were on their way, now. Following his trail, tracking him toward the distant human city that would spell salvation for the entire world. A new beginning. A fresh start to everything. Soon.

He could sense their determination to stop him, their rage and hate. Especially…her. Oh, her anger would be a glorious thing, indeed. His hand slipped to the smooth stub of his left arm, caressing it. He had once thought Kanin a worthy opponent, but the girl, the fierce, relentless, savage little bird, was even more magnificent.

"She is coming," he whispered, a grin stretching his ravaged face. "I cannot wait to see the look on her face when she finds us again. It will be a song for the ages." He chuckled and glanced into the van's interior, where a dark form lay slumped in the corner. "Don't you think so…Ezekiel?"

★ ★ ★ ★ ★

Questions for Discussion

1. In the opening chapter, Allie thought, *I could choose what kind of people I preyed on, but in the end, I had to prey on someone. The lesser of the two evils was still evil.* What would you do if you had to take things from other people—even their lives—in order to survive? What do you think makes someone truly evil?

2. Allie believes she should stay away from Zeke because she will always be a danger to him. What would you do in a similar situation? What would you do if you were the one in danger in a relationship?

3. When Allie first reaches Old D.C., she comes across the Lincoln Memorial, though she doesn't know what it is. What do you think of the way we memorialize our historical figures? Why do you think humans feel the need to create memorials?

4. As Allie and Jackal walk through the sewers when they first enter New Covington, Allie realizes that if she hadn't become a vampire, she would never have met Zeke. Throughout human history, terrible events have also opened the way to good things that would not have happened without tragedy. How do we reconcile the worst life has to offer with the good that sometimes comes in the aftermath?

5. When Allie first finds Kanin, there is nothing left of the mentor she respected and admired. What do you think makes her continue to believe in him and try to help him?

6. Toward the end of the story, Allie faces the fact that the only two people she cares about who are left on earth are going to die. She will be alone. What do you think Allie would do if that did happen? What would you do in her situation?

7. Imagine losing power, including refrigeration, hot water, television and the internet, for the foreseeable future. What would your primary concerns be for basic survival? How would you get news and contact friends and family? What else would you have to think about on a day-to-day basis?

8. What does "eternity" mean to you? Under what circumstances, if any, would you want to live forever? What would we all have to think about, if we could live for eternity?

We hope you enjoy this exclusive excerpt from Julie Kagawa's next book, *THE IRON TRAITOR*, the sixth full-length novel in The Iron Fey series, continuing Ethan Chase's adventures with the Forgotten. Ethan, Kenzie, Keirran and Annwyl recently escaped from the Forgotten fey in New York City. But getting back to daily life isn't going to be easy for any of them, human or faery…

The Iron Traitor

"Do you know why we've brought you here, Mr. Chase?" the principal said, pursing his thin mouth at me. I shrugged. I'd been in this office once, on my very first day, and knew the principal thought I was a lost cause. No point in trying to change his mind. Besides, the two officers, peering down at me from either side of my chair, were far more worrisome.

"We'd like to ask you a few questions about Todd Wyndham," one of the policemen stated, making my stomach clench. "As you already know, he disappeared last Friday, and his mother filed a missing-persons report when he didn't return from school. According to her, you were the last person to speak to him before he vanished."

I swallowed. Todd Wyndham was a classmate of mine, and I knew exactly what had happened to him that night. But there was no way I was going to tell the police officers. Todd was part fey, a half-breed, who had been kidnapped by the Forgotten and drained of his glamour. Problem was, draining his glamour had also robbed him of his memories, his emotions and his sense of self. By the time Kenzie and I found him, his magic was gone, leaving him dazed, passive and completely human.

Keeping my voice steady, I faced the officer who had spoken. "Yeah, I saw him at school that day. Everyone did. What's the big deal?"

"The big deal," the officer continued, frowning, "is that Todd Wyndham showed up at his home last week completely shell-shocked. He can't remember very much, but he has told us that he was kidnapped, and there were other kidnap victims. His symptoms are on par with one who has witnessed a violent crime, and we fear the kidnapper could strike again. We're hoping that you can shed some light on Todd's condition."

"Why me?"

The policeman narrowed his eyes. "Because on the day after Todd's disappearance, Mrs. St. James reported her daughter, Mackenzie, missing, as well. She was last seen at a martial arts tournament, speaking to *you.* Witnesses say that you pulled her out of the building, into the parking lot, and then you both disappeared. Care to tell me what happened, Ethan?"

My heart pounded, but I kept my cool, sticking to the script Kenzie and I had come up with. "Kenzie wanted to see New York City," I said casually. "Her dad didn't want her to go. But she really wanted to see it, you know…before she *died.*" They blinked, not knowing if I was being serious or overly dramatic. I shrugged again. "She asked me to take her, so I did. I didn't know she never told her dad she was leaving."

Kind of a lame excuse, but I couldn't tell them the real

reason, of course. That a bunch of murderous Forgotten had found us at the tournament and chased us into the parking lot, and I'd had to send us both into the Nevernever to escape.

The policeman's lips thinned, and I crossed my arms. "If you don't believe me, ask Kenzie. She'll tell you the same thing."

"We intend to do that." They straightened and backed away, making gestures to let me know we were done here. "You can go on back to class, but we'll be watching you, Ethan. Keep your nose out of trouble, you hear?"

Relieved, I stood, though I could feel the principal's glare on me as I headed for the door. Probably hoping I'd be arrested and carted off to Juvie—one less delinquent for him to deal with. I certainly gave off the image of the sullen, brooding troublemaker—ripped jeans, shirt turned inside out, pierced ears and defiant smirk firmly in place. But whatever. I wasn't here to be a perfect student, to star on the football team or win any trophies. I just wanted to get through the year without any major disasters.

I slipped out of the principal's office with a sigh of relief. Another bullet dodged. I was good at lying to cover up the truth no one else could see. That the fey were out there and couldn't seem to leave me alone. In order to keep the people around me safe, I'd become someone no one wanted to be around. I'd driven away potential friends and was basically a dick to anyone who tried to get close. And it usually worked. Once I made it clear that I wanted to be left alone, people did. No one wanted to deal with the rude, hostile jerk.

Except one.

Dammit, I hope she's okay. Where are you, Kenzie? I hope you didn't get into trouble because of me.

Oh, and here's another fun fact about the Nevernever: time flows differently there than in the real world, usually much faster. So a whole week had gone by in the real world before Kenzie and I could get home again. A whole week of being gone, vanished from the face of the earth. With one exception, no one had seen any trace or heard from us from the time we left the tournament until the night we came home several days later.

So Kenzie and I had had to come up with a good story for when we got back.

Kenzie. I sighed, scrubbing my hand through my hair, worried again. I hadn't seen her since the night she went back home, back to her dad and her stepmom. I'd tried calling her over the weekend, but either her phone was still dead or it had been taken away, because my calls went straight to voice mail. Worried and restless, I'd gotten to school early this morning in the hopes of seeing her, finding out how her family had taken her abrupt disappearance, but I'd been pulled into the principal's office before I could catch a glimpse of the girl who was very suddenly my whole world.

Morose, I headed back to class, still scanning the hall for any glimpses of blue-streaked black hair, irrationally hoping to run into her on her way to the principal's office. I didn't see her, of course, but I did pass a group of girls in the hall, talking and laughing beneath the bathroom sign. They fell silent as I passed, staring at me with wide eyes, and I heard the murmurs erupt as soon as my back was to them.

"Oh my God, that's him."

"Did you hear he forced Kenzie to run away with him last week? They were on the other side of the country before the police finally caught them."

"So that's why the cops are here. Why isn't he in jail?"

I clenched my jaw and kept walking. Rumors and gossip rarely bothered me, I was so used to it. And some of the more colorful rumors I'd heard were so far off it was laughable. But I hated the thought that Kenzie, just by being around me, would be the target of gossip and speculation. It was already starting.

She wasn't in any of our shared classes, which made it difficult to concentrate on what was happening around me. Even so, I caught suspicious glances thrown my way, whispers whenever I slid into my desk, the hard stares of some of the popular kids. Kenzie's friends. I kept my head down and my usual "leave me the hell alone" posture going, until the bell rang for lunch.

I almost went to the cafeteria, just to see if she was there, before catching myself with a grimace. *Jeez, what are you doing, Ethan? You've gone completely stupid for this girl. She's not here, just accept that already.*

As I hesitated in the corridor, trying to decide which direction to go, my nerves prickled and the hair on the back of my neck stood up, a sure warning that I was being watched—or stalked. Wary, I casually glanced up, scanning the surging throng of teenagers for anything that might belong to the Invisible World, the world only I could see. It wasn't a faery, however. It was worse.

Football star Brian Kingston and three of his friends were pushing their way through the corridor, broad shoulders and thick arms parting the crowd with ease. By their faces and the way they were also scanning the halls, they hadn't seen me yet, but it was obvious they were on the warpath. Or at least the quarterback was, his ruddy face and thick jaw set for a fight. And I could just guess who the target of his wrath was.

Great.

I turned and melted into the throng, heading in the opposite direction, hoping to disappear and find someplace I could be alone. Where vengeful football jocks and their cronies couldn't smash my face into lockers, where I didn't have to hear whispers of how I'd kidnapped Kenzie and forced her to go to New York with me.

Once more, maybe by fate, I found myself back in the library, the quiet murmurs and rustle of paper bringing with it a storm of memories. I'd come here the first week of school in an attempt to avoid Kingston then, too. It was also here that I'd promised to meet Kenzie for one of her infamous interviews. And it was here that I'd held my last lucid conversation with Todd, right before he vanished.

Hiding my lunch under my jacket, I ignored the No Food or Drink sign on the front desk and sauntered into the back aisles. I earned a suspicious glare from the librarian, watching me over her glasses, but at least Kingston and his thugs wouldn't follow me here.

With a sigh, I found a quiet corner and sank down against the wall, engulfed in déjà vu. Dammit, I just wanted to be left alone. Was that too much to ask for? I wanted to get through a school day without getting beat up, threatened with expulsion or arrested. And I wanted, for once, to just have a normal day where I could take my girlfriend out to the movies or to dinner without some faery messing everything up. Something like normal. Was that ever going to happen?

When the last bell rang, I quickly grabbed my books and hurried into the parking lot, hoping to make it out before running into Brian Kingston or any one of Kenzie's friends. No one stopped me in the halls, though when I reached my beat-up truck, parked on the far end of the lot, my stomach tightened.

Brian Kingston sat on the hood, legs swinging off the edge, smirking at me. Two of his football buddies leaned against the side, blocking access to the doors.

"Where do you think you're going, freak?" Kingston asked, sliding off the hood. His cronies pressed behind him, and I took a deep breath to calm down. At least they hadn't damaged my truck in any way, yet. The tires didn't look slashed, and I couldn't see any key marks in the paint, so that was something. "Been wanting to talk to you all afternoon."

I tensed, shifting my weight to the balls of my feet. He didn't want to talk. Everything about him said he was itching for a fight. "Do we really have to do this, now?" I asked, keeping a wary eye on all three of them. Dammit, I did *not* need this, but if the choices were "fight" or "get my ass kicked," I wasn't going to get stomped on. I supposed I could have run away like a pansy, but the fallout of that might be even worse. These three didn't scare me; I'd faced down goblins, redcaps, a lindwurm and a whole legion of murderous, ghostly fey who sucked the glamour out of their normal kin. I'd fought things that were trying their best to kill me, and I was still here. A trio of unarmed humans, thick-necked and muscle-headed as they were, didn't register very high on my threat meter, but I'd rather not get expelled on my first day back if I could help it.

"This is stupid, Kingston," I snapped, backing away as his cronies tried to flank me. If they lunged, I'd need to get out of the way fast before they could tackle me. "What the hell do you want? What do you think I've done now?"

"Like you don't know." Kingston sneered, curling his lip in disgust. "Don't play stupid, freak. I told you to stay away from Mackenzie, didn't I? I warned you what would happen, and you didn't listen. Everyone knows you dragged her off to New York last week. I don't know why the cops didn't toss your ass in jail for kidnapping."

"She *asked* me to take her," I argued. "I didn't drag her anywhere. She wanted to see New York, and her dad wouldn't let her go, so she asked me." Lies to cover up more lies. I wondered, very briefly, if there would ever come a point where I didn't have to lie to everyone.

"Yeah, and now look where she is," Kingston shot back. "I don't know what you did to her while you were gone, but you're gonna wish you never came here."

"Wait. What?" I frowned, still trying to keep the cronies in my sights, but something Kingston said distracted me. "What do you mean? Where is Kenzie now?"

Kingston shook his head. "You didn't hear, freak? God, you are a bastard." He stepped forward, eyes narrowing in pure contempt. "Kenzie is in the hospital."

★ ★ ★ ★ ★

mira
Ink